Cruel Music

Also by the author
Interrupted Aria
Painted Veil

Cruel Music

The Third Baroque Mystery

Beverle Graves Myers

Poisoned Pen Press

First Edition 2006

10 9 8 7 6 5 4 3 2 1

Library of Congress Catalog Card Number: 2006900734

ISBN: 1-59058-230-6   Hardcover

Poisoned Pen Press
6962 E. First Ave., Ste. 103
Scottsdale, AZ 85251
www.poisonedpenpress.com
info@poisonedpenpress.com

Printed in the United States of America

To Matthew

Characters

Venice

Tito Amato	a well-known singer
Benito	Tito's manservant
Annetta	Tito's sister
Augustus (Gussie) Rumbolt	her husband, an English artist
Alessandro Amato	Tito's brother, a merchant seaman
Messer Grande	a police official
Senator Antonio Montorio	head of the noble Montorio family

Rome—Villa Fabiani

Cardinal Lorenzo Fabiani	the Cardinal Padrone
Marchesa Olimpia Fabiani	his mother
Abate Pio Rossobelli	his private secretary
Gemma Farussi	the marchesa's maid

Guido, Roberto, Teresa, and various other servants and musicians

Rome—Palazzo Pompetti

Prince Aurelio Pompetti	an aristocrat
Lady Mary Sysonby	English intellectual and antiquarian

Rome—Palazzo Venezia

Cardinal Stefano Montorio	Venetian Ambassador to the Papal States, Antonio's brother
Abate Massimo Lenci	a Montorio nephew

Rome—others

Clement XII	the reigning pope
Cardinal Silvano Di Noce	administrator of Roman charities
Liya Del'Vecchio/Pellegrina	a Jewess from Venice
Maddelena	her friend
Gaetano Tucci	a singer
Mario Sertori	a magistrate

Part One

"It is cruel, you know, that music should be so beautiful."

—Benjamin Britten

Chapter 1

"Zio Tito," asked my four-year-old nephew, "what do you think Befana will leave in my stocking?"

Little Matteo clung to my knee with candy-stickened hands and searched my face with grave brown eyes. It was the eve of Epiphany, only five days into the new year of 1740 and the night that the good witch Befana raced her flying goat all over the skies of Italy. In the morning, good children would awaken to find stockings stuffed with candy and trinkets. Naughty children would be rewarded with a single, bleak lump of coal. While I'd never actually known a child consigned to that terrible fate, Epiphany Eve could be an anxious time for a little boy whose curiosity often overcame his mother's admonitions.

"Befana may not leave you anything." I addressed the boy with mock severity, settling back into a stuffed chair after helping him hang two stockings over the sitting room stove. "It depends on how you've behaved."

His huge eyes grew even larger as I pulled him onto my lap. "Now, you must tell your uncle the truth. While I've been away in Dresden, have you been into any mischief?"

Matteo shook his head quickly and tried to distract me with a question of his own. "What were you doing in Dresden, Zio?" The name of the unfamiliar Saxon town came out with a decided lisp.

"I was singing at the royal opera house. I played a knight in love with the sister of a wicked sorceress. For weeks and weeks, I sang every night and lots of people came to see me."

"Did they like you?"

"Very much. After every aria, the people clapped and shouted for me to sing it again. They paid me so handsomely and gave me so many presents that now I can stay home in Venice and have a nice long rest."

My nephew shrugged his shoulders with a contented sigh and began to twist the sparkling crystal buttons on my waistcoat. I raised his chin with my forefinger. "But tell me, little man, have you been behaving yourself? If you speak the truth, I may put in a good word for you with Befana."

He darted a look toward my sister Annetta, who was bent over an embroidery frame trying to work by the flickering glow of a table lamp. "Have I been good, Mama?" he asked. "I tried to be."

Annetta pushed her sewing aside, resisting a smile. The last few years had been kind to my sister. Marriage to my friend Augustus Rumbolt had erased the shadows of old worries from her eyes, and I was glad to see that she had traded her severely coiled braids for a loose chignon. As soon as I had stepped over our threshold, I had also noticed a new plumpness about the front of her apron that hinted I might soon have another niece or nephew to indulge. There couldn't be too many for me. Since the knife that created my voice and my livelihood had also severed any hope of fathering my own children, my sister's family was the only one I was ever likely to enjoy.

Annetta raised an eyebrow at the squirming, sticky bundle in my lap. "Have you forgotten that just this morning you hit your sister and took the sugar stick that Papa brought her from the market?"

Matteo sent me a stricken look. His nurse, Lucia, had come downstairs and was bearing down on him to commence the nightly ritual of undressing, washing, and bedside prayers.

I bent my mouth to his dark curls and whispered, "If you let Mama and Lucia put you to bed without a fuss, I think I can persuade Befana to overlook this morning. I'll make that old witch jump down the chimney and stuff your stocking with more presents than you can carry."

Annetta carried the grinning boy away, stopping in the hall-way to allow him an enthusiastic hug for his Papa, who was just coming in from a long day at his easel.

Gussie Rumbolt was a second son of English gentry. Drawn to Italy by dreams of painting like the great masters, my friend and brother-in-law seemed to grow more Venetian with each passing year. It wasn't his unruly yellow hair, blue eyes, or honest, pink-cheeked goodness that had changed. The signs of his transformation were much more subtle. Gussie's walk had grown liquid and languid, his laughter more ready, and except for a few favorite exclamations, our soft Venetian idiom had gradually replaced his mongrel speech of English tidbits and schoolbook Italian.

When he caught sight of me, Gussie spread his arms and crossed the faded Persian carpet with long strides. As further proof that Venice was seeping into his soul, he did not pump my arm in his customary fashion but embraced me warmly and graciously endured a kiss on both cheeks.

"Tito, how long have you been here? Annetta should have sent to the studio for me."

"My coach reached Mestre last night, but I couldn't find passage on a boat crossing the lagoon until this afternoon. After I landed, I had to stop at the Post and call at my tailor's. By the time I reached our door, it was almost dark. I wouldn't let Annetta send old Lupo after you. She said you are swamped with work."

"Rather!" His blue eyes twinkled. "I've secured a commission from one of my countrymen. The Duke of Richmond wants ten views of the Grand Canal as a memento of his visit to the sunny South."

"An ambitious project."

"Quite so, especially as the duke is in a hurry. I've had to hire several assistants—a boy to stretch the canvases and grind the pigments and another man to lay out the perspective and sketch the architecture. Of course, I'll do all the painting myself."

Gussie warmed his hands before the stove's glowing coals, then moved to the cabinet that held some glasses and a decanter of Cyprus wine. In our case, the difficulties that are apt to arise when an extended family shares a house had been avoided by a fortuitous mixture of mutual affection and happenstance.

After the death of our father, this modest house on the Campo dei Polli had passed equally to Alessandro, Annetta, and me. Our younger sister, Grisella, had been lost to us long ago. Alessandro was the eldest, a merchant seaman. After years of sailing on ships owned by the great trading houses, he had finally amassed enough capital to purchase his own vessel. Venice might no longer be the complete mistress of Mediterranean trade that she once was, but my enterprising brother had managed to locate an exporter of Turkish tobacco who also provided a ready market for Venetian goods. Thanks to his loyal business partner in Constantinople, Alessandro reaped a tidy profit on glass chandeliers, books bound in gilded leather, exquisitely woven lace, and other luxuries produced on the islands of our lagoon republic.

I had not been seeing nearly as much of my brother as I would have liked. These days, Alessandro spent more time in Constantinople than Venice. Though he denied it, we half believed that he had set up housekeeping with a dusky Turkish beauty. At any rate, Alessandro occupied his room in the house on the Campo dei Polli only several months of the year, and when he sailed, he left no wife behind to foster strife by challenging Annetta's domestic arrangements.

Traveling almost as often as my brother, I was as much of an Italian export as the Murano glass nestled in Alessandro's straw-filled crates. Europe had gone mad for Italian opera. From Handel's theater in London, to the chilly courts of Sweden and Russia, right down to the sunnier stages of Madrid, music lovers clamored for the vocal fireworks that only Italian singers could produce. Great sums were offered to engage the best singers, and I was counted among their ranks.

The best meant *castrati*—male singers gelded as boys to outwit nature and produce sopranos who could deliver angelic song with the powerful lungs of fully grown men. In addition to the surgery, the process of creating a *castrato* voice separated us from our families for years of intense musical training. It was a brutal system, but the public seemed to think that the end results outweighed our suffering.

There had been a time when I shrank from the role of musical eunuch, but I had given up my doubts and my meekness long ago. I was what I was. If that disturbed some people, so be it. Music was as much my delight as my master, and I was proud to be one of its most exclusive servants. However, I had to admit that my latest round of travels had been less than uplifting. Dresden had left me tired to the core of my being.

"How was the journey, Tito?" Gussie handed me a glass of wine as we settled ourselves in a pair of chairs by the stove.

I merely shrugged.

"You must have come over the Brenner," he continued, "then down the valley to Bolzano. Not an easy journey over those mountains on winter roads."

"Traveling wasn't the worst of it." I thought back to the endless hours in the hired coach, swaying and jogging over rutted roads with only the irreverent comments of my manservant, Benito, for amusement. "Though once we'd crossed the pass, the postilion trotted the horses downhill so fast, I fear my backside may never recover." Gingerly, I shifted forward and contemplated the garnet liquid in my glass. "No, what I'm feeling is more than road weariness."

"What is it then? You look quite done in."

"Dresden doesn't have public theaters like we do in Venice. There is only one opera house—wholly supported by the Elector, Prince Frederick Augustus. The singers and musicians are obliged to perform at His Majesty's pleasure, and his royal pain in the ass desires the pleasure of music at all hours. He would keep us at the theater until midnight and beyond, then demand a performance while he took a late supper. Mornings, I had to report to the palace for lessons."

"You had pupils there?"

"Yes, two young ladies. The Elector's daughter and her companion." I shook my head at the memory. "It was absolute torture! No matter how I encouraged or demonstrated, I couldn't convince the girls that moderation was a virtue. They insisted on shrieking their notes as if they were playing to the fifth-tier boxes at the opera house. To make matters worse, the older one decided to fall in love with me. She started by brushing my hand as I turned the pages on her music book. Before I knew it, she was calling me her angel and tucking fervent notes in my pockets. I practically had to perform acrobatics to keep the clavier between us."

Gussie's paint-stained waistcoat rumbled with a deep chuckle. "Was the journey as profitable as you hoped?"

I nodded. "Mainly thanks to the concerts in private homes. Everyone was vying to have the Prince's latest favorite, and the Saxons are a generous lot. Besides my fees, I collected a whole trunkful of snuffboxes and other costly gifts."

"What's next for our famous virtuoso?"

Instead of answering, I closed my eyes and let the familiar sounds of home surround me: the sighing of the coal in the plastered stove; a child's laugh from the floor above; the muffled clatter of dishes as Lupo, our ancient factotum, set the dining table for the evening meal. A lump swelled in my throat. Why was it so hard to say that I simply needed to wrap myself in the warm mantle of home and family?

I answered Gussie's question with a weak joke. "I suppose I'll just rest in Venice until I grow fat as a sow and lazy as a Calabrian mule." I stretched my arms above my head. "Thank God I'm not at the everlasting mercy of a patron. Not so many years ago, my entire career would have been spent singing for my supper at some noble court, dancing attendance on a master who wouldn't know a decent *portamento* from a pisspot. But now that opera has become a business, theater managers are fighting to engage me. Thank God I'm free to make my own arrangements."

I sank lower in my chair, smiling at the prospect of long mornings in my dressing gown, sipping chocolate and catching up on the gazettes. In the afternoons, Alessandro and I could loaf on the Piazza, and in the evenings, we'd all see what the Venetian opera houses had to offer. I'd eventually cast around for work that suited me. But only when I was fully ready.

My brother-in-law poked a pin in one of my lovely dream bubbles. "Alessandro isn't here. His ship sailed this morning, but you can come with me to the studio tomorrow. This new project is really quite interesting. I'm starting with the Rialto Bridge at sunset. The light is tricky, but..."

I let Gussie chatter on. Watching paint dry wasn't the sort of relaxation I had in mind. My thoughts sprang to the ghetto that lay a few squares away. It was an Israelite enclave, gated, and ringed by walls and wide canals. I'd befriended a family of Hebrews who kept an old clothing shop there. Perhaps tomorrow I'd make a visit to the Del'Vecchio household and inquire after their wandering daughter. I had not seen Liya for almost five years, since the unhappy events surrounding the murder of her lover, Luca Cavalieri.

I pictured the lovely Jewess as she had been at our last meeting: angry, grieving, poised to flee the stifling confines of tradition and religious prejudice for a freer life in the wild mountains of the mainland. Not for the first time, I puzzled over what might have happened to her and the child she carried.

A loud banging on our street door jerked me back to the present. I shot a questioning look toward Gussie. He shook his head, forehead wrinkled.

Lupo hobbled the few steps from dining room to front hall. The front door creaked, and the sitting room lamps flickered in the rush of cold air. The clatter of many boots filled the hall.

Gussie and I jumped up. Before we'd taken two steps, a uniformed constable burst into the room and ordered us to stand still. Ignoring our surprised protests, a dozen of these rough *sbirri* fanned out through the ground floor, overturning chairs and scattering papers and bric-a-brac.

Several made for the stairs. When a feminine scream sounded and was sharply cut off, Gussie and I pushed our way to the hall. On the stair landing, Annetta and Lucia each held a frightened, whimpering child. One constable had my manservant Benito by the collar and was threatening the little man with a thick truncheon. Old Lupo had collapsed in a heap by the front door. "Annetta," Gussie bellowed, charging the stairs. A bull-necked constable blocked his path. The man flashed his dagger, and my brother-in-law halted with the blade inches from his nose.

I ran to kneel beside old Lupo. His face was pale and a trickle of blood ran down his forehead, but he nodded to show that he still had his wits about him.

"What's the meaning of this?" I cried to the assembled sbirri. "You have no right to barge in and terrorize decent citizens."

"They have every right," someone snapped from the front door.

Gussie and I turned to see Messer Grande, the chief of Venice's constabulary. His red robe of office lent his weasel face an eminence it otherwise lacked. I had sparred with the man over the investigation of Luca Cavalieri's murder. I would always remember his haughty incompetence, and I was certain that he had not forgotten what he had described as my amateurish meddling and lack of respect for my betters.

An unpleasant smile danced across Messer Grande's lips as he entered and began to unfold an official-looking document. "My men are doing what they're paid to do," he said. "Securing the household of a wanted man. I have a warrant here—for the arrest of one Tito Amato, virtuoso."

"What?" I cried.

Lupo weakly pressed my shoulder, urging me to stand. I propped the old servant's back against the wall and went to face Messer Grande.

"I advise you to come quietly, Signor Amato." His gaze was stony. "There is no reason why anyone else should be hurt."

I was dumbfounded. I had committed no crime. When I'd set out for Dresden, I'd just finished a successful run in an opera by Maestro Vivaldi. I'd been the toast of Venice, everyone's darling. Who could I have crossed in the few short hours since my return?

Gussie approached and extended his hand. "Let me see this warrant. Who authorized it?"

Messer Grande ignored Gussie and handed the paper to me, holding it by his fingertips as if he couldn't bear to brush hands with a eunuch. As Gussie hung over my shoulder, I skimmed through the flowery legal language to the signature at the bottom of the page.

My heart sank.

"Montorio," I whispered.

Gussie was suitably impressed. "Senator Montorio? The State Inquisitor?"

I nodded. Doge Alvise Pisani and the senate elected by the heads of noble families were the titular rulers of the Venetian Republic. But everybody knew that the real power was concentrated in a secretive body of powerful senators called the Council of Ten. No unacceptable act or opinion escaped the notice of the inexorable Ten. With their well-paid network of spies and informers, they kept an ear to every café, church pew, and, it was rumored, bedroom. The Ten were a law unto themselves, and the instrument of their absolute authority was the Tribunal of State Inquisitors. In chamber, two inquisitors dressed in black robes and one in red. Senator Montorio wore the red.

Gussie stared in wordless bewilderment. Messer Grande waited by the door, smacking a limp pair of leather gloves against his palm.

"What am I accused of?" I asked. "Why was the warrant issued?"

"I'm not here to answer questions." Messer Grande shrugged disdainfully, but his voice softened a trace. "I will, however, conduct you to someone who can."

Despite the hackles rising on the back of my neck, I forced myself to lower the pitch of my natural speaking voice and calmly announce, "Don't worry, Gussie. Someone has simply made an unfortunate mistake. I expect to sort things out and be home by tomorrow morning."

Messer Grande didn't even try to conceal his smirk.

Chapter 2

A pair of sbirri seized me under the arms and dragged me, half-walking, half-stumbling, into the night. Messer Grande murmured orders to their sergeant, who relayed his commands in a parade ground bellow. Dense clouds had swept in from the sea, obscuring the stars and turning the sky into an endless mantle of black velvet. The shadowy mass of houses that crowded around the Campo dei Polli provided the only light. Even their friendly dots of yellow lamplight winked out as my neighbors heard the commotion and came to their windows to watch my ignoble progress across the square and down the *calle* toward the canal.

Three gondolas bobbed at the landing. Their lanterns threw streaks of silver lightning across the black water. My captors dumped me into the middle boat, and Messer Grande ordered two more men to join us. The other boats, manned by archers, escorted us fore and aft.

I shivered from more than the sharp breeze whistling down the canal. Why send so many men to secure the person of one less than robust singer? It was not as if I were a prizefighter or some nobleman's bravo. My strength lay in my throat, not my limbs. The authorities had spared no resources in staging this grand show, but its purpose had me completely baffled.

The trio of gondolas slowly navigated the narrow channels of my domestic quarter, then picked up speed once we reached the wider waters of the Grand Canal. The nine o'clock bells had only just rung, so there was still plenty of blaze and bustle on Venice's main throughway. With our boatmen straining at the oars, we flitted around hulking barges bound for the Rialto markets as if they were standing still. Their shadowy crewmen pointed and whispered among themselves. I could imagine the curious questions: Who is this criminal under such stalwart guard? A traitor to the Republic? A murderer?

I wasn't surprised when our little fleet turned left at the mouth of the Grand Canal and passed alongside the gothic arcades of the doge's palace. The Quay of Prisons was close at hand, and it was at those dismal stones that I was forced to disembark. At this bastion of government power, Messer Grande retained only four men to persuade me against struggle or flight. He conducted me to a small room. Not a cell, but a bleak chamber furnished with a wooden table and one straight chair. When I saw he intended to shut me in without a word, I confess I abandoned my last shred of dignity and begged to be told why I was being held.

"You have a reputation for cleverness," he answered, digging under his red robe for a tinderbox to light the squat tallow candle on the table. "Let's see if you can come up with a guess. I'll give you a few minutes to think about it."

The door thudded shut, and the rasp of the key in the lock sounded a note of cold finality. Surrounded by silence, I had ample time to review the last few months: every house I'd visited, every acquaintance I'd dined with, every triumph, every tiff. Then, one leg gone numb from perching on the hard chair, I paced the flagstone floor until I could simply think no longer.

I must have fallen asleep eventually. When the squeak of door hinges jerked my head from my folded arms, the candle wax had snaked onto the table and the flame was burning low. Two sbirri entered, truncheons bared. Messer Grande followed. He made a short circuit of the room, peering into the bare, dark corners as if he expected assassins to materialize out of the grimy plaster at any moment. When he was satisfied that my little prison was secure, he opened the door and bowed low.

Senator Antonio Montorio—it could be no other—sauntered toward me on elegant court shoes with high red heels and diamond-studded buckles. Above his coat of silver brocade, his beautifully dressed wig covered his head at a clumsy angle. Heavy bags pulled his bloodshot eyes low, and his neckcloth was in disarray. While I had been agonizing, the senator had been indulging himself at some casino or pleasure hall.

He stopped just a few inches from my chair and towered over me with hands on hips. He spoke without introduction or preamble. "What do you know about the situation in Rome?"

"Rome? I know nothing of the opera houses of Rome. I've never had occasion to sing there."

"Santa Maria! It's not music that concerns me, man. It's the pope. Surely you've heard he is ill."

I nodded. Everyone knew that Pope Clement had gone blind early in his reign and suffered from a host of ills. At every Mass, the priests offered endless prayers for his recovery. "Yes, of course," I answered. "But what does that have to do with me? Why have I been arrested?"

Senator Montorio placed his balled fists on the table and leaned on his knuckles. "The pope is dying. The old man's been going by inches for months. In Rome, they say the cardinals will be electing a new pope by Easter."

I nodded, still mystified.

"It's high time for another Venetian pope," he continued. "Pietro Ottoboni was the last we sent to Rome. That was over fifty years ago, and the man took pneumonia and died before he could send any significant subsidies our way. We're not going to miss our next chance with the Sacred Conclave, and this time, it won't be an old man with one foot in the grave."

I cocked my head. "It sounds like you already have a candidate in mind."

He took a deep breath. "My brother Stefano desires the papal tiara and I will see that he gets it."

Montorio's resolution didn't surprise me. Like all the nobility of my mercantile city, the Montorio fortune was built on trade. In their case, spices. Europe's taste for Malabar pepper and other Indian seasonings had made the Montorio family a power to reckon with. At one time or another, members of their numerous clan had filled every post in the Venetian Republic from the doge on down. Senator Montorio's younger brother Stefano was already a cardinal who served as Venice's ambassador to the Papal States. Again and again, the industrious Montorios had distinguished themselves from the usual run of charming wastrels who made up the current bulk of Venetian nobility. A Montorio on St. Peter's throne? Why not? Lesser men had certainly been elevated to the role.

But why had the senator ordered my arrest? I swallowed hard and asked that very question.

Montorio straightened and eyed me narrowly. Then he ordered Messer Grande to find two glasses of wine as if the chief of police were his personal footman. If only the circumstances had been different, how I would have relished that moment.

The wine was fetched, as well as several lanterns with brightly burning wicks to hang from wall hooks. Smiling amiably, Montorio sat one hip on the edge of the table and set his free leg swinging back and forth. I recognized the parts we were to play. Just two men having a friendly chat over our glasses. I touched my lips to mine but found I couldn't drink. I waited for his next words with gritted teeth.

"Allow me to elaborate," he began. "The next papal election is by no means a foregone conclusion. When the pope's infirmities confined him to bed, he appointed Lorenzo Fabiani as the Cardinal Padrone to act in his stead. That makes Fabiani one of the most powerful men in Rome, if not all of Italy. Though he's collected a few enemies along the way, Fabiani has enough cardinals in his pocket to control who will be the next pontiff."

"Will he back Cardinal Montorio?"

"We thought so. Certain promises were made, certain favors given." Montorio regarded me thoughtfully, rolling the stem of his glass between his fingers. "Don't be shocked. That is the way papal elections have been decided for centuries."

I wasn't shocked. Only an infant could fail to understand that the Church was as much about politics as salvation. No, what Montorio saw in my expression was the dawning realization that my long rest in Venice was threatened by forces far beyond my control.

He went on. "The election was looking good for Stefano. We'd secured the loyalty of the Spanish cardinals and were prepared to reward Fabiani most handsomely for all the other votes he could swing our way. We were assured of the Cardinal Padrone's loyalty. But…" Montorio dropped his companionable manner and stared into space with a clenched jaw.

"But?" I prompted.

"Besides Stefano, there is another that is often mentioned as a contender for St. Peter's throne. A Cardinal Di Noce." Montorio seasoned the name with a liberal helping of venom. "He's an upstart from some insignificant village in the Alban hills, with no family connections to speak of. Lucky coincidence seems to have advanced his career more than anything else. Yet, Di Noce has his supporters. He administers the poorhouses and charity hospitals of Rome. Quite liberal he is with the beggars. So, of course, the populace loves him."

"Has Cardinal Fabiani switched his allegiance to Di Noce?"

"Ah, Signor Amato, you've hit upon the question of the hour. It shouldn't be so damned difficult to answer, but the situation has become…murky. In public, Fabiani is scrupulously careful to favor both candidates in equal measure. We still have his private assurance that all is well, but his promises have become rather feeble. Combine that with information that Prince Pompetti, Di Noce's most influential supporter, has been visiting Fabiani's villa at all hours, and you see why we are beginning to question the strength of the alliance."

He paused to stare intently into the dwindling candle flame, then flicked his slack, red-rimmed eyes back to me. "That is where you are going to help us. Cardinal Lorenzo Fabiani is a great music lover. He keeps a box at every opera house in Rome and rarely misses a performance. As a goodwill gesture, the

Republic is going to make Fabiani a present of Venice's finest singer." He dipped his chin toward me. "You will travel to Rome, be installed at the Villa Fabiani, and become the cardinal's pet nightingale."

"What?" I jumped up, knocking my wineglass to the floor. The sbirri who had been leaning against the wall with bored expressions sprang to attention, but Montorio only smiled and waved them back.

"You heard me, Signor Amato. You are bound for Rome and the Villa Fabiani. I'm sure they will make you quite comfortable. Since the pope's infirmities handed the reins of power to Lorenzo Fabiani, his palace has become one of the finest in the city."

I shook my head. "Opera lover or not, I can't imagine that Fabiani would trot back to the fold in gratitude for a few arias."

Montorio answered with a sour chuckle. "I see we'll have to teach you a thing or two about papal intrigue. The cardinal's besetting infatuation with music only opens the door to opportunity. Fabiani will have you serenading day and night, at everything from formal receptions to intimate dinners. At those particularly, you will use your eyes and ears as cleverly as your mouth."

"You want me to act as your spy."

"Call it what you will." He shrugged. "We need information and we're sending you to get it. Use your incomparable voice to best advantage. Ingratiate yourself with Fabiani…impress him with your taste and refinement. Make him ask for you when he is relaxing, amusing himself with family and closest friends. We're especially interested in visits from Prince Aurelio Pompetti. Listen well. Every innuendo, every hint of which direction the cardinal will throw his support in the conclave is valuable to us."

I fought the impulse to knock the smug smile from Montorio's face. "You think Fabiani wouldn't see through such an obvious ploy?"

"He may have his suspicions, but he won't refuse your services. He would never turn down one of the most sought after castrati in all of Europe, and once he's heard you sing, he cannot fail to be enchanted. Myself, I have no ear for music, but everyone knows what Maestro Vivaldi said after your last opera at the San Marco. While you were taking your bows, the great maestro clutched his heart and whispered, 'Tonight Tito has wafted our ears to Paradise.'"

I shook my head, fists clenched. "No, I won't do it. I've been touring for months and I've made up my mind to spend some time with my family. Even if I weren't exhausted, I wouldn't go to Rome. I'm a performer, not a spy."

Montorio's nostrils flared with a long inhalation of breath. His glass made an impatient clink as he deposited it on the table. "You don't seem to understand, Amato. This is not a request, it's an order."

"You have no authority to order me to Rome. Use the power of your rank to intimidate me as you may, but I'm a free citizen of Venice with no crime to my credit. You have no right to hold me—I demand to be released immediately."

"I was afraid you might take that attitude. Your fame has given you an independent streak, but I wager we have something that will change your mind." He gestured to Messer Grande, who raced from the room with his red robe streaking behind him. The sbirri roused and took up positions at my flanks. One forced me down on the chair with a heavy hand on my shoulder.

Montorio took the opportunity to enjoy a pinch of snuff. He placed the weed on the little platform of skin between his thumb and forefinger, bent his nose to his hand, and snuffed the treat into his lungs. A froth of lace jiggled at his wrist as he sneezed and shook the debris to the floor. He had not changed his seat on the edge of the table, but the charade of tavern comrades was over. He was a senator, the Red Inquisitor, patriarch of the noble Montorio clan, and blood relation to half the government ministers. I was only a common citizen of undistinguished lineage, an entertainer who had been favored by the fortunes of popular taste. I might be king of the stage at the opera house, but cries of bravo and flowers strewn at my feet couldn't protect me against whatever Montorio was planning.

I heard the sound of heavy boots marching down the corridor, then a soft moan. Sbirri dragged in an unfortunate being who looked and smelled more like a sack of refuse than a man. His shirt was caked with dried blood and his breeches with filth. Matted brown hair covered the face that hung upon his chest. Messer Grande grabbed a hunk of that hair and jerked the man's bearded chin up.

"Alessandro!" I cried.

My brother's cheeks were lumpy and swollen. One eye was squeezed shut by glistening purple flesh. The other rolled frantically in its socket. Alessandro gave no sign that he could see or even hear me. The sbirri dumped his battered body a few paces from my chair.

I struggled against the strong arms of the sbirri who kept me pinioned. Montorio continued to swing one leg, inspecting the large ruby on his forefinger and shaking his head. Finally he said, "It's always sad to see a promising young man turn greedy."

"What are you talking about?" I sputtered. "What have you done to Alessandro?"

"We've been watching your brother. Such a clever, industrious fellow. Alessandro Amato has laid the foundations of a tidy little fortune, sailing every few months with a load of Venetian merchandise and returning with a good grade of Turkish tobacco."

"There's nothing illegal in that."

"There is when his ship carries salt."

I looked at Alessandro, curled in a ball on the stone floor, chest weakly rising and falling. Blood pounded against my eardrums, and my breath came in ragged pants. My brother had never transported salt. It was strictly contraband. The cultivation of the salt marshes and their prized product was a monopoly of the Venetian government. Any citizen cutting into that profitable trade was considered a traitor to the Republic. Alessandro would never have taken such a grave risk. He didn't need to.

"You know my brother is no smuggler." I flung the words at Montorio with all the force of my well-developed lungs. "You had him arrested because you suspected I wouldn't play your game."

Montorio shrugged and moved to loom over Alessandro. He applied an elegant shoe to my brother's midsection and rolled him onto his back. A weak groan was Alessandro's only response.

"Nevertheless, the harbor inspector found a trunk of salt in the hold of your brother's ship," Montorio said, cocking an eyebrow at me.

"Planted," I replied fiercely.

He gave another shrug, another wolfish smile. "I admire you boys. I truly do. Your brother on the seas and you on the stage. Each in your way hearkens back to that enterprising spirit that made our Republic great. I'd like to reach out to you as a friend, to help your family out of this terrible predicament." He spread his hands. "But I need a sign that my favor would be appreciated and awarded the gratitude it deserves. Do you understand?"

I unclenched my strained neck muscles long enough to nod my assent.

"Excellent! I knew we'd talk you around eventually." The disheveled nobleman nodded at Messer Grande, then continued. "Smuggling is a serious offense, of course, but I have the resources to see that Alessandro's trial is delayed. Once you've set out for Rome, I'll see that a doctor is called and Alessandro is moved to a cell with a modicum of comfort. Who knows, if your reports advance my brother's cause, perhaps the evidence against your brother may even disappear. What's one more trunkful of salt in the lagoon?"

Montorio stepped over Alessandro and moved to straighten the fabric of my jacket that the sbirri had rumpled. I could barely stop myself from spitting in his face as he tidied my neckcloth and gave me his last command. "Better have your man pack some warm clothing, my friend. Rome can be quite windy in January. We wouldn't want a cold settling into this golden throat of yours."

Chapter 3

The morning of Epiphany found me aboard a sleek, single-masted tartan bound for Ancona, the eastern port of the Papal States. Before sailing, I'd been allowed a quick visit home, under guard. I thanked heaven that Montorio had not dispatched uniformed constables; a return of the sbirri would have scared the children out of a year's growth. Instead, the man who hovered at my shoulder while I delivered my bad news to Gussie and Annetta was a clerical gentleman of Montorio's own retinue, a young *abate* who would escort me all the way to Rome.

Abate Lenci was a youth of twenty or so years who looked more like an overgrown choir boy than a career ecclesiastic. His brown curls framed flushed cheeks, and his freckled nose stuck up at a jaunty angle. Only his blue-eyed gaze, wary and shrewd beyond his years, revealed his Montorio character. High-strung as a whippet, the abate guided me through my goodbyes and down to the docks with an insistent hand at the small of my back. I quickly saw that his primary task was to prevent me from dawdling, not escaping. How could I possibly flee, after seeing Alessandro in such a state?

As dawn's weak light challenged the night sky with the faintest tinge of mother-of-pearl, we left our cramped quarters and ascended to the wind-swept deck. My manservant, Benito, followed me to the rail, while Lenci pestered a busy sailor with questions about the ship's capacity. Watching Venice's familiar domes and towers fade into the mist, numb from anger and exhaustion, I was barely aware of Benito arranging an extra scarf around my throat.

"Don't bother," I whispered. "I don't care whether I ever sing a note again."

Benito thrust his hands back into the woolly muff that hung from a cord around his neck. He cocked his head in bird-like fashion. "Why do you say that, Master?"

"If it weren't for my voice, Alessandro would be on his way to Constantinople, not bleeding onto the cold stones of the doge's prison."

"Senator Montorio said that Signor Alessandro would be taken care of as long as you sang for Cardinal Fabiani."

I nodded, pretending that the railing I grasped so tightly was Montorio's sagging, rope-veined neck.

"And if your throat becomes inflamed," Benito continued in his calm, motherly fashion, "Fabiani will think you sound like a bullfrog and send you packing. Then Signor Alessandro will be in even worse trouble." He emphasized his advice by pushing the scarf up closer under my chin.

Benito was right, of course. He usually was. In his youth, Benito had submitted to the knife and trained as a singer, but his voice had lacked the power needed for a stage career and he'd drifted into personal service. His new career was an excellent fit; Benito had always had an uncanny knack for divining people's needs and finding ways to fulfill them. This clever, delicate castrato, whose full name was Benedetto Benaducci, had been with me for seven years. He dressed my hair to perfection, had saved my life twice, and never told me less than the truth, even when I fished mightily for compliments.

I released the railing with a reluctant sigh, and Benito leaned close to whisper, "Is that busybody over there one of Senator Montorio's sons?"

I glanced toward Abate Lenci, who was knocking on a stack of casks as if he were a customs inspector. "No, I think the senator's sons all have government posts. Lenci must be connected through a Montorio sister. I seem to recall that one of the younger ones fell in love with a vineyard owner from the mainland. The alliance caused quite a stir at the time because he was merely *nobilita da terra firma*...not a founding family and not particularly wealthy. She was allowed to marry for love only because her other sisters had already made such advantageous alliances. Lenci must be her son. And by the by, watch what you say when he's in earshot. I think he's cleverer than that boyish face would suggest."

As Benito winked to let me know that he had reached the same conclusion, a sail unfurled with the sudden crack of a pistol shot and Lenci's heavy traveling boots stumbled into a coil of rope that was rapidly unwinding. The hemp slithered around his ankle like a malevolent yellow snake. A pair of sailors elbowed each other in anticipation of an abate swinging from the rigging, but Lenci was quick on his feet. He freed himself with an acrobatic leap and inserted himself on the railing between Benito and me.

"Why so gloomy, Signor Amato?" Lenci had a honeyed baritone. "We are bound for the most exciting city in the world."

"Before your uncle's men invaded my home last night, excitement was the last thing on my mind."

Lenci's mouth pulled to one side in a knowing grimace. "You'd best find out early, the senator seldom fails to get what he wants. I wanted to travel and see the world...perhaps inspect the wine fields of France and bring some new ideas back to our farm. But my uncle the senator hatched a different plan. When I turned sixteen, Zio Antonio pressed my mother to have me inducted into the church so I could serve my uncle the cardinal. I was less than keen, and Papa protested, but..." He wiped a hand over his mouth.

Did I detect a rebellious sneer?

"Before the year was out," he continued, "I received minor orders and was made an abate. I've been at the end of the senator's leash ever since."

"The senator must have a long leash, to stretch all the way from Venice to Rome."

"So he does, Signore. Zio Antonio is the head of our family. He may be harsh, but he knows what's best and keeps us on course…one way or another." He fixed me with a pointed look. "As you have seen."

An oath rose to my lips, but I cleared my throat instead. "Do you live at the Embassy?"

"Yes, unless I'm away from Rome on some errand, I stay at the ambassador's palace on the Piazza Venezia. They keep me close the better to run me off my feet. Zio Stefano…I mean, my uncle the cardinal takes a lot of looking after. But really, the palace isn't so bad. It's absolutely at the center of all the action in Rome—especially at carnival time. When they run a horse race on the Corso, the beasts finish right under our windows. We're so close we can see their hooves striking sparks from the pavement."

I had to smile at his burst of enthusiasm. "If your uncles have their way, you will be moving to an even grander palace."

Lenci wrinkled his brow. "Leave the Embassy?" he asked slowly.

"For the Quirinal," I answered, naming the palace favored by recent occupants of the papal throne. "If the Cardinal Ambassador is elected pope, won't you be serving him at the Quirinal instead of the Embassy?"

Abate Lenci removed his oversize tricorne and ran his hand over the curls that trailed down into a plait buried beneath the collars of his greatcoat. He studied the watery patterns created by the ship's wake. "Of course," he finally whispered. "Zio Stefano as pope…I suppose it really could happen…if he doesn't blow himself up first."

He sent me a sidelong glance, grinning at the confusion he saw in my expression. "My uncle the cardinal fancies himself a natural philosopher, you see. If he's not on the roof peering at the stars through his telescope, he's in his workroom making a big stink and noise. He calls it 'experimentation.'"

"That seems an odd pastime for a churchman. The priests in Venice never stop fuming over this new fad for exploring nature's mysteries."

He shrugged. "I doubt that my uncle the cardinal will be unraveling much of God's handiwork. He subscribes to journals from the Royal Society in London and its counterpart in Paris. He gets very excited about duplicating the experiments they record. But being Zio Stefano, he thinks he's ever so much more intelligent than those foreign fellows. To improve on their theories, he adds a bit here or changes something there, so his efforts generally come to naught. A quiet, calm naught if we're lucky."

"What does Senator Montorio think of these experimentations?"

"When Zio Antonio is around, Zio Stefano keeps his scientific enthusiasms to himself. He knows where his bread is buttered. My uncle the senator would be furious if he knew how much time Zio Stefano spends in his workroom. After all, what could possibly be gained by blowing up glass vials or making sparks dance on a wire?"

I nodded slowly, and Benito raised a knowing eyebrow. I fancy we shared the same thought: Tito Amato, virtuoso soprano, was not the only unwilling creature at the end of Antonio Montorio's leash.

⌒☉☉⌒

The next two days brought calm seas and favorable winds that delivered us to Ancona in good speed. The port dated back to the Roman emperor Trajan's time and had been built on a thumb of land that jutted into the Adriatic Sea well south of Venice. Though Ancona's harbor was a marvel of ancient engineering, the silt and refuse of the intervening centuries had accumulated to the point that ships of greater tonnage than our small tartan could no longer cross the harbor bar.

Several years ago Pope Clement had instituted the Herculean project of dredging out the channel and reconstructing the breakwaters. The news had caused an uproar on the Rialto. Venice was already losing valuable trade to cities better situated to take advantage of the expanding Atlantic commerce. Like the Montorios who sailed to the Levant to meet spice caravans that had crossed the desert from India, most of the great trading houses had fallen back on their traditional eastward trade routes.

The restoration of a rival port that would cut precious days off a run to the eastern Mediterranean threatened the livelihood of nearly every Venetian. Never a city known to bend a willing knee to Rome, Venice's senators had reviled Pope Clement in the Great Council, and her common citizens had staged a bloody riot before the residence of the Papal Nuncio.

When our little party disembarked at the pier, Abate Lenci first produced papers for the customs inspector, then roused some porters drowsing beneath a canvas awning. Leaving the abate to negotiate fees, I strolled along the water. The town enjoyed a fine aspect. Green and brown hills snaked down from the rocky uplands to curl around a cuplike harbor of sparkling blue water. The day was pleasantly warm, so I decided to take a closer look at the scaffolds and cranes on the rubble-strewn dike that had caused such a stir. Before I'd covered three more strides, Lenci grabbed the back of my cloak and jerked me to a standstill.

"No time for sightseeing," he said. "A coach will be waiting for us at the Mercantile Exchange. It's been arranged."

"Surely another hour won't make any difference. I'd like to see how the breakwaters are progressing and have a look at the ruins of the Roman arch on the hill over the town."

The dogged abate pulled me in the opposite direction. "My orders are to convey you to the Villa Fabiani with all possible speed. I must do as I am instructed, Signore. Perhaps that is a lesson you should be learning as well."

Lenci located the Exchange, and while my trunks were being secured to the roof of the coach, he sat us down to a sloppy, hurried meal at a nearby inn. To further add to my humiliation, he sent the porters back to the ship to retrieve another gift for Cardinal Fabiani, a basket containing a prize ham that had been cured on a Montorio estate. When the coach set out for the highroad that led across the Italian peninsula to Rome, I was rubbing shoulders with a forty-pound hunk of pork that reeked of garlic and rosemary.

Though the way was steep, we covered forty miles that day. Abate Lenci inquired about the cities I'd visited on my operatic tours but soon fell silent after receiving only irritated grunts in response. The road flattened the next morning, allowing the coach to fly through the miles. Lenci had procured excellent horses, and we had no difficulties changing teams. At every post station, the young abate produced a document strung with an impressive number of red seals that the stablers honored without question.

Prudence finally conquered my foul mood and prodded me to fish for information. I knew that Cardinal Fabiani, my future host, was an opera lover, but that could describe almost any inhabitant of Italy. Regions might vary in food and drink, in dialect and ruler, but every Italian from Venice to Palermo loved the opera. It was our home-grown spectacle. I needed to know more about the cardinal's political dealings. Donning a courtier's smile, I raised the subject with Abate Lenci.

"In Rome, Fabiani lives like a prince," he replied, "a prince of the church surrounded by a priestly retinue. The Cardinal Padrone is only the foremost of his titles. He holds so many offices and benefices it would take several minutes for me to recite them all.

"But at his ancestral home in Tuscany, his family amounts to very little." Lenci sniffed as he waved a well-manicured hand. "You must know the sort—minor nobility, barely tolerated at court."

I nodded, having encountered many down-at-the-heels aristocrats in my time.

"For years, the Fabiani nibbled on the Medici largesse like mice on cheese. When the death of the last grand duke made way for the Hapsburg governors, the cardinal's relatives were tossed out of the Pitti Palace without a crumb. Of course, Lorenzo Fabiani was well established in Rome by that time. I'll let you guess, Signor Amato. Did the Cardinal Padrone shed any tears over his cousins' retreat to their hereditary estate in the marshy middle of nowhere? Loosen his purse strings to ease their disgrace?"

Not knowing the man, I could only shrug.

"In a word—no. Where his family is concerned, Cardinal Fabiani observes only one rule—loyalty to his mother. It was the

Marchesa Fabiani who pushed him into Pope Clement's sphere of influence and paved the way for his brilliant career. She reaps her reward by living in luxury with an army of servants at her beck and call."

I pushed my lap robe aside and leaned forward. "The pope's family are also from Tuscany, are they not?"

"The Corsini." Lenci nodded, a study in wide-eyed innocence.

"Quite a few rungs above the Fabiani, I believe."

"Nearly at the top of the ladder. With a Corsini on his father's side and a Strozzi on his mother's, some of the bluest blood of Tuscany flows through the pope's veins."

"Then how...?"

Lenci interrupted with a schoolboy giggle. "The time-honored way...they say the marchesa was quite a beauty in her youth."

"Fabiani is the pope's bastard son?"

"So some say."

"Do you believe them?"

He gave a short nod. "It seems the most reasonable explanation for Fabiani's rapid rise. Connection is everything in Rome."

"Pope Clement has reigned only nine years. Cardinal Fabiani would have been born many years before he became pope."

"True. Makes you wonder if the old lady simply made a lucky bedding or if she had a soothsayer tucked away on the Fabiani estate. Whatever the source of her good fortune, when the pope's poor health and lack of Corsini nephews created a crack in the wall of papal power, the marchesa hurried to Rome and plastered her son right in."

"And her husband?"

"Dead. Fell off a horse, I think. Broke his neck."

"I see. Is Cardinal Fabiani an able man?"

"Oh, quite. In every sphere. He seems to handle cardinals and bishops as easily as foreign heads of state and is immensely proud of his exalted position."

"Um, that doesn't bode well," I muttered more to myself than to Lenci.

"What doesn't?" the abate asked.

"You know what the Bible says—pride goeth before a fall."

"A fall rather goes with the territory, doesn't it? If your power rests on one man—and that man is hovering at death's door…" He shrugged his shoulders.

"That is one thing I don't understand. Why doesn't Fabiani use his power with the Sacred College to ensure his own election?"

Lenci scratched his chin. "It's a delicate balancing act. My uncles haven't favored me with all the details, but I gather that the Spanish cardinals are adding their weight to our side. An equal number of the Italians, especially the Romans who are loyal to Prince Pompetti, are throwing their lot in with Di Noce."

"What about the French?"

"You can't trust the Frogs." He laughed. "They'll do exactly as they please, as usual. Probably vote for one of their own, even though they have no chance. It's the block of votes that Fabiani controls that will tip the scale, but he doesn't have enough cardinals in his pocket to be elected himself."

I nodded. Unfortunately, my companion could shed no light on the cardinal's current favorite to succeed his benefactor.

"I believe that's your lookout," he told me when pressed.

Repeated questions only drew descriptions of Fabiani's fashionable carriages and lavish banquets and receptions. In short, nothing I deemed useful. I soon fell into a moody silence, and Lenci closed his eyes. In a few moments, he began to snore with shallow, wincing breaths—the sound of a fox hibernating in its den.

Benito sat across from me. Though he had been gazing out the window in cool repose, I knew he had been following the conversation closely. He gestured toward Lenci. "Is the abate to take reports on your progress?" Benito asked in a murmur.

"Lenci will serve as my day-to-day contact, but if I manage to discover anything of substance, I'm to give my information directly to Cardinal Montorio. The senator instructed me to ask leave to hear Mass at San Marco every Sunday. It's the church attached to the *palazzo* that serves as the Venetian Embassy. All the Venetians in Rome attend services there, so I won't be likely to attract any attention. After Mass, the Cardinal Ambassador will meet with me in private."

"Zio Stefano," Benito whispered with a saucy smile.

I nodded grimly. "Zio Stefano…who takes a lot of looking after and seems in imminent danger of blowing himself to bits. I wonder what he makes of his brother's scheme to worm me into Fabiani's household?"

"You'll soon find out. Today is Thursday. Cardinal Montorio will expect some information in three days time."

I groaned softly, gave the ham a vicious shove, and bent to furious thought while chewing on a knuckle. Benito went back to looking out the window. "What a benighted country this is," he observed after a few minutes.

I had to agree. The lands of the Papal States were wrapped in a ragged cloak of wintering flax, but even in the fullness of summer, these rocky fields wouldn't compare to Venice's fertile mainland holdings. In an effort to wrest what they could from the poor soil, the peasants cultivated the hills nearly to the top. Here and there, I spotted a wretched hut unfurling a wisp of smoke into a colorless sky. Nearer to the road, an occasional goat nibbled at a tussock of withered grass. As we jolted along, we passed one of the pope's subjects bent under a massive load of dry sticks. The toothless visage he raised to our streaking coach was the face of poverty itself.

The hours rolled on in weary monotony, and by the time we had reached Italy's ancient capital, I was snoring along with Lenci. I woke with Benito shaking my shoulder. Dusk had fallen, and our coach had come to a halt in the forecourt of a large villa. Still muddled from sleep, I slid the glass in the door open and leaned out to see an arched colonnade lit by a hanging lamp. Its flames threw wavering reflections across tall bronze doors. At each end of the colonnade, a wing of polished stone projected into the fuzzy twilight. Somewhere close by, a fountain gurgled in noisy hiccups. As I rubbed my eyes, the towering doors parted noiselessly and a pair of footmen in sky blue livery shot down a short flight of marble stairs and bent to unfold the coach steps. With a sinking feeling, I realized that I had reached my destination.

Chapter 4

Benito and the prize ham were conveyed around to the back of the villa. Lenci and I were escorted through the bronze doors into an immense hall. Marble columns rose to the vaulted ceiling and beautifully stitched tapestries decorated the walls. Instead of the religious themes I might have expected, the needlework drew its subjects from ancient myth. On the largest, a lifelike Diana gazed across the hall with raised chin and parted lips, as if she expected worshipers to file in and lay tribute at her feet at any moment. I was admiring the workmanship of the tiny stitches when a fleeting movement caught my eye.

It could have been a denizen of the tapestries come to life, a nymph flitting from column to column, white robe and scarves trailing behind her, silver hair unpinned, streaming wildly. Then I saw the truth: not a nymph, merely a weak-minded old woman wandering in her nightdress. A pretty, apple-cheeked girl in the drab gown and linen cap of a servant pursued her.

Lenci ignored the elderly nymph, but brightened as the dark-haired girl drew near. He extended his hand to greet her, calling "Gemma" as she barreled past. But Gemma was too intent on her prey to spare a word for the young abate. In an uncharacteristically unguarded moment, his cherub face made his disappointment obvious.

My curiosity was forestalled by the arrival of a lean man in a jacket and waistcoat of unrelieved black. He advanced in mincing steps, putting one foot precisely in front of the other as if he walked a springy tightrope instead of a solid, mosaicked floor. Abate Lenci presented me to Cardinal Fabiani's private secretary and general factotum, Abate Pio Rossobelli.

"Ah, Signor Amato, how delightful. Our much-awaited songbird has arrived just in time." Rossobelli spoke in oily tones, surprising me with a courtly bow that was a few rungs above the station of a hired musician, even a relatively famous one. "The cardinal wished to welcome you himself, but alas, he has been called to the Quirinal on pressing business. I'm afraid that you will have to content yourself with my humble services."

Returning his bow, I voiced the usual pleasantries.

Dismissing the abate who had guided me to Rome, Rossobelli hooked his long fingers under my elbow and ushered me toward the grand staircase. I was almost sorry to see Lenci go. A Montorio he might be, but I reckoned him a more pleasant companion than the one who imprisoned my arm in a strangle hold.

As we mounted the cascade of marble steps, I took the opportunity to observe this Abate Rossobelli at close quarters. The first part of his name fit him well. The stray hairs escaping from under his short clerical wig were a dull brick red and the blood flowing under his pale skin seemed to pool in ruddy blotches at the crest of his sharp cheekbones. As to *belli*...I thought not. A less handsome man would be hard to find.

Fabiani's secretary observed me with the same level of scrutiny. His lank jaws maintained a perfectly proper smile, but his bulging, pink-rimmed eyes glowed with curiosity. Not, I thought, with the curiosity of a whole man observing a castrato at close range—I am well used to that look—but with a much more cunning appraisal.

Once on the second level, Rossobelli covered the maze of corridors hung with portraits and tapestries in long strides, chattering about the history of the villa and the wealthy Genoese banker who had built it. At the rear of the house, he opened the door to a luxurious suite. The first chamber was furnished with comfortable sofas and had its own balcony that overlooked an orchard garden lit with torches set on iron pikes. The bedroom contained a canopied bed hung in turquoise damask, a marquetry dressing table, and an open secretary furnished with a liberal supply of quills, ink, and paper. There was even a dressing room with a cozy nook for Benito. The reason behind this extraordinary favor became clear when the abate pointed to a bell over the bed's carved headboard.

"This will be your clarion call, Signore. The bell connects to a cord in the cardinal's suite, right along the corridor at the corner of the southwest wing. His Eminence will ring when he wants you. Warn your man to be ready. The cardinal doesn't appreciate being serenaded by a man in a dressing gown and nightcap. No matter what hour, you'll have to be presentable."

My jaw dropped. "I'm expected to sing at all hours?"

Rossobelli lifted his eyes heavenward, as if praying for patience. "You've been told nothing of this?"

"No, nothing."

"What else could I expect from Lenci? Too busy chasing skirts to have a care for anyone else's troubles. Ah well, it's all in a day's work…unpleasant details fall through the cracks and Rossobelli comes along with the dustpan." He gave a tight smile, then lowered his voice as the door opened on Benito and a sturdy footman lugging my trunk and bags. "It's like this, Signore. His Eminence often finds difficulty falling asleep. By trial and error, he has devised a helpful bedtime ritual. Cardinal Fabiani reads or studies his papers until his eyelids are heavy, then he requires a dim room, a cool cloth across his forehead, and most important of all, a soothing song. You understand?"

I nodded. A bit bewildered, I'll admit.

"Cardinal Fabiani will be so happy that you have arrived. When Cardinal Montorio told us of your coming visit, His Eminence was absolutely astounded…quite overcome…I mean with joy, of course."

I tried to hide my dismay, but Rossobelli's eyes were sharp. "Come, come. You're displeased. Will it be so difficult? Singing for the man who has had all the responsibilities of Christendom piled upon his shoulders? Lightening his sleepless misery with a little midnight serenade?"

"No, of course not. It's just that I'm not accustomed to giving concerts in the middle of the night. And not for an audience of one. My voice is trained to reach the top tiers of a theater."

"Oh, you will have plenty of opportunity to show off your voice before a crowd. This evening, in fact."

"Sing tonight?" I croaked in distress.

He plucked a watch from his fob pocket. "Yes, it's just gone seven. His Eminence is hosting a little reception at nine. You will need to report to the music room at thirty minutes 'til. I've left some scores of the cardinal's favorite arias on the harpsichord."

Behind Rossobelli's back, the footman was unpacking my trunk and handing clothing to Benito to brush and put away. It looked as if my manservant had already formed a bond with the footman whose muscular thighs seemed in danger of splitting the cheap fabric of his breeches. As Rossobelli elaborated on my marching orders, the two servants shared some rueful headshaking and eyerolling, ending with Benito aiming a rude gesture at the oblivious secretary.

Wishing I could do the same, I said, "But I've been traveling for days. My throat is coated with the dust of the road."

"How unfortunate," Rossobelli answered, flicking his hand as if to disperse any dust particles that might still be circling. "It does pain me to ask, but His Eminence would be so happy…so grateful if you would but try. Cardinal Montorio will be among the guests. I'm sure the Cardinal Ambassador is eager to enjoy the voice that his good Venetian *zecchini* have purchased." The abate widened his eyes dramatically. "The Montorio brothers are providing suitable compensation, are they not? Woe upon my foolish head if I've misjudged your circumstances…I just assumed…since they are making a gift of your services…"

I stared at the floor as he trailed off into silence. Suitable compensation? Alessandro's safety in exchange for a bit of wear and tear on my throat? There was no arguing against that bargain.

I raised my chin and answered, "I will, of course, be delighted to comply with Cardinal Fabiani's wishes."

∽∾

The music room that Rossobelli had so casually mentioned was a crimson and gold salon the size of a small amphitheater. The same stocky footman had fetched me after Benito had brewed a pot of his throat-reviving tea and worked his decorative magic on my person and attire. When I caught sight of my reflection in the long mirrors of the music room, I was almost shocked.

I saw a long-limbed eunuch of remote mien and noble bearing clad in his finest court dress, looking as if he had nothing in his head but the melodies he would soon sing. No one would guess that I was prey to emotions that had my stomach in knots and my heart in despair. Without even being aware of the transformation, I had slipped into my stage demeanor along with my brocade jacket and powdered wig.

The cardinal's harpsichord was in excellent tune. I assumed that a keyboard musician would arrive to accompany me, and a few string players as well, if the music stands on the dais were any clue. But just then I was alone. Determined to make the most of my time, I set to work on some simple scales. Despite Benito's herb-laced tea, my chest felt tight and the tones that bounced off the mirrored walls sounded strident and harsh. My natural voice was an unforced, agile soprano that could master any ornamentation a composer could invent. It wouldn't be at its best tonight, but if I could just complete a proper warm-up, it would do.

I'd finished my vocalises and was playing through one of the well-worn sheets of music when the back of my neck began to crawl. Someone was observing me. I was sure of it. People stared at me every night on the stage, but this was a different sensation—oppressive, vaguely malevolent. My hands sank away from the keyboard, and I slowly pivoted from the waist. Candlelight from chandeliers and wall brackets played over a completely empty room.

I turned back to the harpsichord. To regain my concentration and clear my head cavities, I opened my jaws in a huge yawn and sounded a series of ascending high notes. When a length of white silk drifted over my shoulder, I almost swallowed my tongue.

"What a mouth you have," came a whisper by my ear.

In one motion, I shot off the bench, turned, and pressed my rump against the keyboard. The old woman from the entry hall giggled and raised a mottled hand to stroke my jaw. Her cheeks were wrinkled and sunken, but she fluttered her sparse eyelashes like a girl of sixteen.

"Can you crack a nut with those jaws?" she asked. "I had a groom once…a tall fellow…with a wide mouth like yours. He could crack a walnut between his teeth. He showed me every time he saddled my big bay. How he could make me laugh."

I relaxed. The wandering lady had escaped her keeper. I had only to find the girl with the plump cheeks and I could get on with my warm-up.

"Allow me to assist you, Signora," I began, taking her outstretched hand in both of mine. "Where is your maid?"

Her vacant eyes held my gaze for a moment, then questioned the air with sharp, darting looks.

"Come, Signora. I'll help you find her." I stepped off the low dais and gave her hand a gentle tug. She descended, but twisted out of my grasp. Her pipestem arms swooped in rhythmic circles, setting her sheer draperies and the loose skin beneath them into quivering motion.

"Sing," she whispered. "Pretend nothing's amiss. Or *she* will come. She'll bring her rope and tie my ankle to the bedpost. She makes it tight, tight. Like this." The increasingly distraught woman clamped her fingers around my wrist, her heavy ring pressing my flesh to the bone.

When I winced, she threw my hand aside to raise the hem of her gown. I looked down. Blue veins snaked over her bare, withered foot. Sobbing now, she pointed to an ankle encircled by a ring of bruised, chafed skin.

A door slammed. Two footmen followed the girl that Abate Lenci had called Gemma across the shiny parquet floor. This time I noticed more than her coloring. Gemma's skirts swelled over shapely hips before nipping to a slender waist, and a generous bosom peeked over her tightly laced bodice. She would have been a welcome sight for any man if she hadn't been scowling and pushing up her sleeves like a pint-sized Sicilian ready for a brawl.

"Marchesa, you've been a very naughty girl." Gemma could have been chastising a five-year-old.

My companion whimpered and tried to hide behind me.

"You have chocolate and biscuits waiting in your room, My Lady. And Guido has made up a nice fire," Gemma continued. "Look, you're shivering. Your feet are turning blue from these cold floors. Come along now. Do be a good girl for once."

Gemma reached around me to grab her charge's wrist. The unhappy lady balled a handful of my jacket in her other fist and gave me a pitiful look. While Gemma tugged at her arm, she tugged equally hard at my brocade.

"Marchesa…" Gemma's tone sharpened to a warning.

The determined marchesa stretched her mouth in a croaking cry until her old face matched the classical mask of tragedy that decorated so many theaters. "Signore, help me, please," she wailed.

Gemma jerked her chin at the footmen.

"Wait," I stammered, acutely aware that my lack of status in the household gave me no right to comment, let alone intervene. "This lady has committed no wrong. She just came in to hear me sing. Let her stay and listen a moment."

I might as well have addressed empty air. Without so much as a nod, the footmen circled the marchesa with their arms and herded her away, sobbing softly and mumbling incoherently.

Gemma bent to the floor to retrieve one of the marchesa's errant scarves. Tucking the silk into her sleeve, she drew herself up to full height. Even then, the girl barely came up to the middle of my chest. "You are new here, Signore," she observed coldly.

I admitted as much, then added, "But I don't want to see the poor old lady mistreated."

"Do you even know who you are rushing to defend?"

I shook my head.

"Your *poor old lady* is Marchesa Olimpia Fabiani, the cardinal's mother. She occupies the warmest suite of rooms in the villa, receives every comfort she so much as mentions, and dines off dishes of gold." Gemma tossed her dark head. "Solid gold, mind you, not plate. The pope himself is not better taken care of."

"She showed me her ankle. It was bruised."

Gemma sighed. "You must understand. The marchesa is slowly losing her mind, and it's my job to see that she comes to no harm. Sometimes she has a good day. Then she allows me to dress her, and the cardinal takes her for a walk in the garden. Except that her conversation is confined to long-ago events, you would never guess how addled she truly is. But on a bad day…oh, Signore, you have no idea."

"Today is a bad day?"

"One of her worst."

"She does seem harmless, though."

Gemma snorted. "Tell that to Guido, the footman she chased through the garden this very afternoon. When I caught up with them, she had him cornered by the pavilion. She was brandishing a pistol in one hand and a hatchet in the other. The Blessed Virgin knows where she got those weapons…had them hidden in one of her hidey holes, I suppose. At any rate, I got there before harm was done."

"Perhaps the marchesa was defending herself as best she knew how. This man could have been rough with her."

"Rough with the marchesa?" Gemma rolled her eyes. "Guido wouldn't dare. The cardinal dotes on his mother and allows only so much restraint as needed to ensure her safety. He would have any footman who manhandled the marchesa whipped and thrown into prison. No, I'll tell you what Guido's crime was. The marchesa had ordered a strawberry ice. The kitchen was out of strawberries, so he brought her lemon instead."

As I hung my head, feeling foolish, Gemma softened her tone. "Would you like some advice, Signore?"

I nodded.

"You have no idea of the things that go on at the Villa Fabiani. If you want to stay out of trouble, you'd best to stick to your business and let others stick to theirs."

I sighed. If only that were possible.

⌒⟋⟍⟍⟍

Ten minutes before the concert, like players in a well-rehearsed show, more footmen appeared to dust the rows of chairs and replace guttering tapers with fresh. The musicians who made up the small orchestra entered with similarly practiced moves.

The harpsichordist shuffled the musical scores, placing a light, lilting piece by Scarlatti on top. "By the cardinal's standing order, we always start with this one." He was a round-faced man wearing a starched linen stock that cut into the abundant flesh of his neck. His tone could have frozen a mountain stream in midflow. "Do you know it?"

"Yes."

"And the others?"

I nodded. I'd studied most of these songs at the Conservatorio San Remo where I'd spent my boyhood. Each of the seemingly straightforward arias carried a subtle challenge that could easily expose a mediocre singer's limitations. The cardinal's favorites revealed a high degree of musical sophistication. I understood why he'd chosen them, but the collectively cool demeanor of my fellow musicians presented a puzzle.

A gong sounded, signaling the entrance of a splendid procession. The villa's rules of concert etiquette were more involved than any I had encountered in my previous travels. A pair of Swiss guards in striped uniforms and ceremonial helmets led the way. A double train of brightly dressed ladies and gentlemen interspersed with black-cassocked priests followed, separating to fill the rows of chairs in orderly fashion. Lastly, a quartet of pages bearing heraldic standards marched down the aisle and stationed themselves at the corners of the dais.

Without being told, I stiffened my spine like a soldier on review. At another gong, two cardinals clad in robes of scarlet silk topped by frothy capes of white lace started down the aisle.

I took a hard gulp. One of these men held the papal election, and my brother's freedom, in his bejeweled hands. I searched their faces as they neared the dais. With many bows, gracious smiles, and conspicuous protestations of humility, they invited each other to take the seat of honor.

One cardinal was tall and broad shouldered, with dark good looks that were ruined by bags under his eyes and a pointed nose that continually sniffed the air like an alley cat on the prowl. The other cardinal was short and stooped, with a vacant, bemused expression, and well-padded torso. Which was Lorenzo Fabiani, the man I must captivate with my song?

Abate Lenci provided the telling clue when the shorter cardinal finally succumbed to the other's urgings. He applied his scarlet backside to the gilded chair, rocked from side to side to settle his bulk, then patted his robe for something that was clearly missing. The abate who'd guided me to Rome hustled forward and produced a snuff box and lace-edged handkerchief for the man who must surely be Stefano Montorio, the uncle who took a good bit of looking after. Bowing back out of the way with a tactful mixture of apology and concern, Lenci seemed determined to ignore me—until he sent me a surreptitious wink that brought an unguarded grin to my lips.

The grin dissolved when I realized that the other cardinal was staring at me. So this was my host, Lorenzo Fabiani. Light from hundreds of candles glinted off the jeweled cross on his breast, but it was the gleam from his deep-set brown eyes that captured my attention. The noise of an audience preparing to be entertained—the rustling of robes and gowns, the discreet coughs, the scraping of chairs—all faded to nothing. The only sound in my ears was a roar like the waves of the Adriatic breaking over the sandbars of my island home. The only sight before my eyes was the cardinal's face with his restless nose, and those shadowed, searching eyes. For a moment I was breathless, drowning in his gaze.

Fabiani broke the spell by inclining his head in a gracious gesture. Behind me, the harpsichordist sounded a flourish. My song broke like a hound loosed for the hunt, and Scarlatti's brilliant notes streaked across the salon.

Chapter 5

Long after the line of elegant carriages had collected the cardinal's guests and rattled away into the chill Roman night, I remained awake. The fire in my bedroom crackled cheerily, but I found its warmth more oppressive than cozy. Seeking air, I donned my cloak and stepped onto the balcony off my sitting room. The garden torches had been extinguished; the only light came from the almost full moon. Its beams turned the paths below to silver ribbons strewn among the blue black rectangles of terraced herb beds and feathery silhouettes of cypress trees. Here and there, a pond shimmered. I leaned into the railing, straining my eyes to make out the lines of the pavilion set into the thick garden wall.

The Villa Fabiani, as I'd learned from Rossobelli, sat on the Janiculum Hill at the edge of Rome. Settled much later than the ancient city's famed seven hills on the east side of the Tiber, the Janiculum rose steeply from the river's western bank. Its healthy air and scenic views had attracted Renaissance builders who sought to avoid the unsavory alleyways of the central city. Wealthy bankers, well-endowed monastic orders, and leading prelates cleared patches of the forested pinnacle, created magnificent dwellings, and left the rest in parkland. The villa I'd been forced to call my new home shared the crest of the hill with several other estates that stretched north to the Vatican and south to the old Aurelian wall. To the east, beyond the fuzzy strip of mist I fancied must be rising from the Tiber, somewhere in the blackness relieved by only a few wavering dots of orange flame, lay the heart of Rome.

A tingle of expectation leapt to my throat, but I forced it down, reminding myself that I was hardly a tourist. I turned my thoughts back to that evening's concert. From the beginning, Cardinal Fabiani had fixed his expression in a coolly attentive smile and dispensed his applause in carefully measured doses. His guests followed his lead to perfection.

I wasn't immediately concerned. It often takes an audience some minutes to put the cares of the day aside and open their ears and hearts. But after receiving the same response for the next three arias, each more lovely than its predecessor, I started to worry. An evil genie popped onto my shoulder with the suggestion that Fabiani was guarding his response because he enjoyed keeping me in suspense.

The concert rapidly became a duel of wills. The cardinal might be a master at hiding his emotions, but I'd been performing since I was a boy of twelve. If I didn't know how to read an audience after sixteen years on the stage, I never would. The next song opened as a trivial piece that flew along at a hurdy-gurdy clip until it slowed to reveal surprising depths of musical poignancy that couldn't fail to move a true music lover.

I trained my gaze on my host. During the first section, Cardinal Fabiani closed his eyes and took a deep breath like a man steeling himself to have an abscessed tooth pulled. At the same time, I couldn't help noticing that my fellow Venetian, Cardinal Montorio, began tapping the toe of his satin slipper to the lively beat.

I sang the solemn bit with every ounce of conviction I possessed. Montorio's eyes glazed over like a fish on a market slab, but Fabiani's gaze locked onto mine as it had at the start of the concert. Only this time I was in charge. Now Fabiani was the one who was drowning, swept along by my heartbreaking lament, sucked beneath waves of sublime song until I chose to release him with one golden note that shimmered in the air long after the harpsichord had fallen silent.

The tension that had girded my chest ever since I'd left Venice suddenly relaxed. My host was nodding, applauding vigorously. If the occasion had been less formal, I would have expected him to jump to his feet and yell "Bravissimo."

A gust of wind raked the midnight garden, agitating the moon's reflection in the silver pools and making me clutch the woolen cloak to my throat. I knew I should seek the warmth of my bed, but this was the first time in many days that I had been completely alone, and I had much to consider. Pressing my back against the smooth stones of the villa, I drew in a breath of moist night air and tried to make sense of Fabiani's perplexing behavior at the supper that had followed the concert.

It was a simple buffet with dishes set out for the guests to partake of as they liked, but even so, I'd been surprised when Abate Rossobelli delivered the message that the cardinal desired my presence. I followed the abate through the unfamiliar corridors to a crowded dining room. He slipped away as soon as we entered, but it wasn't hard to locate Cardinal Fabiani holding court near the fire. The cardinal occupied a raised chair and wasn't eating or drinking. He was deep in conversation with two purple-clad bishops. As I approached, he waved them away and regarded me with an impenetrable stare. I sank to one knee, took his right hand, and kissed his ring of office.

I'm not sure what I expected. A word of welcome? A compliment on my performance? What I got was a slight pressure on my hand signaling me to rise, then a definite nod of dismissal. As I shuffled backward, as red-faced as if I'd made a stage entrance on the wrong cue, a nobleman in a lavender coat and black velvet breeches took my place.

"Here he is, my lost lamb. Better late than never," the cardinal announced, his pointed face breaking into a smile. He proffered his ring for the kiss in a casual gesture, then kept the man's hand in his while he waved an admonishing finger. "I know, I know. You have an excuse at the tip of your tongue. What was it this time? Some gypsy with an old pot he swears is an Etruscan antiquity?"

"Not this time, Your Eminence—" He would have continued, but Fabiani pressed his hand more tightly.

"Let me take another guess," the cardinal said. "Some old woman from the hills with a song to trade for her supper? Some ditty her people have been singing since the Caesars ruled?"

"Not that either. Though I assure Your Eminence that an old ballad can teach as much about a vanished race as an inscription carved in stone."

"Whatever the excuse, my friend, I wish you'd pull your head out of the dusty past. The delights of the present are so much more…" The cardinal released the nobleman's hand and shrugged his shoulders. "…immediate. For instance, you just missed an amazing concert. The Venetian castrato is enchanting."

I had to stop my mouth from dropping open. Enchanting was I? Would it have killed him to tell me so?

"Your Eminence," the man replied. "I offer no excuses, because there can be no excuse for missing a moment of your generous hospitality."

The cardinal chuckled. "Ah, Pompetti, where will you be if that silver tongue of yours ever goes mute?"

My breath caught in my throat. Back in Venice—it seemed a hundred years ago—Senator Montorio had warned me to be on the lookout for this man. Prince Pompetti led the cabal that supported Cardinal Di Noce.

I observed the prince even more closely. His carriage was exquisite: upright and commanding, yet graceful as a dancer's. But he had not acquired that weather-beaten skin practicing minuets and galliards in a ballroom. The lines at his eyes and mouth, plus the abundant gray threads in his natural black hair, led me to put his age at about fifty. A decidedly healthy and energetic fifty.

I suddenly realized I was staring more than good taste allowed. If I didn't want to be chucked out of the villa posthaste, I would have to be more prudent. A footman glided past with a two-handled tray. I plucked a wineglass off its silver expanse and moved closer to the immense fireplace. Because the space directly before the blaze became uncomfortably hot after just a few minutes, there was a constant flow of ladies in wide, pan-niered gowns edging forward to warm their bare shoulders, then retreating with fluttering fans. I tucked myself among them. With my eyes lowered to my glass, I tuned my ears toward Cardinal Fabiani and Prince Pompetti.

"…on your own, tonight?" the cardinal was asking.

"For the moment." Pompetti's response held the promise of infinite possibility.

"I had hoped to meet the lady who is so often at your side these days. They tell me her beauty is most remarkable, for an Englishwoman."

"Lady Mary is blessed with both beauty and brains. Her father subscribes to radical notions about the education of females. Mary Sysonby reads Latin as easily as English or Italian and is as well versed in history as any male scholar of my acquaintance. She is assisting me in compiling a catalogue of my collection."

"I see," the cardinal said regretfully. "She must be one of those tiresome women who are constantly at war with their irrational natures. Are you certain her society does you credit?"

"I find Lady Mary's company quite charming," Pompetti answered smoothly. "As I'm sure you will, once you've met her. Unfortunately, the lady had other business to attend to tonight."

"Ah-ha, I knew it." The cardinal thumbed the cleft in his well-formed chin. "It's all part of a plan. You sent your petticoat antiquarian on the trail of the Etruscan pot, so you could politick without distraction."

The prince laughed. A little too loudly, I thought. Then he bent his head to the cardinal's shoulder and continued to converse in low tones.

Santa Maria! How was I supposed to learn anything if people insisted on whispering?

I had to get closer. Letting the crush of satin and damask skirts sweep me farther from the fire, I circled around to a per-fect listening post at the back of Fabiani's throne-like chair. The phrases "a great devotion to the Blessed Mother" and "willing to bow to wiser heads" had barely met my ear when I felt a pecking tap on my shoulder.

"Signor Amato, found you at last." Abate Lenci was grinning like a sailor released from his ship after a four-month voyage. "I've been looking everywhere. Zio Stefano wants me to present you."

Lenci swept his arm toward the buffet table, where Cardinal Stefano Montorio was digging into a plate piled high with orange and scarlet balls of melon. I cast a glance toward the golden chair. Pompetti was still whispering and Fabiani was nodding seriously. But there was nothing for it. I allowed myself to be led away.

In a moment I was kneeling to kiss Montorio's ring, grimacing from the sticky juice that covered his flabby hand. The cardinal barely attended to Lenci's introduction. He waved his fork as words of praise competed for limited mouth space with morsels of half-chewed melon.

"You did us proud, Signore," he finished in a loud monotone intended to be heard by as many as possible. "Naples may boast of her Caffarelli and Siena of her Senesino, but you reminded everyone that the very best singers come from Venice."

"You are too kind, Eminence."

"No, no. I'll admit to a tin ear where music is concerned, but Fabiani was impressed and he's a connoisseur. He likes to be mysterious, but I could see that you fascinated him, and that's all that matters. Eh?"

Montorio didn't bother to lower his voice, and I caught a definite flick of his eyelid as he speared another chunk of melon. My God, was the man actually winking at me? Didn't he understand the need for discretion? I made a quick survey of the group clustered around the table and was relieved to note that all the guests appeared deep in conversation with their neighbors.

"Tell me," Cardinal Montorio continued in a forced, hearty tone, "why have you not adopted a name for the stage? Your fellow singers usually take a name to honor their patron or their birthplace."

"I had no patron. In the beginning, my father made arrangements for my...ahm...career and for my initial training at the *conservatorio.* After he died and I found work, I paid the maestros the balance owed in small installments."

"Then you need a name that reflects the glory of Venice."

"I prefer using my own."

"Let's see," he said, ignoring my statement and twirling his fork with a thoughtful gleam in his eye. "How about Veneziello?"

I shook my head.

"No? Then something to honor our republic's patron saint. Marco...Marciano. I have it...Marcolini. The perfect name for a castrato from Venice. What say you?" Cardinal Montorio smiled expansively.

I took a sip from my glass, then raised my chin. "With Your Eminence's indulgence, the Amato family settled in Venice even before the bones of our revered saint were enshrined in the basilica that bears his name. Since I won't be leaving any sons to carry on the family name, I can at least honor my ancestors by singing as an Amato."

"I see." The cardinal's lumpy face lost its vapid expression. He wrinkled his forehead in a questioning frown, and for the first time, I caught a glimpse of the intelligent curiosity that led him to probe nature's mysteries. Cardinal Montorio glanced at Abate Lenci, who had been hovering anxiously. "My nephew warned me that you're a bit of a free-thinker. An independent mind is an admirable trait. But for someone in your position, Signore, it could be more liability than virtue."

Before I could form a reply, the cardinal abandoned his thoughtful mien and inquired about my journey to Rome. I quickly launched into a description of our travels, relieved to have hit on a safer topic of conversation. Lenci chimed in with a few amusing observations about the sea voyage and had his uncle smiling and chuckling in no time. It was my mention of the Ancona project that turned the smiles to frowns again.

"Ancona," growled Cardinal Montorio. He slapped his plate down on the spotless tablecloth, sending melon balls on a careening course among the silver serving platters.

As a white-gloved footman swooped in to herd the melon into a napkin, Lenci caught my eye and shook his head in a warning gesture. He was not the only one to react. Abate Rossobelli had reappeared, still in his black day jacket. At the mention of Ancona, his lanky form jerked like a fish on a hook.

"How far has the work progressed at that teacup they call a harbor?" Cardinal Montorio grumbled.

I thought back to the spit of land that hooked around the silted-up bay. "That would be hard to say," I answered, very aware of Rossobelli standing across the table, staring at an epergne piled with frosted grapes as if they were rubies and emeralds coated with diamond dust. "Engineering isn't in my line at all. I remember seeing several large machines, but I have no idea what they were doing."

Montorio turned to his nephew. "You always have your nose into everything. What did you see?"

"As you may recall, we were in a bit of a hurry to put Ancona behind us," Lenci replied dryly. "But I did notice a pair of dredgers at work on the mouth of the harbor, and the walls of the dike were being widened and reinforced."

"Have they started on the lighthouse, yet?"

"Barely."

"How long will it take to complete the project?"

The abate shrugged. "There's a lot of work remaining, at least a quarter mile of dike that hasn't been touched. The better part of a year, I should think."

His uncle nodded sagely. Finally lowering his tone to a conspiratorial whisper, he replied, "Well and good. Antonio can bide his time, then."

Leaning back against the cold masonry, I forced my thoughts back to the present. I wished I could say that my labors over the long evening had borne fruit, but I would only be lying to myself. When Cardinal Fabiani's departure from the dining hall had signaled the assembly to disperse, my head was bursting with new faces and new information, little of which seemed likely to advance my progress.

The door to the balcony rattled and Benito came out, looking for all the world like Matteo's nurse when the boy had overstayed his bedtime.

"It's late, Master."

"I know."

"The breeze is picking up."

"So it is."

"I've warmed your bed."

"Thank you. I won't need anything else. Retire if you like."

Instead of retreating, Benito closed the door and moved to lean over the balcony railing. He craned his neck up and down, right and left.

"Checking for eavesdroppers? I think even Rossobelli must be in his bed by now."

"It never hurts to be sure."

I smiled in the darkness. In his varied adventures, my manservant had learned to be wary. I should take a leaf from his book.

The lowering moon shone on Benito's smooth forehead. "Come to bed, Master. You've done everything you can do for tonight."

"I've accomplished nothing."

"Cardinal Fabiani enjoyed your singing. That gives you a start."

"How do you know that Fabiani was pleased?"

"I spent most of the evening in the servants' hall."

I cocked my head in a silent question.

"They just knew," he answered. "It's hard to hide anything from people who dress you, drive you, feed you, and clean up all your messes."

I nodded. I'd experienced the relationship of master and servant from both sides. Though my calling provided me with an income sufficient to hire Benito's services and contribute to the running of our house on the Campo dei Polli, many of the wealthy who engaged me to sing treated me more like a servant paid to amuse than the artist I was.

Benito raised a gracefully plucked eyebrow. "If I tell you I've already found out an interesting thing or two, will you go to bed?"

"It depends. How interesting are these things?"

"You be the judge. The first is that Cardinal Fabiani had a favorite singer who occupied these very rooms. A castrato named Gaetano Tucci, by all accounts a pleasant fellow. Even the cook had a good word for him, and she's a harridan who spouts nothing but complaints. Fabiani dismissed Tucci when he learned that you were coming."

"I see." That explained the coolness of the other concert musicians. To them, I was an unwanted interloper. "And the other interesting thing?"

"Prince Pompetti is a frequent visitor at the villa."

"Senator Montorio is already aware of that."

"Is he also aware that the prince changes coachmen and footmen as often as a woman changes her hat?"

"Why?"

"That I don't know."

"How did you hear of this?"

Benito sent me a pert smile. "I didn't waste my time downstairs. I've been making friends."

"Would your friend be the broad-backed footman who brought up my trunks and lingered to help you unpack?"

He nodded. "That's Guido."

"Ah, Guido is it?" I rubbed my eyes and stretched my neck. Fatigue was finally taking hold. "Be careful, Benito. Rome isn't Venice. People don't come here for pleasure—they come on pilgrimages to display their Christian virtues. The power rests in the hands of the churchmen."

Benito snorted. "Guido's already told me all about how it works."

"Oh?"

"Yes." Benito smoothed his hair, preening like a proud canary. "Guido says that in Rome everybody gives orders, but nobody obeys them, so it all works out well enough."

At least some things never changed. I would sooner expect the stars to fall from the sky as Benito to start behaving against his nature. We had never landed in a new place without my manservant entering into some fleeting liaison. I rubbed my eyes again, then lurched forward, my attention caught by a sudden trick of moonlight.

A gauzy phantom seemed to float through the garden, a pale luminescence against dark shadows. It circled a reflecting pool, danced on the breeze, and finally paused to hover at the top of an evergreen cypress. Benito and I peered wonderingly, and we both jumped when a spectral arm shot out. It pointed straight to the pavilion by the garden wall and was answered by a quavering glow that winked out almost immediately. The light could have been a candle from the main villa reflecting off a window in the pavilion, but that phantom was more substantial than mere moonshine. Did a ghost haunt the Villa Fabiani?

The breeze suddenly calmed, and a laugh burbled from my manservant's lips. "It's nothing. How silly. We're shivering over a scarf blowing in the wind. Look, it's caught in the top of the tree."

"And here comes its owner," I replied. The old marchesa flitted around a shoulder-high hedge with Gemma panting in hot pursuit.

"The crazy lady. Guido told me about her, too."

I nodded slowly, giving vent to a mammoth yawn.

Deciding that the hour was fit only for lunatics, Benito and I sought the comfort of our respective beds. As my head sank into the goose-feather pillow, I contemplated the bell mounted above. Would the cardinal have trouble sleeping tonight? Would I have to face his cool stare at close quarters? My body was too tired to let my mind worry over it. The bell remained silent and I slept the sleep of the dead.

Chapter 6

The new day began with an ancient gargoyle of a footman named Roberto banging on my door. He had come to summon me for Mass. In my travels, I'd become quite negligent in my devotions, much preferring a cup of chocolate in bed to a tiresome session on my knees. I'd also convinced myself that God heard my prayers no matter where I said them. But when Roberto insisted with an air as proud as his master's, I reluctantly pushed my warm covers aside and applied my feet to the cold floor.

The villa's chapel lay at right angles to the tapestried entry hall. I hovered at the entrance while the servants arranged themselves according to some preordained pecking order. The housekeeper led the above-stairs servants into the middle range of pews: valets first, then maids and footmen. The kitchen crew followed, led by the cook in her towering white kerchief. Next came the coachmen and grooms, these last attended by more than a hint of stable odor. Most of the staff took little notice of me, but my appearance seemed to amuse a pair of young scullery maids. They took one look at my smooth throat and beardless cheeks and giggled behind their prayer books until the cook rapped her knuckles on their heads.

Wondering where I fit in, feeling uncomfortably neither fish nor fowl, I looked around for the musicians who had accompanied me the night before. Down front, among the priests, the old marchesa was dozing next to the altar rail, attended by a middle-aged woman with graying hair scraped back under a white cap. Did the cardinal allow Gemma a day off now and again? If the marchesa's late night wanderings were anything to judge by, the girl certainly deserved one. Unable to locate my fellow musicians, I decided they must live out, in their own homes. When a courier in leather breeches and riding boots pushed me aside, I trotted past the servants and squeezed into a pew filled with clerks, much relieved that no one admonished me for taking a place above my station.

At the altar, Cardinal Fabiani commenced his rituals under an image of the Christ writhing in anguish on a huge crucifix. By contrast, the cardinal appeared well-rested and untroubled by the insomnia that Rossobelli had warned me of. Mass unfolded in businesslike fashion. The Latin phrases flew off the cardinal's tongue, and fewer clerics than I expected approached the rail for communion.

After Cardinal Fabiani had wiped the golden chalice, polished it to high shine, and folded each piece of linen so that no drop of the Blood or crumb of the Host would fall unnoticed, he raised his right hand. He bestowed the final blessing with three fingers springing from a glove so white that it fairly shone and then marched straight from the chapel to the audience chamber across the hall.

For two hours every morning, I learned, the cardinal's door was open to all petitioners. I paused to observe the mismatched group waiting in the anteroom. Churchmen in black or purple silk tried to avoid rubbing shoulders with barefoot monks. Rough peasants who looked as if they had just arrived from the country gazed open-mouthed at the clouds and cherubs on the frescoed ceiling. A lady of quality, accompanied by her maid, took care not to notice a very pregnant girl quailing under her father's stern gaze. If the cardinal was going to sort out this lot, he must possess the wisdom and diplomacy of a Solomon.

Just as my rumbling stomach propelled me in search of my morning chocolate and rolls, Rossobelli appeared from some obscure corner, all hand-wringing and humility. "Are we making you welcome, then? In our small way?" Without waiting for a response, he continued, "If you require anything you must let me know at once. Perhaps you would like an instrument for practice…I could arrange for a harpsichord to be moved into your suite."

I agreed readily, then added, "I'm surprised one hasn't been installed already. Since I'm not the first singer to occupy the rooms."

"Ah, someone told you about Signor Tucci."

"Yes, someone," I replied, refusing to gratify his very evident curiosity. "I hate to think that I was the cause of a fellow musician's dismissal."

"You mustn't worry on Tucci's account."

"Why? Has he found other employment so soon?"

Rossobelli put two fingers to his temple and shook his head with a tolerant smile. "Signor Tucci didn't confide his plans to me. For a performer, he is a most retiring man, gentlemanly, almost meek. Nobody's enemy but his own, you might say."

I questioned the abate with a look, but he dispensed with the topic of my predecessor by assuring me that Tucci had been given a suitable pension. Rossobelli then urged me to explore Rome. He lavished praise on ruins, churches, fountains, and gardens, and even offered to put a carriage at my disposal.

"You're free for the day," he said. "After his daily visit with His Holiness, Cardinal Fabiani will dine at the Quirinal and conduct business from his office there. He won't want you until this evening."

That clinched it. Not the recital of Rome's treasures, but the promise of freedom. I'd passed only one night under Cardinal Fabiani's roof, but already the prospect of a day on my own was too tempting to refuse.

☙❦❧

A short hour later, I found myself strolling the paths of the Janiculum under a brilliant blue sky partitioned by thin, streaky clouds. The chill morning air provided a few shivers, but the milky sun hinted at a warmer day to come. Benito was my only companion. I'd refused Rossobelli's offer of a carriage and footman to act as guide. Besides wanting to forget about the Villa Fabiani for the next few hours, I needed to walk. Men of my kind had an unfortunate tendency to acquire extra flesh. Sometimes it seemed that simply looking at a plate of rich food made my waistline expand. This could work to the advantage of some castrati, particularly those who portrayed women on the stage, as here in Rome, where women were barred from theatrical performance by papal decree. A plump chest and generous hips went a long way in creating the proper illusion. But I'd never been drawn to female roles, and I had no intention of spending my old age as one of those fat eunuchs who lumber about looking like a cow swollen with calf.

A brisk, ten-minute walk took Benito and me through a massive gateway in the ancient wall that had once defended Rome against northern barbarians and into the twisting streets of a working class district populated from all points of the compass. In the space of a few blocks, I saw Syrians, Turks, even several black-skinned Ethiopians—all mixing easily with the short, sturdy Romans. The houses grew farther apart as the road broadened and dipped toward the foot of the hill. Before us, a bridge supported by four arched vaults crossed the muddy waters of the Tiber.

I paused for a moment to study the starburst of roads that sprang from the opposite end of the bridge. The main road continued straight on toward the east. The others angled off and disappeared amidst buildings that dwarfed the ones we'd just passed. With a sinking feeling, I realized I had no idea where we were going.

A stone bench at the base of a drooping evergreen offered a convenient resting place. I sent Benito back to the shops in search of a guidebook, then propped my chin on my walking stick to watch the steady stream of traffic cross the bridge. It quickly struck me that Rome was a city of horses. In Venice, men were carried by sleek boats and goods by hand carts or barges. Here, the horses did the work. Low-slung ponies, draft horses with wide backs and muscular hindquarters, and spirited teams of matched Arabians that carried themselves as proudly as the men riding in the carriages they pulled: horses were everywhere. So were their droppings. The unpaved street was thick with dust topped by a repellent layer of flattened dung. My Venice was no model of hygiene, but at least her watery roadways were cleansed by daily tides. It looked as if the Romans depended on the rain to be their broom. By the time Benito returned, I had worked up a sorrowful case of longing for my city of water and stone.

"The Trastevere," Benito said, stabbing a finger at the crude map in a book meant for pilgrims to the Holy City. "That's the quarter we just came through. And that bridge is the Ponte Sisto."

I roused myself to nod.

"Where do you want to go?" my manservant asked. "If you want to visit St. Peter's, we've come the wrong direction. The Vatican sits on a hill to the north."

"We'll save St. Peter's for another time. I've already done enough praying for today. Gussie told me to be sure to take in the Pantheon. Here, let me see if I can find it."

As I flipped between the map and listings of popular attractions, Benito asked, "What's the Pantheon? Some kind of monument?"

"A temple, it says here. Dedicated to the entire array of ancient gods and goddesses. It was saved from destruction when Pope Boniface consecrated it as a church of Santa Maria."

"What? Christians worshiping in a pagan temple?"

I shrugged at his surprise. "I think that happens quite often, especially in a place like Rome, a city that's been inhabited for thousands of years. Old buildings put to new uses—ah, here it is. Across the Tiber, but not too far." My finger traced the route on the map. "Gussie raves about the Pantheon. He did a lot of sketching there when he was making his Grand Tour. He calls it an architectural miracle—a dome with a coffered ceiling that's almost as big as St. Peter's, but predates it by centuries."

Benito nodded, jumped up, and pointed eastward. "Then across the bridge we go. Mind your boots. This road is filthy."

As we picked our way through the muck, Benito rose on tiptoes to whisper near my ear. "Do you think we should invite our friend to join us?"

I immediately knew who he meant. Back in the Trastevere, I'd spotted a tallish man in a gray cloak and the sort of circular, wide-brimmed hat that many Romans prefer to the more fashionable tricorne. His height was the only remarkable thing about him. That is, of what I could see. He was careful to keep his chin lowered so that his hat brim shadowed his face. Until I'd rested by the bridge, I thought he was simply someone going our way. He raised my suspicion when he followed Benito back to get the map. Now he was trailing at a distance, abruptly halting to gaze over the bridge railing every time I glanced back.

Of course, my presence at the Villa Fabiani had raised suspicions. When I declined Rossobelli's offer of a carriage, the abate could have made speedy rearrangements to dispatch someone to follow me. Or was I being trailed by one of my own countrymen? Perhaps a Montorio bravo to ensure that I didn't grow too independent. I let Benito take the map and lead the way. I had much to ponder, and in my current frame of mind, I could have waded straight through one of Rome's numerous fountains without realizing that my feet were wet.

The Pantheon was just as magnificent as my brother-in-law had promised. Later in my stay, I would search for the old Roman Forum and find it teeming with cattle waiting for the market, its skeletal fragments and broken arches half-buried in rubbish and weeds. Most of the other classical ruins had suffered similar treatment. Over the years, the great baths and amphitheaters and triumphal arches had been pillaged of their marble facings and smoothly cut building stones. Everything that could be torn out had been incorporated into new buildings or sent to the lime kilns. Latter-day Romans were only just beginning to appreciate the wantonness of the destruction.

The Pantheon had been spared by grace of its diversion to a Christian purpose, but to me, it still felt more like a pagan temple, somehow sacred and unnerving at the same time. I sucked in a breath as we mounted its steps, moving from the filthy, bustling square to the cool shadows of its covered portico.

Benito shivered. "It's like a forest," he whispered. "A forest of stone."

I raised my eyes. Massive columns of red and gray granite soared above us, expanding to meet the roof in capitals of sculpted leaves and foliage. The noise of the city receded as latticed grills directed us through the open doors and into an immense, domed rotunda. Somewhere along the curved expanse of the encircling walls was the tomb of the artist Raphael. The guidebook said it was not to be missed, but I had eyes for only one thing: the oculus.

At the zenith of the coffered dome, the builder had created a circular window to the sky. A shaft of sunlight streamed through the opening like a beam of divine substance. It burnished the floating dust motes into tiny diamonds and made everyone who stepped into its brilliance shimmer like beings fashioned of light. If any deity was worshiped in this space, Apollo seemed the obvious choice.

Coming back out into the square was like leaving an enchanted land for the most prosaic scene imaginable. It was Friday—market day—and an array of stalls and barrows fanned out from the central fountain. The residents of this quarter must have been working since cockcrow. The results of their labors assaulted our senses: bread fresh from wood-fired ovens, papery garlic bulbs woven into braids, fish with scales of shimmering green and blue, and bright red blood dripping from severed joints piled on butchers' carts. The splendor of the Pantheon had made me forget about our mysterious friend in the wide-brimmed hat, but I caught sight of him again as Benito and I wandered among the merchandise.

Jostling shoulders with housewives intent on filling baskets with ingredients for the family dinner, I resisted the temptation of the roast chestnut seller and started down an aisle displaying household goods. A trio of wide-hipped women haggling with the proprietor of a junk stall soon blocked my path. Over their heads, I saw customers inspecting pots hanging from a tinker's cart, and farther on, towering stacks of folded fabrics in every hue and texture. I twisted around to tell Benito to go back, but

my nimble manservant was already ducking under my elbow.
Without missing a step, he pinched the nearest padded bottom
and darted through the resulting cleft. I sucked in my stomach
and wriggled after him.

"What is it, Benito?" I cried as I crashed into his back. "Move
along." The ladies were squealing, and one lifted her basket as
if she might use it as a weapon. Yet my manservant stood stock
still. He clutched my cloak. "Master, do you see?"

I saw. She was examining fabrics halfway down the aisle,
pointing out a bolt of silk the color of the lagoon on a summer
day. As the merchant unfurled the blue green cloth, the sun that
filtered through holes in his canvas awning turned the silk to
rippling water. She laughed in delight. Despite the raucous cries
swirling around me, every note of that silvery laugh hit my ears
like a blow from a sledgehammer.

"Liya Del'Vecchio," I whispered. "How on earth?"

Benito's anxious gaze searched my face. "Are you going to
speak to her?"

I took a deep breath. Liya gathered the silk to her chest and
trailed a length over one arm. The olive skin of her smooth
cheeks and forehead seemed to glow in the dappled sunlight. I
remembered her heavy dark hair done in coiled plaits secured
with gold pins. Her tresses still shone like a raven's wing, but
now they were shorter, loose on her shoulders, confined only by
a cap tied under her chin. A white cap, not the yellow kerchief
I'd seen other Jews wearing as we'd come through the city. She
laughed again, but shook her head. The tradesman spread his
arms, entreating. She smiled sadly, as if the price of the cloth
was much too dear, then handed it back in a bright bundle.
She turned to go up the aisle, away from where we stood. Still
I hesitated.

"Master?" Benito's voice was tight. He bounced from foot to
foot. "Shall I follow her?"

"No. It has to be me. Only…" I glanced back over my shoulder. The three ladies had turned back to their shopping and were
bending to cram their prizes in deep baskets already laden with

meat and produce. Other women pushed and shoved to get by. I could just see the round brim of our follower's hat, dipping up and down several stalls back.

I sighed in frustration. Liya Del'Vecchio was part of my past. She was my business and mine alone. I didn't know whether my shadow took orders from Rossobelli, Montorio, or someone else, but he was clearly up to no good. I had no intention of putting Liya under his notice.

A barrel at my right hand held a display of mops and brooms. Moving quickly, I tossed its owner a coin and grabbed a long-handled mop. Benito gazed open-mouthed, wondering if I'd lost my wits. He soon understood. That morning, for our sightseeing tour, he'd brought out a tricorne edged with gold *point d'Espagne* and a fringe of ostrich feathers. As it wasn't my favorite hat, I'd demurred and we'd had a good-natured skirmish. Now I was glad I'd deferred to my manservant's fashion dictum. Shielded by the mob, I transferred my tricorne to the mop's wooly head and secured my cloak beneath it.

While Benito went snaking down the crowded aisle with my eye-catching headgear bobbing beside him, I made sure that my shadow was still well behind. Then I ducked between two stalls and out into the square.

I trotted back toward the Pantheon and mounted its steps. Streets exited the square alongside the huge building, branching to the east and west. A solid wall of buildings bounded the square beyond the temporary market. If I kept an eagle eye from my position, it would be impossible for Liya to leave without my notice. I didn't have long to wait. I spotted her straight back and determined gait just as a new disturbance was moving down a side street.

I shot down the stairs to collide with a group in rough clothing just bounding onto the square. Beggars in rags, porters, bargemen, rope makers, and other laborers were followed by women of the same class. Their eyes gleamed with anticipation and every tongue uttered the identical cry: "Di Noce…our papa cardinal…he comes…he comes."

Liya whirled, shaded her eyes with her hand, and gazed in my direction. I waved frantically, jumping up and down as the noise and energy of the throng intensified. Her expression did not change.

I shouted, but the chaos swallowed my words. The crowd around me contracted, flowing toward the source of the excitement. It was like swimming a river against a powerful current. The traffic of bodies from the side street met the mass of people hastening from the market, and they all swirled together in one great cataract. The crush trapped my arms at my sides and buffeted me farther and farther away from the woman I sought, until suddenly, as if by magic, I was thrown straight into her arms.

"Liya!" I cried, struggling to hold my footing.

She responded with wide-eyed wonder. "Tito Amato!" She grabbed my arm fiercely. "Can it be? What are you doing here?"

The cries of "Di Noce, Di Noce" became a swelling chorus. As the object of their frenzy neared, a new surge rippled through the crowd. A bulky man in a tattered jacket, intent on witnessing the procession, pushed between us and broke our hold.

I grabbed for Liya's sleeve, but the press of the crowd threatened to carry her away. With a bursting leap, she threw an arm around my neck and pulled me close. Her breath was warm on my cheek. I heard "Teatro Argentina, tomorrow afternoon," and then she was gone.

I stood unheeding and unmoving as the tumult quieted and the crowd suddenly parted. With my heart drumming in my ears, I dimly realized I was about to see the cardinal who was expected to challenge Stefano Montorio for the papal crown. I looked around for a formal procession, Swiss Guards on the march, a stately gentleman in crimson waving from the window of a gleaming carriage. But there was none of that.

Cardinal Di Noce didn't ride. Escorted by only three priests, Di Noce walked among the people. His simple black cassock was faded and dusty, and his broad-brimmed hat had slipped back to expose a skullcap surrounded by a few tufts of gray hair. A short, chunky man, Di Noce shuffled along with the humble steps of a poor parish priest returning from an all-night vigil. Nevertheless, my neighbors gazed in rapt attention. Some fell to their knees and made the sign of the cross; others scurried forward to touch medals and rosaries to the hem of his garment.

As Di Noce progressed across the square, I tried to see what it was about this unkempt, balding, middle-aged cleric that inspired such devotion. Yes, the blessings he pronounced brimmed with humility and concern. And his slanted, wide-set eyes seemed to radiate good cheer. But, after all, he was just a man.

I tapped the shoulder of the fellow next to me, a baker in a flour-caked apron pushing his young son forward. "Who is this Di Noce?" I asked. "Why is everyone so excited?"

My neighbor dropped his beard-shadowed jaw. "Is there a man alive who hasn't heard of Di Noce?"

"I'm new to Rome. Just arrived from Venice."

He shot me a contemptuous glance that lingered on the ruffles of fine lawn falling over my shirt front. "Perhaps Venice hasn't heard. Cardinal Di Noce will be our next pope."

"Is it true?" I made my eyebrows arc in surprise. "I thought our ambassador, Cardinal Montorio, was the man to replace Pope Clement."

"Montorio? Not likely. Rome will riot if that ball of lard wins out over our…" He clamped his mouth shut abruptly, narrowing his gaze as if to say: I'll shut up because I don't know who you are, but your ambassador might as well be a piece of shit floating on the Tiber.

I smiled broadly, trying to win his confidence. "It's all right. I'll grant that Cardinal Di Noce may gain the papal throne. But tell me, what is so special about him?"

My simple question seemed to tax the man's power of speech. He opened his mouth, closed it just as fast, and stood thumbing his stubbled chin. His son pulled at my sleeve. I looked down.

With the pitiful innocence of youth beaming from his face, the boy answered eagerly, "Di Noce is special because he loves us, Signore. Loves us like a papa. And wants to make us happy."

Chapter 7

Later that evening, Cardinal Fabiani returned from the Quirinal to host his weekly *conversazioni*. In the music salon, the harpsichordist and I provided entertainment as the guests gathered to sit in circles of upright chairs and nibble on wafers and ices.

In contrast to his coolness of the previous evening, my fellow musician unbent sufficiently to enlighten me as to the identity of a number of the guests. A young fop reading aloud from a slim volume of poetry was the eldest son of Prince Orsini. Another who propped his elbow on the overmantel and gazed over the room with a bored expression represented the house of Barberini-Colonna, his linked names signifying ancestry from both papal and aristocratic lines. Every guest, my informant whispered in reverential tones, was a Person of the Highest Quality. Reigning over them all, Cardinal Fabiani seemed to enjoy himself mightily as he swanned from group to group.

As before, the cardinal's musical selections had been waiting by the keyboard. Rubbish this time, not a standout among them, and designed so that I would sing only every other set of pieces. My talents had been relegated to the musical equivalent of the tapestries and mirrors that decorated the villa's walls, a pleasing background and nothing more. At least I could focus on the guests' conversation while the harpsichordist was having his solo.

I sang my bit, then took a seat at the edge of the dais. Pretending to peruse the score of my next selection, I opened my ears to the nearest group. Gossip concerning people unknown to me ran to coarse lengths until Cardinal Fabiani joined the circle. Then the talk turned to the state of Pope Clement's health.

"How is the old man doing?" asked a custard-faced woman in a gown of French blue much too bright for her complexion.

"A bit better, today," Fabiani answered smoothly. "He took some ox-tail soup for dinner."

"Of course," responded the Orsini stripling, his volume of poetry splayed over his knee. "That's what you always say. He's better and better, but still on his deathbed. At this rate our esteemed pontiff will be the healthiest corpse ever."

An older man winked at the woman in blue and said, "If you want to know how the pope really is, you had best go to Mass at the Lateran."

"Whatever for?" she asked, snapping her fan open.

"Have you not heard the old story? When the Holy Father is about to die, the bones of Pope Sylvester the Second rattle in his tomb under the floor."

"Stuff and nonsense," she whispered over the fluttering fan, but her eyes were shining with curiosity.

"It is true. Long ago, when the Moors still held sway in Spain, the future Pope Sylvester studied the art of divination with one of their learned wizards. He made a pact with a demon that ensured his elevation to the papacy, but his wicked sorcery prevents his bones from achieving eternal rest. When Pope Clement's predecessor went, Sylvester's bones jumped and bumped so hard that the choir could not be heard over the clatter."

"Were you there?" she asked in a tone of amazement.

"Unfortunately not. But a friend of my cousin swears that he witnessed the strange event."

"But how could moldy old bones know when the pope is going to die?"

"Only the Lord knows. And perhaps the demon that Sylvester bargained with."

Behind her fan, the woman in blue buzzed in conversation with a friend. They both appeared ready to jump up and call for their carriages to race across the city to press their ears to Sylvester's tomb.

Fabiani sent the speaker a jaundiced look, then addressed the credulous woman. "He's teasing, my dear. The legend of Sylvester's bones is just a story crafted to entertain pilgrims. Every famous church has some such tale to its credit. The more fantastic the tale, the more coins the sacristan can collect in the telling."

"But his cousin's friend..." she started doubtfully.

"Superstition makes fools of the gullible and unwary," Fabiani intoned sharply. "If anyone heard anything, we must blame superstition."

"It goes beyond superstition," a new voice chimed in. I hadn't noticed Cardinal Montorio enter the salon, but there he was, squeezing his bulk between the gilt chairs. Abate Lenci hovered nearby as usual.

"It's pure ignorance," the cardinal said. "When I first came to Rome, I heard of this so-called legend and set about to gather the true facts. Consider this—back in 1694, the priests of the Lateran opened Sylvester's tomb to lay the rumors to rest for good. The body was intact, but disintegrated the moment it came in contact with the air. Obviously, the tomb now holds nothing but the dust of Sylvester's earthly remains. We all know that dust doesn't rattle. The story is pure poppycock."

Cardinal Fabiani inclined his head with a smile, but the rest of the company were clearly vexed at Montorio's pronouncement. An intriguing mystery with a whiff of brimstone is always more interesting than bare fact. As their disappointed clucks quickly turned back to gossip, I focused my attention on the other nests of gold chairs and the ladies and gentlemen milling among them. I was looking for Prince Pompetti's handsome head and graceful bearing, but Di Noce's champion was not in attendance. An elbow poked my ribs: my turn again. After I'd sung my way through a few more innocuous melodies, the footmen stopped serving ices, giving the guests their cue to depart.

The harpsichordist, perhaps recalling my displacement of Signor Tucci, once more cooled. Folding the music into a neat stack, he left without a word. In a few moments, the last satin gown rustled through the main door and I was alone with the maids who crept in to erase the traces of guests and restore the room to its immaculate splendor. Crumbs were whisked, candle wax scraped, spills mopped, and bibelots rearranged in perfect order. Not for the first time, I marveled at the sheer number of working hands required to keep one man living in luxury.

A pair of maids sweeping the parquet floor at the other end of the salon paused when Gemma trotted through a side doorway. I was too far away to hear, but the girl's gestures were unmistakable. She was searching for the marchesa—an urgent matter if Gemma's flushed face and strained expression were any indication. Trading sneers, the pair bent to their brooms and turned their backs on Gemma without a word. Their gestures were also eloquent: We'll do your job when you start doing ours.

Gemma looked as if she might argue the point, but then Guido came in and spoke a few words. She cocked her head and regarded him with a doubtful expression.

He nodded impatiently. Gemma shook her head. I fancied she mouthed the words, *not now.*

Guido moved closer, smiling seductively. The footman wanted something—that much was evident. But I doubted it had anything to do with romance. The maid arranged herself so their bodies wouldn't touch as he whispered in her ear.

Something he said managed to turn the tide. After a brief moment, Gemma pivoted on her heel, and they left together.

Feeling a bit lost, I made my way to the main hall, where I found Abate Lenci trying to look as if he had a reason to be dawdling there. He greeted me with a touch of irritation. "Signor Amato," he whispered, "Fabiani's gone to his library to take brandy with Orsini and several others. How can you take the measure of his political designs if you're not with them?"

I sighed. "I can't follow Fabiani around like a spaniel. I have to wait until I'm called to his presence. Your uncles don't realize what a task they've handed me."

The arrival of Rossobelli prevented any response that Lenci might have made. When the secretary pointed out that Cardinal Montorio's carriage was waiting, Lenci scampered for the door. Rossobelli had a few words for me as well: Cardinal Fabiani appreciated my performance at the conversazioni but would not be needing me again tonight. Not sure whether to be relieved or concerned, I went to my room, changed to a dressing gown, and sent Benito to the kitchens to arrange a supper tray.

⁂

I was writing a letter to Gussie when Benito and Guido wheeled in a cart of covered dishes wreathed in mouth-watering aromas. Having a manservant who was well liked in the kitchen was proving to be a distinct advantage. I wasted no time in settling myself at a table before the sitting room fire and uncovering the largest platter. A trout grilled to perfection nestled atop a bed of saffron rice; its mottled skin glistened with lemon butter. Just as the first forkful touched my lips, Guido gave Benito a departing caress that he obviously intended to escape my notice. My attendant responded with a coquettish smile and a few whispered words.

Flooded by a sudden rush of sadness, I abandoned my fork and sank back to stare into the flames dancing in the fireplace. How was it that my manservant fell into these easy romances while my love affairs were continually fraught with difficulty? Back in Venice, I'd gradually resigned myself to a future without Liya. I'd put my dreams aside and concentrated on my music, taking occasional solace in the arms of one of the numerous ladies who haunted my dressing room door. Now, after one brief touch, one hurried exchange, my thoughts were again obsessed by the beautiful Jewess—for such I would always think of her, even if she had rejected her heritage. I finished my meal in a somber frame of mind, perhaps allowing Benito to fill my wineglass with rich Montepulciano a few too many times.

After I pushed away from the table and carried my coffee to the sofa, Benito cleared the dishes and wheeled the cart into the hall. Then he flung himself onto a footstool before me. He had read my sadness like a book.

"Master," he said, leaning forward and placing his hands under his chin in a prayerful position. "Back in Venice, when Signorina Liya ran away, you told me she was seeking a safe haven."

"That's right. Liya's mother vowed to reject the child she was carrying. Her lover was a Christian, and a deliberate scoundrel besides."

"But Luca was no worse than Liya's own cousin. Those two were up to their elbows in schemes."

My coffee spoon tinkled against the delicate porcelain as I reflected on the events that had resulted in the disastrous ghetto fire. "I know, but people don't like to blame their own. Luca was the outsider, so the Jews cast him as the villain. Liya's mother demanded that she make plans to send Luca's child to a Christian orphanage—a most unusual stance, I'm told. Liya's father tried to bridge the gap and make peace between them, but the two strong women snapped him like a dried chicken bone. Soon, the whole family was threatening to disown Liya. She was at her wit's end."

"You never told anyone where she was headed."

I sipped at the smooth brew. At the time, the Jewess' choice had astonished me. Perhaps it still did. Sharing her secret for the first time, I spoke slowly, reluctantly. "Liya fled to a wise woman who lives on one of the deserted islands out in the lagoon."

"A woman who doles out potions and philters?"

I nodded. "This woman arranged for Liya to travel to a village high in the mountains of the mainland. A village where they don't care who is Christian or Jew."

"Does such a place exist?"

"Apparently, yes. The people of such villages keep to themselves and follow *la vecchia religione*."

"My grandmother used to tell stories about peasants who keep to the old religion and still worship Diana as the queen of the moon and the forests. She warned us to avoid them like the plague." Benito glanced around with a shiver. I remembered how superstitious my manservant could be: salt over the shoulder, dire predictions over a broken mirror, firm reminders about tempting fortune if I happened to whistle in the theater. "Diana's followers have the power of the evil eye," he said, lowering his voice a notch. "They're *streghe*. Witches."

"I suppose," I answered, staring into my coffee, finding it difficult to imagine the sensible, clever seamstress I'd known dancing around a bubbling cauldron, invoking whatever deities such simple, unlettered people believed in. For the thousandth time, I wondered if Liya had found what she sought and if she ever spared a thought for me.

"Then tell me this." Benito raised an eyebrow. "If Signorina Liya follows the old religion, what is she doing in Rome, the center of Christian power? Surely Rome deals with heathens even more harshly than Venice."

Not having the answer to that question, I sent Benito to fetch another bottle of Montepulciano and directed him to fill a glass for both of us. Under the wine's beneficent influence, we talked of nothing but happier days until the flaming logs collapsed into glowing embers.

Later, as I tottered to bed and pulled the coverlet up to my chin, I realized I'd let Liya's baffling appearance chase the real reason for my visit to Rome from my mind. I admonished myself with stern resolve: freeing Alessandro was the important thing, not rekindling a romance that had been impossible from the start. My head sank into the pillow and my eyelids eased shut. I couldn't have slept more than a few minutes until the bell above my bed leapt to life with a clanging vengeance, jerking me upright and hurling my heart against my ribs.

Cardinal Fabiani wanted me.

Still muzzy from consuming an unaccustomed amount of the grape, I fumbled for my underclothes and stockings. By the time I had them on, Benito had arrived with a clean shirt and some soft wool breeches. He reached for my formal wig, but I shook my head. I'd give this midnight concert with my own hair loose on my shoulders.

The broad corridor was deserted except for my own intersecting shadows cast by the flickering wall lamps. Reaching the cardinal's door, I swayed a bit as I straightened my clumsily assembled attire. The door opened on Rossobelli, pink-rimmed eyes bulging in agitation.

"Quick," he whispered on a sharp breath. "There's no time to lose."

I stepped inside. Metal rasped on metal as Rossobelli shot the bolt home. The sitting room was darker than the hallway. I formed a fleeting impression of heavy tables and overstuffed sofas as the abate hustled me through to the bed chamber. There I approached a canopied bed twice the size of mine and was surprised to find it empty, its pillows and bedclothes in perfect array.

In a corner, Rossobelli was fidgeting with a bookcase that rose up from behind the cardinal's priedieu.

"Where is His Eminence?" I asked.

"I'll take you to him. This way, if you please."

The bookcase creaked, then swung outward. A gust of cool air met my cheeks. Rossobelli lit a hand-held lantern from a little candle illuminating a statue of the Virgin and motioned me toward a gaping dark rectangle that had appeared in the plastered wall. "Come…he's waiting."

I hesitated. It had penetrated my addled brain that there was more here than a sleepless cardinal. Rossobelli was frightened—frightened enough to have totally dropped his habitual fawning persona.

"Where does that lead?" I asked.

"To the pavilion in the garden. Follow me. The cardinal needs you."

The passage that swallowed my reluctant steps descended in a series of enclosed, sharply angled staircases: no dusty cobwebs or skeletons hanging in irons, simply a hidden access designed to ensure privacy. It was at the bottom that my real qualms began. Several windowless corridors branched off into the ground floor of the house, but Rossobelli dove to the left, into a mouth of stone that reeked of stagnation and mold.

"What is this place?" I asked, stooping to follow his crabbed form.

"An old aqueduct. The Romans built it as a conduit for water to drive grain mills on the Janiculum. It runs above ground outside the city, then dips underground at the Aurelian wall."

I froze. We were traversing a centuries-old tunnel? With how many tons of dirt over our heads? A cold clamminess raced down my spine. Involuntarily, my feet shuffled backward.

The lantern swung around. Rossobelli's long fingers encircled my wrist. His nails dug into my flesh. "Don't be a fool. It's perfectly safe. I've been through here more times than I can count. Look—" He swept the lamp in an arc, illuminating neatly reticulated blocks. "The Romans knew how to build. The only bits that are impassable are where they intentionally collapsed the walls so the Goths couldn't sneak through in the Siege of 537."

Nodding, I remembered that I'd been impressed by a triumph of Roman engineering just that day. Both the Pantheon and this aqueduct would probably survive until my nephew's grandchildren had grandchildren of their own. I moved forward gingerly and was soon scuttling beneath the garden like a creature of the dirt. I almost crashed into Rossobelli when he stopped at a staircase of roughhewn rock that intersected the tunnel. The aqueduct continued downward, in the direction of the Tiber, I surmised. I wasn't sorry that we climbed the stairs.

A vertical slit of light descended to meet the glow from our lamp. Rossobelli seized my shoulder. "I trust you aren't squeamish."

"Not particularly," I answered, attempting to suppress a hiccup.

"Good. The last thing His Eminence needs is a fancy boy with a weak stomach."

Rossobelli widened the crack of light by opening a door that formed part of the thick garden wall. We entered the pavilion that I had seen from my balcony. It was an artfully rusticated retreat, rather like a tiny hunting lodge built of pale stucco and floored with a mosaic of black and white pebbles. The night air circulated through the garden entrance and the lattices covering the unglazed windows. Empty pots awaiting spring planting were stacked in a terra cotta pyramid beside a trio of low ironwork benches.

The effect was charming—except that the nearest bench held one very dead girl. She was curled on her side with her face to the wall and one pale arm flung back at an odd angle. Loose dark hair obscured her features, but her mode of death was obvious. She'd been strangled from behind. A long white scarf bit into the soft flesh of her neck; its free ends trailed limply on the pebbled floor.

Cardinal Fabiani towered above the corpse, standing as still as a marble statue. Praying? Without wig or cap, his bowed head was bald as an egg. His chin was buried in the fur-lined collar of his dressing gown and his hands wrapped in a cloak of rough, brown wool that he clutched to his chest. At Rossobelli's quiet cough, he roused and sent me a look that bore right through the remnants of my wine-induced haze.

Part Two

"A dirge for her the doubly dead in that she died so young."

—Edgar Allan Poe

Chapter 8

"Gemma Farussi," Fabiani said offhandedly, as if introducing a tiresome courtier, "my mother's maid."

"Yes, I recognize her gown." The calmness of my tone astonished me. Inside, my heart was hammering on my ribs.

Fabiani's pointed nose twitched in surprise.

"We met before the concert last night. The marchesa had wandered into the music room…" I paused to drum up a bit of courage. "What happened here?"

"We don't know. Rossobelli found her, just like this." The cardinal shook his head and resumed his silent contemplation.

As slender as she was, Gemma's corpse seemed to take up a great deal of space. After a moment, Cardinal Fabiani knelt and gently unwound the fatal length of silk from her neck. He examined it closely before directing his next remark to Rossobelli. "Did you find my mother?"

The abate answered with a brisk nod. "She'd hidden herself in the larder off the kitchens. If the fringe of her shawl hadn't caught in the door, I'd be looking still."

"Anyone about?"

"Only the footman at the front entrance. He didn't seem to realize that anything was amiss."

"And Matilda?"

"When I returned Marchesa Fabiani to her bed chamber, Matilda was sleeping in her chair by the fire."

Still kneeling, Fabiani crumpled the scarf into a ball, molding the delicate fabric in his restless grasp. "You didn't wake her, did you?"

"No. The marchesa sought her bed without a whimper, so I left Matilda as I found her."

"Good man. With God's favor, my plan may just work."

Fabiani shot me a keen glance. "You seek to worm your way into my most intimate circle, Signor Amato. I cannot think of a better place for you to begin."

"Your Eminence," I stuttered. "I was sent to entertain, not—"

He cut me off with a wave of his hand. "Time is too short to fence with words. It is already well past midnight. I know why Antonio Montorio made me a present of you, and I know all about your brother's arrest." He sighed. "Perhaps your depth of family feeling will give you some sympathy for my position."

Rising, he unfurled the cloak, laid the length of coarse wool beside the bench, and rolled poor Gemma onto her back. "Help me, Rossobelli. She's so small, her cloak will cover her form."

The abate averted his face. "Hideous," he whispered. "She was so young, so lovely."

"I'll grant you she was beautiful." Fabiani stroked Gemma's chin with his thumb and gazed at her contorted face for a long moment. "But she's also dead, and we have work to do. Grab her feet, man."

As Rossobelli moved to do as he was told, the cardinal addressed me. "Tito, I want you to run down the lane to the Via della Lungara. Do you know the Porta Settimiana?" He referred to the gateway to the Trastevere that Benito and I had passed through that morning.

I nodded.

"Right before the Settimiana, on the left side of the Lungara, you will find Atto Benelli's hut. He's an old woodsman who fishes the Tiber and tends a market garden by the river's edge. Wake him. Tell him you are from the villa and need him to bring his boat round to the mouth of the old aqueduct. Tell him to bring some chains. Heavy ones."

I didn't answer. Gemma's death mask had robbed me of speech.

"Well?" Cardinal Fabiani scowled. "Do you need an encore?"

I shook my head miserably. "No, I understand."

"Go on, then. Down the first garden path to your left and straight out to the lane. Get back here as quickly as you can. You won't have any trouble. Benelli will follow orders…I own the land where he grows his cabbages."

I did as I was told. The night air was brisk and I had no cloak, but I don't think I would have felt the cold, even if I had not been running. I might have been moving through a nightmare. I heard my steps pound the graveled lane as if from a great distance—likewise my ragged breathing—but my body was numb. The little maid who had seemed so full of pluck and vigor lay dead, strangled by another's hand. Fabiani should have roused the household, summoned a magistrate, sent a messenger to Gemma's family. Instead, he had hastened to conceal the crime and had drafted Rossobelli and me to help him. The reason was obvious: he believed the old marchesa had done the deed and wanted to protect her.

Protecting family I could understand. The face that floated before me, all through my headlong flight to Benelli's hut, was Alessandro as I'd last seen him—my brave brother bruised and beaten to further the Montorio cause. Would cooperating with Fabiani help me gain Alessandro's freedom? I wasn't sure, but I did judge it certain that failing Fabiani would mean the end of my usefulness to Antonio Montorio. In that eventuality, Alessandro would be tried and executed as a smuggler before the month was out.

The old woodsman's hut was easy to find, waking its owner more difficult. I pounded as hard as I dared, hoping the good people of the Lungara were all fast asleep. When Benelli finally opened the door, the odor of cheap wine and old sweat clung to his nightshirt. His rheumy eyes opened wider at each repetition of my request, and he muttered excuses about a pain in his shoulder and a leaky boat. It required the invocation of Cardinal Fabiani's name to turn the tide and secure his promise that a serviceable boat would be waiting.

I returned to the pavilion as quickly as I could. The cardinal had vanished. Rossobelli was pacing nervously. The abate must have returned to the villa while I'd been off waking Benelli, for he now wore a short, hooded cloak. He ran to me and clapped my cheeks between cold, damp palms. "Thank God," he squeaked. "Is it all arranged?"

I nodded.

He opened his watch, then closed it with a decisive click. Gemma's body stretched full-length on the floor, cocooned in her cloak like the larva of a giant moth. "Grab her head," ordered Rossobelli. "I'll take the feet."

"Must we?" I swallowed hard. "I mean, isn't this going to make things even worse? Surely a magistrate could see that the marchesa is not in her right mind. She wouldn't be hauled before the criminal court. She could be secured somewhere...a comfortable place where she can't hurt anyone else."

The abate simply rolled his eyes and tapped his watch with a meaningful frown.

The girl made a light burden. Even so, it was a job getting her down the hidden stairway and through the portion of the aqueduct that descended to the Tiber. As we picked our way along, I asked, "How did you happen to discover her?"

Rossobelli shifted his hold on the lantern, throwing a harlequin pattern of light and shadow over the damp walls. "I was making my midnight rounds, checking to see that all the doors were locked and all the servants where they should be."

"I would expect the housekeeper to perform that chore."

"Signora Battista is a lazy cow, in bed by ten almost every night. While she snores the evening away, footmen gamble at cards, maids sneak out to meet lovers, and the bootboy makes himself sick trying to learn to smoke a pipe."

"You check the pavilion every night?"

"No. I look out for Cardinal Fabiani's interests as best I can, but even I cannot do everything. I secure the house and leave the gardener to see to the grounds."

"And the stables?"

"They are beyond the stand of trees on the other side of the villa from the garden. Well away from the house, thank heaven."

"Then—oof." I stumbled over a rough juncture. Falling to my knees, I struggled to keep the maid's head from hitting the hard floor.

Rossobelli seemed glad of the short respite. He was breathing hard and continued his story in ragged gasps. "I went out to the pavilion...because the footman on duty at the front door said that Marchesa Fabiani had been tearing through the hall, mumbling about going to the garden for an ice...when I found a back door standing open...I knew it would be easier for me to retrieve the marchesa myself rather than track down Matilda."

Having secured my hold on our burden, I rose shakily. "Did you meet anyone on the way out to the garden?"

"No."

"Hear anything, see anything?"

"Such as?"

"Footsteps, someone running away."

"Of course not. I'm sure Marchesa Fabiani was in the larder by then. By the time I found her, she'd spilled flour all over the tiles and had eaten her way through an entire cold pie. She must have run away and found her hiding place as soon as she saw what she'd done."

"Matilda was supposed to be watching the marchesa?"

"That is true. His Eminence had given Gemma the night off."

"When did she leave the villa?"

"Not long after the conversazioni—after I assured myself that the marchesa was settled in her room with Matilda."

"Where was Gemma going?"

"How would I know? It's not my business to keep track of the servants when they're out of the villa."

"But she was on the grounds, in the pavilion. At least she was when she was killed. What do you suppose Gemma was doing there?"

Rossobelli heaved a deep sigh and suddenly became very busy rearranging his hold on Gemma and the lantern. As he resumed his reverse march through the tunnel, his feet seemed to slip and he threw out a hand to break his fall.

After more grunting and fumbling, I repeated the question.

"I wouldn't know," he finally replied, shrugging under Gemma's weight. "Why don't you ask your friend Abate Lenci?"

Before I could speak again, Rossobelli bade me shut my mouth so he could mind his footing. Thus, we pushed on toward the Tiber in silence, soon emerging to fight our way through a thicket of bushes and brush that lined the riverside. Once on the bank, we set Gemma down, then straightened to rub our arms and stretch our backs.

A full moon hovered over the dark bulk of the Janiculum, casting a net of silver threads on the waters of the Tiber. Straining my eyes, I saw Benelli and his rowboat standing out as a dark form bobbing in the channel. Rossobelli pulled his hood forward, raised the lantern, and moved it back and forth.

"This is as far as I go." Rossobelli's whisper was tentative, as if he didn't quite believe what he was saying.

"What? I can't manage alone."

"You won't be alone," he answered with more determination. "Benelli is old, but the girl is tiny. He will help you get her into the boat and row you out to the river's deepest pool." Turning swiftly, Rossobelli blended back into the shadows before I could voice further protests.

I hardly like to recall the rest of that terrible night. Acutely aware that mine was the only face the old woodsman could associate with this criminal undertaking, I presided over Gemma's watery, unsanctified burial on a deserted stretch of river north of the city. As her weighted corpse sank with barely a gurgle, it seemed to take the few remaining scraps of my youthful innocence with it. I couldn't have felt more befouled if I'd murdered the girl myself.

After Benelli had returned me to the dry land of his vegetable garden, I headed back to the villa at a dirgelike pace. Bare winter branches formed a skeletal canopy over the gravel lane and filtered the moonlight into pale, angled shafts. With the chill air sweeping the cobwebs from between my ears, I reached a worrisome conclusion: Cardinal Fabiani's theory about Gemma's murder was as full of holes as a fisherman's net.

At first, in the rush to conceal the deed, I'd accepted his belief that the old marchesa had strangled Gemma in a fit of lunacy, but the more I considered, the more I doubted. The scarf around Gemma's neck had indeed appeared to be one of the marchesa's, but I'd seen the old lady shed her shawls and scarves as easily as a tree scatters autumn leaves. Gemma was always picking them up. Until she could return them to her charge's shoulders, she would tuck them in her sleeve or tie them about her waist. Poor Gemma could have been carrying the instrument of her demise on her own person.

That was only the starting point for my questions. As I reached the edge of the wooded Fabiani estate, I paused to picture the marchesa's pipestem arms and bony shoulders. Even in the fury of madness, could the elderly woman have possibly mustered the bodily strength to overcome a strong, healthy girl? To tighten the silk around her neck until she grew limp and still? I had never witnessed a strangling, but I supposed that it must take several minutes.

With the wind soughing in the limbs above, I left the lane and ascended the narrow path to a gate that I'd barely noticed on my wild flight to Benelli's hut. The gate stood half open, its iron bars set in a corner of the stout garden wall well away from the house. I gave the gate a shove, but the hinges didn't budge. Wrapping both hands around the bars, I redoubled my efforts. The gate barely moved. Looking down, I saw why. Tussocks of dried grass and weeds were matted thickly around its base. I'd wager this gate hadn't been shut since last spring.

I picked my way through the terraced herb beds and shining pools, anxious to return to my chamber, but the moonlit paths were deceptive. Rounding a tall evergreen, I found myself in the graveled yard that surrounded the pavilion on three sides. With pulse pounding, I approached the miniature lodge and stopped at the doorway. The interior was totally black; I had no desire to go farther. Like a perfumed scent that lingers once a woman has passed, an air of menace hung over this place.

Hanging my head, profoundly wishing that I had never followed Rossobelli down the hidden stair in the first place, my gaze was caught by a piece of metal that glinted in the moonlight. A thick, leaf-bare vine arose from one side of the doorway to twine over the arched entrance. Something dangled from a low tendril: a good-sized pendant worked in silver and attached to a leather cord. Faster than a Monte dealer, I palmed the bauble and gave a tug. The light was too dim to examine my prize properly so I transferred it to the pocket of my breeches.

A few false starts set me on the path that led to the villa, but one last surprise awaited: the doors were locked front and back. Even if I screwed up my courage to return to the pavilion, I had no lamp to locate the catch on the hidden entrance or to navigate the blackness of the aqueduct.

Ringing the bell cord at the main portico seemed to be my only option. A sleepy Guido answered. I'd concocted a tale about becoming lost on a midnight walk, but Benito's friend handed me a better story. With a knowing smirk, Guido couldn't resist making a joke about a eunuch stumbling home after trying his luck in the bordellos of the Trastevere.

"Ah, you caught me out. See here…" I ran my hands over my sweat-stained shirt and torn lace. "Your Roman whores are even more dangerous than our Venetian ones. The jades fought among themselves as if they couldn't wait to bed me, but once I was at their mercy, they stole my purse and rolled me out the door without jacket or cloak."

Guido laughed, and I saw that his looks were more remarkable than I had first thought. He had removed his cheap servant's wig to reveal thick, almost blue black curls, and the pleasing proportions of his features were marred only by the vestiges of a fight that had once rearranged his nose. I could see why Benito was smitten.

He said, "You should have let me know what you wanted. Your man could have easily arranged it. I can supply you with a woman who won't pilfer your pockets, one who knows some jolly tricks that might suit you most particularly." With a leer, he added, "Like our Lord, she performs the miracle of bringing the dead to life."

"I'll remember that." I nodded, forcing a smile. "Have you been on duty here all night?"

"Since ten o'clock."

"Am I the first to disturb your rest?"

He shrugged. "The old lady got loose."

"Oh, what time was that?"

"Halfway between eleven and midnight. I told Rossobelli about it, then I didn't see her anymore. All in all, nothing out of the ordinary."

Perhaps for you, I thought, but instead asked, "How did you have the bad luck to draw night porter's duty?"

"Night duty's a nevermind for me. After Rossobelli comes around there's hardly anyone about, and a fellow can follow his thoughts without getting sent on a hundred errands." A cocky grin contorted his well-shaped lips. "But old Red Chaps does give me more than my share."

"Are you in Abate Rossobelli's bad graces, then?"

"I think he sees it as a kind of penance." Guido winked. "For my sins."

Heaving a parting chuckle, I directed my weary steps toward the upper floors. By the time I reached my room and lit a lamp to examine the silver pendant, dawn was breaking over the hills of Rome.

Chapter 9

The morning was nearly spent when I arose with a pounding headache. Refusing solid food, I sipped at a cup of warm chocolate while I dressed to go out. No unwilling service, be it disposing of a body or warbling a serenade, was going to keep me from seeing Liya.

Using my map, I found the Teatro Argentina on a busy corner at the intersection of two streets lined with churches and shuttered houses painted in muted shades of russet and ocher. In contrast to the theaters of Venice, it was of modest size and presented an unassuming face to the street. A graceful young man with bleached hair governed the stage door. He clearly saw me as an irritant in his well-oiled day. "No one here by that name," he answered curtly when I asked for Signorina Del'Vecchio.

"But I saw her only yesterday. She told me to meet her. I had the idea that she works here."

"Don't know the lady." He shrugged and moved to shut the door.

From the depths of the theater, the familiar sounds of an opera company preparing for a performance met my ears. Suddenly, Liya's throaty laugh separated itself from the general din, and her smiling face popped over the doorkeeper's shoulder.

"Tito, wait there. I'll just be a minute. I need my shawl."

The straw-haired young man swept me from head to toe with a curious glance. "If that's who you want, why didn't you just say so?" he muttered before slouching off.

Waiting, I massaged my temples in the gloomy alley that ran between the theater and a taller building that blocked the early afternoon sun. I couldn't help comparing the Argentina with my theater back in Venice. If I had appeared at the San Marco stage door, colleagues and friends would have gathered round and embraced me, hustled me to the green room, broken out bottle and glasses. Old wives caution the young: Take care how you wish. I was learning that lesson on a bitter road. After the drudgery of Dresden, it had been my heartfelt wish to shun the theater for months on end. Now, I would sing a four-act opera every night rather than be subject to Cardinal Fabiani's sinister intrigues.

When the door opened again, Liya's apologetic smile sent those thoughts flying. "I didn't have a chance to tell you before," she said. "I'm Liya Pellegrina now."

My breath hung in my throat. What fresh torment was this? "You're married?" I stammered. "Who? How long?"

"Still leaping to conclusions, I see." She slipped an arm under mine and started our progress to the street. "I took a new name when I left the ghetto. I feared that Papa would send someone to bring me back, and that's the last thing I wanted. A clean break was best…or so I thought at the time."

"I see," I murmured in relief. "A new name for a new life. And Pellegrina—*pilgrim*—what could be more apt?"

She nodded.

I confess I stared at her profile like a boy entranced by his first fireworks display. Liya was even more beautiful than the image I had treasured in my mind these past five years. Her loose black hair made a striking frame for the exotic plane of her cheekbones, and her olive skin seemed as soft and supple as rose petals. Her eyes were the only thing that truly surprised me. Their black orbs had changed—for the better. In Venice, they'd often flamed with bonfires of resentment and frustration. Now they shone with a quiet, steady contentment. Whatever new life Liya had found seemed to suit her.

"Do you make masks and headdresses for the Argentina?" I asked.

"Yes, but I sew on the costumes as well. The boys' gowns mainly. I've developed quite a knack for creating a bosom where there is none. And giving sixteen-year-olds who have no hips the swell of—" Liya broke off at my look of alarm. "Surely you've seen an opera here in Rome."

"I haven't had time—I just arrived several days ago—but I know the Church forbids women on the stage. It was the same at my conservatorio in Naples. We all had to take our turns playing the women's parts."

I fancy Liya had never thought of me in that light. She raised an inquiring eyebrow, but there was something more important afoot. My mysterious follower had returned and was studying the theater's front entrance from the pavement across the street. I didn't like the intensity of his gaze or the way he was muttering to himself.

"Liya," I whispered, dropping my mouth to her ear. "That man over there, the tall one in the Roman hat." She half turned. "No, don't look at him. He was following me yesterday, when I saw you outside the Pantheon. Now he's on my heels again. I want to shake him off, but I barely know my way around Rome. Which way should we go?"

She made a moue of concern. With eyes lowered under lush lashes, she took a quick peek, then astounded me by raising her hand in a friendly wave. The tall stranger responded in kind. Smiling, he stepped into the street, but almost immediately paused. He extended his long neck forward and back, like a goose scooping up grain. A carriage rolled by, and when it had passed, he was gone.

"That's odd." Liya cocked her head, trailing her fragrant hair on my sleeve. "He'll usually risk life and limb to run across the street and tell you his troubles."

"You know the man?"

"Of course. That's our poor Tucci. He sang with the company here until a wealthy cardinal hired him away. Those who know music say Tucci's voice has no equal, and I suppose he does sing admirably fine. I just know that he's a lamb—always pleasant—never raised a fuss over his costumes like so many singers. Everyone makes a pet of him. But lately he's gone a bit round the bend. His patron turned him out several weeks ago, and Maestro Ucellini won't hire him back. He says it would be financial folly to engage a singer that Cardinal Fabiani has discarded. Now, poor Tucci acts like a woefully lost lamb. He's been coming to the theater every day, bleating about his sad tale and begging for scraps of news."

We'd been strolling as Liya recounted Tucci's story. Now she stopped and dropped my arm. "But Tito, what makes you think Tucci is following you? You've just come to Rome. He couldn't even know you…unless you've sung together in other cities, perhaps?"

"No, I've not encountered the man before." I draped her arm over mine again and gave her an account of my business in Rome. The abbreviated version, I fear: the one that cast me in the role of goodwill ambassador rather than spy. Seeing Liya, and finding her so obviously pleased to see me, had set my good sense teetering on a precipice. I longed to carry her away to some private place, bury my face in her lap, and pour out all the terrible events of the past few days. But what did I really know of her present situation and frame of mind? I reluctantly determined that my smartest course of action would be to conceal the dire details of my trip to Rome and see what turn our renewed acquaintance would take.

She thought a moment as we strolled in the direction of the Tiber. "I'm sure Signor Tucci means you no harm. His dismissal may have left him unsettled in his humors, but the man doesn't have a wicked bone in his body. I think he's only curious to view the singer who supplanted him at the villa."

"I'd be pleased to give him a closer look. His advice on how to satisfy Fabiani would be most welcome. So far, the cardinal has been less than overwhelmed by my songs. Do you know where this Tucci keeps his lodging?"

"He has rooms at Number 38, Piazza di Spagna. When he's not pestering Maestro Ucellini to regain his old position, he

entertains the children of his neighborhood with puppet operas.
They're quite charming. He's fixed a miniature stage that he carries to a certain park on sunny afternoons. While he manipulates
the strings from behind, he announces the characters and sings
all their parts."

"You've seen them?"

"Several times." She hesitated, suddenly shy, then added, "I
thought they would amuse...my son."

"Ah, Luca's child." I hesitated as well, but not from shyness. "He
must be nearing five by now. Is that what you call him? Luca?"

She gave a peculiar laugh. "I broke tradition in that way, too.
He isn't named for his father."

She fell silent, so I prodded her. "He does have a name?"

"Oh, yes." She fixed me with a penetrating look. "I call him
Tito."

I digested that surprising bit of information as we turned
several corners and entered a noisy café. After we ordered grappa
and sweet biscuits, I asked her why.

"When I went to Monteborgo, I had plenty of time to ponder
a number of things. The village was amazingly quiet compared to
the ghetto, and I didn't have my mother's constant nagging and
nitpicking ringing in my ears. Monteborgo was the sanctuary I
needed. By the time Tito was born, I had gradually come to see
that my love for Luca was really a blindfold that kept me from
seeing him as he really was."

"Luca reeked of charm," I said, "but his pleasing ways hid
a selfish heart."

She smiled wryly. "There was a time when I would have
smacked your cheeks for saying such a thing. But you're right,
Tito, quite right." She took a sip of grappa that left a smudge of
syrupy purple over her finely chiseled lip. "That's why I refused
to name my son after a rogue. I asked myself, 'Who is the most
admirable man I know? Who possesses the sensibility and fine
feelings that I would seek to bestow on my child?'"

"And you settled on me?" I asked in wonderment.

She nodded. "You were at the top of my list."

My hand sought hers across the white tablecloth. "Liya, why did you not return to Venice? The last time we met, I made my feelings abundantly clear."

"I did come back. Several years ago…"

"But your family never said."

"You see them?"

"Often—when I'm home." I shrugged. My voice became husky. "They are my only link to you."

She clenched my hand and pulled herself up very straight. "Did they sit shiva for me?"

I shook my head. "In this, your father has been adamant. He refuses to go into mourning because he believes you will return someday."

"How are they?" Her black eyes shone, but if they held tears, they did not wet her cheeks.

"Your mother and father are well. Your grandmother still sits by the stove, pretending to do needlework but really keeping an eye on everyone's activities."

Liya smiled a little, so I went on, "Mara and Sara married men of the ghetto, and Fortunata has become quite the little lady. She helps your father in the shop."

"Then Papa must be happy." Liya sighed. "Fortunata was always his favorite."

I thought Pincas would be happier if his eldest daughter would pay him a visit with the grandson he had never seen, but I didn't say so. Instead, I asked, "You didn't see them at all?"

"No. I was in Venice only a short time. I went to the theater to look for you, only to find you'd gone to England for an extended engagement at the opera house in Covent Garden." She dropped her gaze. "And that you were traveling in the company of a certain lady."

I groaned. "What wretched luck. I returned from London almost immediately. The vile taste of that gloomy town has turned against Italian singers, and there's no point in staying where you're not wanted." I leaned across the tablecloth. "More importantly, the lady you heard about was a miserable mistake. She lasted no longer than my London engagement."

Liya sent me an enigmatic smile. "Our luck appears to have changed for the good. We have found each other once again. In Rome, of all places."

I returned her smile. "Have you left Monteborgo behind for good, then?"

"I've left the village, but not its ways."

"You're still a devotee of the old religion?" I asked, lowering my voice to a whisper. Even the mention of the streghe made me itch to look over my shoulder to see who might be listening.

It was her turn to nod. She took another sip of grappa before answering, "There are more of us than you might think. Not all in remote villages."

"Wise women?"

"Not just women. Many men follow the old path along with us."

I opened my mouth to ask another question, but she silenced me with a shake of her head. "If you care to listen, I have marvelous things to tell you. But here is not the place."

She was right. The placement of the café tables allowed only enough space for the waiters to squeeze through with their trays balanced high on one hand. We were closely surrounded by black-clad abati, all sipping coffee and offering conflicting rumors about the state of Pope Clement's health: he had rallied and appeared on a balcony of the Quirinal—no, he was sinking and had lost the power of speech—no, he was raving night and day like a madman.

Summoning a waiter, I said to Liya, "I do have something I'd like to show you. It's a strange relic—you may be able to enlighten me about its meaning. Shall we walk?"

"Yes, of course." Liya pulled her shawl over her shoulders. "But back toward the theater. A new opera opens tonight—the first performance since before Christmas. I've been gone too long already."

I nodded, suddenly aware that my headache seemed to have entirely disappeared, then answered, "I saw the play-bill—*Ricimero* by Jommelli. I'd like to see what that Neapolitan butterball has come up with. When I left Naples, Jommelli was full of boasts but had yet to make his mark."

"You must come. Maestro Ucellini expects a twenty day run."

"Whether or not I see *Ricimero* depends on Cardinal Fabiani."

"He will see it several times, I'm sure. The cardinal keeps a fine box, overlooking the stage from the third tier."

"But will he bring his caged nightingale along?" I was unable to keep the bitterness from my tone.

She tossed her black curls. "Tito, why have you shackled yourself to Fabiani? As I recall, you always valued your liberty to make your own arrangements. Does having a Venetian as pope really matter so much?"

I took a deep sigh. "That's another thing we must save for later discussion." Digging into my waistcoat pocket, I clasped the pendant I had found at the entrance to the garden pavilion. I paused on the pavement to transfer it to Liya's palm. "Here, tell me what you can about this."

While I pretended to admire the feathery creations in a milliner's window, Liya studied the intricately worked silver. "It's called a *cimaruta*. Many followers of the old religion keep one as an amulet, either sewn into a hidden pocket or on a chain under a shirt. Where did you get it, Tito?"

I'd given my story some thought. Not wanting to involve Liya in any unpleasantness, I lied like a trooper reporting for duty after an all-night drunk. "The necklace came from a trinket stall at the market. I thought it might make a nice souvenir of Rome for Annetta, but when I gave it a good look, I wondered if it might not have some pagan significance."

I wasn't sure if Liya gave any credence to my tale, but she did explain the symbolism. "It's a sprig of rue fashioned of silver. Both the plant and the metal are sacred to the goddess Diana."

"What are these charms dangling from the branches?"

"Let's see. Each cimaruta is different, made according to the wearer's inclinations." She turned the bright amulet to catch the sunlight. "Here's a half moon, in its waning phase, to banish evil. And this little five-petaled flower is vervain, for purification. The fish is for health and strength. And…what's this one?" She wrinkled her brow.

I bent my gaze to her palm and poked at the tiny charm with my forefinger. Telling her what I'd already observed, I said, "It seems to be a cross."

"So it is," she whispered under her breath, "a Christian cross."

She raised her chin to look me in the eye. "Tito," she said with grim foreboding. "What have you gotten yourself into?"

⁂

After delivering Liya to the theater and making plans to meet again, I spent the rest of the afternoon snooping. My first stop was No. 38, Piazza di Spagna, but Tucci had not returned home. It must have given the singer quite a turn to see the rival he had been following in the company of someone he counted as a friend. Nearby, I spotted several boys playing tag on the magnificent flight of steps that swoops up to a twin-towered church overlooking the square. The boys knew Tucci as "the scarecrow man with the puppets" and showed me the little park where he often staged a show on Sunday afternoons.

With nothing more to be done in that quarter, I hired a carriage to return to the villa. On my order, the driver set me down when we reached the edge of the estate. I wanted to take another look at the pavilion without Rossobelli hanging over my shoulder. I raced up the path until I reached the half open gate, then slowed to slink from tree to tree. This part of the garden seemed deserted, but voices from the hothouse that served the villa's kitchen floated over the hedges and cypress trees. Realizing that I was behaving in a ridiculously suspicious manner, I forced myself to stand tall and stroll toward the pavilion as if I had every right to be enjoying the cardinal's garden.

Once inside the rustic little building, I hesitated a moment to let my eyes adjust to the dim light admitted by the thick ivy lacing the window lattices. Gradually I saw that little had changed in the few hours since I'd first viewed Gemma's corpse. The three benches made a circle in the center of the pebbled floor, and the pyramid of terra cotta pots sat to one side. No more gauzy scarves or pagan amulets were in evidence, either inside or out.

The hidden doorway was shut, its stucco front tight against carved pilasters of dark wood on each side. It failed to yield to my prodding and poking, so I stood back to study the swags of flowers and festoons of fruit chiseled into the oak. About knee level, a cornucopia of oranges contained one piece of fruit that looked slightly different from the rest. I bent to look closely: not an orange depicted there, but a coin bearing the crest of some long-ago ruler. Of course, a coin made perfect sense. Rossobelli had told me that the original owner of the palazzo was a banker. Using two fingers, I pressed the circle into the wood and was rewarded with a grating creak and a sliver of damp darkness.

My skin prickled at the thought of traversing the old aqueduct again, but I forced my feet onto the stone stairway nevertheless. Rossobelli had seemed quite at home in the tunnel; I doubted that he was the only resident of the villa who knew of its existence. I ran my hands around the inside of the jamb and soon discovered a used, but serviceable candle in a holder complete with flint box. I struck a spark and got a feeble light going. Not yet cognizant of the door's mechanism from the inside, I folded my handkerchief into a tight square and wedged it in the catch before descending the steps.

I took a deep breath as I lowered my head to enter the aqueduct itself. The air was different here: thin, cold, with a metallic tang that coated the back of my throat. The stillness was profound, so deep that my breathing sounded as loud as the wheeze of a blacksmith's bellows. I moved haltingly forward on a downward slope, keeping my eyes alert for I knew not what. If the damp walls held any secrets, they did not reveal them to me.

At my feet, the seam that I had stumbled over the night before was the only irregular feature in the blocks polished smooth by slow-dragging centuries of flowing water.

After what seemed like an eternity of groping through the chill gloom, daylight from the distal end of the tunnel shone as a dim pinprick and quickly expanded to a welcome thumbprint of blue. In the growing light, my attention was drawn by some curious shading on the ceiling between me and the mouth of the tunnel.

I raised my candle and my stomach contracted into a tight ball. Bats—hundreds of them—clustered in furry knots not a foot from my head.

By reflex, I jerked my head into my collar and scrambled my way to the opening as fast as my feet would move. I dropped the candle in my ignominious flight, but it was of no consequence. Nothing could tempt me to enter that aqueduct again.

Blinking my eyes in the afternoon sun, heartily glad that the bats had slumbered on, I brushed myself off and searched the densely packed bushes for a way to the river bank. Opposite the mouth of the tunnel, broken branches marked the spot where Rossobelli had pushed through last night, but a quick inspection revealed something more promising. A short distance away, a sinuous path snaked its way through the brush. I examined the tips of the branches as I passed. No ragged edges or broken twigs here; they were as smoothly clipped as the hedges in the villa's garden.

The Tiber's yellow waters lapped at the bank where Rossobelli and I had laid Gemma's body. I paused there for a few moments, hanging my head at the thought of her rowboat cortege and final resting place. A bell from a church across the river tolled the hour. Five o'clock. The cardinal would soon be calling for his nightingale. With a sense of unease, as if I'd left something important undone, I followed the bank until I found a steep path up to the Lungara and flew back to my cage on swift wings.

Chapter 10

A footman whose face I didn't recognize was manning the main entrance. The bronze doors had barely thudded shut behind me when Rossobelli appeared and fastened himself to my elbow. Before keeping my appointment with Liya, I'd been obliged to ask his permission for an excursion across the Tiber. He'd given me leave with a return of his fawning manner, which was now joined by a nauseating whiff of collusion that he conveyed by resting his pink-rimmed eyes on mine in long, meaningful stares. I attempted to shrink away from him with even more determination than I had that morning.

"I know I'm later than I said, Rossobelli, but I had…er, some business to attend to…"

"Indeed, and a fine day it is for…business," he interrupted, tightening his grip.

"Has Cardinal Fabiani asked for me?"

He nodded, writhing in mock deference. "As much as it pains me to hurry you—with so many matters of import that must require your attention—but His Eminence is lying down and would very much enjoy a serenade. I would take it as a particular favor if you would go right up."

"Of course." I swallowed a sigh.

He released me with an encouraging nod.

I started toward the stairs, but not before I'd taken a good look at the secretary's spider-fingered hands. Back in the garden, I'd tried to picture the fatal attack. I imagined Gemma wandering the paths in search of the marchesa or perhaps waiting for some-one on one of the ironwork benches in the pavilion. The girl must have been taken by surprise, or have known her assailant well enough to let him draw close. Either way, when the scarf tightened around her neck, she would have put up a desper-ate fight. Anyone with access to the villa and grounds could have wielded one of the marchesa's discarded scarves, but only Gemma's killer would have scratches from her clawing fingernails on his hands and wrists.

Rossobelli was sending me on my way to the cardinal's suite with one of his obsequious half-bows. Angry-looking red scabs decorated the fleshy mound of his out-stretched palm.

"Goodness." I halted in my tracks. "You've hurt your hand."

"No, not at all." He immediately straightened, making tight fists right and left. "It's nothing."

"But it is. You must have that seen to."

The abate shot his gaze around the hall, making sure that the footman was well away at his post, then whispered in a most unservile growl. "Shut up, you fool. When I fell last night, I caught myself with my hand. The less said about it the better."

It was my turn to bow and continue up the stairs.

The cardinal's commodious suite was awhirl with sky blue livery, as full of people as I had expected to find it the night before. Amid the stuffy grandeur, several footmen adjusted widow draperies, while another arranged a vase of flowers. From a sweating silver carafe, the cardinal's valet poured a golden ribbon of wine into a cup on a nightstand already crowded with vials of drops and potions. Fabiani was abed, squirming and thrashing in an effort to find a comfortable resting place. Even for a nap, he capped his head with the cardinalate scarlet, a satin nightcap of Turkish style whose folds gleamed against the snow-white pillow case. When his servants saw me, they paused in mid-activity and seemed to heave a collective sigh of relief.

I approached the bed. The cardinal beckoned with a clawing gesture.

"Ah, my songbird. You've come at last. I need rest if I'm to last through the opera tonight. Sing something that will soothe me to sleep." Fabiani stretched his lips in a beatific smile and addressed me as if Gemma's horrifying death had never occurred.

"Do you enjoy Vivaldi, Your Eminence?"

He frowned. "Too gaudy. Give me simple melody, not fireworks."

I knew just the thing. I modulated my voice to its softest tone and began a sweet rendition of a *canzonetta* by one of my old maestros, a tender reflection on unrequited love. The valet applied a cloth to Fabiani's brow, and the cardinal sighed and snuggled into his pillows. Before I reached the end of the second stanza, the cardinal was the picture of repose: eyes closed; catlike nose no longer twitching; lips parted to emit deep, regular breaths. I took particular note of the pale, unblemished hands crossed loosely on the coverlet.

Before sleep totally prevailed, Fabiani opened one eye to whisper, "You'd best rest, as well, Tito. You're coming to the Argentina with me tonight."

⁂

"Guido's saying that Gemma quit. Just demanded her wages, threw her clothes in a bag, and walked out." Benito frowned at the velvet patch which refused to adhere to the skin between my right eye and temple.

"Doesn't that strike anyone as odd?" I was trying to talk and hold my head still at the same time. "Are positions in service so easy to find in Rome? Judging by the number of beggars I've seen in the street, I'd guess that jobs are hard to come by."

"Guido says that Rome is a dole town. There's a free bread ration, and the religious confraternities fall all over themselves to fulfill their charitable duties. Plenty of free hospitals, too. Why should a man work when everything is provided?"

"Why is Guido working, then?"

Benito grinned as he applied another dot of mastic to the star-shaped patch. "Ambition. Guido says he wants more than a crust of bread and a spot of sunshine to nap in."

"Your new friend seems to say a great deal. I trust you're not revealing any of our secrets in return." I had recounted the details of the midnight tragedy when Benito found me puzzling over the cimaruta that morning.

"Don't worry about me, Master. I understand what will befall Signor Alessandro if we fail. As far as Guido is concerned, I'm valet to a dimwitted but kindly castrato who thinks of little besides the health of his throat and his next good meal."

"Dimwitted? Me?" My jerk of annoyance dislodged the tiny patch that Benito had labored over.

Licking his forefinger, Benito nudged the reluctant patch back to its original position. As he reached for more mastic, he calmly stated, "You know how it is—people tend to discount castrati as vain, self-absorbed songsters—as if cutting off our balls removed any other interests or pleasures besides music. It will work to our advantage if people believe we're a pair of lightweight fools. They'll be less on guard and the more we'll learn in the end."

Sighing through my nose, I gave his strategy a nod of assent. "Did Guido mention how the staff learned of Gemma's supposed decampment?"

"Rossobelli announced it this morning, at breakfast in the house servants' dining hall. Said that Matilda would be seeing to the old lady's needs from now on. That's why nobody wondered. The marchesa gave Gemma fits—the girl had threatened to quit a hundred times. Now, Guido's taking bets on how long Matilda will last. I put ten *paoli* down on three weeks."

"There is something else. Guido called Gemma away from the music room, right after the conversazioni. Why, I wonder."

"Oh, I know why. He found the marchesa outside without her shawl. Gemma and Matilda were still trying to coax her inside when I went down to the kitchen for your dinner."

I nodded thoughtfully.

Benito curled his tongue over his upper lip, intent on his task. "Good God, but this patch would try St. Peter's soul."

"Just put it back in the box—it's time I should get downstairs. It hardly fits my mood tonight, anyway." I was, of course, referring to the convention that a patch placed at the corner of the eye denotes a man of passionate temperament.

"Is that so? I would have thought that spending the afternoon with Signorina Del'Vecchio would have raised a bit of passion in your breast...or perhaps lower down."

"Oh, Benito. What am I going to do with you?" I moaned in mock exasperation as I shrugged into my coat. "Do try to remember, she's Signorina Pellegrina now, and we're just getting to know each other again."

"She may have changed her religion and her name, but she's still Liya, daughter of a ghetto rag merchant."

"Not a fair statement. Her family deals in high quality used clothing."

He rolled his expressive eyes. "You know what I mean—it's like the old saying about a leopard and his spots. We are who we are, though we may try mightily to convince ourselves and others that we're not."

I nodded, assessing my reflection in the mirror. Even without the beauty patch, I looked a fine sight: coat of claret-colored brocade that I'd worn for my first concert at the villa; shirtfront of Burano-lace ruffles; full dress bob-wig, powdered to a starch white; and a subtle dewing of cosmetics to give my skin the lily-and-rose complexion that was fashionable for both men and women. But was that really me? Somehow I pictured my true self at about nine years old, chasing Alessandro and his friends through the calli and campi of Venice, dreaming of sailing away on a pirate ship and discovering buried treasure. Back then, becoming one of those peculiar eunuchs that I'd seen singing the high parts of Mass at the Basilica was the farthest thing from my mind.

I dragged myself back to the present and addressed Benito's back as he rummaged through a drawer. "While I'm at the opera, perhaps you can get this loquacious Guido talking about Gemma. Was she friendly with the rest of the staff? Or were there feuds?

"And…" I fingered my neckcloth thoughtfully. "I'd also be interested to know if there's any possibility that her relationship with the cardinal went beyond master and servant."

Benito flashed a saucy grin over his shoulder. "It will be my pleasure, Master. Here…" He stood up and unfurled a handkerchief for my perusal. "Silk, don't you think? For the opera?"

I gazed at the lace-edged fabric in horror.

"Master?"

"Oh, Benito, I must be the biggest fool in all of Italy. I've left my handkerchief stuffed in the secret door of the pavilion."

"Not one with a monogram?" Benito's expression mirrored my own.

"I'm not sure." I took off at a run. "I'll have to get it."

Darting past me, Benito pressed his back against the door. "No, let me. The back stairs will be quicker, and no one will think twice about me running up and down."

I hesitated. It was my mistake and I should be the one to rectify it.

"Besides, it's time for you to go down."

"It is, but I would like to be sure that all is well before I leave the villa."

"I'll bring it to you in the front hall, as if I had forgotten to supply a handkerchief for your pocket." My manservant nodded decisively.

We entered the long corridor. While Benito trotted toward the servant's staircase, I made my way downstairs by the sweeping marble cascade. I'd been told that Cardinal Fabiani's box at the opera house contained six seats. Rossobelli and I were to ride with the cardinal in his black and gilt coach; a small party from Prince Pompetti's circle would meet us at the theater.

Fabiani greeted me with a nod, obviously anxious to be off. But as he donned an ermine-trimmed cloak, the old marchesa came loping through the grand hall. A diamond headpiece circled her tangled locks and scarlet dots of rouge decorated her cheeks. Even more startling was the outdated ball gown of crushed velvet that covered her bony form. No one had done the laces up the back, so the bodice had slithered down to reveal breasts as limp and flat as two empty meal sacks.

Holding her skirts bunched in two fists, she made a beeline for her son. "Lorenzo, *caro*. Don't leave without me," she entreated in a rasping croak. "I want to see the opera…I'm all dressed."

The cardinal's mouth fell open. "Merciful Heaven! What nonsense is this? Rossobelli, find Matilda at once."

The abate scurried off, knees pumping awkwardly from side to side.

Fabiani fixed an apprehensive smile on his lips. With tentative fingers, he tugged the marchesa's bodice to a less revealing position, then took his mother's hands in his. I observed her hands with interest. A thick ring, embossed with the Fabiani crest framed in tiny seed pearls, sprouted from her forefinger like an ornamental carbuncle. Blue veins snaked between wrinkles and spots of brown discoloration, but the skin on the back of her hands was unbroken. "Mama," he said, "you can't…that is, you wouldn't want to come. This opera will be very dreary. And long, very long. You would be bored to tears."

The old woman drew one hand away. She plucked at her gown, then at her straggling hair. "I want everyone to see my diamonds. Especially the Marchesa Albioni. She brags on her jewels, but they aren't nearly so fine as these."

Fabiani spoke slowly and firmly, "Mama, just think a moment. It's 1740. The Marchesa Albioni has been dead for five years. And you are ill—in no shape to go to the opera. You must go back to your room with Matilda."

The marchesa's new nursemaid had arrived. Quailing under the cardinal's dagger-like gaze, Matilda patted her charge's bare shoulder. "Yes, My Lady, back to your room. I'll make you some chocolate. And we'll play a game. Any one you like."

The marchesa gave the woman a gaping smile, but her milky eyes darted this way and that, searching the air, wordlessly asking: Who on earth are you, and what am I doing here? Hugging her velvet bodice up under her neck, she allowed Matilda to guide her. They were turning toward the stairs when the marchesa's gaze caught mine. She wriggled away from her keeper and threw herself in my arms.

"I know you. You'll take me, won't you? We'll see the opera together."

"Mama, stop," Fabiani gasped.

But the marchesa did not stop. "Yes, my pretty tall one." She rose to her tiptoes and pressed her fingers to my lips. "Your beautiful mouth. Kiss me now, carissimo, show me all the wonderful things you can do with that mouth."

"My Lady, please…" I stammered as footmen came running and Matilda flapped her arms in useless agitation.

The marchesa fought like a tigress. Her memory may have betrayed her, but her will endured. By the time she was carried away, one footman was limping, one had a bloodied nose, and Matilda had been knocked flat on her skinny rump.

I hardly knew what to say. Should I beg my patron's pardon for being the unwitting spur to his mother's outburst? Or pretend that nothing out of the ordinary had just occurred? Rossobelli offered no clue. He merely shuffled a nervous tattoo on the marble tiles, bleated a cough, and announced several times that the carriage was waiting. And where was Benito? The unfortunate drama had given him more than enough time to run to the pavilion and back.

Fabiani no longer seemed to be in a hurry. While Rossobelli dithered, the cardinal stepped closer to me. He stopped only when his face was inches from mine. Like a scholar examining an ancient parchment, he studied my features with narrowed eyes, parted lips, and quivering alley cat nose. Somehow I sensed that silence was the only proper response.

After an uncomfortable moment, rapid steps clattered over the terrazzo and Benito appeared at my elbow.

The cardinal broke his gaze. "I'm sorry, Tito. As you know, my mother can be quite…unpredictable." With that, he turned abruptly, his scarlet cloak billowing in his wake. The bronze doors parted. Over his shoulder, he flung a glittering smile. "Come, Signori. An evening of music and magic awaits."

"Did you find it?" I whispered out of the side of my mouth.

Benito slapped a folded square of fabric in my hand. Glancing down, I was puzzled to see the silk handkerchief that he had removed from my drawer earlier in the evening.

Rossobelli sidled close. "If your ensemble is complete, Signor Amato, His Eminence is waiting."

I followed Rossobelli, but watched Benito over my shoulder.

My manservant shook his head and silently mouthed: Not there.

⁂

We entered the cardinal's box at the Argentina just as perfunctory applause rose to greet the composer taking his place at the harpsichord. Fabiani settled himself in the best seat and gestured for me to sit at his left hand. We overlooked the stage so closely I could see the cast as they waited in the wings gargling spring water and adjusting costumes. The stage was set with a scene from ancient Rome. The buildings of the Forum rose against a backdrop of impossibly blue sky, cotton wool clouds billowed from the rafters, and an avenue of triumphal obelisks seemed to stretch to infinity. When two singers joined hands and entered stage right, I leaned forward with avid curiosity.

The *recitativo* that set up the opera's story line went well enough and the first solo was rewarded with loyal cheers, but it was the following duet that let me know I was in for a treat. The castrato who sang Ricimero, a barbarian king who hastened the fall of the Roman Empire, was a sound musician and even better actor. He commanded attention with every noble gesture, and the immense chest beneath his costume armor swelled with a voice of compelling resonance. More than a few ladies swooned when he directed his powerful soprano toward their boxes. The castrato who filled the prima donna role was even more interesting.

The playbill listed his name as Albertini, an obvious nod to an influential patron. He must have been almost straight from the conservatory—more boy than man—certainly not a day over eighteen. His youthful beauty made him a natural to play a female. The corseted waist, padded bodice, and porcelain face paint only gilded the lily that he already was. But it was his voice that had me hugging the box railing.

Any intelligent person can learn the language of music. It's a sort of code. Blobs of ink on the staff signify certain sounds that the human throat has the capability of creating. Learn what each blob means and you can sing. The result can be dull, plodding, competent, or inspired. Every singer imbues the process with his own style and personality. Albertini's contribution to Jomelli's score was playful delight. The boy sang with melodious abandon, his face shining with the joy of producing such marvelous sounds. His agile soprano ran up and down trills with astonishing ease and filled the auditorium like a peal of perfectly tuned church bells. Albertini's only sin was excess. With undisciplined enthusiasm, he improvised embellishments that overshadowed Jomelli's melodic line. I found myself adjusting and correcting his performance in my head—how I would love to take on a pupil of his caliber. I had become so engrossed that I failed to notice two latecomers entering the box.

When Rossobelli hissed and gave me a sharp poke in the ribs, I whirled around to shush him and instead found myself staring into the amused brown eyes of Prince Aurelio Pompetti.

"Amazing, isn't he?" The prince nodded toward Albertini. The duet had concluded with a stirring cadenza, and the singers were basking in wild applause and collecting the flowers that admirers tossed on the stage.

I nodded, still half-entranced by the music. "The best I've heard in many months."

Another poke from Rossobelli reminded me that I was addressing one of Rome's elite aristocracy. I quickly scrambled from my seat and gave the prince the bow that was his due. He responded with an abbreviation of the usual courtesies and presented me to his female companion.

Like most of the English, Lady Mary Sysonby was blond, rosy, and well-washed. She also possessed strong features and a vigorous frame which would have told well on a prima donna but struck me as overbearing in the small confines of the box.

"I've seen you before, Signor Amato, on the stage in London," she said in precisely enunciated Italian.

I bowed my acknowledgment.

"My father took me to Covent Garden to celebrate the birthday that occasioned the opening of my third decade of life. Though never inclined to novelties, Father thought I should see the Italian Opera before the fever for eunuchs abated."

"I hope we provided a fitting accompaniment for your special day."

She tossed her head in an equine gesture. "I admit to finding your songs extremely skilled. Some touching, even. But still, I must condemn your mutilation. Nature undoubtedly intended you to have a fine, deep voice. Why not leave it at that? This fad for frivolous trilling has robbed you of your generative organs and deprived you of posterity."

I clenched my teeth to keep my jaw from dropping. Few Italian women would have expressed themselves so boldly, but Prince Pompetti didn't seem troubled. Indeed, he inclined his handsome head in a series of nods, as if encouraging a star pupil in a recitation. As Albertini favored the audience with an encore, Lady Mary amplified her assertion with a detailed history of what she called "illegitimate eunuchism."

It was Cardinal Fabiani who insisted on the last word. Finally tearing his eyes away from the stage, he spoke regretfully. "My dear Lady Mary, if your ears were as keen as your intellect, we wouldn't be having this conversation."

Chapter 11

I confess I swelled with pride at Fabiani's comment. The cardinal might be up to his neck in secrets and schemes, but it warmed my heart to know that he appreciated splendid music and the pleasure it could bestow. I sent him a grateful look which he returned with an amicable smile. Perhaps I was working my way into his good graces at last.

Down below, a double row of dancers whirled in to replace the singers. Given that Rome had banished women players from the stage, there was a twisted logic in casting castrati in the prima donna roles, but an all-male ballet troupe held little charm. Throughout the scarlet and gold auditorium, the audience turned from the box railings to other pursuits. Cards, romance, gossip, suppers: all proceeded apace in these miniature drawing rooms.

I excused myself with every indication of needing to find the water closet. In reality, I meant to search for the ungainly figure I'd spotted standing at the back of the pit where Rome's poorer sort watched the show. I was going to have a word with Gaetano Tucci, whether he liked it or not.

I found the singer in the first-tier corridor, gazing mournfully at one of the framed playbills that decorated its walls. He started when I spoke his name, and his deep-set brown eyes displayed the look of a frightened animal.

"I must talk with you, Signore," I said.

He threw up his hands as if to shield his face. "I don't need your gloating, I'm low enough already."

"I'm not here to gloat," I answered, surprised. "Why would you think that?"

"His Eminence told me all about you. Your insolence, your vanity, your cruelty towards your fellow singers. He warned me to be on my guard."

"Fabiani told you that? When?"

"Before he dismissed me. The cardinal said he regretted letting me go, but he couldn't resist engaging such a celebrated singer—even if he did call you 'the most jealous of all the virtuosi.'"

"He maligns me, Signore. I've never been less than fair with my colleagues, even the ones who behave as you just described."

Tucci straightened his sloping shoulders. His nostrils flared. "You challenged Caffarelli to a duel because he corrected your tempo, then left him standing in the morning mist, catching a ruinous cold when you cowardly failed to show."

"What? I never."

"Well, you can't deny that you've lately performed in Dresden."

"That's true."

He fixed me with an accusing stare. "Where you had Signora Campanini fired when she dared insert your famous *bomba* into one of her arias."

"I had nothing to do with that. Prince Frederick dismissed her because she is too lazy to invent embellishments of her own. She stole musical feats from all of us. I'll write to Dresden if you don't believe me. Many there know the truth and won't mind telling it."

Tucci shuffled his feet and fumbled with the libretto he had rolled up in his hands. "Is it possible that His Eminence misled me?"

I nodded gravely. "It would seem so."

"Why would he do such a thing?"

"Perhaps he didn't want you talking to me."

"But why?"

I shrugged, feigning ignorance, but I thought I knew. If Fabiani had declared his support for Di Noce within Tucci's hearing, the cardinal might well wish to prevent me from conferring with his former singer.

"See here, Signore," I said. "I bear you no ill will. In fact, I wish to gain your friendship."

The singer frowned.

"Hear me out. I understand that your stock is low in Rome at present. But you are still in your prime. You must engage yourself elsewhere, conquer the stages of distant cities, then march back to Rome in glory. That's how careers are managed these days."

He shook his head so hard that the queue on his wig wagged like the tail of an excited dog. "I haven't sung anywhere else for years. I know no one of any influence outside Rome."

"I do. I'll furnish you with a letter of introduction to the director of the Teatro San Marco in Venice. I've sung under Rinaldo Torani off and on for almost ten years. If I give my recommendation, you can be sure of receiving an offer."

"You would do that for me? I doubt that you've ever heard me utter a note."

"I haven't, but I don't need to. Cardinal Fabiani is a musical connoisseur, and he chose you as his personal songster."

"Then showed me the door six months later. I did my best to please him, but still he tired of me..." Tucci trailed off in a quavering tone, then whispered, "He has obviously grown fond of you in just a few days—sitting in the cardinal's private box is a singular honor. I wondered what sort of man you would be, and if he would find your company more pleasant than mine."

"Is that why you were trailing me through the city?"

"Yes. My friend Giovanni, the harpsichord player, told me you'd arrived. I tried to stay away, but couldn't help myself. I hid on the grounds, hoping for a glimpse of you. When I saw two men who were obviously castrati come out of the villa and stroll down the path to the Lungara, I knew one of them must be you, so I followed."

"Looking for what? Were you hoping that I would beat my servant or show myself a monster in some other way?"

"I don't know. I suppose I was just trying to distract myself from the truth."

"The truth? What are you talking about?"

Tucci screwed up his face as if he were about to cry. "The truth is that His Eminence must have let me go because my voice is not what it used to be."

"Don't think that." I shook my head firmly. "It is not your voice that caused your dismissal. Politics are to blame."

"Politics?" His mournful features grew puzzled.

"Fabiani didn't hire me," I responded. "I was thrust upon him. In return for some information from you, I will try to explain."

The opera's first act must have come to a close; elegant ladies on the arms of their dashing escorts poured into the corridor. Recognizing the theater's former star or perhaps simply curious about two castrati having an intimate conversation, people stared, whispered behind fans or cupped hands, or sidled close with eager ears. Tucci and I were immediately of one mind.

"This way," he said and led me toward the back of the theater. We passed through an out-of-the-way door to halt on a drab stairway landing. Footmen in varied livery hurried by, quietly ignoring us, but a platform caged by rough wooden supports rattled up and down the open stairwell, making a fearful racket.

"What on earth?" I asked.

"It's a new innovation," he replied. "Instead of carrying food and drink from the street to the upper tiers, the servants place the boxed-up dinners on this. Someone hauls it up and down with ropes from the top."

"Ingenious," I murmured as the platform clattered past, "but noisy."

"They only use it during intermission. Its racket will cover anything we might say."

"Ah, yes…before I tell you what really brought me to Rome, let me satisfy my curiosity about a trifling matter. Were you by chance concealing yourself in the garden pavilion on the night I arrived?"

"No. In fact, I didn't even know you were at the villa until Giovanni stopped by my rooms early the next morning. Why do you ask?"

"I was on my balcony quite late and noticed a light in the pavilion. At the time, I thought it must be a reflection from the villa, perhaps a lantern carried by the night footman as he checked the doors. But later, when I had the opportunity to stroll around the garden, I saw that the pavilion's windows were covered with lattice, not glass."

"Wasn't me. Most likely a couple from the staff having a tumble." He shrugged. "Now, please...you promised to explain how politics led to my undoing."

Tucci showed little surprise as I recounted my tale of being pressed into service as a Montorio spy. He clucked his tongue over Alessandro's rough treatment and nodded his head sympathetically.

"I well remember the Montorio brothers," he said. "They hovered around His Eminence like flies on a goat. Quite a scheming pair, I thought, especially the senator."

"You met Antonio Montorio as well as his brother the Cardinal Ambassador?"

"Antonio visited Rome several months ago. Cardinal Fabiani honored the entire Venetian entourage with a magnificent ball and spent many hours closeted in his library with both brothers. Antonio made lavish promises, but His Eminence holds him and his word in little esteem."

"How did you learn of this? Did Fabiani request entertainment during these discussions?"

"No." Tucci smiled coyly. "But His Eminence told me about them. In the long nights, when he despaired of sleep, the cardinal would send everyone else away. Then he'd have me sing his three favorite songs, over and over. In between, he would talk, drifting from topic to topic, almost as if he had forgotten I was there."

"You learned much," I prodded.

He drew himself up proudly. "I probably know as much about the government as any state minister. Certainly as much as that self-important paper pusher Rossobelli."

"Then you must hold the answer to my most pressing question. When the Sacred College goes into conclave, which cardinal will have Fabiani's support? Montorio or Di Noce?"

Tucci rubbed his long jaw, keeping me in suspense. Then he answered, "It's not so easy to say. His Eminence speculated on a host of different scenarios, not all involving the two cardinals that everyone seems to be talking about." He chuckled. "Some men count sheep to fall asleep. Cardinal Fabiani tallies votes."

He saw my look of disappointment and quickly added, "But I can assure you that there is one question that drives Cardinal Fabiani's thinking as surely as water turns a mill wheel—which pope could he control? He was searching for a lever—a tool he could use to retain power and continue to live as well as he likes." Tucci shook his head, but a smile at the corner of his lips betrayed his admiration for Fabiani's tactics. He continued, "His Eminence said that the bonds of loyalty are easily broken, but fear can bind a man to you forever. He also said that the Montorios know no fear. They are too accustomed to power."

I nodded. The sound of a trumpet voluntary came through the wall. The opera was recommencing, and I needed to get back to the cardinal's box. I'd been away too long as it was.

Tucci was also anxious to leave, but I put a light hand on his sleeve and asked quickly, "When you were at the villa, did you become acquainted with a maid named Gemma Farussi?"

"Of course, I was often called to serenade the cardinal as he visited with the marchesa. Gemma was always in attendance."

"Did the cardinal show her particular favor?"

"He relied on her to keep the marchesa from harm."

"I'm speaking of something more personal." Strings joined the trumpets in an overture to Act Two. "In short, did Gemma share Fabiani's bed?"

Tucci shook his head. "His Eminence has honed his taste for many fine things. He demands beautiful rooms, good food, and fine wine, but music is his overriding passion. Human entanglements don't seem to interest him." Tucci smiled ruefully. "He welcomes neither woman nor man to his bed."

Interesting, I thought as I took leave of the singer with a promise to send his letter of introduction to Number 38, Piazza di Spagna. If Tucci knew what he was talking about, Fabiani was one of a rare breed: a high-ranking churchman who actually kept to his vow of celibacy.

⁂

With the good manners typical of his breeding, the cardinal greeted my delayed return with barely a lift of his eyebrow. Prince Pompetti and Lady Mary ignored me entirely. Rossobelli might have had something to say, but his attention was consumed with supervising the villa servants who had brought a light meal of hothouse asparagus and roasted duck. Though there were only five of us at the small table in the narrow box, the cardinal's cook had provided enough food to feed ten. I wondered if the duck had ridden up on the efficient hoist I'd just seen.

Roberto, the chilly old fellow who had awakened me on my first morning at the villa, offered a platter to Fabiani. The cardinal took a liberal helping and addressed his guests. "I miss the good company of my brother cardinal. Di Noce always brings a genial air to any occasion. Does his absence indicate that he shares Lady Mary's dread of musical eunuchs?"

"Not at all, Your Eminence," Pompetti replied smoothly. "My carriage stopped at the hospital of Santa Maria della Consolazione to fetch him, but he sent a nursing sister out to offer his regrets. A small boy had been run down by a coach, his legs crushed by the horses' hooves and his abdomen by the wheels. The pain must be horrific. Cardinal Di Noce is determined to stay at his bedside until the end."

Fabiani gave a solemn nod. "Di Noce is a true pastor, always at his duties among the people."

"An inspiring leader for the worldwide Church, wouldn't you say?" Pompetti put one elbow on the table and leaned over his untouched plate.

"His Eminence the Cardinal Di Noce does set a wonderful example of providing charity for the poor and comfort for the sick," Rossobelli added with surprising vehemence.

"Not only comfort," said Lady Mary.

We all eyed her questioningly.

"They say his hands have the gift of healing, especially where young children are concerned. Mothers line up before his residence with croupy babies and listless infants. Even hopeless cases often find relief."

"The man is a saint," intoned Rossobelli. Then he squirmed and added, "If I may be so forward as to say so."

"I tend to agree with you." Fabiani filled his mouth with duck. Melted fat oozed from between his lips to course down the cleft in his chin. Swabbing with a napkin, he said, "Unfortunately, a saint is of little use in collecting taxes, recruiting an army, or conducting any of the other business required to run a state. Can a saint cudgel the Finance Minister into preparing a workable budget? Argue the annual Peter's Pence out of the Archbishop of Paris? And what of your pet project, Rossobelli?"

"You are speaking of the port at Ancona?"

Fabiani nodded. "Would a pope who immerses himself in pastoral duties interest himself in the completion of a dike in a distant town?"

The abate answered forcefully. "Such a generous pope would surely do what is necessary to ensure the welfare of his subjects. The land around Ancona is poor and rocky—its inhabitants live in miserable conditions. Reviving the port would bring prosperity to the entire eastern half of the Papal States. Of course…" Rossobelli shot a venomous look at me. "Some would rather see Ancona's blue waters silted up forever and her good citizens in rags."

"Why Abate Rossobelli, I believe you must hail from Ancona," Lady Mary said shrewdly.

He looked away for a moment, then nodded. "It's true. My father is harbor master there, though his duties amount to little at this point."

Fabiani sat back in his chair. A smile played about his lips. "So it seems that we have three staunch Di Noce supporters at table. What about you, Tito? You've been very quiet. Who would you like to see as the next pope?"

"That's hardly for me to say," I murmured in surprise. "I'm just a musician. I know nothing of church administration."

Fabiani spread his hands. "Come, come. I invited you all to enjoy the evening in the spirit of brotherhood and equality. You are free to state your opinion." He narrowed his eyes over the flames of the candles that lit our table. "As a Venetian, you surely have one."

I swallowed the food in my mouth. The succulent duck might as well have been a lump of gristle. The cardinal was toying with me, with all of us. He would not allow me to remain silent. "I've seen the crowds cheering for Cardinal Di Noce," I replied slowly. "I'm sure he's most virtuous and wise in his way, but Cardinal Montorio has many strengths, as well. He comes from a long line of statesmen—the Montorio family has been in the Golden Book since the founding of Venice. You might say that governing is in his blood."

The cardinal nodded sagely, encouraging me to continue. I'd barely started to praise the Montorio clan's industry in the spice trade when Pompetti interrupted.

"Family," the prince said darkly. "That will be Montorio's downfall. If he wins the throne, just imagine all the brothers, nephews, and uncles who will scramble for the new pope's grace and favor. Cousins of cousins will pull themselves out of the Venetian muck and hurry to Rome with yawning, empty purses."

"Prince Pompetti makes an astute observation. Don't you agree, Eminence? There's no one more grasping than a Venetian who scents gold in the air." That came from Rossobelli, flushing and goggling over his portion of duck, but the cardinal paid him no heed.

Lady Mary regarded Fabiani with a cocked eyebrow. "Besieged by relations, would Cardinal Montorio even bother to remember those loyal supporters who don't share his name or birthplace?"

Fabiani threw his head back. Laughter rumbled from his broad chest. "Don't bother, Pompetti. I know the drill by heart. That was your cue to remind me that Di Noce is an orphan, raised and educated by a house of friars who take their vows of poverty more seriously than the rest of us."

The prince made a sheepish shrug. "Perhaps it is time to speak of other matters."

"Exactly, no more politicking for tonight. Amuse me, Pompetti. Tell me of your latest find. What ancient scrap of bric-a-brac will soon be taking its place in your vast collection?"

"Ah, nothing could be easier. The treasures are right here, dangling from Lady Mary's lovely ears."

I'd noticed the lady's unusual jewelry earlier. Her blond hair had been powdered and pinned up in a lofty arrangement that seemed in danger of imminent collapse. While her messy curls sported a trifling nosegay of pink and blue blossoms, her exposed ear lobes glowed with the elegant reflection of old gold. The metal had been expertly worked into a twisted loop that widened to form the torso of a bare-breasted woman.

"Quite unusual," Fabiani said. "Are they Roman?"

"Etruscan," Pompetti countered. "The metal was mined and the earrings crafted while the Romans were still living in huts on the banks of the Tiber."

"Don't tell me those baubles have been buried in the dirt since then."

Pompetti smiled. "Not at all. They've been cherished and handed down through the centuries. The Etruscan elite didn't disappear when the Romans traded their plows for swords and overran Italy. The more intelligent among them welcomed their conquerors, accepted the new government, then simply continued with their old ways."

Lady Mary cleared her throat. "The Roman Senate was full of representatives from Etruscan families. Faliscan and Umbrian, too. Many of them settled in the capital and took Roman brides." She beamed at the prince. "Aurelio's own lineage dates back to the ancient rulers of Arretium."

"As did the previous owners of the earrings," Pompetti said. "It wasn't an antiquarian's spade that acquired them. Merely newly minted gold, a large purse of it." He shrugged, gazing at Lady Mary's ears. "But it was worth it, well worth it."

The prince needed no prodding to elaborate on the exploits of his ancestors. A Pompetti officer, it seemed, had commanded a legion that fought Hannibal and his elephants during the Carthaginian war, and a later Pompetti soldier had helped Caesar scour Gaul. After the fall of Rome, the family turned from military to diplomatic endeavors. According to the prince, it was a Pompetti who filled Charlemagne's head with visions of a Christian empire as great as that of the Caesars and watched as Pope Leo crowned the Frankish king as Emperor of the Romans. Oblivious to Fabiani's growing restlessness, Pompetti lectured us with rising vehemence and a fervent gleam in his eyes. He might have gone on forever if the cardinal hadn't interrupted by calling for the servants to clear the table.

Roberto winced as a fellow footman piled his tray with soiled china and silver. My eyes were on his bent, retreating back as I did some sums in my head. "How can you trace your lineage back so many centuries?" I asked the prince.

Pompetti shrugged. "It is each generation's duty to preserve our unique history. My family has been telling the same stories for well over a thousand years."

Cardinal Fabiani raised his wineglass. "Before we have the pleasure of hearing Albertini again, let us toast the illustrious house of Pompetti that has brought so much to our venerable city." His words were pretty, but the expression on his face had turned peevish, I thought.

The prince must have agreed with me. Like the skilled diplomat he was, Pompetti matched Fabiani's toast with a compliment of his own. "Though my family history may stretch back to the misty reaches of time, it will never be as exalted as Your Eminence's."

Fabiani smiled broadly. I supposed the bastard son of a pope trumped an Etruscan descendant every time.

Chapter 12

The next morning being Sunday, I presented myself as instructed for Mass at San Marco, a medieval church attached to the sprawling complex that housed the Venetian delegation to the Papal court. The palazzo itself was a massive building of three stories topped by a crenellated roof and square tower that made it look more like a fortress than a residence. The church was much less forbidding and immediately reminded me of home. As I took my place, it did my heart good to see our patron saint's winged lion depicted in stone and stained glass, and to hear the soft Venetian dialect whispered among my countrymen. Once settled in a pew towards the back of the church, I slid to my knees and offered a heartfelt prayer for Alessandro and all those I'd left behind. An organ soon wheezed to life, and a column of clerics marched down the aisle, swaying in time to the stately processional, wafting incense from brass censers.

It surprised me when an elderly bishop took the celebrant's place at the high altar where I had expected to see Cardinal Stefano Montorio. Puzzled, I let my gaze drift around the church's dim interior. On the left side of the nave, an abate peered around the third column from the entrance. His suit of dour black was enlivened by generous ruffles of lace at the neck and wrist. Lenci, of course. He pointed toward the door and crooked a finger in an unmistakable gesture for me to follow. Excellent. I was anxious to put several questions to the young man.

Murmuring apologies as I trod on feet and disarranged the hats of the ladies crowding the pew before me, I made my way to the side aisle and followed Lenci outside to a colonnade that spanned the church and palazzo. He halted in the exact center of the columned walk. Through the archways, I saw a garden courtyard planted with rose trees stripped bare by winter. Gray clouds filled the patch of visible sky, and a damp chill made me shiver in my cloak. No one else was about. The only sounds were the muffled clatter of carriages from the Corso on the other side of the palazzo and the droning of the choir from the church behind us.

Lenci's freckled face appeared paler than usual, but he gave me a lopsided grin and said, "Zio Stefano is a bit…indisposed. He's still in his rooms and sent me to fetch you. I hope you don't mind missing Mass."

"Not at all. I'm anxious to get this interview with Cardinal Montorio over as soon as possible."

Lenci nodded, sucking at his lower lip. "You have news for my uncle?"

"It's been difficult. Cardinal Fabiani is as self-contained as an oyster. But, yes, there are a few things I've noticed."

Lenci started toward the entrance to the palazzo but stopped when I sank down on a bench in the archway.

"I thought you were in a hurry," he said.

"I am. It's just…I thought you might be able to help me. Something has happened at the villa…something puzzling."

"What?"

Watching his face closely, I chose my words with care. "A girl disappeared rather suddenly, a servant who takes care of the old marchesa. Gemma is her name. Do you know her?"

Lenci furrowed his smooth brow and scratched his head with theatrical aplomb. Finally he replied, "I think I know who you mean."

"I noticed that you greeted her quite warmly on the evening I arrived at the villa."

The abate cleared his throat. "You have a sharp eye, Signor Amato. I might as well admit it—I know Gemma."

"How well?"

"Well enough. I see her whenever we can both get away." He shrugged and smiled. "A man needs an outlet, and it's no secret that I was pushed into holy orders. Still, I'd rather that Zio Stefano not know about Gemma."

"He wouldn't approve?"

"Definitely not, but only because he takes his pleasure with professionals and advises that those around him do the same. Zio Stefano says that only a fool risks having a serving wench with a big belly follow him around demanding money to raise an unborn child."

I nodded. That sounded like typical Montorio logic. "Are you in love with Gemma?"

"How romantic you are. Let's just say I'm fond of her. If she'd been born to a higher station, perhaps things would be different. But Gemma is a servant, she serves a purpose..." He looked me quickly up and down, as if he'd just been reminded that I was a castrato "...perhaps one you can't appreciate."

How little the boy knew. I smothered a sharp reply and instead inquired, "Is that what she would say of you, Lenci? You serve a purpose?"

He chuckled mirthlessly. "I don't know. Why don't you ask her?"

"I can't. She's gone."

He gave a faint shrug.

"Rossobelli told the other servants that Gemma left without warning, but not one of them saw her go."

Another shrug.

"You're not worried?"

"Not really. Gemma will be back."

I thought of the watery grave, the ripples of moonlight on the Tiber as Benelli and I rolled Gemma's body out of the boat. Still I asked, "Perhaps you know where she is?"

"I can only guess. I can't meet Gemma as often as I'd like. As you know, my time is hardly my own. Looking after the old lady doesn't give Gemma many excuses to slip away, either. Last time we met, she was excited about a new task that Fabiani had set her to."

"What new task?"

Lenci didn't answer right away. He gazed out at the barren garden, then put one foot on the bench and pulled a snuffbox from his waistcoat. He offered it to me. A cube of tortoiseshell with silver mounts nestled in the extravagant lace cuffs that brushed his fingertips. I shook my head.

Busying himself with his tobacco, he replied, "Let me see. She was babbling from the moment we met, but I confess that I was more interested in unlacing her bodice and getting her out of her shift than attending to her words. Surely you've noticed her incomparable…oh, never mind. Of course, you're only interested in Fabiani's intrigues." He bent his nose to his hand, covered one nostril, and inhaled the weed with the other. On a sneeze, he continued, "After, when we were both in a half-doze, she said that Fabiani was loaning her out to the Palazzo Pompetti. An English lady staying there as a guest had need of a hairdresser for special occasions."

"Lady Mary Sysonby."

"Yes, that was the name. Gemma said that Lady Mary's petticoats were ragged at the hem and her head was stuffed with unfashionable interests—intellectual pursuits that you'd expect from a literary gentleman, or even a schoolmaster. Despite her worn linen and tiresome discourse, the lady possessed enough vanity to demand coiffures that could compete with the acknowledged beauties of Roman society."

"Surely Lady Mary has her own maid."

"Alas, not one skilled in creating the edifices currently fashionable in Rome. Have you seen the things ladies are putting on their heads these days? Not just flowers, but whole bouquets, and they've gone from using one plume to the whole bird. What's next? Live canaries in cages?"

"Why did Fabiani send Gemma?"

"She's a skilled coiffeur. When the marchesa still went out in society, Gemma dressed her hair to perfection."

"I mean…"

"I know what you mean," he put in as he bent to treat his other nostril. "Why would Fabiani want to give up his mother's experienced keeper?"

"Yes."

After a resounding sneeze, Lenci answered, "Gemma was absolutely preening her feathers about that. Bragged about gaining the cardinal's trust and being sent on an important mission. She was already drooling over the gold crowns that Fabiani promised as a reward."

"For arranging hair?"

Lenci raised an eyebrow. "Gemma was to be as much a hair dresser as you are a singer."

I nodded. "Fabiani sent her to spy in the Pompetti household."

"Of course. Have you not wondered why a prince of Rome's highest nobility is championing a dusty little cardinal with no connections and no lineage?"

"I have."

"Apparently so has Fabiani. Di Noce's piety and generosity impress the rabble, but it takes more than virtue to gain the patronage of a prince. Gemma was to do some digging at the Palazzo Pompetti and report back. That's probably where she is now. Knowing my clever girl, I'd guess that she's made herself indispensable to Lady Mary and been hired on full-time."

"When did she tell you about this new commission?"

"New Year's Day. Right before I left for Venice to collect you."

My fingernails scraped the stone of the bench as my hands balled into fists. At the dawn of the new year, I'd been on the other side of the Alps, happily speeding towards the refuge of home and family. What a fool I'd been! As I'd enjoyed the mountain scenery unfolding through the coach window, I might as well have been a witless beast being carted to the slaughter pen. My nails dug into my palms. Suddenly, I wanted to lash out and hit something, or someone, very hard.

Lenci regarded me with his head cocked to one side, blue eyes questioning. Throughout our conversation, I'd seen no deceit or guile in those eyes. Where Gemma was concerned, the abate displayed the manners of a budding cad, but that made him no different than most aristocratic tyros. If he were guilty of her murder, I very much doubted that he'd have been able to answer my questions without some sign of distress. And Lenci was not the cause of my family's disaster. He was merely another hapless creature herded along by his uncles' lust for power. I exhaled deeply, relaxed my hands, and stood.

"We should be going," I said.

"Absolutely. God forbid that Zio Stefano be kept waiting." The abate produced a cambric handkerchief and flipped his cuffs back to wipe his hands clean of tobacco. My fists clenched again. Perhaps I was an even bigger fool than I thought. Both of Lenci's hands displayed a ladder of scabbed scratches.

"Where did you go night before last, after Cardinal Fabiani's conversazioni?" I forced my tongue to form the words casually, but Lenci leapt to his guard.

He drew his chin back. "Is that any of your business?"

"Maybe not, but would it hurt to tell me?"

He answered with a roll of his eyes. "Zio Stefano required my help in his workroom. We supped in haste as soon as we arrived back at the palazzo. Then he had me set up one of his infernal electrical experiments. We were making sparks until well past midnight."

"Is that where you injured your hands?"

He glanced down. "Yes, this electricity seems to have a mind of its own. There was a lot of broken glass—another one of Zio Stefano's projects gone awry."

I inclined my head with a smile that I hoped he would interpret as sympathetic.

⁂

Moving at a dogtrot, Lenci led me through a network of resplendent hallways and staircases. Footmen in liveries of bright ultramarine sprang to open doors, and maids balancing loads of linen or lugging buckets of coal scurried out of our path. By the time we reached Stefano Montorio's suite, I was panting for breath.

"What took you so long?" the cardinal snapped. He paced in his dressing gown and glanced from Lenci to the fourpost bed where a young blond of ample proportions made no effort to cover her naked bosom or thighs. She beamed us a smile, then pink flesh jiggled and quivered as she rose to her knees to ransack the tangled counterpane for her underclothes and stockings. Lenci ogled unabashedly, while I attempted to cover my embarrassment by moving to one of the long windows and gazing down on the Corso as intently as if Pope Clement himself were turning handsprings down that famous avenue.

"The girl needs paying," Montorio continued, "and I need my breakfast. I sent for it nearly an hour ago."

Lenci extracted some coins from his calfskin purse. Rattling the silver in his fist to speed the lady's desultory efforts to dress herself, he pulled the nearest bellcord. I heard Lenci upbraid the footman who had the bad luck to answer his ring, and mercifully soon, the arrival of the cardinal's breakfast cart coincided with the departure of his nighttime companion.

"Tito, what are you doing over in that corner?" Montorio asked. "Come talk to me while I see what the cook has decided to poison me with this morning."

I moved to the center of the handsome apartment of old-fashioned oak paneling. A Persian carpet the size of a small campo covered the floor; parchment maps of Venice and her imperial territories decorated the dark walls.

The cardinal dug his fingers into the flesh under his ribs. "I swear, everything I eat turns to wind these days." Then, snapping his fingers at Lenci, he said, "Massimo, chairs if you please."

I sat in the chair that Lenci shoved my way but remained silent as Montorio gulped his chocolate and gobbled fried pastries. He had a habit of filling one cheek, munching slowly, then sliding the mass into the other cheek to savor every last morsel. As the wind began to rattle the window panes, I tried mightily to rid my mind of the image of a piglet being fattened for the Easter table. Montorio demolished a plate of eggs and several other dishes before he sat back to clean his teeth with an ivory pick. Finally, he got down to business.

"So, Tito. How are you faring at the Villa Fabiani?"

Intent on making my scraps of information seem as significant as possible, I had rehearsed my piece a hundred times. But after watching Montorio stuff his belly amid the luxuries of his bed chamber, and comparing that with what my brother must be existing on while confined in a damp cell of the doge's prison, my carefully crafted words dissolved on my tongue. To my astonishment, I heard myself snarl, "Better than Alessandro, surely. At least I'm warm and dry."

Montorio lowered his pick and swung his gaze to his nephew. "What's he talking about?"

"Alessandro, the sailor brother. You remember. Zio Antonio felt Tito would need additional inducement to support your cause."

"Yes, quite." The cardinal gave a small burp, then fixed me with a calculating look. "You're on a mission of sorts, eh Tito? Your goal is not so much to see me elected pope as to gain your brother's freedom."

"I admit it. Who is elevated to St. Peter's throne means little to me, but Alessandro means a great deal."

The corpulent cardinal took another sip of chocolate, then waved his hand toward Lenci. "Go set up my microscope in the workroom, boy. I have something to show Tito after we've finished our conversation."

"But, Zio…"

"Now, Massimo. Don't make me ask again."

Lenci grimaced and trudged off with the mutinous pout of a youth ordered to his bed chamber for punishment. After he'd slammed a door at the back of the room just a little too loudly, Cardinal Montorio shook his head and smiled. "Massimo is my sister Julia's youngest. A good boy, really. But Julia spoiled him immeasurably—let him run wild all over the estate instead of schooling him with a tutor. Now, my nephew is paying the price. He finds the conduct of official life much duller than tending his father's grapes. But he'll learn…as we all do."

Montorio set his cup down, propped an elbow on the arm of his chair, and drummed his fingers against his cheek. "Now, have you managed to uncover Fabiani's intentions regarding the election?"

"The cardinal is a man of great taste and diplomacy. He seldom brings politics into social conversation."

"Half the city observed you at the opera last night." He grinned at my surprise. "Surely you realize that Romans find the drama in the boxes even more interesting than the action on the stage. Did you learn nothing in the hours you spent in close confines with Fabiani and Pompetti?"

"Several things struck me, but as an outsider, I can't vouch for their certainty."

"I'll be the judge of that. Proceed."

"Though his parentage comes from the left side of the blanket, the Cardinal Padrone is exceedingly proud of his connection to Pope Clement and most anxious to hold onto the privilege that comes with it. When a new pope takes the throne, Fabiani won't be content to be swept out the doors with the rest of the current crop of officials. He desires an important role in the next administration."

Montorio nodded. "That's well understood and promises have been exchanged. Tell me something I don't know."

"Prince Pompetti is sowing seeds of doubt. At every opportunity, he reminds Fabiani that you have numerous relatives and associates who would expect an advantageous redistribution of appointments, benefices, and offices. Relatives who would resent rewards going to a non-Venetian."

A hollow laugh escaped the cardinal's mouth. "Fabiani knows the game. A papal election is like a fresh hand of cards. Every new deal brings on a different set of punters to replace those whose luck has run out."

"But Prince Pompetti is quick to point out that Cardinal Di Noce has no family or hangers-on and that he may well be open to the guiding hand of one well-versed in statecraft."

Montorio reached for a fork and drew trails through a yellow splash of congealed egg yolk on the plate before him. "Is Fabiani swayed by Pompetti's arguments?"

"He's listening. I know that."

The cardinal rose, showering the floor with crumbs. He crossed to the hallway door and cracked it open. Satisfying himself that no one was hovering on the other side, he returned to his chair and pushed his breakfast cart away. Leaning forward with elbows on knees, he said, "Antonio will be livid if Fabiani reneges on our agreement." He dropped his voice to a whisper. "But for me, it would be a gift from heaven."

Surprise welded my tongue to the roof of my mouth.

"I have other interests, you see. I'm quite comfortable here, studying the marvels of the natural world and devising new experimentations. My ambassador's duties are few. I attend the necessary events, say a few Masses, and my staff of clerks handles the paperwork. But the Quirinal…it's a different world! Has Fabiani taken you there?"

I shook my head.

"The formality is excruciating. Every act of daily life has its own ceremonial practice. The pope can't even evacuate his bowels without a squad of *monsignori* and macebearers in attendance."

"Surely it's not as bad as all that?"

"Perhaps I exaggerate. But the rules of behavior are rigorous and enforced by court officials whose highest ambition is to bolster the status of their pontiff and thus improve their own lots. They would give me no latitude for natural philosophy. Or…" He jerked his head toward the bed "…some of my baser pleasures. No, I want to go on as I am. Being elected pope is my nightmare."

Cardinal Montorio gazed at me in stony silence. I realized that I'd been holding my breath. I let it out with a sigh that was met by a draft of air from some unseen place. The drapes on the bed frame gently rose and fell. When I spoke, my voice held a tremor. "Senator Antonio Montorio believes otherwise."

"My brother is accustomed to having his way. I've heard of special ships that explorers use in northern waters. Icecutters they call them. With prows of iron for breaking through ice-bound seas. That is how I think of Antonio. Because it is easier to break than resist, most everyone in the family lets him plow right through. But not me, not this time."

"What are you going to do?"

"I'm already doing it. Clement isn't dead yet, and a few Italian cardinals who believe in a godly Church remain undecided on his successor. I'm working on them."

"On Di Noce's behalf?"

He nodded.

"But…I'm supposed to be pushing your cause with Fabiani. Alessandro's freedom, perhaps his very life, depends on it."

"I'm giving you a different charge. I want you to feed Fabiani information that will send him running straight to Di Noce's camp. Tell him that Antonio means to cut him out entirely." Montorio jumped up and started to pace. As he warmed to his plan, his words spilled out faster and faster and his eyes held a feverish gleam. "Once Clement is dead, there will be no need for a Cardinal Padrone. I'm a man in my prime, not a blind invalid dependant on his bastard son. Tell Fabiani that I'll make Antonio a cardinal—there's nothing to stand in my way—my brother's wife died last year. Then I'll appoint him as my Secretary of State, and together we'll plunder the papal treasury for Venice."

He came to rest behind my chair. I turned my head, and he placed his lumpy face only inches from mine. "Are you agreed?"

"I can't tell Fabiani that," I cried. "Don't you understand what will happen to Alessandro if I oppose the senator?"

Montorio straightened and pushed back the sleeves of his dressing gown. "Antonio is powerful, but he doesn't control every last cousin and nephew. Besides Massimo, there are others loyal to me. One works in the doge's prison. Help me, and I'll have him arrange Alessandro's escape."

"Escape?" I sprang from my chair. "But then Alessandro could never return to Venice. His ship is there, his livelihood. Venice is our home, for God's sake." I gave my head a violent shake. "An escape is no good. Alessandro needs to be released with his name cleared. Anything else would be a travesty of justice."

"At least Alessandro would be alive." Montorio crossed his arms over his round belly. He eyed me with a sorrowful gaze. "In your case, Tito, a brother without a home is much preferable to one swinging from a gibbet."

I thought desperately. How could I be sure that the cardinal was telling the truth? Even if he did have a confederate in the prison, switching loyalty from Antonio to Stefano could be a dangerous strategy. Besides, the thought of a Montorio turning down a position of almost infinite power was hard to believe.

"What about Ancona?" I asked finally. "Venice is counting on you to stop the port project. If Ancona is revived, Venice will see her trade move south. Your own family's business would suffer."

Montorio crossed the floor to a map of the Venetian Empire. Toying with a ring on his forefinger, he stared at the puzzle of interlacing territories for a few long moments. Turning his attention back to me, he said, "Our city has always found a way to enrich herself. Whether ferrying crusaders to the Holy Land or penetrating the remotest regions of Asia for silks and oriental luxuries, Venice has managed to survive in glory."

"It's not so easy these days. Even Doge Pisani is cash strapped, they say."

"Don't worry." He shrugged. "Venice is making a new name for herself as the whoremistress of Europe. The rise of Ancona can't stop that any more than a mosquito could drop an African elephant. Venice will survive as the city of endless Carnival and so will the house of Montorio."

"Then what about…God?" I hesitated, struggling to come to grips with notions I usually left to the priests. "Perhaps God means for you to do great things as pope. Maybe that's what all this is about."

He frowned. "Come with me," he ordered, pivoting on his heel.

Chapter 13

Whether they rise from shining canals or paved avenues, the palazzi of Venice and Rome share a similar design. The gardens and ground floor rooms are spacious and formal, dedicated to public life. The next level, the *piano nobile* with its salons and dining rooms, is used to entertain extended family and friends. The owners of these grand bastions of privilege, and the servants who wait on them, occupy the upper floors. A personal suite consists of several rooms connected in linear fashion that move from the most public to the most private. A visitor is first received into an antechamber attended by under footmen. The more important the visitor, the more quickly senior servants conduct him to the sitting room. In most cases, the bed chamber lies at the end of the line, but at the Venetian ambassador's residence, Cardinal Montorio had reserved the most secluded retreat for his scientific workroom.

As he pushed open the door at the back of his bed chamber, we stood on the threshold of a world unknown to me. The door was padded with thick batting and the windows draped with heavy fabric. An acrid, musty odor met my nose, and light from several lamps glinted off brass instruments whose purpose had me completely mystified. Animals in glass cases, frozen in time by the taxidermist's art, hung from the ceiling and sat on shelves. I searched the shadows for Lenci, but couldn't locate him. He must have hared off once he had carried out his uncle's command. The abate hadn't passed through the bed chamber, so I assumed the thick drapery must conceal another entrance.

The cardinal strode straight to a table which held a tubular cylinder fashioned of mahogany and green leather rising from a brass tripod. "Here, Tito. You spoke of God. Have you ever seen him?"

I shook my head, wondering what game Montorio was playing at.

"Come, take a look. Observe the face of our creator."

I approached gingerly. Lenci had illuminated a lamp that shone onto a tilted mirror positioned at the base of the tripod. I now saw that the upright cylinder overhung a saucer, and on that saucer was a flat strip of wood punctuated by transparent circles the size of a coin. At Montorio's urging, I closed one eye and screwed the other to the eyepiece. A fuzzy blob swam in a circle of light.

"I can't make anything out," I said.

"Adjust the tilt of the mirror. The light must strike the specimen directly."

My fumblings only made the circle of light disappear entirely. Montorio took charge of the instrument, and after twisting this and tweaking that, bade me try again.

I bent to the eyepiece. My stomach lurched. A monstrous beast lay at the other end of the tube. Its huge eyes bulged, two sharp horns stabbed the air, and six furry legs ended in claws that clutched a tree branch.

"What is that?" I asked, springing back.

Montorio chuckled. "A louse. On a human hair."

"Impossible."

"It's more than possible, it's true. This is an enlarging instrument. Some call it a microscope. There are lenses in that tube that can magnify a flea to the size of a camel."

I met his words with a dubious expression.

"You're familiar with spectacles, aren't you?"

"My father couldn't read without them."

"This is the same idea, only these lenses possess a stronger magnifying capability. My telescope on the roof is even more powerful. With it, I can examine the moon as if it were a wheel of cheese suspended right in front of my face."

I had never been a much of a student. The priest at our little parish school taught me letters and simple sums, but once I'd been exiled to the conservatorio in Naples, lessons in vocalizing occupied most of my waking hours. The maestros fed us only scraps of humanities, rhetoric, and philosophy. Why waste time on academics when our golden throats were all that really mattered? Cardinal Montorio was delving into realms of knowledge that I'd barely heard of.

"A louse, you say?" I stepped back toward the instrument. "I had no idea. This little fellow is so intricate, so detailed. I can see the joints on his legs, like double pairs of knees. And he has whiskers on his chin." Intrigued, I studied the specimen for some minutes in silence. Then I remembered Montorio's earlier claim. "But what does this insect have to do with God?"

"Everything. The microscope proves that we're part and parcel of an awesome creation—a universe of marvels that we can only see the tiniest part of. Even the smallest creatures among us display the most elaborate symmetry and rationality of intent." He clapped a hand on my shoulder. "I want you to observe the louse's whiskers again. See them?"

"Yes."

"Now imagine that he is infested with his own lice clinging to those whiskers. And that those animalcules have more hairs and even smaller lice. And so on and so on."

I straightened and shook my head, dizzied by the thought.

"That's where God is," Montorio stated emphatically. "Not in the ancient superstitions of the Church, not in the dusty words I repeat at every Mass, but in the elegance and beauty of an ordinary louse. We live in wondrous times, Tito, that such instruments as this can act as a signpost on the path toward truth."

"And what is the truth, Your Eminence?"

"Isn't it obvious? The revelation for the coming age is that the Almighty has a plan far beyond our ken, much more important than the salvation of our meager souls."

I cleared my throat, suddenly uncomfortable. An icy shiver ran up my spine. Though he was a servant of the church, Cardinal Montorio embraced a philosophy as blasphemous as Liya's pagan beliefs.

"I must go," I said, turning toward the padded door.

"Yes, you must," he agreed. "Go convince Fabiani to muster his forces for Cardinal Di Noce. I don't care how you do it. Pretend you're angry and paint Antonio and me to be as bad as you wish. Or use your guile and make Fabiani think you're letting secrets slip. Just do as I ask and your brother will go free." He winked. "You can count on me."

I tarried long enough for one more question. "Your nephew must be a great help in your scientific endeavors. Abate Lenci told me about an experiment you conducted night before last—an electrical experiment that resulted in a lot of broken glass. Did he get it all cleaned up?"

A frown creased Montorio's forehead. "You must be speaking of the Leyden jars. In the proper conditions, glass jars can be forced to condense electrical fluid. You see…" He gestured to a wooden case holding a quartet of jars stoppered with ball-tipped metal rods. "All the jars are present and accounted for. Not even cracked. I am a master of electrical experimentations, hardly likely to break anything. I wonder why Massimo saw fit to mention such a thing."

Suspecting I might know why, I merely nodded, tucked my hat under my arm, and left Cardinal Montorio to his contemplation of the universe.

꙰

Outside the Palazzo Venezia, a cold rain fell in intermittent bursts, forcing me to turn up the collar of my cloak and pull my tricorne low on my forehead. Hugging the building to shield myself from the drops and avoid the muck thrown by hooves and carriage wheels, I turned in the direction of the Tiber. If the day had turned out fine, Liya was to meet me at the park where Signor Tucci staged his puppet operas. We'd made no plans to cover the eventuality of bad weather. Nevertheless, I was unable to contemplate setting off for any destination other than the lodging she shared with a woman who ran a cookshop in the Trastevere. Liya had described its location with the exactitude of the fine, neat stitches she'd always used to fashion my head-dresses at the Teatro San Marco: two blocks straight up from the Ponte Sisto, a sharp left at the Via Della Scala, left again at the first alley, third doorway on the right.

I made haste until I reached the bridge, then found my steps flagging. It required no stretch of the imagination to blame the blustery afternoon for my growing ill humor. All around me, eaves dripped, chimneys howled with ghostly wails, and streets ran with rivulets of stinking filth. Everyone with good sense had shuttered themselves into a room with a warm fire. But as I hopped a murky stream descending from the Trastevere, I had to admit that it was more likely the unsettling session with Cardinal Montorio that had raised all my doubts and insecurities to a fever pitch.

From childhood, I'd attended Mass with my family and schoolmates as a thing of habit. But what did I believe, really? I certainly knew right from wrong and suffered pangs of conscience when I was selfish or less than kind. I suppose I'd always felt that if I made things right in my corner of the world, God and his angels and saints would take care of the rest. Cardinal Montorio had opened my eyes to a much wider view. Lighting a candle at the foot of a plaster saint or confessing my sins of profanity or impure thoughts seemed almost irrelevant when compared to his study of the boundless marvels of the natural world.

Liya undoubtedly held still different beliefs, a strange creed that I could only guess at. As the overhanging balconies of the alley off the Via Della Scala closed over my head, I wondered why I was so anxious to keep company with a woman who had given herself over to sorcery. My uneasy thoughts fixed on visions of

Liya in a circle of black-hooded crones, muttering incantations and summoning evil spirits—eerie, impish things with leather wings and burning eyes. I proceeded even more slowly.

When I located the cookshop, a deep building only ten to twelve feet in width, I didn't go in. A handpainted sign nailed between the one window and the solid door read "The Laughing Frog—cooked meat and sauce," and carried the crudely executed drawing of a frog with a gaping grin. Many of the poor lacked ovens and frequented shops like these to either eat their dinner or carry it home. Indeed, the alley was ripe with the smell of garlic, oregano, and braised beef. A long whiff made my head swim, and my stomach reminded me that I'd had nothing to eat since the night before. No one had yet seen me; the warm interior and chill outside air had turned the panes of the narrow window to clouded squares. Perhaps I should just return to the Villa Fabiani, have my dinner, and consider where an association with a strega might lead.

I was turning to go when a movement at the misted window caught my eye. A vertical line appeared on one of the lower panes and was decisively crossed at its topmost point: a *T* etched by someone inside. Was this a message? My curiosity grew as another line, topped by a dot, appeared to the left. When the pink fingertip pressed the window again, I squatted low and joined it with my own. Together, we traced the last two letters of my name, fingers separated by only a thin pane of glass.

I'd barely straightened up when the door to the cookshop banged open and a small boy ran out. From inside, a feminine voice yelled, "Don't go far. And mind the door, *diavoletto*, you'll freeze us all." The boy turned back to pull the door closed, then greeted me with a shy grin.

"How do you know my name?" he asked, with eyes as big and round as dark moons.

I squatted again, so we could talk man to man. "Your name? But that is my name you were drawing."

The toe of his laced boot dug at the paving stones. He crossed his arms over his short jacket. "Tito is *my* name," he asserted.

"And mine, too."

He ducked his chin and eyed me from under a fringe of lashes that any woman would covet.

"Look, I'll prove it." I pulled out my watch, which was attached to a ribbon fob that Annetta had embroidered as a present for my last name day. Spreading the ribbon on my knee, I asked, "Can you read the letters?"

"Of course, I'm not a baby. It says *Tito*. Is that really your name?"

"That's my watch ribbon, made by my sister, so it must be my name."

He gazed at me solemnly and whispered, "Do you want to know a secret?"

I nodded.

"I know where a big spider lives."

"Show me," I grunted, rising to my feet.

Little Tito grabbed my hand and pulled me to the crevice that separated the cookshop from the next building. A large black spider had built its web across the narrow opening. The remains of several spider dinners clung to the wispy strands. I picked Tito up so he could have a better look.

"He's been here for three days," the boy observed, throwing his arms around my neck. "I keep telling him to move."

"Why?"

"If Nonna Maddelena finds him, she'll knock him down with her broom."

"Who is Nonna Maddelena?"

"She takes care of me when Mama goes to work. She's not my real grandmother, but I call her Nonna because Mama told me to."

"Is she nice?"

"Yes…to everybody except spiders."

We'd just reached the point of bestowing the hairy spider with the aptly descriptive name of Arruffato when Tito squealed and wriggled to the ground. Liya was coming down the alleyway, her wet shawl dragging her shoulders low. Her expression was as dark as the sky that peeked through the crowded, rain-soaked buildings of the Trastevere. She brightened when she caught sight of her son running to meet her and positively glowed when her eyes met mine. "I've been looking for you," she cried over the boy's bobbing head.

I smiled, remembering how I used to dawdle at the Teatro San Marco for hours, waiting to catch a word with Liya, pining for a glance from her flashing dark eyes. She had fascinated me then: her musky scent, the soft roundness of her shoulders and breasts, the curving line from slender ankle to muscular calf that lost itself in the skirts shielding her most intimate mysteries. She fascinated me still. I took a hard gulp. All at once, it didn't matter if Liya conjured up Satan himself. My doubts floated down the gutter with the chill Roman rain, and love flooded over me.

⚬⚭⚬

"Your handsome abate murdered Gemma!" said Liya, once I'd revealed the unhappy details of my last few days in Rome.

"Lenci?" I asked.

"He must have. He lied about the scratches on his hands, didn't he? And how clever, using the old woman's scarf. Gemma must have told him plenty of stories about the marchesa's tantrums, so he knew that Cardinal Fabiani would assume his mother strangled the girl and rush to cover it up."

I moved my damp feet closer to the *scaldino* that occupied the space between our two stools. We had settled in Liya's attic quarters after filling our stomachs with bread smothered in spicy meat sauce and consigning little Tito to the care of Nonna Maddelena, a pleasant, gray-haired woman of wide hips and meaty forearms. No stove or fire graced this room, so we warmed ourselves at the ceramic pot filled with smoldering charcoal that kept the chill away from many a poor household.

"I don't know, Liya. I find it difficult to imagine Lenci driven to such violence. He talked about the girl in a callous vein, but I put that down to immature boasting. I've seen the way he looked at her. Underneath the arrogant posturing, I think Lenci truly cared for Gemma. *Cares*, I should say. If he didn't murder her, the boy doesn't even know she's dead. He thinks she's serving Lady Mary at the Palazzo Pompetti."

"Perhaps Gemma was pushing for more than Lenci wanted to give."

"Money? Lenci said that Fabiani was giving her a handsome bonus for gleaning information about Pompetti."

"I was thinking of marriage."

"How could she expect that? Lenci is a cleric."

"These young men in Rome seem to jump in and out of holy orders as easily as a bird hops from branch to branch. The Quirinal and the Vatican abound with opportunities for place and prefer-ment, but the Church is not the only game going. Perhaps Gemma was trying to convince her lover to shed his cassock."

I shook my head. "Marrying a girl from the servant's hall would hardly advance Lenci's prospects. At present, he has little money of his own, but if he remains loyal to his uncles, he will surely come into his share of the Montorio wealth."

"Ah." Liya sent me a tight grin. "Which uncle? The one intent on snaring a Montorio papacy? Or the one running from that prospect with all his might?"

I shrugged, unsure. I was still reeling from Stefano Montorio's startling declaration, and Lenci's loyalty was yet to be deter-mined. "At any rate," I responded. "If Gemma's demands grew too strident, Lenci could have just walked away. It happens every day—a servant romanced, fed on dreams of class-blind love, then left with a broken heart—and not just the women. Why would Lenci stoop to murder?"

Liya returned my shrug. "If there is an explanation, the Tito I used to know wouldn't rest until he discovered what it is."

"If I were smart, I'd forget the entire sorry affair. Gemma's murder really has nothing to do with me."

"Except that Cardinal Fabiani set you squarely in the middle." Liya sat forward, hands on her knees. The glow from the pot lit her chin and gently rounded cheeks, casting her eyes into shadow. "Why do you think he had Rossobelli summon you of all people? A loyal footman or stableman would have provided more muscle to carry the body to the river."

"Fabiani knew I was a Montorio man from the beginning. He must have been seething, being forced to welcome someone who wasn't under his absolute authority into his household. He maneuvered me into disposing of Gemma's corpse to counterbalance Antonio Montorio's influence. I've done Fabiani's dirty work—now he has a hold on me, too."

"Poor Tito, being pulled in two directions. No," she quickly corrected herself. "Three directions."

I glanced uneasily around the angled ceilings and shadowed nooks of Liya's attic, then at the woman before me. For so many years I'd longed for this easy intimacy with Liya. I'd wanted to share my life with her: the life I'd led before Messer Grande had dragged me from my home, not the life of desperate papal politics. But how was that to be, with so many obstacles blocking our way? I pushed up from my stool and began to pace the open space between Liya's bed and the low couch that served her son.

"It's poor Alessandro, really," I said. "If I can't resolve this mess, he will be the one to suffer. Except for Cardinal Di Noce, all the churchmen I've encountered seem more anxious for pleasure or promotion in this world than salvation in the next. And they aren't worried about who might get hurt in their drive to realize their ambitions."

"What you need is information—something that will tip the scales back in your favor." Liya stirred the coals in the scaldino with a short iron poker.

I nodded. We'd been talking a long time. The candles were burning low and the room was beginning to get smoky, making my eyes sting and tear. I pushed the casement window over her bed open a crack. The rain had stopped, giving way to a foggy, early dusk. In a window across the way, someone lit a lamp, a beacon of ocher light shining through the gray mist. I took in a deep breath of fresh air and rested my forehead on the corner of the cool windowsill.

When I turned back, Liya was opening a battered trunk set in one of the nooks formed by the sloping eaves. She removed a small calfskin pouch. I watched with interest as she moved to stand over the scaldino, took a generous pinch of some powdery substance from the pouch, then let a glittering stream fall from her fingers onto the coals. Flames of blue and silver sprang to meet her hand. No sooner had they been swallowed back into the pot than a pungent, exotic odor invaded my nose and a shudder ran over me.

"What are you doing?" I whispered, suddenly recalling my visions of winged imps.

She swept her arm in a beckoning gesture. "Tito, come sit. I think I may have an idea, but I must ponder it in my own way."

I slowly returned to my stool, eyes wide and nerves tingling.

"Do you still have the cimaruta you found outside the pavilion?" Liya asked, settling across from me with her gaze trained on the coals that now glowed in bright shifting hues.

"Yes," I answered, digging in my waistcoat. "I thought it would be safer in my pocket than back at the Villa Fabiani." I gave the amulet and its dangling charms another close look before handing it to Liya. "You said that these branches worked in silver represent a plant sacred to Diana."

"Rue, the herb of grace. Besides conferring good fortune and protection, a cimaruta shows the wearer to be a disciple of the good goddess."

"The same Diana that the ancient Romans worshiped as the goddess of the moon and the hunt?"

She nodded, never shifting her gaze from the pot. "Diana is only one of her names. The people of Florence call her Tana. In Naples, she's known as Jana. By all her names, she's far older than Rome, as old as Mother Earth herself. The priests of the new religion drove her from her temples and put up new statues of virgins and martyrs, but Diana never forgets her people. Centuries ago, she sent her daughter Aradia to teach us and free us."

Realizing I'd been holding my breath, I snatched some air to ask a question, but Liya shook her head and pressed a finger to her lips. "Quiet, I must have quiet." Cupping the cimaruta in her left palm, she pressed it to her heart and began to rock gently back and forth. I had seen fortune tellers at carnival booths strike a similar pose, but this was different. Liya was not play-acting; she was allowing me a peek at her cherished beliefs.

When she spoke again, her voice was harsh, panting, as if she had just run a great distance. "I see a woman, tall, blond, with a long chin...she wears classical robes...heavy golden rings hang from her ears."

My mouth was dry. "Lady Mary," I croaked.

"A man stands behind her with his hand on her shoulder... he's dressed the same way..." Liya fell silent. Beads of sweat broke out on her forehead.

"What does he look like?"

"An older man...very upright and proud...black hair threaded with gray. I've seen him before, at the theater."

"Prince Pompetti!" I peered down into the scaldino. The humble chafing pot held no visions for me, but it was telling Liya quite a tale.

"They stand before a golden door embossed with crossed keys," she cried. "The woman smiles and spreads her arms, but the man shakes his head. He's saying something."

"What?"

Liya swayed on the stool. "Don't know...it fades." Her lips went slack, her eyes closed. She slumped with a groan, and I sprang to catch her before she fell to the floor. Her faint was fleeting. As I held her, she burrowed into my chest and reached up to stroke my cheek with her hand. Tightening my arms, I kissed the top of her head.

"Are you all right?" I asked.

She raised her chin and smiled. "Perfectly all right. And now I know what you must do."

I wondered if the scene Liya had described had come more from her own head than from the pot, but either way, I was interested to hear her advice.

"Pompetti and his lady are hiding a secret. The keys of St. Peter tell us that it concerns the papal throne. While she was waiting on Lady Mary at the palazzo, Gemma must have uncovered something of great import…"

"Something worth killing for," I said, finishing her thought.

Liya sat up and crossed her legs under her skirt. Her black eyes glittered in the candlelight. "Tito, tell me again exactly when Gemma was killed."

"It was late on January eleventh, or perhaps the first minutes of the twelfth."

"Around midnight, then?"

"Yes."

"The night of the full moon," she said thoughtfully.

"So it was," I replied, shifting uneasily at the recollection of the silvery light that had bathed the waters of Gemma's final resting place.

She bobbed a decisive nod. "You have to follow in Gemma's footsteps, Tito."

"I agree, but how? Fabiani would never give me leave to go snooping at the Palazzo Pompetti."

Her fingers tightened around the cimaruta. "Leave it to me, caro. I'll find a way."

Nodding slowly, I pulled her close again. This time it was her mouth that I kissed.

Chapter 14

The days that followed dragged by at a snail's pace, each seeming longer than the one before. Never had I felt so much a prisoner of another man's routine. Singing at supper parties and conversazioni filled my evenings, and I was often summoned to serenade Fabiani throughout the small hours of the night.

During those intimate concerts, I tarried as long as I dared between songs, speaking of this and that, hoping that Fabiani would start musing about the coming conclave as he had with Tucci. Not surprisingly, the cardinal saw through my stratagem right away. "Let music reign here," he commanded, deep-set eyes staring from under his scarlet nightcap. "I won't allow the cares of the day to follow me into my bed chamber. Sing as I bid you, otherwise be silent."

The gossip mongers announced that Pope Clement had fallen into a prolonged sleep and was taking no nourishment. Spurred by the approach of the inevitable, Cardinal Montorio pressed me harder than ever. Abate Lenci confirmed that a Montorio cousin was the vice-superintendent of prisons, but whether this man was Zio Stefano's pawn, I dared not ask. And so I temporized as best I could, following the news from the Quirinal as avidly as the Roman oddsmakers. Day by day we all waited, but the old man must have been made of stern stuff. Unable to discuss my worries with anyone in the villa besides Benito, I plastered a smile on my face and went about my duties.

During the day, Fabiani spent much of his time at the Quirinal. Still, my time was not my own. Before he left, I was always presented with a list: transpose and copy a bundle of scores, learn the arias from *Ricimero* and other recent operas which had captured his fancy, entertain the marchesa.

That last occupied a good bit of my time. Matilda was not as skilled at keeping the old lady out of trouble as Gemma had been. When she was awake, Marchesa Fabiani displayed only two states of being. She either sat in a silent trance with her mouth hanging open or rambled about the villa with a furious energy fueled by impulses known only to her. The kitchen had lately become one of her favorite haunts. Several times a day, a scullery maid reeking of smoke and grease ran through the villa's pristine upper hallways, calling for Matilda to come and collect her charge before the cook started throwing pots and pans. When it was discovered that a lively dance tune could keep the marchesa amused, my fate was sealed.

"Another *volta*," she begged one morning after toeing and dipping her way around the music room to a sedate minuet. She had already breakfasted with her son and was feeling especially playful. When the cardinal had gone off to receive his morning callers, the marchesa had demanded music and I was summoned.

I attacked the harpsichord keys with more vigor, accelerating the tempo. The marchesa whirled and kicked. Her silver hair came loose from its pins, spreading out like a ragged curtain blown by the wind. The sight of her multiple reflections in the wall mirrors delighted her as much as it would a five-year-old. But in a short time, her breathing became harsh and her whirling slowed.

I patted the space beside me on the bench. "Take a rest, My Lady. I'll play one of my favorites for you."

Hoisting the skirts of her day dress above her knees, Marchesa Fabiani ascended the dais and plopped down on the bench. Her new maid had withdrawn to a distant corner of the salon. Matilda had her head bent to a piece of mending, showing only the crown of her white cap. For the moment I had the cardinal's mother all to myself.

"And how are you doing today, My Lady?" My fingers ranged over the keys as I favored Marchesa Fabiani with a smile that had disarmed many a princess and prima donna. She responded with a flirtatious look that took ten years off her age. In her prime, I thought, the old lady must have been quite something.

"I'm in fine spirits, Signor Amato, thanks to your lovely music."

So she remembered who I was. It must be one of her better days. I was eager to discover what else she might remember.

"I was sorry to hear that Gemma is no longer with us," I ventured. "I hope you're not missing your maid too much."

She made a face. "That slyboots. She left without a word to me, you know. On our Tuscany estate, the servants understood that loyalty to the family came first. They did everything they could to oblige and protect us. These Romans follow their whims and do exactly as they please."

"Did Gemma have whims?"

"More than whims. A lover! She thought I didn't know, but the stupid girl was transparent as glass." The marchesa cackled with glee. "I caught him once, coming away from the back stairway setting his breeches to rights. Gemma came up a moment later. You must know him—the young man who serves the Venetian ambassador—the one who looks like an angel in a Botticelli painting."

"Ah," I murmured. "You are speaking of Abate Massimo Lenci."

"Is that his name?" She plucked at her straggling silver locks. "A beautiful boy, but a bit womanish and pale. He dresses far too well for an abate and looks like he runs from the sunshine. Not the rugged sort at all..." She trailed off with a dreamy smile.

"I'm told that Abate Lenci enjoyed tending the grapevines on his father's farm—before he was brought to Rome by his uncles, that is."

"Hm..." The marchesa was still lost in her thoughts but suddenly roused and shook her head. "With that pretty face, he could have any woman he wants, I should think. I wonder why he wastes his time on a dirty little thief."

My hands faltered on the keys. "A thief? Gemma?"

"Stole my things she did. Took my chocolate pot and the cups that go with it. Took my silver brush and put a cheap one in its place." The marchesa's voice rose. "Thought I wouldn't notice. Crazy—that's what they call me, don't they?" Her gaze suddenly darted to the corners of the salon and her fists clenched. "Don't they? Don't they?"

"Who, My Lady? Who would say such a thing?" I patted her arm in a vain effort to calm her.

"Everyone. Even the footman at the door taunts me." She jumped up, poised for flight. "Even you. You think I'm crazy, too. I can see it in your face."

"No, no, My Lady. Not at all. I'm concerned for you. If things are missing, you must tell the cardinal. Your son will sort it all out."

"I have told him," she wailed. "Lorenzo doesn't believe me. He says I just forget where I put things. But Lorenzo doesn't know. He doesn't understand. Gemma steals my things and hides them, then I have to steal them back and hide them from her."

"My Lady…" I started helplessly. But the marchesa had taken off. She ran headlong across the shiny floor, stumbling and weeping. Matilda threw her mending aside. With a surprising burst of speed, she intercepted the marchesa before the old woman covered half the distance to the door. I trotted toward the struggling pair, but before I could reach them, the marchesa surrendered with barely a whimper. Matilda warned me away with a shake of her head and a finger to her lips. Then she guided the marchesa toward the upper floors, promising a trayful of sweets and ices.

I made quick use of my newfound freedom. It had been several days since my visit to the opera house, but I had been too disturbed to write Tucci's letter of introduction or to finish my oft-interrupted missive to Gussie. I returned to my room and opened the secretary to sharpen a quill. Benito must have been attending to duties elsewhere in the great house, so I was blessed with peace and quiet for the first time in days.

Tucci's letter flowed easily from my pen, but Gussie's presented a problem. I was accustomed to pouring out all my thoughts to my friend and brother-in-law, and I knew that he and Annetta must be hungering for news, but I didn't fancy consigning a candid letter to the pouch on the mail coach bound for Venice. A letter brandishing my home address could easily fall into the hands of a Montorio minion. I shook my head, wondering if I was merely being cautious or if the marchesa's unwarranted suspicions were rubbing off on me.

While I was warming the wax to seal Tucci's letter, a happy thought struck me. The singer planned to set out for Venice as soon as I furnished him with the introduction to my old musical director. He surely wouldn't mind carrying an extra letter. After all, I was doing the man a generous favor. I took Gussie's letter out of my writing case and launched into a detailed account of the misfortunes that had befallen me since my arrival in Rome. I indulged my errant speculations about all and sundry, then closed with a bracing note meant for Alessandro. I thought it unlikely that my brother would be allowed any messages, but if anyone could convince a guard to show some compassion and pass the note to Alessandro, it would be my sweet sister Annetta.

I was sealing the second letter when Benito arrived with a basket full of freshly laundered shirts and underclothes.

"Ah, just in time. Do you know the Piazza d'Espagna?" I asked my manservant. If I could evade Rossobelli's sharp eyes, I might be able to get away long enough to visit Liya.

Benito shook his head.

I sighed, drumming the letters against my palm. "I want to stop by the theater, but there won't be time to deliver these as well. The Piazza d'Espagna lies on the opposite side of the city from the Teatro Argentina."

"I'll go, Master. I'll ask someone the way. The Piazza d'Espagna shouldn't be hard to find."

I had not seen Liya since her vision at the scaldino. She had sent two messages by a Trastevere urchin, each a scrap of paper bearing the single word *Patience*. That virtue was wearing thin.

I was more anxious than ever to gain admission to the Palazzo Pompetti. I was also dying to hold Liya once again in my arms. The apostate Jewess was the one bright spot in the sorry travesty my life had become.

Benito extended his palm. His eagerness was almost palpable. My manservant must have felt as caged as I did.

"These go to Signor Tucci at Number 38. You must explain that he's to deliver one to the Campo di Polli." I handed the letters over. "Be careful," I cautioned as the little man grabbed his cloak and disappeared through the door.

I'd donned my jacket and was searching for my watch when I heard a soft scraping at my door, almost as if a dog was pawing to be let in. I crossed the room with light steps and halted with my hand on the doorknob. The knob moved slowly under my fingers, but it wasn't my hand that supplied the power. I ground my teeth, full of anger. The person on the other side of the door must have seen Benito leave. Assuming that I must still be with the marchesa, he thought he could safely search my room. Of course it was a *he*. It was Rossobelli—fearful, earnest Rossobelli, absolutely convinced that I meant to ruin Di Noce's chance to be the next pope and thus destroy his home city of Ancona for good.

I pulled the knob with all my might. A black-clad abate stumbled over the threshold. He swung around to latch the door, then clapped a hand on my shoulder. I was staring into the wide blue eyes of Massimo Lenci.

"Thank God, you're still here," he cried. "I just met Benito on the stairs. He told me you were going out. Zio Stefano is downstairs with Cardinal Fabiani. I have only a few minutes."

⁂

"Gemma's gone. I made inquiries at the Palazzo Pompetti. She hasn't been there for over a week." Lenci's boyish face had turned hard. He paced my small balcony. Three strides forward, turn, and three back. "Why did you bring me out here, anyway?"

I jerked my chin toward my chamber. "In there, the walls have ears. Here, we're in little danger of being overheard if you keep your voice down."

Nodding and modulating his tone, he said, "You told me she disappeared, and I thought you didn't know what you were talking about. Now it seems you know more than I do."

"How did you get in the palazzo?"

"Walked up to the service door as bold as brass. I bought a box of powder from a wigmaker's shop—French, the best there is. I announced that Gemma had ordered it and insisted that it be delivered only to her hands."

"What happened?"

"I got an earful. Gemma hasn't been to the palazzo since a week ago Friday. She was supposed to dress Lady Mary's hair for the opera premiere the next evening, but she failed to keep the appointment. Lady Mary had every maid in the house lending a hand, but they say she still went out looking like a mare with a nosegay of flowers stuck in her mane."

A smile crept to my lips. "An apt description. I was there. Lady Mary and Prince Pompetti joined us in Cardinal Fabiani's box."

"The prince was furious because all the attempts to coif his lady made them late."

I nodded. "Weren't you afraid you'd be recognized at the palazzo? Surely some of Pompetti's servants have seen you in the ambassador's retinue. They would wonder why the nephew of Di Noce's arch rival would appear at their master's door with a box of hair powder."

"Don't think me a fool, Signore. I played the part of a messenger—quite well, actually. I put on my oldest breeches and a jacket I used to wear to ride out to check the grapes. I even smeared some dirt on my stockings, tied my hair back with a piece of string, and wore a battered hat I'd dug out of the trash." He shuddered and shrugged at the same time. "Besides, it was worth the risk."

"Worth the risk to find the whereabouts of a girl who only... what did you tell me? Serves your needs?"

Lenci's cheeks flushed brick red. "I wish I'd never said that," he said miserably.

I stared at the young abate, taking in the tight jaw, the shadows under his eyes, the leanness of his cheeks. Gemma's disappearance seemed to have played on his deepest emotions. But there were still the scratches on his hands. Almost healed, barely visible now.

"Your hands seem much improved," I observed.

Lenci glanced down, shaking his head impatiently. "That's of no consequence."

"It could be."

"Why?"

"In determining whether or not I'm going to trust you."

"I don't understand."

I crossed my arms with a sigh. "You said you cut your hands on broken glass, but when Cardinal Montorio took me into his workroom, he denied that there had been any accident with the electrical jars."

Lenci rolled his eyes. "Zio Stefano thinks he's the greatest natural philosopher since Galileo. He never admits to a mistake, and he won't be gainsaid. If he tells you the sky is green, he expects you to agree. No matter what he told you, the truth is that I cut my hands on his shattered Leyden jars. He merely replaced them with fresh ones that he had on hand."

I stared at Lenci's serious young face, then gazed at the roof of the pavilion over the garden's bare branches. The cool breeze ruffled my hair and I pushed it back into place. Should I tell Lenci what befell his lover in the garden, or was he leading me down another blind alley in this maze of deception?

"Why do my hands matter, anyway?"

I remained silent, still unsure.

"Signor Amato, you must tell me. I fear for Gemma. And I am not the only one. Her mother is beside herself with worry."

"Gemma has family in Rome?"

He nodded. "Her mother is a widow who depends on her children's wages. Gemma has several brothers who are in the pope's army. Her sister works as a laundress at a foundling home. It actually took me several days to find the house—Gemma had only mentioned the general neighborhood. It's a ramshackle place on the Tiber near the Hebrew ghetto, the smelliest, most pestilential place in Rome."

"I gather that Gemma's mother hasn't seen her, either."

"No. Gemma stops by every Sunday. She's missed two Sundays, now, and the last was her mother's name day—unheard of for Gemma to miss that."

"Has her family searched for her?" I asked, still hesitating.

"Absolutely. The sister came here to the Villa Fabiani at the end of last week. She questioned the housekeeper, who turned her over to Rossobelli. He fed her some story about Gemma walking out without giving notice. He showed no concern for Gemma's welfare—as much as called her a whore. Said he 'thinks there might be a man involved—a bargeman from the river.' Ha!" Lenci hit his fist into his palm. "He's more than a sanctimonious clod. He's an outright liar."

I raised my eyebrows. "Are you so sure?"

Lenci was silent for a moment. His pink tongue flicked around his lips. "You speak of trust, Signor Amato. I'm giving you mine by telling you that I'm absolutely certain Gemma never left here of her own free will. Gemma shared quarters with Teresa, the head house maid. They were friends…Gemma was supposed to keep me a secret, but…you know how women talk. Yesterday, when Zio Stefano dismissed me before he went in to Cardinal Fabiani, I saw my chance to seek Teresa out. I found her brushing the carpet in the second floor hallway. She didn't want to talk at first, but when she saw I wouldn't be put off, she told me about the night Gemma disappeared. Gemma didn't pack her bags, Rossobelli did. He did his dirty work in the dark. Teresa pretended to be asleep, but she wasn't. She watched from under the covers as he whisked Gemma's things into a bag and crept out the door."

"Has she told anyone else of this?"

"Not yet. Teresa rather fancies keeping her position, but I don't think she'll lie to a magistrate. Unemployment is far superior to prison."

"A magistrate?" Hearing my voice raise to a squeak, I cleared my throat and asked as calmly as I could, "How did a magistrate get involved?"

"Since Gemma's family received no satisfaction from Rossobelli, they called in a city magistrate. So far, he's only checked the hospitals and ordered the constables to be on the alert for...for any bodies in the river or back alleys." Lenci choked over those last words, then toughened his tone. "He'll no doubt widen his investigation once I give him Teresa's information. I wonder how Rossobelli will like being grilled by Mario Sertori? I've heard he's a hard man, not nearly so impressed with churchmen as the rest of Rome."

I displayed what I judged to be an appropriate expression of surprise. Behind my carefully molded features, my mind was racing. Fabiani would protect his mother at all costs and direct his toady Rossobelli to do the same. I'd been in Rome long enough to learn that the city was under the direct regime of its own governor: a prelate, of course, ultimately answerable to the pope, but one who oversaw a cadre of laymen. In the way of petty officials everywhere, these constables, magistrates, and judges enjoyed pulling the noses of their social superiors whenever they were handed the opportunity. I asked myself, how would Fabiani respond if this Mario Sertori pressed the question of Gemma's disappearance?

A cold ball of fear took possession of my stomach and rapidly expanded to chill my entire being. Fabiani's plan was suddenly crystal clear. I saw why I'd been called to carry Gemma's body away. It was more than a simple exercise of power. Gemma was of little account in Fabiani's book, a mere servant, and he hoped she would be quickly forgotten. But if her body did chance to surface or anyone showed up at the villa making troublesome inquiries, Cardinal Fabiani had groomed me as a custom-made scapegoat. By involving old Benelli, the cardinal had even guaranteed a witness to my criminal behavior.

I heard Lenci's voice through the drumming of the blood in my ears. "You've gone pale. Are you ill?" he asked, starting forward in concern.

I made my decision in that instant. Like an understudy tapped to replace an ailing prima donna, the mystery of Gemma's murder suddenly moved from the ranks of the chorus to center-stage. To protect my own neck, I had to discover the maid's killer, and I knew I couldn't do it alone.

"Abate Lenci," I began. "I'm afraid I have some very bad…" I stopped when a persistent pounding on my door penetrated through my chamber to the balcony. "Wait, I must answer that," I murmured. "Stay here, out of sight."

I sprinted across my sitting room. With each resounding knock, the door jumped in its frame. I jerked it open. Another abate greeted me—Rossobelli, his cheeks bright red with exertion.

"Signor Amato," he cried, panting. "You must come right away. Your man Benito's been run down—badly hurt. They took him to the Consolazione."

Part Three

"Pretexts are not wanting when one wishes to use them."

—Carlo Goldoni

Chapter 15

The hospital of Santa Maria della Consolazione lay across the Tiber, at the foot of the Capitoline Hill. Abate Rossobelli had called for a carriage and insisted on climbing in after me.

He perched on the front seat, facing me, canting his head this way and that: a gigantic, white-faced crow exuding an air of genteel concern. "You must allow me to accompany you. Cardinal Fabiani would think me remiss if I allowed you to make this difficult journey alone."

I nodded.

Holding my gaze, he raised his fist and rapped on the roof for the driver to start on.

Out in the streets, a bright sun beamed down on throngs of Romans going about their everyday business. Most of the faces that turned toward the carriage sporting the cardinal's coat of arms mixed a flicker of curiosity with the tedium of oft-repeated activities. At that moment, I would have traded my vocal cords for the boredom of an ordinary day. My mind was in a tumult. Rossobelli explained that a boy had run from the Trastevere with the news that a servant from the Villa Fabiani had been run down by a drayman's cart. The lad's description left no doubt of Benito's identity: *finocchio*, he'd called him, a poof. I peppered Rossobelli with questions about his injuries, but the abate couldn't say. The boy had been more interested in collecting a few coins than furnishing details.

We crossed the river at the Isola Tiberina and soon stopped in a courtyard formed by a soaring church of smooth gray stone and an outflung arm of the same material. A flight of steps bisected the hospital wing; I took them two at a time. Rossobelli followed at a more dignified pace. Bursting through the doors and running toward a long mahogany counter, I cried, "Benedetto Benaducci! Where is he?"

A gnome-like nun wearing a white habit and intricately pleated wimple bent over a ledger. I fidgeted while she ran her skeletal finger down the list of names. She finally shook her head, gazing at me over the top of her spectacles.

"Please," I begged. "He was admitted earlier today. An accident victim."

"They are all accident victims, Signore." She addressed me severely. "That is the only type of patient we accept…but the name you speak is not on the list."

I reached across the desk to turn the heavy book so I could see for myself, only to have my hand smacked with the large crucifix that dangled from her waist.

Rossobelli approached the counter with a solemn frown. His clerical garb seemed to impress the nun more than my fashionable attire.

"We're looking for a small man who was run down in the Trastevere just over an hour ago," Rossobelli said. With a sidelong glance at me, he added even more gravely, "He may not have been able to state his name."

"Wait here." She slid off her stool and scuttled down the corridor like a white crab.

I paced, puzzling over Benito's supposed accident. Carriage mishaps were fairly common. The topheavy, enclosed two seaters were particularly prone to upsets if the driver underestimated his speed around a corner. That's why a pair of grooms was often assigned the duty of riding on the back to counterbalance the weight. But a drayman's cart was hardly a speeding carriage. It was a heavy vehicle, pulled by one plodding horse. When had my nimble, sure-footed manservant not been capable of jumping out of the way of a lumbering cart?

Rossobelli walked over to a small shrine where a plaster Madonna with outstretched arms presided over a bank of flickering candles. The abate surprised me by kneeling to pray. Over his bent head, I saw a plaque blackened with age and a locked metal box chained to the railing.

I stopped pacing. Unable to decipher the plaque and searching for an innocuous topic to keep my fears at bay, I asked, "Do you read Latin?"

"Of course," he replied, raising his chin but keeping his palms pressed together.

"What does that say?"

He translated without hesitation. "All in need, from whatever corner of the world, are welcome here without restriction." He cleared his throat. "This is a charity hospital, Signor Amato, run on the alms and donations of pilgrims."

As Rossobelli's chin again sank to his chest, I took my purse from an interior pocket and slipped a coin through the slot in the box. I was too angry to pray.

In a few minutes, the guardian of the admissions desk returned with a young nursing sister. A gray smock covered her white habit almost entirely, making her rosy cheeks and pink lips the only spots of color about her person.

I hurried to her side while Rossobelli pushed stiffly to his feet.

"Follow me," she commanded in a half-whisper. "The men's ward is this way. If we hurry, the surgeon may still be there. Are you his family?"

"Yes." The word escaped my lips without thought. "Well, the closest to family that he has. Actually, I'm Benito's employer. How is he?"

She set her lips in a firm line. "It's not my place to say. The doctor will explain." Quickening her pace, she led us up one staircase and down a corridor to a cavernous ward lined by beds surrounded by canvas screens. The smell was horrific: putrefaction and the odors of bodily functions permeated the air. Cries and moans rose from all sides.

My manservant lay in a raised bed with roughly squared wooden posts. He had been covered by a thin woolen blanket; the shallow rising and falling of that worn blanket was the only sign that he still lived. Benito's face, normally so alert and expressive, could have been mistaken for a death mask fashioned of polished ivory. A gauze bandage covered the crown of his head, and his left arm was bound up in a sling.

Hot tears bathed my eyes as I groped for Benito's free hand. Several times I called his name, but his frighteningly still expression never wavered.

Rossobelli grasped my shoulder. Starting as if a spider had landed there, I brushed his long fingers away.

"The doctor," he murmured.

A tired looking surgeon in a blood-stained smock lumbered to the bedside. He pulled the covers down and put his ear to Benito's bandaged chest. Clucking his tongue, he turned his attention to his patient's head. After prodding and poking every crevice, he raised Benito's eyelids with a flick of his thumb. I cringed at the filth that covered the doctor's hands.

"Will he live?" I asked tremulously.

The doctor shrugged his sloping shoulders. "This man is gravely injured, probably dragged over the cobblestones by the cart that hit him. I've done what I can—bled him, set the fracture, taped the ribs, and dressed the cuts and scrapes. The head injury rests in God's hands."

"Has he said anything?"

Another shrug.

"No." The nurse spoke for the first time since we had reached the bedside. "He neither speaks nor seems to hear."

The doctor had turned to pass through the opening in the canvas screens. I moved to block his exit. "What happens now? What must I do?"

"Wait," the man growled. "As we all will." He pushed past me, then added in a softer tone, "Sometimes, when the brain has been injured, it goes into hiding. To lick its own wounds, so to speak."

"For how long?"

"As long as it needs," he flung over his shoulder as he disappeared behind another screen.

"Here now," the nurse flared up behind me. "Just what do you think you're doing?"

I whirled. Rossobelli hovered over Benito, rearranging and patting his covers.

"Stop that this minute," she continued.

The abate straightened quickly. His sharp cheekbones made ruddy slashes across his pale face. "I was just trying to make him more comfortable."

"That's my job." The nurse rounded the foot of the bed and inserted her willowy form between the abate and Benito. The fabric of her habit pulled as she stiffened her shoulders. "Perhaps you should wait in the corridor." Her half-whisper carried a hint of steel.

Rossobelli glowered but retreated through the screens and out of the stuffy ward. I suddenly felt much better about leaving my manservant in the care of this capable young woman.

"What is your name, Sister?"

"I'm Sister Regina."

"Will you be tending to Benito all the time?"

She sent me a ghost of a smile. "There are six of us assigned to this ward. Our quarters are at the back, so several of us are always on duty. But as you see, this ward holds forty patients, and the beds don't stay empty for long…" She sighed and folded her hands over her smock. "We do the best we can, Signore."

My fingers again sought the purse in my jacket pocket. My time might not be my own, but thanks to my triumph in Dresden, I did have plenty of money.

The nun flinched when she saw what I was about.

"You mustn't do that," she said. "I can't accept money. I'm not even allowed to touch it. It's a rule of our order."

"Who empties the offertory box I saw downstairs?"

"Father Giancarlo, from the church next door. He's the hospital superintendent."

"Does the Consolazione have a children's ward?"

"Yes." She gestured toward the ceiling. "On the floor above."

I held up a thick gold coin. The nun's eyes widened. It was a Roman crown that could buy ten blankets, many dozens of eggs, or fifteen pounds of prime beef. "I'll visit every afternoon. For each day that I find Benito alive and well cared for, I'll give Father Giancarlo one of these to spend on the children."

"Very generous, Signore," she murmured.

"One more thing." I fixed her clear gray eyes with my own. "If anyone besides me pays my friend a visit, a nurse will find something to do nearby. I want to know who comes, what they do, and what they say."

Sister Regina dipped her chin in a solemn nod. We had struck a bargain.

༄

After leaving my first offering with Father Giancarlo, I found Rossobelli waiting by the carriage. He gave me an icy greeting and bade me climb in to return to the villa.

"No," I replied. "I need to be on my own for a bit. I'll walk, thank you."

Rossobelli looked like he was going to give me an argument but evidently changed his mind, merely saying, "At least I can take that package for you."

I clutched the bundle of Benito's clothing that Sister Regina had wrapped up with twine. "That won't be necessary."

"As you wish." He entered the carriage, slammed the door, then poked his head through the open window. "This unfortunate incident doesn't relieve you of your duties, you know. His Eminence will require you at eight o'clock sharp."

The carriage had barely rolled away when Guido trotted up, his handsome face blotchy with exertion and strain. "Signor Amato, I came as soon as I heard. How is Benito? Is he going to be all right?"

I told the footman all I knew, little as it was, then added, "Did Rossobelli see you? He just left in the carriage."

Guido shook his head. "I saw it coming and stepped into a doorway, but it doesn't matter. I'm not on duty until this evening. He can't stop me from seeing Benito if I want." He cocked a thick eyebrow and asked hesitantly, "You don't mind if I go up, do you, Signore?"

"Of course not."

I must admit to a twinge of jealousy as I watched the footman mount the stairs as quickly as I had. Benito's amorous liaisons were generally casual and short-lived, nothing to compete with his primary occupation of seeing to my needs, but this relationship with Guido seemed more serious. If God's grace allowed Benito to live, Guido might still take my loyal companion and sometime nursemaid from me.

Feeling curiously adrift, I squared my shoulders, reproached myself for my selfishness, and set off for the Trastevere. The Romans were an idle lot. The women always seemed to be gossiping from their windows and the men playing cards or throwing dice on the stairs. Even the shopkeepers spent more time in the doorway than behind the counter. I shouldn't complain. Their laziness might produce an eyewitness who could describe Benito's accident firsthand.

The right place wasn't hard to find; many fingers pointed the way. It seemed that everyone had heard the news and was eager to express an opinion on the dangers of heavily loaded vehicles driven by heedless madmen.

I chose to question a beggar I'd noticed on previous excursions through this quarter. He was a fat, amiable man of middle years who occupied a certain street corner as if it were his personal drawing room, a corner that happened to be directly opposite the site of Benito's misfortune. My beggar decorated his person with tarnished medals and bits of military uniforms from several countries. He balanced his weight between one good leg and a wooden peg that took the place of a missing limb.

"Lost it at the Battle of Parma," he explained cheerfully, "courtesy of an Austrian cannonball. Those sausage eaters did me a favor, really. If I'd stayed a soldier, I probably wouldn't be here at all."

I dropped a few coins in the hat which he'd quickly doffed. "Were you here earlier this morning? When the man was run down?"

"To be sure. You can find me here nine to six every day. I set my time by the bells of the monastery at the top of the street." He showed yellow teeth in a smile, circling his wrist to make the coins dance and jingle. I added to their number. My purse was suddenly getting more of a workout than it had during my entire stay in Rome.

"How did it happen?" I asked.

"You see that wall?" He pointed across the street to a shoulder-high structure that ran the length of the block and surrounded what looked to be a pottery factory. "The poor fellow was right in the middle there—had a canny little smile on his face—bouncing along with a swivel in the hindquarters, almost like a young miss."

I nodded at the particularly apt description of my manservant.

"Along came a cart piled high with casks, the sort that haulers use to shift liquid goods from the warehouse to the shops and fine houses. It was moving at a good clip. Nothing odd in that, we've got a slope here, running down to the river. But when the driver saw the fellow, he cracked his whip…laid into the nag something fierce…drew blood." The beggar fell silent and shook his head.

"It was deliberate, then?"

"Oh, yes. He drove his cart right up by the wall, full speed ahead. His cargo was rocking so hard, I thought we'd have casks cracking like eggs hitting the pavement. The poor fellow ran like the wind, but he couldn't get across the horse's path. And he didn't have nowhere to go, see? It's a solid wall, no doors or gates to jump into."

I took a hard gulp. "Go on."

"He went down with a squawk. Sounded like a goose getting his neck wrung. I couldn't see exactly what happened next. He went bouncing around under the cart, and by then people were screaming and running."

"Did the driver stop?"

"For a minute. Just long enough for the other man to jump down."

"Other man?"

"There was a man sitting at the back of the cart, holding onto the sides, legs dangling. When the cart stopped, he jumped off and ran to the fellow who was down. He turned him over and loosened his shirt. I thought he was going to help him, but I reckon he got scared. Must've thought they'd killed him. He jumped back on the cart and the driver took off like the Devil's legions were on their tail."

"The driver? Had you seen him before?"

"Never."

"You sound very sure."

He leaned against the building and nodded with a confident smile. Of course, I thought, a successful beggar must search the faces of all who pass by, taking their measure for a potential handout.

"What did he look like?"

"A burly man in a jacket of faded blue. And leather gloves with studded gauntlets."

"His face?"

He thought a moment, fingering his chin. "Didn't get a good look at his face, on account of the cap, see? He wore a bright blue knit cap, pulled down low, with the tail flopping over his cheek. All I saw was his chin. It was long and scooping—the kind that's easy broke in a fight."

"Good. What about the other man?"

"He was dressed in citified clothes. Nothing fine, just better than what you'd see on most working men." The beggar paused to rub his good knee. "Young and strong. The way he jumped off and on the cart, he couldn't have been too much over twenty.

No, don't bother to ask. I didn't get a good look at his face, too many people in the way."

"Did a constable come to investigate?"

"A pair of 'em—after all the excitement was over. They organized a litter to take the man to the hospital and haven't been back."

I thanked my informant with another coin and crossed the pavement to make my own inspection. The stamp of passing feet had destroyed any marks on the cobblestones, but the wall of smoothly dressed limestone carried an imprint that set me shivering from head to toe. I squatted low. A rust red handprint, smudged but free of dust or soot, glared out from the stone at the level of my knees. I pressed my palm against it, imagining Benito's terror as he'd been dragged beneath the cart. My anger was so hot, I half expected the stone to sizzle at my touch.

Who had ordered this cowardly attack? And to what purpose? Was I meant to take it as a warning to keep Gemma's murder a secret? Surely not. Cardinal Fabiani knew that my involvement with the disposal of her body was enough to keep me silent.

I stood and tucked my bundle under my arm. There was nothing more to be seen here. Letting my feet wander aimlessly, I considered other possibilities. I had asked Benito to question the servants about Gemma's background and relations. Knowing his dogged persistence in such matters, I wondered if his curiosity had been made known to Rossobelli. The cardinal's secretary was sure to have eyes and ears among the staff. Is that why Rossobelli had been so intent on accompanying me to the hospital? Had he wanted to see what damage his henchmen had dished out?

I'd actually quickened my steps with visions of bursting in the villa and beating Rossobelli's head to a pulp when another thought stopped me. Thanks to Abate Lenci's revelations, Gemma's murder was at the forefront of my mind, but I had to consider that Benito's attack could have been a reminder to stay the course with Antonio Montorio. The Red Inquisitor was not a man to let anything stand in the way of his plans. Had he somehow found out about Stefano Montorio's offer to arrange Alessandro's escape?

I stopped at the entrance to a narrow alley, my head reeling with twisted thoughts. Without a clear message, how was I to decipher the meaning behind the violence? Shifting the bundle of Benito's clothing to my free arm gave me an idea. The beggar said that the younger man had loosened Benito's shirt. Perhaps he had left some sign for me to find.

I attended to my surroundings for the first time in many minutes. My unwitting steps had led me to the alley that held Maddelena's cookshop. Liya was most likely at the theater, but her friend would give me a quiet place to search Benito's clothing. And feed me, too. I could use a meal. I had never done my best thinking on an empty stomach.

Chapter 16

The natural joy of a child yet to be saddled with the world's woes is one of life's everyday miracles. As I opened the door to the crowded cookshop, little Tito reminded me that such happiness still existed. He shot out from behind the counter in the depths of the shop, encircled my waist in a bear hug, and insisted I pick him up so he could gabble his news directly into my ear.

"Arruffato wasn't a boy."

"Arru…" I started questioningly. "Oh, your spider friend."

Tito nodded, eyes as bright and shiny as buttons. "He was a girl. And he…I mean, she had babies. More than I can count."

"Well, this I must see. Will you show me?"

"I can't. They're gone. Nonna Maddelena says they crawled away to find new homes."

"Yes, all gone, but maybe one of their children will come back to visit someday." Maddelena straightened from wiping one of the few empty tables and took little Tito from my arms. She smelled of spices and roasting meat. Smiling, she sent the boy to the kitchen with a playful swat on the seat of his breeches. "Go back to your games, little one, let Signor Amato take a breath."

"Oh, he's all right," I replied.

"But you'll want to talk with your friend." The proprietor of the cookshop nodded sagely. "How did you know that Liya had sent him here? Have you been to the theater?"

"No, I haven't seen Liya for several days." I removed my tricorne and scanned the faces of the working men who were filling their bellies with a late dinner. "My friend, did you say?"

"Back there." She flicked her rag toward a table wedged in a nook between the stairs and the serving counter.

A man sat with his back toward us, assiduously plying knife and fork. I stared at his bulky shoulders and untidy queue of blond hair in disbelief.

"Gussie," I shouted.

My brother-in-law almost knocked his bench over in his rush to greet me. The next few moments passed in a blur of embracing, back slapping, and competing questions. Once settled in the secluded nook, we conversed in whispers too low to be heard over the clatter of cutlery and buzz of louder voices.

I started with a sad recitation of Benito's condition, but interrupted myself when Maddelena brought food and drink. For a few moments, I fell on my plate like a man who hadn't seen food for two days.

"Don't they feed you at that splendid villa?" Gussie asked, accepting Maddelena's offer of more macaroni.

"I thought performing as the cardinal's lap dog had destroyed my appetite," I replied, "but suddenly I'm ravenous." Between bites, I went on to apprise Gussie of all that had happened since I'd sailed from Venice.

He listened with few interruptions but wrinkled his brow so many times that I feared it would settle into permanent creases. Furtive murder and papal intrigue were well outside his honest, straightforward way of thinking. By the time I had succeeded in explaining why it was so important that I discover Gemma's killer, we had demolished a stewed chicken, two huge bowls of buttered macaroni, and a bottle of Frascati.

With a welcome belch, I pushed my empty plate aside and asked, "But Gussie, why have you journeyed to Rome? I thought you were occupied with a large commission."

"Annetta was worried," he explained. "She called at the Roman post every day, expecting a letter. When none came, she imagined every sort of dire possibility. I told her you could take care of yourself, but she gave me no peace."

"What about the paintings for the Duke of…whatever he is?"

"Richmond. He'll just have to wait. If truth be told…" Gussie sent me a severe glance, tapping his fork against the china. "I was getting worried, too."

"Your letter kept growing fatter and fatter. I should have sent it days ago, but I was worried about prying eyes." I patted the bundle of clothing on the bench beside me. "It will be in here, but it contains little I haven't just told."

Gussie nodded, breaking off a hunk of bread to soak up the remains of the garlic-drenched butter. "Alessandro wanted me to come, too. He was almost as insistent as Annetta."

"You've been allowed to see him?"

"His warden has been most cooperative—for a price, of course. Venetian civil servants elevate the practice of bribery to a high art. Five *soldi* would have bought a ten-minute conversation through a grating with a jailer stationed near enough to hear every word, so I gave a zecchino to gain entrance to Alessandro's cell for a more private conversation. For ten more I could have ordered us a meal of boiled beef and decent bread. I was even quoted prices for importing various grades of whores."

"How does Alessandro fare?" I planted my elbows on the table, steeling myself for the worst.

"Remarkably fine. His bruises are fading, and he seems in good spirits."

"I'm glad to hear it, but somewhat surprised, I'll admit. Surely Alessandro is aware of the punishment meted out to convicted salt smugglers." Goosebumps popped out on my arms. The thought of my brother swinging from a gibbet on the Piazzetta chilled me to the depths of my soul.

Gussie followed the bread with a thoughtful sip from his glass. "I can't quite make him out. Everyone in Venice walks in fear of offending the Tribunal of State Inquisitors, but when I talk to Alessandro about his situation, he simply waves his hand as if Senator Montorio is nothing more than an obnoxious mosquito.

Alessandro is keeping something up his sleeve, Tito…or I'm a Dutchman."

"What could it be?"

"I cannot imagine, but I will tell you this—besides coming to Rome, there was one other task Alessandro set for me. He wrote a nice, fat letter of his own, addressed to a Turkish gentleman in Constantinople. He said it concerned business matters too important to consign to the post."

"Venice and Constantinople have shared a reliable mail route for well over a century."

"I know, but that wasn't good enough for Alessandro. He had me locate one of his military friends who is attached to a swift galley that was preparing to set sail for the Ottoman port. The man promised to deliver the letter personally, as soon as his ship dropped anchor. He was greatly exercised by Alessandro's arrest. Called it 'a shocking example of despotism.'"

I nodded. It was heartening to know that some fellow Venetians recognized the injustice. Perhaps I'd not been so alone as I'd felt these past weeks. "When did the galley sail?"

"Two days after you left Venice." Gussie did some counting on his fingers. "That would be January eighth."

"Did you notice the name on the letter?"

"I committed it to memory—Yusuf Ali Muhammad. Alessandro's friend said the address was in a neighborhood that shared a wall with the gardens of the Topkapi Palace—not a shabby place by the sound of it. Does any of this sound familiar?"

I shook my head. "Alessandro has been very close-mouthed about his Turkish doings. Did he send a letter for me?"

"I'm afraid you will have to make do with me as messenger. I'm to ask if you remember the opera that opened last year's carnival season."

"How could I forget? It was *Antonio e Cesare*. Scalzi and I shared the lead roles. In the middle of the first act, he refused to join me on stage unless he received a substantial raise in salary."

"What did you do?"

"Maestro Torani signaled me to play for time. I sang almost every aria I knew before Scalzi deigned to appear. Why? What does that old business have to do with our current difficulties?"

"That is what Alessandro was so anxious that I tell you—you're to play for time as best you know how."

"What?" I stared at Gussie in blank astonishment.

My brother-in-law spread his hands. "That's all I know. Alessandro said, 'Tell Tito to humor the Montorio brothers, keep himself safe, and pray that Pope Clement hangs on for another few weeks.'"

The cookshop had cleared out. The citizens of the Trastevere had consumed their dinners and settled down for the siesta that cuts the daily activities of this southern city into two distinct halves. Maddelena, ignoring little Tito's vigorous objections, had also taken the boy upstairs for his siesta. It was a good time to examine the package I'd carried away from the hospital.

While Gussie conveyed our soiled dishes to the counter, I sawed at Sister Regina's knots with my dagger. The nun had used Benito's relatively clean waistcoat to wrap his bloodied shirt, breeches, and jacket crusted with dirt and filth. These surrounded Benito's underclothes and the shoes that he always kept as scrupulously polished as my own. I ran my thumb over their scarred leather with a sigh.

My search of Benito's pockets was halted by the sudden appearance of Liya coming through the kitchen door and tossing her cloak on the counter.

Gussie had already explained how he had come to Maddelena's cookshop. After securing lodging in a corner of the Trastevere that catered to artists, he had quickly located the Villa Fabiani, but not knowing my situation, he hesitated to present himself at the door. Summoning his utmost powers of deduction, he decided that I might have made myself known at Rome's foremost opera house. Liya had spotted him immediately.

"So you found each other. Good." Her white teeth gleamed in a smile; her black hair shone under a white lace cap. "What is this?" She picked up one of Benito's torn stockings and drew it through her hands. "Are you going into the rag business, Tito?"

I allowed Gussie to tell the story of the malevolent drayman's cart while I mined Benito's pockets. My manservant never liked to be without, so I brought out quite a few treasures: watch; purse; filigreed case containing a stubby pencil, several of my visiting cards, and a scrap of blank paper; comb; small ball of string; a half-eaten biscuit wrapped in a handkerchief; and a fresh tin of violet pastilles. Tucked in the lid of the oval tin was a scrawled note: *a sweet token for my love—G.* Guido had evidently discovered Benito's taste for candy.

Pressing herself onto the bench beside me, Liya stroked my hair and kissed my cheek. "Oh Tito, I'm so sorry…poor little Benito."

I saw Gussie bite the inside of his lip at the intimate gesture. My friend and brother-in-law was guarding his countenance more carefully than usual, but I could see that he was not entirely happy that I was involved with Liya again. Gussie had been at my side when I first wooed her and had sympathetically endured all my moaning over her loss.

Lining the items up on the table before me, I studied them closely, hoping to find a clue to tell me why my manservant had been attacked. I shook my head. There was nothing that shouldn't be there, but…several things were missing. I tore through the garments again, coming up with nothing more than a quantity of lint.

"What is it, Tito?" Gussie asked.

"The letters. I sent Benito out to deliver two letters to a singer bound for Venice—a letter of introduction to Maestro Torani and the letter to be delivered to your hand."

"Perhaps Benito had already been to Tucci's place and was on his way back," Liya offered.

"There wasn't time. Besides, someone who witnessed the attack told me that Benito was walking downhill, towards the Tiber bridge."

"He might have encountered this Tucci fellow on the street—a coincidental meeting." Gussie raised a hopeful smile.

"Unlikely," I replied, "but the next time I'm able to shake Rossobelli off my coattails, I'll seek Signor Tucci out and ask him."

"Let me, Tito. Tucci rarely goes a day without appearing at the theater." Liya followed her words by slipping her hand over mine, but I paid it no heed.

I was thinking back to the scene in my room: sealing the letters, consigning them to Benito. He had been clutching the letters as he went through the door. My manservant had a way of infusing even the most mundane activity with high drama. When encountering someone in the corridors or on the stairs who could give him directions to the Piazza D'Espagna, Benito would have cast himself in the role of royal courier and carried the letters as if they held state secrets. I groaned, burying my face in my hands.

"Tito?" Gussie and Liya cried in unison.

"How could I have been so careless?" Words tumbled from my lips. "I should have made sure Benito tucked those letters away, warned him more sternly. No, I should have delivered them myself. Thanks to me, Benito is hovering at death's door and whoever has Gussie's letter might as well have been taking notes on my every move."

We digested this development and the possibilities it raised in silence. Muffled thumps and squeals from the upper floor told us that little Tito had finished his nap. Liya fixed her dark eyes on mine. "Would it cheer you up to hear that I have a plan to penetrate the Palazzo Pompetti?"

I nodded. "At least I would be taking the lead instead of letting other people push me hither and yon."

"Tomorrow night, then. Can you get away from the villa?"

"I'll find a way." I caught sight of Gussie's raised eyebrows. "Can we all go?"

"No, sorry. I secured an invitation from Lady Mary with some difficulty—for myself and one other only." Liya turned to Gussie with a stiff smile. "But we will dress here. You can help me get Tito properly turned out."

"Won't my usual court attire do?" I asked.

She shook her head, cultivating an air of mystery. "Be here at seven, both of you."

"But—? What are you planning?"

"Just be here, caro."

Studiously silent, Gussie busied himself with flicking crumbs from his waistcoat. Just as well. I very much doubted that I would want to hear what was running through his mind.

⚬⚬⚬

Back in my room at the Villa Fabiani, a fire had been laid, but it still awaited the touch of a taper. So did the lamps. Never had my chamber seemed so dark and cold. Not ready to face preparing for the evening without Benito, I stepped out onto the balcony and wondered what Abate Lenci had made of our interrupted conversation. At least I could be sure that he had nothing to do with the attack on Benito: even if he had noticed the letters my manservant carried, there had been no time for Lenci to arrange to steal them. He had appeared at my door only a minute or so after Benito had walked through it.

I sighed; time was wasting and I must make myself ready. Cardinal Fabiani had planned an excursion to the Capranica, an opera house that rivaled the Argentina. Just he and I. The official reason for the cardinal's invitation was to hear my critique of the production, but I believed that Fabiani really wanted to enjoy the opera without the need to entertain guests who would rather chat than listen. Stepping back into the sitting room, I was surprised to hear someone moving about in my bed chamber.

I approached gingerly and peered around the doorway.

In the shadows, a stocky figure hunched over my wash stand. Crossing to the bedroom window on noiseless cat feet, I threw back the drape. The dim twilight revealed Guido, mouth frozen in a wide circle, clutching a steaming pitcher.

"Ah, Signore. You startled me." The footman recovered himself to bow respectfully. "I've brought some warm water, and I'll have your fire going in a moment."

"Of course, thank you." I sank down on the window seat, feeling more than a little foolish.

Guido continued his work with an industrious air, fetching my dressing gown, arranging my brushes, and laying out soap and towels.

I removed my jacket and began to untie my shirt. The day's exertions had left me feeling sticky and grimy. When Guido left to fetch a taper, I made a beeline for the wash basin, soaped up a cloth, and reveled in the touch of the warm water bathing my skin.

"Which suit of clothing will you be wanting, Signore?" The footman had reappeared to light the lamps.

"I can take care of that, Guido. You can go now—no need to play valet."

"Abate Rossobelli has given me leave to assist you with whatever you need." He drew himself up, chin elevated at a sharp angle. "I may only be a footman, but I've watched the valets often enough. There's nothing they do that I can't."

"Are you sure? It means more work for you."

"A man in my position has few ways to improve himself, Signore."

I searched his young, stubborn face and understood. To move up the servant ranks, a footman must acquire new skills. If Guido didn't take advantage of opportunities as they presented themselves, he could end up like Roberto, still minding the door and running the halls with a bent back and creaky knees.

"All right, Guido. Benito's duties are now yours. You can start by handing me that towel."

He complied with a grateful bow and said, "Now, I don't suppose you will be requiring a shave?"

"No," I answered dryly.

"Then which suit?"

I made my choice, and Guido proceeded to fit me out for the evening. Touched by his determined but clumsy efforts to handle powder and paint, I tried to forget that I didn't particularly care for the man. I sensed a hot temper behind his carefully molded smile, and I could easily picture him in the middle of one of the street fights that I had seen break out over nothing more than an unconsidered glance or chance rubbing of shoulders. Where Venetians of the lower classes confined themselves to wild outbursts of invective, Romans quickly advanced to blows or the brandishing of the wicked little knives that both men and women kept about their persons.

But Benito had taken this coarse Roman to his heart; for my manservant's sake, I tried to be accommodating. "Were you able to spend much time at the hospital?" I asked as Guido draped my shoulders to protect my jacket from the final dusting of wig powder.

"A few minutes only. I don't know if Benito could hear me, but I knelt at his bedside and made him a solemn promise."

"Yes?"

The footman's face darkened. He worked the powder bellows with a vengeance, creating a white cloud above my head. "I vowed that the people who did this will pay. Whatever a man is, he should be able to walk down the street without fearing for his life."

I suppressed a sneeze behind the paper cone that protected my nose. "Are you saying that Benito was attacked because of his feminine ways?"

"It would not be the first time, Signore. Romans like their men to be men and their women…well, you know what I mean."

I immediately thought back to the opera that had starred the lovely Albertini. "Yet your countrymen pile into the opera house to see boys singing women's roles."

"Well, that's different. Everyone knows that the singers are playacting. All in fun, you might say. But a man in the street who looks more like a woman in manly attire—it strikes some as a personal offense—they feel like they're being tricked."

Accustomed to easygoing Venetian ways, that possibility had not occurred to me. I was wondering if Guido's theory could possibly fit the scene the beggar had described when my neophyte valet slammed the bellows on the dressing table with a crash. Over the rim of the paper cone, I beheld three images of his scowling face reflected in my tri-fold mirror.

"By the blood of our Lord, I won't let Benito go unavenged," his deep voice rumbled. "I'll find out who did this and see them pay. Benito can count on me—and so can you, Signore."

"Er, yes. An admirable sentiment," I replied weakly, somewhat shaken by Guido's display of raw emotion. I swallowed the lump that had risen in my throat. "Tell me, how was Benito when you left?"

"No change. The nurse that attended him like a sentry said he may lie like that for some time."

Glad to hear that Sister Regina was keeping her part of our bargain, I nodded thoughtfully. "Guido, did you happen to see Benito earlier today, before he left the villa?"

"Just for a moment."

"Where?"

"He was passing through the back courtyard. I caught his eye, but he didn't stop. He seemed in a hurry."

"Did you see him speak to anyone?"

"He might have done. There was a lot of activity about. Cardinal Montorio's carriage had just arrived. Pope Clement is bad, they say—sinking fast. Whenever *Il Papa* takes another turn for the worse, the Venetians are sure to pay a call."

I snorted into my cone. "Do all the servants understand that Cardinal Fabiani is the lever that could raise either Montorio or Di Noce to the throne?"

"Certainly. We dine and sup on speculation—at least we did until old Red Chaps banned talk of the election." Guido whisked the cloth away with a snap, then seemed unsure of how to deal with the resulting storm of powder.

I handed him a curved brush. He stared at it for a few seconds, then applied its bristles to my back and shoulders.

"Why did Rossobelli do that?" I asked.

"He said it's none of our business—that better men, guided by the Holy Spirit, will make the decision—and that it's blasphemous to talk about the conclave like it's a horse race."

"Hmm. I've seen horse races that were easier to predict." I sought his eyes in the mirror. "What do you think, Guido? Who would you like to see as pope—Di Noce or Montorio?"

"It makes no difference to me. A fresh pope brings fresh promises, but give him several months and all will be forgotten. We have a saying here in Rome—The Tiber stinks no matter who sits in St. Peter's." With an eloquent shrug, he replaced the brush and passed me the hand mirror.

I swiveled my chin this way and that. It was a fine job for an aspiring valet. I told him so and received a humble grin in response.

Leaving Guido to tidy my suite, I hurried downstairs to meet Cardinal Fabiani for our night at the opera. The great hall was empty except for the footman serving as porter. It was old Roberto.

"Is the cardinal not down?" I asked.

"His Eminence has been in his reception room this past half hour," he replied.

"Alone?"

"No, Signore."

"With a gentleman?"

He sniffed. "I wouldn't go so far as to call him that."

"Ah, Tito," Cardinal Fabiani hailed me from across the hall. His scarlet cloak flapped around his ankles as he advanced with a man who was a stranger to me, a solid column of a man with lank, iron gray hair that framed his face like a pair of curtains. The stranger's eyes were gray as well, and their penetrating gaze lingered on everything it touched, as if even the walls were conspiring to hide a guilty secret.

"Don't think I've forsaken you," Fabiani said. "We'll be leaving in a moment. But first, I have someone here who would like to ask you a few questions. I…" Fabiani hesitated as if searching for words or perhaps assessing our societal ranks to decide who should be presented to whom.

His companion had no patience for such niceties. He gave me a clipped bow and gestured back toward the cardinal's reception room. "I am Magistrate Sertori," he informed me. "This way, if you please."

Chapter 17

"Don't worry, Tito." Cardinal Fabiani raised his voice over the rattle and squeak of the carriage, seemingly elated to be on our way to the opera at last. "Where there is no body, there can be no crime."

I glanced out the window. A north wind had blown up, and many of the people we passed on the shadowy pavements were muffled in furs and quilted gowns. I nestled into my cloak, as chilled by the memory of the interrogation I'd just endured as by the weather. Though I'd denied all knowledge of Gemma's whereabouts, Magistrate Sertori had kept me for the better part of an hour, repeating the same questions and drilling me with his icy gaze.

"But Your Eminence," I said, "with all due respect, Magistrate Sertori suspects that there is. He knows that Abate Rossobelli spirited Gemma's things out of her room."

The cardinal fingered his chin. "Yes. I've been wondering how Sertori knew to pressure our little Teresa into telling her tale."

I shrugged, unwilling to name Abate Lenci as the likely informant.

"At any rate," he continued, "what Sertori suspects and what he can prove are two very different matters."

"He will have Teresa's testimony."

"I doubt that. Teresa hails from Naples. Like so many young girls, she came to Rome in search of a rich husband. Since the proper swain has not presented himself, I think it's time for Teresa to return to her family."

"And if Teresa disagrees?"

"She won't," he replied with a pleasant smile. "Teresa is not as fresh as she used to be, and she knows it. Tomorrow, she'll snatch the dowry I offer and be rolling down the Via Campana before Sertori has finished his breakfast. In a few days, she'll be in Bourbon territory, well out of his reach."

"What if Sertori questions old Benelli?"

"Why should he? No one knows of Benelli's involvement besides you and me and Rossobelli."

"Yes," I murmured. "Unfortunately, I'm not Abate Rossobelli's favorite person."

Fabiani drew his brows together. "Is this a personal enmity? Or political?"

"We both know that your secretary is squarely in Prince Pompetti's camp where the next pope is concerned. It's only logical that Rossobelli would resent anyone linked to the Montorio cause."

The cardinal nodded, encouraging me to go on.

I spoke carefully. "Sometimes I think Rossobelli would do anything to see Di Noce elevated to the papacy."

The cardinal considered for a moment, then his scarlet cloak began quaking, and he threw back his head in a deep chuckle. "You see Rossobelli as a murderer? Oh Tito, that's rich."

Laughing outright, he wiped his eyes with the back of his gloves. They were scarlet too, of course, and embroidered with the papal crest. Why not the Fabiani crest, I wondered as the cardinal's laughter filled the carriage.

"Our friend from Ancona doesn't have the backbone for violence, Tito. He's a bookworm, not a ruffian of the streets. Why, the man nearly faints when the cat walks by with a dead mouse."

"Actually, Your Eminence, I was thinking more along the lines of Abate Rossobelli ridding the villa of my pernicious Venetian influence by setting me up as Gemma's murderer."

The cardinal stopped laughing. "Oh, is that what you meant?" He cleared his throat. "Of course, what can I be thinking? Gemma was a servant, a person of no significance in society or government. How could killing a powerless maid help Cardinal Di Noce?"

"How indeed?" I asked quietly.

Like a magic lantern show, the cardinal's face displayed an array of emotions as the carriage passed from light to shadow and back into light. For one brief moment, I felt I had gained the upper hand. Then the cardinal collected himself.

"Tito, we both know why Gemma was killed and who did the deed. My mother rebels against the strictures that her mental state requires, but someone has to look after her and keep her safe. I am most particular about that." He inhaled deeply. "Perhaps Gemma did her job too well. Let's just say that the affair is a tragedy all around—but not one to be compounded by involving a magistrate, eh?"

I nodded slowly.

The cardinal's mood became expansive again. "As far as Sertori knows, Gemma left the villa for parts unknown and Rossobelli cleared out her cupboard. A little servant problem, nothing out of the ordinary. If the three of us keep our heads, there is nothing at all to worry about."

Yes, we three, what a merry trio. Sinking farther down into my cloak, I wondered who had stolen my letter to make it a quartet.

"Cheer up, my young friend." The cardinal braced himself against the leather cushions as we took a sharp turn into the Piazza Capranica. "Tonight, we see *La Serva Padrona*, a comic opera about a maid who turns the tables on her master. I've been told it's quite amusing, so no long faces allowed."

The carriage stopped and the theater loomed above us, a slice of shimmering marble surrounded by a noisy crowd. As soon as the grooms jumped down to lower the stairs, five or six women clutching ragged, inadequate shawls rushed forward clamoring for coins. The grooms raised their elbows to knock them back.

"Stop," Cardinal Fabiani ordered. "Let them come."

Crouching in the carriage, I watched Fabiani stand tall and toss several handfuls of silver from the top step. His regal figure framed against the ebony carriage drawn by a matched pair of Arabian steeds must have made a grand impression. As he descended, the beggars scrambled after his largesse, blessing his name and his soul. The crowd parted to speed his way into the building, and the more richly dressed theater patrons bowed or curtsied. Many broke into spontaneous applause as the cardinal passed.

I followed in his wake, observing his humble protestations and gracious waves, absolutely certain that he had stage managed the whole business.

⌘

Much later, after watching an operatic maid draw laughs for tricking her master in ways that would have had her dismissed, if not beaten, in the real world, I slid wearily between my cool sheets. Considering the heaviness of my limbs and the prickling of my eyelids, I expected sleep to come as soon as my head hit the pillow. Not so. Even though I was well aware that Benito's bed in the adjoining dressing room was empty, I found myself listening for the wheeze of his high-pitched snores. Instead, I heard the sounds of the villa adjusting to the change in temperature: the creak of wooden joists; the chink of stone settling on stone; the pad of stealthy, bare feet.

My eyes flew open. Had I dreamed that last? I strained my ears in the darkness. There it was again: a few steps, then a pause, and more running steps.

It took only a moment to slip into the dressing gown that I'd left folded on top of the covers. I grabbed an unlit candlestick as I shoved my feet in my slippers. Once I was out in the broad corridor with the flickering wall lamps, I illuminated the candle and moved in the direction the steps had taken. Passing the cardinal's suite, I stopped to press my ear to his door. Quiet reigned. A few more steps, and I turned right to enter the long, straight hallway that led to the northwest wing.

Halfway along was a niche that held a large Chinese vase, but it seemed that the vase had been overturned and a gauzy, indistinct figure was struggling to right it. Quickly, I jumped back around the corner and took a more careful look. Lowering the blue and white vase to the carpet, the figure turned a bit, just enough for me to recognize the marchesa.

I raced toward her. "Marchesa Fabiani," I whispered. "What are you doing?"

She sat on the floor with the vase between her legs. A look of alarm spread over her old features when she first caught sight of me, but it quickly faded as I knelt beside her.

"Oh, it's you—the music man. Here, help me—you have long arms."

"What is it?"

"I put something in this vase—some time ago—and I can't reach it." Her arm was buried up to her shoulder.

"Let me see."

She scooted back. I grasped the neck of the vase and tilted it from side to side in the glow of the candle. Only smooth ceramic met my gaze.

"It's empty, My Lady."

"No, it can't be."

As she seemed likely to throw herself on the delicate porcelain once again, I encircled the upturned vase with my arms and stood up. I shook the pot vigorously, to no avail.

"You see," I said, still whispering. "Empty. Now, let me take you back to bed."

A look of desperation glinted from her eyes. Before I could settle the vase in its proper place, she came up on one knee, teetered a bit, and took off down the hall with her nightdress straggling behind. I sprinted after her. How could such an elderly lady move so fast?

I thought I had her cornered when she halted before a floor-length tapestry that pictured a group of ancient Romans reclining at a banquet table. The corridor had come to an end. There was nowhere else to run.

Hoping she didn't have a weapon hidden in her gown, I advanced by inches. I didn't share the cardinal's belief that his mother had killed Gemma, but I hadn't forgotten that she had been ready to do violence to Guido over a lemon ice. As my pulse pounded, the marchesa raised the edge of the tapestry as if she meant to hide herself behind it. She then astonished me by disappearing into what appeared to be solid wall.

I jerked the fabric aside to see a section of wall cocked inward at an acute angle.

"Hurry," she cried as she descended into darkness. "I need your light."

She led me down a hidden staircase, similar to the one that started behind the cardinal's priedieu. No amount of cajoling would convince the marchesa to return to her room, so there was nothing to do but keep on her heels. When I judged that we had reached the first level, the staircase dumped us at a door which opened into the back of yet another tapestry. I took the lead. Slinking between the fabric and the wall, I emerged into the villa's huge dining hall.

The marchesa sped toward the unlit fireplace, but I paused to examine the tapestry. Its faded threads depicted some unfortunate Sabine women being dragged down an ancient staircase in the infamous Roman attack. I was beginning to see a pattern: a passage behind the banqueting tapestry led to the dining hall, this one provided an alternate route upstairs. The close-fitting doors could be opened with the flick of a simple thumb latch. How clever the Renaissance architect had been; the untrained eye would never have spotted the unaccounted for space between the walls.

I turned and held my candle aloft. The tiny panes that made up the French doors in the opposite wall twinkled in my light. Beyond the glass, all was black. I took a few steps toward the marble mantelpiece where the marchesa grunted and groaned, rendered wordless by frustration.

Using the soft, firm tones that seemed to work so well for the cardinal, I said, "It's all right, My Lady. I'll help you. What are you trying to do?"

She beat at the mantel with an open palm.

I gave her shoulder a tentative pat. "Just slow down and think. Tell me what you want."

"The…the…that thing," she finally gasped, pointing to the mantel clock, which was an ormolu elephant carrying an elegant timepiece on its howdah. "A catch…in here." She tapped the footed stand.

We both held our breath as my fingers probed the frets and flutes that supported the elephant. The tick of the clock and the soughing of the wind in the chimney were the only sounds.

"Underneath," she murmured, gradually calming.

"Ah, I have it." By touch, I slid a tiny rod to my right. The elephant swung back, revealing a shallow drawer that harbored a glittering pair of earrings. Emeralds and diamonds, unless I missed my guess.

The marchesa bobbed to her tiptoes and snatched the jewels. She gave them one disgusted glance before throwing them to the floor with a brittle clatter.

"My Lady…?" I asked, thoroughly confused.

Marchesa Fabiani tottered to the dining table and sank down on a heavy oak chair. Shoulders sagging, she sobbed like my two-year-old niece when her brother was teasing her. "It's not there," she wailed. "I'll never find it."

"What, My Lady? What are you looking for?"

Wiping her nose with her trailing sleeve, she gulped and answered, "His portrait—a small one—the only one I have."

"Whose portrait?"

A sly smile spread across her lips as she removed the heavy, crested ring that seemed to enjoy permanent residence on her forefinger. Showing none of the difficulties that she'd had with the clock, she gave the ring a series of twists, and the pearl-rimmed crest popped up to reveal a painted miniature.

"A lover's eye!" I exclaimed, after she'd handed it to me.

She nodded appreciatively.

I bent over the tiny painting and studied it by the candle's wavering glow. It was a fine example of an ingenious token, usually worn as a memento of a distant lover, and popular because it preserved the lover's identity. Instead of picturing the full face, the miniature represented only one eye with its brow and part of a nose. The marchesa's token showed a glittering dark brown eye topped by a shaggy brow.

"I take it you are searching for the full portrait of this man."

She nodded, stretching her hand toward the ring. "The artist painted that while he was doing the portrait."

I snapped the cover shut, stroked her blue-veined finger, and gently replaced the ring. She raised it to her lips and squeezed her eyes shut.

"Who is he, My Lady?" I asked softly.

"Lorenzo's father." She opened her eyes. Unshed tears made them sparkle like a young woman's. "I wrote a note on the back of the portrait, then I put it somewhere for safekeeping…" Her voice cracked and the tears spilled down her cheeks.

"A note, My Lady?"

She pounded her forehead with the heel of her hand. "I forget, you see, and I mustn't ever forget him. He was the love of my life. I wrote both our names and Lorenzo's right on the canvas—as a sort of secret family history—then I signed it. I'll always be able to recognize my own signature, won't I?"

I sighed as she gripped my arm and gave it a little shake. A screech made us both turn our heads toward the arched entry-way.

"Thank the Holy Virgin." Matilda ran into our illuminated circle, closely followed by Guido. "My Lady, we've been looking everywhere."

The marchesa dipped her chin and shrank in on herself like a leaf withered and curled at summer's end. As Matilda tried to rouse her, I backed into the shadows and quietly replaced the elephant on its base. Scooping the earrings from the floor, I stepped back into the light and said, "I heard Marchesa Fabiani running through the hallway and followed her. I've been trying to persuade her to go back to bed." I rattled the earrings in my fist. "She was clutching these."

The strain on Matilda's face eased a bit. "Oh, thank you, Signore. His Eminence has been bothering her to death about losing these earrings."

"Perhaps they should be locked up."

"Yes, Signore, it's just that my lady does so like to play with her jewels. It keeps her amused when nothing else will. The cardinal would hate to take them from her." The maid had raised her charge to her feet. "Can you help me get her upstairs, Guido? She's as limp as a dead trout."

The footman hastened forward. "Of course. That is...will you be requiring anything, Signore?"

"No," I replied, stretching my arms and opening my mouth in a great yawn. "I'm practically falling asleep on my feet. You go with Matilda and I'll see myself to bed."

And so I did, pausing only a moment to take careful note of the tapestries in the entry hall and muse a bit about the color of Pope Clement's eyes.

My dreams should have been filled with speeding carts driven by draymen in blue caps or perhaps hospital wards filled with mangled bodies. Instead, my restless sleep ferried me back to a childhood terror.

Alessandro and I were swimming off the Lido. The undulating blue of the Adriatic stretched to the horizon before us as the light surf lapped a sloshing cadence on the seashore behind. I followed my brother's naked white back, both of us diving and splashing in the sun-glistened water, reveling in our temporary escape from schoolroom lessons.

On that warm carefree day, I had yet to face the knife that would seal my life's fate. Mama and Papa were still alive. They had spread a cloth on the soft sand and were enjoying a meal from a covered basket. Every few minutes Mama would rise, shake the sand from her skirts, and shade her eyes to locate Annetta. As befitting a girl, our sister had to content herself with skipping along the shore instead of stripping to her drawers and taking the delicious plunge into the sea.

Mama spared only a quick wave for her sons in the water. After all, Alessandro and I had been raised on a canal-laced island floating in the middle of a broad lagoon. If we had learned nothing else, we boys of Venice should be able to take care of ourselves in the water. We were bathing in lazy delight, floating on our backs, filling our mouths with salty water and competing to see who could spew the tallest spray. Then the sea monster slithered its tentacles around my leg.

In my dream, the shallow blue water turned into a churning, black abyss. I sucked in a burning lungful of brine as the creature pulled me under. Desperate for air, I twisted and thrashed. A horrible roar emerged from a gaping mouth filled with teeth as sharp as sabers. I struggled mightily, but the more energy I expended, the more tightly I was caught.

Alessandro was my savior. In the capricious realm of the dream, where earthly clocks hold no sway, my brother was suddenly a full-grown man, the bearded seaman that had run afoul of the customs officer only a few weeks ago. Using the stiletto that never left his person, he sliced through the monster's suckered tentacles and delivered me to light and air.

I woke covered in sweat with my heart pumping. Lighting my candle with shaky hands, I reminded myself of the reality of the event. I had become tangled in a dense clump of seagrass, and my ten-year-old brother had used his hands to free me and drag me back to the beach. Mama had nearly hugged the breath out of both of us before extracting a solemn promise: Alessandro and I would always watch out for each other, never hesitating to render aid if one of us found the other in danger.

Throwing the covers back, I moved to sit on the edge of the bed. A slit of gray between the window drapes heralded the start of a new day. Play for time, Alessandro had ordered. That was all very well. But should his advice hold true if someone I loved was brutally attacked? If a magistrate was breathing down my neck? And what would Mama say if she could look down from heaven and see me diddling precious time away while Alessandro waited in a jail cell for we knew not what?

My dream burdened my waking thoughts, creating a malaise that made it easier to put my plan for the day into action. At the end of his midnight shift as porter, Guido came to tend my fire. Forcing my voice into a gravelly whisper, I told the footman that my tonsils were inflamed and that I required only some hot soup, a pot of tea from Benito's private stock, and complete rest until tomorrow at the earliest.

Unfortunately, it was Sunday and Cardinal Montorio would expect me to attend him at the Palazzo Venezia. I wrote a hurried note that I prayed would suffice. Explaining my condition, I stressed that any exposure to the cold outside air could be ruinous to my throat. Guido promised to see to the delivery of my note and inform Rossobelli of my indisposition before he went off duty.

I dreaded the long day in my room, but with all I had to think about, it passed more quickly than I had foreseen. First, I checked the lockbox in my trunk to make sure I had enough funds to keep my promise to Sister Regina. I was relieved to see that my gold would last for several weeks. In the event of Benito's ordeal continuing beyond that, I also opened one of my small satchels that contained a quantity of snuffboxes and other valuable gifts I'd collected in Dresden. It was not as full as I expected. I scratched my head, trying to recall if I had directed Benito to sell any of the baubles before we left Germany. No matter, there was still plenty to keep me going in Rome for quite a while.

Early in the afternoon, I fended off a visit from Rossobelli by pointing to my throat, which I'd wrapped in eucalyptus-soaked flannel, and pretending that I was unable to utter a word. Alone again, I spent several hours playing mournful sonatas on the harpsichord that had been delivered several days earlier. When a solicitous Guido returned with a supper of beef broth and biscuits, I took only a few sips. I whispered that what I really needed was a good night's sleep and instructed him to bank the fire and not disturb me again.

The door had barely clicked shut on Guido's exit before I tore the flannel off my neck and ran to my bed chamber. Vocal flourishes weren't the only tricks I'd learned at the Conservatorio San Remo. A wig stand wearing a nightcap could double for a weary head on a pillow, especially with the cover pulled tight in front. Clothing rolled into a bolster made a convincing body when arranged just so.

Clutching one small candle, I tiptoed down the corridor. Luck was with me. I met no one on my way to the banqueting tapestry in the northwest wing and was soon down the hidden staircase, through the deserted dining room, and out into the night.

Chapter 18

Liya's attic was a cozy haven from the death-cold north wind that still scoured the city. Gussie had arrived before me and hovered over the scaldino with a mischievous smile threatening to break over his studiously solemn countenance.

"This blow may work to our advantage," Liya said. "The more layers of clothing we can wrap you in the better. Stand still—" With a snap, she shook the wrinkles from a flannel petticoat and held it up to my waist. "Perfect. I thought these things of Maddelena's would work."

I took in the skirts tumbling across the bed, the corset of linen and whalebone with its white laces snaking through the dark fabrics. "Oh no. You didn't say anything about this. I'm not setting foot in the Palazzo Pompetti dressed as a woman."

"You must, Tito." She gave me a bemused, impatient look. "The invitation is for myself and another woman. You will be posing as my country friend who's visiting from Monteborgo."

"Why not your *male* friend from the country? And skirts or breeches aside, how is it that they won't recognize me? Prince Pompetti and Lady Mary certainly know my face well enough."

"It's very simple." She folded the petticoat over her arm. "They won't recognize you because everyone wears a mask, and they invited us because the prince's circle is short of women. The rite demands an equal balance of the sexes."

"The rite?"

Gussie's twitching smile erupted into full-blown laughter. "Liya means to take you to a witch's ball, Tito. You're going to howl and cackle and fly up the chimney on your broomsticks."

Throwing the garment aside, Liya rounded on Gussie. "You big oaf, you have no idea what you're talking about. Tonight we celebrate the festival of Lupercus, a holy day for all Diana's followers. This group follows a different tradition than my own, but they're still mystery keepers, and I'll not have you making fun of them."

"Liya, my love." I took her hand and pulled her toward the scaldino. "I want you to sit down and begin at the beginning. How did you wangle an invitation to this…Lupercus celebration?"

She resisted for a moment, then capitulated with a sulky smile. "All right. I suppose you need to know what we're getting into if you're going to play your part without being discovered."

Sinking down on a stool and stirring up the coals in the scaldino, Liya began her tale. "I presented myself to Lady Mary as a seamstress in need of extra work—no untruth in that. My deception began in saying that my friend Gemma had suggested I offer my skills at the Palazzo Pompetti. Lady Mary was kind, but disinclined to take me on—until I dropped the cimaruta that you found outside the pavilion. That made her sit up and take notice."

I shook my head. "That was foolhardy, Liya. For all we know, someone from Pompetti's household may have murdered Gemma."

"Perhaps, Tito, but at any rate, it seemed unlikely that Lady Mary would grab a scarf and strangle me right there in her boudoir. The cimaruta actually produced the opposite effect. She clasped me to her bosom and asked for news of Gemma. She seemed genuinely worried about the girl."

Gussie and I shared a look of concern. "What did you tell her?" I asked.

"Only that no one has seen Gemma since the night of the last full moon—the Wolf Moon." Liya flashed a smile, brief as a falling star. "In the naming of moon cycles, Lady Mary's tradition and mine agree."

Gussie wrinkled his forehead in dismay. "Lady Mary Sysonby embracing witchcraft—it seems impossible."

"Lady Mary is a wonder." Liya tossed her head. "We've met several times, and I find her braver than any woman I've ever known. She has studied the folklore of her homeland and traveled to Germany and Italy learning the languages and ways of ancient peoples." Liya crossed her arms with a sigh. "Somehow, she manages to do exactly as she pleases and yet retain her rank and standing."

Gussie responded to the bitterness that had crept into Liya's tone. "Not somehow, but with money. Lady Mary is the only child of the Earl of Linford, a peer who owns several plantations in the West Indies. Her doting father indulges her vagaries and enthusiasms with a fondness bordering on mania. If she were plain Mary Smith from the hamlet of Linford, her story would be vastly different."

"Do you know her?" I asked.

"Only to look at. When I was at Cambridge, Lady Mary Sysonby was considered quite a catch, though she did have an unfortunate habit of telling fellows exactly what she thought of them. But when she was barely into her twenties, she took it into her head to go to Ireland to explore those heaped-up stones they say are actually Druid temples." He raised his chin, suddenly looking like the very proper English gentleman. "No one wants a wife who finds the past more fascinating than her husband, no matter how many pounds a year she's worth."

"Prince Pompetti may be the exception," I mused. "He seems uncommonly stuck on the past. I wonder how they met?"

Liya raised her eyebrows. "If you two can refrain from interrupting, I'll tell you."

"Beg pardon, I'm sure," Gussie mumbled.

"Yes, please go on," I added.

"In her study of old beliefs, Lady Mary noted that worship of the Great Mother underlies all the later religions that have grown above it. When she heard that clandestine groups of goddess worshipers still existed, she came to Italy to seek them out. Her quest took her to Benevento, a town in the southernmost reaches of the pope's domain. There, she heard tales of Aradia, the Holy Strega, and knew she had found her spiritual destination."

Liya looked from me to Gussie. "I suppose you know nothing of Aradia?"

We shook our heads.

"Some people call her the Beautiful Pilgrim. Four centuries ago, she came to teach the people enslaved on the lands owned by the monasteries and the feudal princes. She revived the old tales of their mother Diana, whose worshipers had been driven into hiding by the Christian usurpers. With a small band of followers, Aradia traveled the length and breadth of Italy, taking pity on the poor and instructing them in the magic arts. She taught peasants worked to death in the fields and starved by the tithes demanded by the priests and abbots. She came to my people, the Jews, and to the Gypsies, also. To all who would listen, she gave Diana's gifts—the power to bless or curse, to converse with spirits, to divine the future, to attract love and bend fortune to your will."

Liya paused, so I felt safe in asking a question. "Surely the Church had something to say about this?"

"Of course, when have Christians ever tolerated dissenting opinions on matters of faith? With the bishops nipping at her heels, Aradia was forced to leave Italy and travel east, but she left a great legacy. The Old Religion had reclaimed its own and wouldn't be put down by the burnings and torture to come. Aradia's teachings spread to all levels of society, where they have remained to this day—you might be surprised to learn exactly where."

She tilted her head with a satisfied smile. "Naturally, worship of Diana thrives in the forests and isolated valleys and mountain villages, but it also flourishes right under the pope's nose. That's where Prince Pompetti comes in. He leads a cult of Roman nobles who trace their ancestry back to the earliest people—the people who lived as one with the land so long ago that time wasn't even measured. They call themselves the Academy of Italia and seek to emulate the pure ideals of their ancient ancestors in all things, even religion. When Aurelio Pompetti encountered Mary Sysonby on one of his antiquarian jaunts to Benevento, it was a match made in heaven. They returned to Rome and were soon holding private worship services on full moon nights."

Gussie was scratching his head. "I don't understand. If Pompetti and his lady are secret pagans, why has he set himself up as the champion of Cardinal Di Noce? Why does the prince meddle in Christian politics at all?"

"Perhaps it's all a cover," I said. "They don't burn heretics any more, but I'm sure the punishment could be severe, even for someone of the prince's stature." I looked to Liya, who had lived in Rome long enough to know.

"His lands and possessions could be confiscated," she said. "At the very least, he would be thrown into the prison at the Castel Sant'Angelo. It is certainly to Prince Pompetti's benefit to keep the appearance of being a good Catholic. Still…" Liya paused and stared into the coals of the scaldino as if searching for inspiration. "I sense there's something more that we don't know."

"Gemma was killed on the night of the full moon," I observed.

Gussie clapped his hands on his knees. "But tonight's moon isn't full. It's past the final quarter, almost new. Why is the prince hosting a celebration now?"

"The festival of Lupercus is a *treguenda*, a fertility rite that is celebrated around this time every year, no matter what the phase of the moon." Liya stood and pushed up her sleeves. "It's time to go to work, Tito. We'll have to hurry if we're going to get you ready in time."

She held out one hand. "Breeches and shirt, please."

I don't like to ponder the details: the padding strapped to my naked chest, the shift of fine cambric that went over it. The corset that Gussie laced so tightly I could barely breathe. The panniers that fell from a belt affixed to my waist to give me the hips of a peasant matron who had borne a hovel full of children. The worst was the wig Liya had borrowed from the theater. It was fashioned of frowsy gray hair and topped with a kerchief of rough linen.

"Why do I have to be an old woman?" I asked, thinking I might have made a rather attractive young woman if only Liya had provided the proper clothing.

"People will take less notice of you. Nobody pays much attention to women past their prime. Also, it will give you a reason to stoop. You're very tall for a woman, you know."

The next step was employing greasepaint to give my face the semblance of age. Liya directed Gussie to hold a lamp over my head as I sat at her dressing table. After studying the intense highlights and shadows created by its descending rays, she reached into a tin make-up box, also from the Argentina.

"Close your eyes," she murmured.

I complied and felt the drag of the grease sticks against my skin, followed by the caress of her thumb as she blended the colors over my cheekbones, along my jaw line, and down each side of my nose.

Out of the corner of my mouth, I asked, "Were you able to speak to Tucci today?"

"Yes," Liya answered. "He was hanging around as usual, complaining because you hadn't sent the letter you promised. I set him straight."

It was as I'd feared. My letters were in the hands of the mysterious man who had jumped off the back of the drayman's cart to rifle Benito's pockets. When Liya instructed me to frown for all I was worth, the expression came naturally.

Wielding a pointed brush loaded with blue gray, Liya enhanced my natural wrinkles with a delicate hand. Finally, she handed me a mirror.

"You'll do," she said. "Especially if you pretend to be shy and keep in the background." With a sigh, she added, "Benito could have done a better job. He would have added bushy eyebrows and a nice wart sprouting from your nose."

I nodded, pleased with her efforts but weighed down by the memory of Benito so small and still under his bandages. The one drawback of my plan to escape the villa for the night was that I'd not been able to get to the hospital. What if Sister Regina decided I had reneged on our bargain?

"Gussie?" I asked.

My friend had set his lamp down and was gazing at me open-mouthed. He shook his head like a wet dog, then replied, "Sorry, Tito. I've seen you as a soldier, a slave, an Egyptian pharaoh, the king of Crete, even Apollo, but I've never seen you like this."

"If we are to find Gemma's killer, we all have our parts to play." With a rueful grimace, I shook out my skirts and crossed the floor, attempting a bent, limping gait. "I have a job for you, if you will."

"Whatever you wish."

"Go to the Consolazione and see how Benito is faring. The hour is late for a visit, but some silver should gain your admittance. If the nuns are doing as they promised, give this gold piece to Father Giancarlo." I reached for my waistcoat which held my purse. "And if there's anything you can do to make him more comfortable..." The helpless tone of my voice seemed to waver in the close air of Liya's attic chamber.

Gussie's big fist closed around the coin as his other hand squeezed my shoulder. "Don't worry, Tito. You are no longer alone—your friends are here and everything that can be done will be done."

Nodding, Liya looked up from extinguishing the scaldino. Its dying embers lit the planes of her face with a reddish glow and lent her beauty a wild, demonic edge, as if the coals in the pot had been borrowed from the Devil's own bonfires.

⊙πχ℗

The midwinter night, blue black and clear, displayed an array of stars scoured to peak brilliance by the biting wind. Liya supplied me with a heavy cloak and a muff folded around a flat stone that had been warmed in the oven. Neither prevented my feet from turning to blocks of ice by the time we reached the Palazzo Pompetti.

For most gatherings, the forecourt of such a handsome palazzo would have been lit by torches and bustling with carriages and footmen, but Pompetti's pagan celebrations clearly took a different tack. Not a soul was stirring, and the arched windows that punctuated the marble façade were dark. A casual passerby might think that Pompetti and his household were visiting the country.

Liya went straight to a side gate bearing a shield ornamented with a frog wearing a royal crown. The gate's hinges had been well-oiled; nary a squeak sounded as we passed through. I followed her billowing cloak across the gravel-strewn drive. She stopped at a secluded doorway and donned a stiff satin mask that covered the upper part of her face. She handed a similar mask to me. I hesitated, fumbling with its ties to cover my indecision. What was I doing? Just weeks ago, I had been secure in the world of the opera house that I knew so well, and now I was disguised as a peasant woman, about to throw myself into…what had Liya called it, a fertility rite?

A few more moments and I might have backed out, but Liya gave my hand a quick squeeze and knocked on the door—three quick raps, then two slow. We were admitted by a man in a full mask whose identity was further shrouded by a hooded, wine red cloak. We traded our outdoor cloaks for similar garb and were directed toward the great hall.

The scene was not as alien as I had supposed. In fact, it felt very like the celebration of the blood miracle of San Gennaro that I had witnessed during my conservatorio days in Naples. In that centuries-old ritual, a silver bust of the saint that contained an ampoule of his blood was conveyed to the cathedral in a grand procession. In growing waves of ecstasy, the faithful prayed for the blood to liquefy so that Naples would be blessed with a year of good fortune. If the blood should remain solid, the pest, an earthquake, or some other catastrophe was sure to befall the city. The wild rejoicing that followed the miracle of liquefaction and the fervor of the believers pushing forward to kiss the holy ampoule had been a sight to see. Now that I thought of it, I seemed to recall that the miracle-working San Gennaro had been a bishop of Benevento before his martyrdom. A curious coincidence.

Prince Pompetti's hall was swathed in drapes of dark velvet and dominated by a bronze tripod that supported a brazier as big around as a coach wheel. A steady flame glowed at its center. At least thirty figures in masks and robes identical to ours surrounded it, swaying and chanting in a pleasant blend of soprano and deeper voices. Following Liya's lead, I tucked myself in at the back of the group.

The red robes covered Pompetti's guests from head to toe, but they couldn't disguise the forms beneath. The women stood out by virtue of the fashion of the times which emphasized breasts and hips. Observing closely, I soon noticed something else: shoes. The toes peeking from beneath the robes could tell me as much about their wearers' status as the gold, or lack of it, in their purses. I saw dainty pointed toes of silk brocade, bulging rounds of scuffed leather on thick soles, and many examples of footwear in between. The prince and his lady had gathered quite a collection of followers from all walks of life. A maid like Gemma would have fit in just fine.

The chanting continued for some time; praise of Lupercus was intermingled with specific requests. A woman would beg, "Lord Lupercus quicken my womb," and all would take up the plea, voices rising and falling around the ring until a new request was made. As near as I could tell, this Lupercus was a god of all living, flowering things: the special protector of farmers and shepherds as well as a potent fertility symbol.

After a number of worshipers had approached the brazier and passed their cimarute, other amulets, and small animal statues through its flames, someone produced a violin, one of the pocket variety that dance masters employed. The lilting rhythm of a roundelay sounded, and I stumbled as a hairy, ham-fisted paw tugged at my left hand. Another masculine hand with soft, uncalloused palms grasped my right, and the entire circle spun into a whirling, skipping dance that moved clockwise around the fire.

For a moment of panic, I thought I had lost track of Liya but soon spotted her smiling mouth between two taller, gamboling figures. Feeling rather silly and tripping on the hem of my unaccustomed skirts, I tried to skip like a child at play. Once I had the hang of it, the dance was actually rather fun. We spun faster and faster, following the escalating tempo, and at last, the dance became a wild rout. My companions whooped and shrieked over the now discordant fiddle, and the circle broke apart. Red robes spun alone or in pairs to the four corners of the hall. I saw Liya backing into the shadows and moved toward her with a stitch in my side.

"What now?" I whispered once I'd reached her.

"The priest who represents Lupercus should appear at any moment. Be prepared to—" The portentous clang of a gong interrupted, and all eyes turned to the astounding figure who was entering the smoky hall.

The pagan priest was garbed in a flowing orange robe embroidered with gold thread that reflected the flames of the brazier. A wolf mask of terrifying realism covered his entire face and rose to meet a conical headdress painted with squiggles and shapes of foreign symbols. I was surprised to see that he snapped a flagellant's cord every few paces.

Placing my mouth next to Liya's hood, I whispered, "Why does he have a whip? Is someone going to be punished?"

She shook her head. "To invoke Diana's power, the women who want a child will remove their garments and dance again. He'll whip them along to heighten their ecstasy."

At this, my curiosity knew no bounds. I observed the priest closely as he proceeded toward the brazier and measured his height with my eyes. I had not been able to identify any of the red-robed figures as Prince Pompetti and had been on the watch for his arrival. Taking the lead role would match Pompetti's character, but the man in the flame-colored robe was a good three inches shorter than the prince, and though his flock clearly regarded him with awe, his bearing was far from regal.

"Liya," I whispered, drawing her still farther away from the group, "who do you suppose…" I stopped when I backed into something sharp.

Turning, I found the very man I sought. Prince Pompetti had withdrawn his red hood and pushed his mask onto his forehead. His handsome face had turned ugly in the flickering light. His dagger hovered directly over my liver.

Chapter 19

Pompetti jerked Liya's arm. Directing us out of the great hall with wordless jabs of his blade, he herded us both down the corridor to a smaller chamber lined with bookshelves and display cases full of ancient bric-a-brac. Before the fireplace, Lady Mary sprawled in a deep leather armchair, idly flipping through the pages of a ponderous-looking volume. As Pompetti closed and locked the door, she shot me a look that wavered between derision and anger.

"Remove that mask and ridiculous wig," she ordered, laying the book aside.

I slowly complied. She heaved herself up, leaving the chair emblazoned with the red slash of her discarded robe. Coming to stand directly before Liya, she said, "You, too, Signora Pellegrina…if that is your true name. I want to see your face."

Recovering more quickly than I, Liya whipped off her concealing garments. "We can explain, My Lady."

Prince Pompetti crossed the room and deposited the iron key that had locked the door in one of the clay pots arrayed along the mantel. Liya dropped a hurried curtsy in his direction. "We deeply regret distressing Your Highness with this intrusion, but gaining access to the palazzo was…necessary. Much depends on it."

"Yes," I added. "Absolutely necessary or we would never have—"

The prince cut me off with an irritated slice of his hand. "I don't understand why Fabiani sent you. I thought the cardinal and I were in perfect agreement."

Lady Mary shushed him with a whisper. "Let Tito explain, my dear."

I bowed, painfully conscious that the manly gesture and my padded bodice created a laughable contradiction. "Cardinal Fabiani didn't send us. This was all my idea. My friend Liya merely agreed to help. We're…looking for someone. A maid I believe you know well, Lady Mary. Gemma Farussi."

"Now, what possible interest could an emasculated singer have in a lady's maid?" Lady Mary crossed her arms over her damask gown and glanced toward Liya. "I don't suppose for a moment that Gemma is actually a friend of yours."

"No, My Lady," Liya replied softly. "Gemma wasn't my friend. We never even met."

"Wasn't? What do you mean—wasn't?" The clever Englishwoman seized on Liya's use of the past tense. "Has something happened to Gemma?" Lady Mary whirled to face Pompetti. "I told you—I warned you. That sly friend of yours has done something with her." She turned back to me. "What do you know?"

Liya and I traded uneasy glances. Our assault on the Palazzo Pompetti was not going at all as expected. I gulped hard. How much to reveal?

"Out with it." Lady Mary's voice rang out imperiously. Pompetti stepped to her side. Thoughtfully, he tapped his dagger against his cheek. The steel blade gleamed in the firelight.

"I have reason to believe that Gemma is dead—murdered." My words hit the air like leaden weights.

"Are you certain?" Lady Mary asked with a strangled groan. I nodded.

She began to pace, heels clicking on the parquet floor. Pompetti watched her with a pained expression. "Fabiani did away with her," she muttered, talking more to herself than to us. "He could have sent her back to me—or stowed her somewhere away from Rome—but no, that conniving servant of the Christian god decided his interests must be protected at all costs."

She clenched her fists and put her face inches from mine. "Now I understand why you're here. Somehow you discovered our bargain, and you saw any chance of a Venetian pope going straight down the drain. You're nosing around for scandal, heresy, some proof that you can use to disgrace Di Noce and put your precious Stefano Montorio on the throne."

"No," I protested. "I know nothing of any bargain. I'm probably the last person that Cardinal Fabiani would confide his plans to."

"Then why are you here?" Pompetti inquired in a biting tone.

Frustration made me rash. Without thought, I flung back, "To find out if you murdered Gemma."

The back of Lady Mary's hand met my ear with a resounding smack. As I staggered, left ear ringing, she loosed a torrent of English oaths. Thanks to my long association with Gussie, I understood roughly half.

Liya blocked my stumble and pressed her body close to mine. My arm encircled her waist as Lady Mary slowed and switched her rant to Italian.

"We were helping the girl," she said. "Like so many of her countrymen, Gemma knew nothing of her natural heritage. Marvelous relics abound, but she didn't know how to see them. A present-day Roman goes to Santa Maria in Aracoeli and sees a Christian church, but it was once a temple to Juno, and before that a grove sacred to the goddess of the earliest times. Half the churches in Rome have a similar history writ in their very construction—Pan of the Woods carved on pew ends and under the eaves—"

"The Madonna statues by the north door," Liya interrupted, nodding forcefully, but keeping within the small circle of protection that my arm bestowed. "Not all of us are ignorant, you see." For my benefit she added, "To us, the north is a place of power, the source of deep magic. The Christians call the north doors of their churches the Devil's doors. They brick them up, and allow only unbaptized children and suicides to be buried at their thresholds."

206 Beverle Graves Myers

Lady Mary reclaimed her lesson. "In areas where the old traditions are strong, a Madonna by the north door represents the goddess. On many a statue, her secret worshippers have literally kissed the paint off her feet."

"Was introducing Gemma to the Old Religion the only way you were helping her?" I asked.

Lady Mary shook her head with a sorrowful smile. "Unfortunately, Gemma was more interested in charms than the deities that give them power."

"What sort of charms?"

"The sort that all young girls long for. Gemma had a lover who wasn't as attentive as she wished." Lady Mary sighed. "I had almost finished collecting the supplies I needed to make a salve that would make her irresistible to him."

I thought Abate Lenci had been more entranced by Gemma's own person than she realized and that a balm of exotic ingredients would do nothing more than make her skin smell sweet, but Liya was clearly a believer.

"Were you waiting for the new moon to gather orris root?"

"No, I prefer yarrow. Simmered with a bit of her—"

Prince Pompetti broke in with a nod of annoyance toward Liya. "All right, enough—you've convinced me. You are a *strega*, then. Not everything you told Mary was a lie."

"I sacrificed my home and turned my back on my family to follow the old path," Liya replied, proudly raising her chin. "I christened myself with a new name to honor Aradia, the Beautiful Pilgrim."

"What is the name you discarded?" Pompetti asked.

"Del'Vecchio."

He drew near, studying Liya's profile. "Yes, I thought I detected a whiff of Abraham."

Liya stiffened in my embrace. "Do the circumstances of my birth make me unwelcome at the Lupercan rites?"

The prince thought for a moment, then shook his head. "We are all equal in the eyes of the goddess, but that is not the issue. You entered my home under false pretenses. When surrounded by enemies, it is folly to trust outsiders, especially those who might hinder our plans."

He glanced at Lady Mary; a frown formed between his heavy brows. She returned his gaze with a tight, straight-lipped expression. I pulled Liya even closer as the fire crackled in a malevolent dance and the air in the overly warm room seemed to vibrate with tension. Despite Lady Mary's obvious fondness for Gemma, I still wondered if Pompetti didn't have a hand in the girl's death. He had struck a bargain with Cardinal Fabiani—was Gemma's murder part of the transaction? One point stood out clearly: Pompetti was quite capable of ensuring that Liya and I never saw the light of day.

A sharp knock at the door made us all jump.

The door handle rattled. "Aurelio? Mary?" A light, pleasant voice called from the corridor.

"Just a moment," the prince responded, stepping toward the vase that held the key.

Before he could reach it, the lock made a series of clicks, as if the wards were turning at the command of an invisible key. The paneled oak swung back to reveal the priest of Lupercus still sporting the face of a wolf, complete with fur, yellow eyes, and horrific fangs. My heart galloped in my chest, and I sensed Liya's performing the same maneuver.

"Oh, forgive me." The priest removed his conical hat and unfastened the straps that held the heavy mask in place. "I forget what a sight this must be for those who don't understand its meaning." He revealed his face, wreathed in a smile and covered with a sheen of sweat. He continued while mopping it with a darned handkerchief, "I believe you must be one of the initiates, my dear."

Liya nodded, shoulders relaxing at the priest's surprisingly friendly demeanor.

"And you, Tito." His black eyes crinkled at the corners as they looked my female attire up and down. "You're obviously no stranger to disguise."

"That is so," I replied, struggling to reconcile the evidence of my eyes with what I knew of the man before me. I'd seen that smiling face before, felt its radiating goodwill, and noted the profound effect it had on others. The priest of Lupercus was Cardinal Di Noce.

⚭

"I was born in a tiny hamlet outside Benevento." Cardinal Di Noce spoke with an air of serene detachment after he'd bade us all be seated and take our ease. "A lacy membrane covered my head as I was delivered into this world. This caul, and other signs divined by the wise woman who attended my mother, convinced the elders that I was destined for great things. A gift for healing birds with bent wings and other ailing creatures confirmed their early prediction."

He paused to drink from the crystal goblet in his hand. "Please, join me," he invited, gesturing to the tray that Pompetti had fetched from a nearby cabinet.

I reached for a glass and took a sip of the bright yellow liquid. Anise, mint, dandelion, and other unidentifiable flavors exploded on my tongue in rapid succession. Soft yet stimulating, it tasted like the first day of spring had been captured in a bottle.

"Liquore Strega." Di Noce nodded toward the decanter. "Distilled in Benevento and infused with over seventy herbs sown and harvested at the proper seasons of the moon. Wonderful, isn't it?

"Now, where was I? Ah, yes—my boyhood. Carefully sheltered and schooled in the teachings of the Holy Strega, I knew much of the forest but little of the outside world until I reached my twelfth year. Then life took a dramatic turn—Marzetta, the village wise woman, told me the time had come to fulfill my destiny. I took tearful leave of my family, but was secretly anxious to leave the bounds of what I then thought was a very boring, ordinary village. Marzetta and I traveled many miles north to a Christian monastery where I was consigned with the story that I was an orphan in need of a vocation."

He paused, regarding the four of us with raised eyebrows, as if inviting query. Prince Pompetti and Lady Mary displayed the polite but distant expressions of those who had heard this tale many times before.

Never one to miss my cue, I asked, "For what possible purpose?"

Di Noce answered by holding his glass aloft and turning it to catch the firelight. The golden liqueur swirled with reflected flames; amplified with the orange hue of the cardinal's robe, it shone like a goblet of liquid sunlight. "I was to be like one of the herbs in this delightful concoction. Unbeknownst to the good monks, I would infuse the Church with the flavor of the Old Religion."

"The Church wouldn't exist without a dash of the old beliefs mixed in here and there," Liya said with a judicious nod.

"Of course, my dear, you know your history. From the beginning of their ascendancy, the Christian masters accommodated the traditional beliefs to make the new religion seem more palatable. What is the birthday of Jesus the Savior, after all?" He quickly answered his own question. "December twenty-fifth, an arbitrary date chosen to coincide with Saturnalia, the celebration of the winter solstice—the return of the sun and lengthening of days, a sign that winter won't hold the earth in its cold grip forever. You see?"

I scratched my head. "Yes, I understand that. It only makes sense that the new religion would incorporate bits of the old. But centuries later, what influence can one lone pagan have on the vast machinery of the Church?"

Prince Pompetti snorted, then sat forward with a hand on his knee. He gestured with his empty goblet. "You think our friend Di Noce is the only one?"

I shrugged, amazed at the thought of even one pagan infiltrating a Christian institution.

Di Noce favored me with one of his infectious smiles, again raising his glass. "There are many more than the herbs in this cordial. Hundreds more. And have been for centuries."

"How is this possible?" I asked, sure they were toying with me. "Such things could not go on without being discovered."

"Sometimes they are." Di Noce's face fell into a solemn frown. "Have you not heard of the massacre of the Cathars?"

Observing my furrowed brow, he continued, "In the south of France? A Christian sect whose priests favored mountain groves over cathedrals and preached tolerance, peace, and the equality of women?" His voice took on a bitter tone. "Naturally, they had to be stopped. They were burned by the thousands and their lands laid waste by the dread Inquisitor, Simon de Montfort."

I shook my head. Not for the first time, my lack of education shamed me.

"Or the Bogomils of Carpathia?" Pompetti chimed in. "Or King Phillip's suppression of the Knights Templar?"

"No, I'll have to take your word that such things occurred," I responded. "Still, how has a devotee of the Old Religion managed to rise so high in the ranks of a church he despises?"

My question propelled Di Noce out of his chair to hover over mine. Bracing his hands on the arms, he spoke with such vehemence that my cheeks were sprayed with fine drops of spittle. "The people I love—it's the vanity and greed of their masters that I hate."

Lady Mary spoke for the first time since Di Noce had entered the room. "I know what you're asking, Tito, and the answer is simple. The time has come and the chosen one stands before you. The winds of change are blowing and will soon scour the earth. The Freemasons know it and so do we." A flush rose to her cheeks. She produced a fan from a capacious pocket, fluttered it into action, and continued excitedly, "France is a powder keg of discontent. Many expect it will explode within a few years. The people will rise and pull the bloated aristocrats from their palaces and the grasping bishops from their churches."

Pompetti broke in, eyes glittering. "Italy will follow. Our petty dukedoms and principalities will fall like a house of cards. With a pope ready to lead us back to the Golden Age, Italia will reunite and rise again."

I sat thunderstruck—what nonsense they were gabbling—
heresy, revolution, the very destruction of society. I might
have been listening to lunatics raving from behind the bars of
a madhouse. I remembered what Gussie had said about Lady
Mary's father gleaning his wealth from plantations in the West
Indies. How did she reconcile living off the sweat of African
slaves with the ideals she spouted? And Prince Pompetti—if
he desired equality, why didn't he sell his treasures and his fine
palazzo and live as a common man?

These questions and more crowded my mouth, but I bit my
tongue and instead asked, "You spoke of a bargain with Cardinal
Fabiani. Had Gemma alerted him to your…activities?"

A rueful expression crossed Lady Mary's face. "Gemma may
have been sent here as a spy, but she quickly became one of us.
We're not the only ones with secrets, you see. Fabiani has a few
of his own that Gemma was only too pleased to reveal."

"She became your go-between?" I asked.

Pompetti nodded. "We were weaving a pattern of strange alliances, and Gemma acted as the shuttle. It's odd, really. I hate the
behemoth of a church that Lorenzo Fabiani serves, yet I find the
man generous and charming. I don't mind playing his game for
the nonce—if it guarantees that our goals will be attained."

"The papal throne for Cardinal Di Noce," I observed, glancing up at the orange-robed figure who still hovered above me.
Stepping back, he folded his hands under his robe and arranged
his lips into the serene smile of an oriental deity.

Pompetti agreed with a short nod. "It's within our grasp—if
the old man in the Quirinal would just see fit to die."

"And Fabiani plays your game," I mused, "because he values his
luxurious way of life above all else. He believes Cardinal Di Noce
will allow him to retain his position." A position also endangered
by some secret that Gemma had revealed, I reminded myself.

Lady Mary was fanning herself in irritated jerks, darting angry
looks at Pompetti. I addressed her.

"I fancy you don't share His Highness' assessment of Cardinal
Fabiani."

"I don't doubt that Fabiani will keep his part of the bargain," she replied, fanning furiously, "but I'd hardly call it charming to murder a defenseless girl."

Pompetti went red in the face and mumbled, "Cara mia, we mustn't leap to conclusions."

Lady Mary snapped her fan shut. "My deduction is based on sound logic. Gemma's description of our full moon gathering was valuable to your friend Fabiani in one respect—in someone else's hands, it could be employed to ensure a very different result." Shooting me a look, she flipped the fan open again. "Some would use it to see Di Noce disgraced and excommunicated. We know that no one from our circle would have dared harm a girl under our protection. So who is left to benefit from her death?"

Pompetti rose, mouth hardening. "And now two more are privy to our secret."

The air of camaraderie that Di Noce's benevolent disposition had created vanished in an instant. The atmosphere in the room once again grew close and tense. Without thinking, I let my hand stray to the place where I usually kept my dagger only to find the belt that supported the curve-making panniers. I threw Liya a glance that held as much longing as apology.

"I'll not condone violence, Aurelio." Di Noce's black eyes flashed and his voice sliced the air like a saber. In a heartbeat, the mild-mannered priest had changed to a leader capable of commanding an army, or at least one proud Roman aristocrat.

In the end they let us leave, Liya clinging to my arm with trembling fingers. Di Noce and Lady Mary stayed behind, but Pompetti saw us down the long corridor. Just before we reached the door that led to the forecourt and freedom, he ordered me to a halt.

I felt his hot breath as he whispered at my shoulder, "If my plans go awry, I'll know who to blame—and no one, not even the goddess herself, will stop me from killing you in the most painful way I can devise."

Chapter 20

The next morning, I crept into Mass like a man still unsteady from his sickbed. As I expected, Rossobelli pulled me aside the minute that Cardinal Fabiani had recited the Dismissal.

"I hope your voice is returning," the abate said. "His Eminence tossed and turned all night, pining for your sweet songs."

"I'm doing much better," I replied in a carefully modulated croak. "But to speed my full recovery, I intend to consult a physician."

"Oh, my feeble brain. You should have said something. The shame—" Rossobelli pressed the heel of his hand to his forehead. "—that I did not give a thought to calling for a doctor the moment I heard you were ill. I'll send at once—for His Eminence's personal physician."

"No," I answered quickly. "I require a doctor well-versed in vocal ailments. I'm going to the Argentina to inquire who treats the leading singers there. That will be the man to put my throat in order."

Rossobelli offered me the use of a carriage. This time I accepted. I had much to accomplish, yet my excuse of finding a doctor would only stretch so far. Otherwise, I wouldn't have minded walking. The Romans advise that if you don't like the weather you need only wait a few hours. How true. As I climbed into Fabiani's third-best carriage, the sun warmed my back like a day in May, and it was hard to believe that the banks of the Tiber had glistened with ice only the night before.

The doorman at the theater passed me in with a nod of recognition, and I soon found Liya sewing ruffles on a flouncey gown worn by a headless dressmaker's dummy. She greeted me with a kiss, and I held her for a too-brief moment of dizzying delight. There was no time for more. She took me to the empty auditorium where Gaetano Tucci sat with his chin on his walking stick. He looked as mournful as a criminal hearing himself sentenced to the galleys.

"You must have thought I neglected my promise," I began by way of greeting.

He gazed at me through half-closed eyes. "I can't say I was surprised…considering that Cardinal Fabiani warned me of your treachery."

"As Liya surely explained, I did write your letter. It was stolen from my manservant, along with another." I handed him several folded pages. "I've rewritten it, even better than the first. Go on, read it. It's not sealed."

Holding the letter at arm's length, Tucci read silently, then sat up tall, much cheered. "Thank you. It's a generous recommendation. With this, I should have no problem finding a position in Venice." He surprised me by popping out of the seat as if he meant to start his journey that very moment.

"Will you answer one more question about the Villa Fabiani before you set off?" I gave him no chance to refuse, tacking one question onto the heels of another. "If the marchesa wanted to hide something important, where would she put it?"

"Small or large," he asked quickly.

"Medium, I think, but flat."

"Try the kitchen—the larders are her favorite." He turned to go, then paused. Before I knew it, he was hugging my neck, suddenly overflowing with emotion. "I'm going to sing again. My career isn't over, after all."

I patted his back awkwardly. "Venice will love you—your arias will have the gondoliers in tears."

Tucci cracked a huge grin and nearly ran for the door.

I watched him go with more than a hint of envy. Tucci would have an entire opera house luxuriating in ecstatic bliss, while my talents were restricted to playing operatic nanny to one fussy cardinal.

⊙⊙⊙⊙⊙

Despite my longing for the stage, helping a fellow singer regain his confidence improved my mood considerably. I returned to the carriage with a jaunty step. "They have recommended an English specialist of great renown," I rasped to the driver. "On to this address at once."

The carriage clattered through the sunny streets and back over the Tiber. We soon drew up before the lodgings of the famous Dr. Augustus Rumbolt. I found Gussie in banyan and breeches, ostensibly perusing morning journals and nibbling toast, but actually fretting over my excursion to the palazzo.

"Tito," he asked immediately, "what happened? Did you discover anything useful?"

"All will be revealed in time, but just now, we have to hurry." Tugging at his sleeve, I spun him out of the light gown, and pulled a clean shirt over his head. Gussie in turn tucked the tails into his breeches and made quick work of his neckcloth.

"Here," I cried, spotting a black satchel peeking from beneath his bed. "What's in that bag?"

"My supplies. I brought a sketch block and some charcoal and paints in case I found time to do some work."

"Perfect—carry it with you. It looks just like a doctor's."

"Whoa, Tito. I can't keep up with you." Gussie slicked his tousled hair down with water from a basin, leaving off to catch a black ribbon I retrieved from the floor and tossed across the room. "What are we playacting now? Doctors?"

"Only you, for the driver's benefit—just long enough to get across the city." I plucked a somber jacket from a peg, and with Gussie appearing suitably learned and wise, we descended to the street and set out for the Consolazione.

The ride gave me more than enough time to recount the events of the Lupercan celebration. Gussie appeared more startled with each revelation, but agreed to postpone further discussion until after we had visited Benito.

On reaching our destination, I sent our conveyance back to the villa. Gussie and I mounted the steps. Thanks to the genial morning sunshine streaming through high windows, Benito's ward had a more cheerful appearance. Unfortunately, the nauseous smells and painful groans were as unsettling as before.

Benito lay like a wax effigy. His eyelids were sunken and lips cracked, but at least fresh bandages wrapped his head and his arms rested on tightly tucked, clean sheets.

I called his name several times, in increasingly strident tones, but he made no response. I'd barely registered a deep qualm of misgiving when Sister Regina bustled between the screens.

"Oh, it's you," she said, moving to gauge my manservant's temperature with the back of her hand on his brow.

"How his he?"

"Holding his own." Her hand jumped to his cheek, then to his wrist. "He's stronger than he looks."

"Has he spoken?"

The nurse straightened, keeping two fingers on Benito's pulse. Her face was swollen, as if she'd passed the night without sleep, and the borders of her wimple cut into her rounded cheeks. She shook her head. "He rouses a bit when his other friend comes, flutters his eyes and moans, but we've not been able to distinguish any words."

"His other friend would be a footman in sky blue livery?"

"That's right. A stocky fellow, built like a prize fighter. He tries to give orders like he's one of the doctors."

"You're joking."

"Not at all," she assured me gravely. "He asks for a damp cloth, a fresh chamber pot, a cup of tea—as if we would let him try to pour tea down the throat of a head injury."

"Surely Benito has had some sort of sustenance?" Gussie broke in.

"Of course. We've managed to get some broth down him—but then, we're trained to administer fluids without choking him."

I stroked Benito's uninjured arm, willing him to open his eyes and inquire what all the fuss was about. It was several moments before I could force myself back to the business at hand. "How many times has the footman been here?"

"Three. Twice yesterday and once the day before. As you requested, he's not been allowed to be alone with the patient. Nor have any of the other visitors."

"There have been others?"

She nodded her chin toward Gussie. "He came last night."

"Oh, yes. I know about him."

"And the abate who was with you the first day. He's been back once."

Rossobelli—that was a surprise. "What did the abate do while he was here?"

"Tried to roll him about, as if he were merely sleeping and a bit of shaking would wake him." Angry dots of reds sprang to her cheeks. "Of course, I stopped him immediately and ordered him out in no uncertain terms."

"You've done very well, Sister. You're as fierce as a Hyrcanian tiger, but a good deal more attractive."

"Oh—" Her flush deepened and she lowered her gaze. "It's for the children. I don't mind extra work if it will help the little ones."

I stayed a few more minutes, patting Benito's hands and cheeks and murmuring reassurance. Despite my best efforts, he failed to rouse for me as he had for Guido. As a parting gesture, I leaned close and promised that he would be home before the first swallows of spring returned to nest on the Campo dei Polli. No matter what Fate had in store for me, I had resolved to send Benito back to Venice as soon as he was well enough to travel.

As far as the men who ran my dear manservant down, if I managed to find them, they would have as much to fear from me as from Benito's hotheaded Guido. It was unfortunate that the beggar had not noticed the name of a business on the cart.

Countless such carts ply the streets of Rome, and since the driver of this one was not known in the Trastevere, I had no starting point for a search.

⌇

It was barely midday, but I left the hospital in the mood for a bracing glass of wine. Gussie knew just the place.

"If it still exists—" he said, covering the sloped pavement with rapid strides, swinging his black satchel. "—a café where the barman discourages prying eyes and ears, and each man keeps his business to himself. I spent quite a bit of time there when I was visiting Rome in the clutches of my tutor. The old fellow couldn't make the climb."

I soon saw what he meant. The narrow street ascended through brick and stucco caverns filled with lines of laundry and squealing children, then funneled into a staircase that seemed to be an endless flight to nowhere. With an anonymous stone wall on one side and dense vegetation on the other, I was unable to discern which of Rome's many hills we were climbing. By the time we reached a square that contained a small fountain and a few homes with ground floors let out to shops, I was huffing and puffing.

"Ah, there it is." Gussie smiled for the first time that day.

We passed through a smoky, dim interior and stepped onto a sun-flooded terrace. Following a waiter's gesture, we took an empty table by the stone railing. I blinked at the sky of enameled blue, and a springlike breeze ruffled my hair. Before us spread a panorama of brown-tiled roofs, treetops, and square church towers. Between the buildings, the Tiber glinted in short stretches, and in the distance, the white dome of St. Peter's towered over its neighbors, blending into pale ivory clouds.

Caught up in the view, I didn't speak until a glass of Montepulciano was in my hand and Gussie had asked me if last night's confrontation at the Palazzo Pompetti had brought me any closer to identifying Gemma's murderer.

"At least we know the sort of ritual Gemma witnessed on the night of her death," I answered.

"Do you think she realized that Cardinal Di Noce is part of Pompetti's cult?"

"It seems likely. According to Liya, the group doesn't wear masks for their full moon devotions—that ritual is more informal, almost like a party. There's a bit of business around the fire, then they share a meal of cakes and wine, all at the same table, in perfect equality."

"That put Gemma in possession of some damning information."

I nodded, taking a sip of the mellow, ruby wine.

"Then we must take a look at the people who would want to ensure that Gemma would never be able to discredit Di Noce."

I held up a forefinger. "Number one is Abate Rossobelli. He is adamant that the Ancona port project proceed to completion and well understands that Stefano Montorio is as much against it as Cardinal Di Noce is in favor. If Rossobelli knew that Gemma could scuttle Di Noce's chances of winning the election, he would have considered it his civic duty to murder her on the spot."

"Could he have known? Wasn't he the one who discovered her body?"

"So I was led to believe. He said he checked the pavilion while he was hunting the marchesa after a footman had spied her out of her room." My gaze followed a small striped lizard as it crept out from a crack to sun itself on the railing. "I wish I knew more about what had happened in that pavilion before Rossobelli summoned me. I suspect that Gemma met the cardinal there to tell him about Pompetti's gathering. Given the dark garden and open windows, nearly anyone could have overheard her report."

"What about Stefano Montorio? If Di Noce were out of the running, the Venetian would surely be elected. He would be torn away from his beloved experiments and forced into a position he describes as…what did you tell me?"

"His worst nightmare—yes. But Lenci said that he and his uncle left Fabiani's *conversazioni* together. They supped, and then conducted experiments at the Palazzo Venezia until the small hours of the night."

The waiter reappeared and raised his bottle questioningly. Gussie nodded toward our glasses. He held his tongue until the man was well away, then asked, "How far are you willing to trust this young abate? It strikes me that he has divided loyalties. Zio Antonio is determined to have a Montorio pope, while Zio Stefano is just as determined to avoid that fate. Which uncle does Lenci serve?"

"Like any bred in the bone Montorio, he serves himself. He's ready to jump any way that brings him benefit, but I've come to believe that neither he, nor anyone else from outside the villa, killed Gemma."

"Because of the attack on Benito?" Gussie's friendly face darkened.

I nodded. "The Montorio faction would have loved to get their hands on my letters, but there simply wasn't time for Lenci to have arranged to steal them in such a fashion. Benito approached someone in the villa for directions. The sight of him waving those fat letters made someone very nervous—someone with the connections to order a hauler's cart into a wild ride."

"Given the time constraints, the cart must have been making deliveries in the area, maybe even at the villa itself."

I nodded. Gussie brought up a good point. Why hadn't I been keeping an eye out for casks being unloaded at the kitchen entrance?

"That brings us back to Rossobelli," he said. "In keeping Fabiani's affairs in order, he must come in contact with many tradesmen."

I took a long draft of wine and allowed fragments of past conversations and fugitive sensations to form into one definitive thought. "Or Cardinal Fabiani himself," I said, focusing my gaze on the basking lizard. "That's who Lady Mary blames."

"Fabiani? Why?" Gussie ran a hand over his face and shook his head as he continued, "It all grows more and more twisted—worse than the plots of your operas where a god descending from the heavens is the only way to cut through the complications."

"It makes a certain sense. Just listen." I planted my elbows on the table. "Fabiani sent Gemma to spy out the palazzo in the first place—I can just imagine the look of relish on his face when she told him that Di Noce presided over streghe cavorting in Pompetti's ballroom as naked as the day they were born."

Gussie rolled his eyes and looked as if he had heard quite enough.

"No, hear me out. You might expect Fabiani to use Di Noce's secret to run him out of Rome in disgrace, but our clever cardinal is much more devious than that. Fabiani apparently intends to hold Gemma's information over Di Noce's head—he is willing to see the secret pagan voted in as pope as long as Di Noce allows him to continue in the role of Cardinal Padrone."

"You know I'm a come-lately Catholic—I left the religion of my birth for Annetta's sake only. But even for me, this is almost unthinkable. A high-ranking cardinal condoning such a sacrilege? I can't even find the words. What kind of holy man would behave in this fashion?"

"There's no holiness about Fabiani. I've watched him for some time now and concluded that the only code he lives by is his own exquisite taste. Music is his overriding passion, but he also enjoys being the center of fashionable society and never refuses fine food or drink. For him, the Church has been nothing more than a means to an end."

"More dilettante than priest, eh?"

"Exactly."

"But why would he kill Gemma?" Gussie pushed his wineglass aside in frustration. "Wouldn't it make more sense for him to keep her in reserve? As a spur to ensure that Di Noce made good on his promises? Gemma was an eyewitness to the pagan revels."

"I see what you mean. Still, he wouldn't have wanted her to fall into others' hands, and he wouldn't need her if she had supplied other evidence."

"What? Like an affidavit or something of the sort?"

"Perhaps. But I believe Fabiani had another reason for wanting Gemma dead—it's that other secret Lady Mary alluded to.

Gemma told her and Prince Pompetti something about Fabiani that he definitely wouldn't want known."

"Did Lady Mary give you any hint as to what that secret might be?"

"No, but I've come up with my own idea, and I mean to test it out as soon as I can wangle my way into the Quirinal."

The English have a reputation for reticence, but after knowing Gussie as a friend and living with him as my sister's husband, I knew how those banked embers could blaze into a firestorm under the proper provocation. My statement provided the critical spark.

Gussie popped to his feet and slammed both hands on the table. "Alessandro said play for time, not run all over Rome collecting a score of powerful men who want your head."

"Gussie, simmer down." I glanced around. All over the terrace, heads had turned our way. "And sit down. I can assure you…this won't be dangerous…"

Gussie didn't sit, but he did lower his voice. "Last night wasn't supposed to be dangerous either, but the prince and his lady saw right through you."

"That was my fault." I sighed. "I think I caught their attention by dancing a bit too sprightly for an old lady. I'll be much more careful from now on—"

"So you mean to pursue this wild goose chase?" Gussie broke in. "No matter what I advise?"

"I must. Don't you see?"

Shaking his head, Gussie muttered something about pigheaded singers and threw down some coins. He wound his way through the tables and ducked into the dim tavern interior.

"Just listen, Gussie," I continued as I scurried after him. "This part will be easy…and no disguise will be needed…all I have to do is discover the color of Pope Clement's eyes."

But Gussie didn't hear; his angry strides had already taken him outside to the little piazza.

Chapter 21

Cardinal Fabiani fell in with my plan as easily as one might wish. That evening, after I had entertained a small supper party with a few songs delivered at half strength, I asked if it would be possible for me to serenade Pope Clement at the Quirinal.

"He's very ill, Tito," Fabiani replied at first.

I persisted. "Just as music eases Your Eminence to sleep, its charms can lighten almost any burden or suffering. I would consider it the crowning jewel in my career to know that I brought some measure of solace to the Vicar of Christ in his final days."

Fabiani fingered the cleft in his chin. "It's difficult to know what brings His Holiness solace these days—but yes, your singing does move swiftly from ear to heart. I see no reason why you shouldn't serenade him. When will your voice be back to full strength?"

I thought quickly. Time was of the essence, but it wouldn't do to appear overeager. I suggested two days hence, and after a hurried consultation with Abate Rossobelli, the cardinal agreed.

The time passed slowly. The marchesa descended more deeply into her elderly childhood and didn't even dress to leave her room. Both days I presented myself to ask if I could be of service, but Matilda sent me away with a tense shake of her head and an invitation to try again tomorrow.

With more free time at my command, I strolled the garden as often as I dared. From behind the hedges, I kept watch on the back of the villa, but no carts driven by men with blue caps or prominent chins dropped off goods. The deliveries seemed to take place during the morning hours, so I visited the hospital in the afternoons, once in Liya's company. Unfortunately, we saw no change in Benito's condition. I fretted anxiously, wondering how long my manservant could survive in this state.

I also attempted to make amends with Gussie. My brother-in-law proved to be a hard man to catch up with. His landlady told me he'd gone off to paint the Ponte Rotto, a forlorn ruined arch in the middle of the Tiber that was the only standing remnant of the river's first stone span. I followed her directions, but when I reached the broken bridge, Gussie was nowhere to be found.

Wandering the tangle of streets near the river, I finally stumbled onto the latest scene that had caught his fancy. On some granite stairs, Gussie had set up an outdoor studio, box of colors and water jar at his side and block of grainy paper on his lap. Oblivious of the racket in the street, he was sizing up a black cat with a red leather collar who perched atop a disused crate like a specimen of feline royalty.

I squatted beside him, but Gussie didn't acknowledge me. I watched as he swabbed a water-filled brush over the paper and built up the color in rapid, sweeping strokes.

I finally asked, "Since it's a black cat, why don't you use black paint?"

He grunted. "Black makes the painting look flat. For dark colors, it's better to layer the washes—start with raw umber, then go to green, and its complement red. Let the white paper furnish the highlights. See?" His hand never stopped moving, and in the space of a few moments, his two-dimensional cat had taken lifelike shape. A slash of scarlet for the collar was the finishing touch.

"Is this how you've been spending your time?"

"It suits me most admirably—considerably less trying than watching you march straight into trouble."

"I'm doing what I must to get Alessandro out from under that ridiculous smuggling charge."

"Alessandro said—"

"I know what Alessandro said, but how can he judge what I should do? He's locked away. He has no idea what we're up against here."

"We?" Gussie used a charcoal pencil to make a notation in the sketch's upper left-hand corner. He tore the damp page from the block and waved it through the air to dry.

"Are you removing yourself from this enterprise, then?"

"No, merely inquiring who you are including in the *we*."

I resisted a sudden impulse to send his paints flying. "I see what this argument is really about. Why don't you just come out with it—you don't want me involved with Liya."

At my angry tone, the cat made a leap and stalked away with its tale held in a rigid shepherd's crook. Gussie watched it disappear between the legs of passers-by, then began to gather his supplies.

He said, "Your love for her was difficult enough when she lived in the ghetto. A Christian and a Jew—you told me yourself that such unions always end in tragedy. Now she's fled the support of her father and has a bastard child—and taken up pagan ways. How can you countenance that?"

"I hardly know what I believe anymore, Gussie. I'm certainly in no position to criticize Liya's philosophy."

"That's too dignified a word for it. This so-called Academy of Italia or Liya's band of wise women, can't you see that they are nothing more than revolutionaries in disguise? All they want is to upset the existing order of things for their own ends, whatever those might be." He raised his chin and regarded me with unconcealed anguish. "Tito, what can you be thinking?"

I stared at my feet for a moment, then handed him a brush that had rolled down the stairsteps. "I once knew a young Englishman who enraged his very proper family by interrupting his Grand Tour to marry a Venetian girl they were certain would lead him to ruin."

"My situation was quite different."

"How? Your mother and your brother and sisters have no more regard for Annetta than you do for Liya. They have never been to Italy to visit and rarely write."

He shook his head. "It's not the same. You and Liya have problems on both sides."

"Why do you say that? Because I'm a castrato? I thought you'd known me long enough to realize that doesn't mean I'm completely dead below the waist." In the silence that followed I became aware that housewives and loiterers were observing us with interest. Gussie had finished packing his satchel, so I towed him out of earshot and kept walking.

He answered in a low, intense tone. "I have no doubt that you and Liya could arrange that side of things to your mutual satisfaction, but how can you live with any degree of comfort in society? The Church will not allow you to wed. The most Liya can ever be is your acknowledged mistress, gossiped about by every matron from the Piazza San Marco to the Campo dei Polli and not welcome in any decent household."

"There's one possible solution."

"What's that?"

"In the past, several castrati have petitioned the pope for special dispensation to marry."

"Has it been granted?"

"No. In the last case I heard of, the pope sent a courier back advising the poor fellow to have the surgeon finish the job he'd obviously botched."

Gussie's thick eyebrows drew together. After we had walked in silence for a moment, he asked, "So, where's the solution in that?"

"As we're painfully aware, we'll soon have a new pope, one who might take a more sympathetic view."

"I'll accept that possibility, but there's something else that worries me. Liya sent you away before, and I watched you nurse a broken heart for years. How can you be sure she won't do so again?"

"It's different this time—for both of us. I've been convinced of that ever since I laid eyes on her in the market near the Pantheon."

"Are you positive that you're not simply wishing it were so? You overcalculated the depth of her affection before. And have you considered the possibility that you're using romance as a balm to counter the difficult circumstances you face here in Rome?"

"I'm not the callow youth I was when I knew Liya in Venice. I've learned a bit more about women, and I know my own feelings, Gussie."

"Are you willing to put that to the test?"

I nodded, puzzled. What was he talking about?

"We've come to the right place, then."

We had wandered into a busy, asymmetrical square with a hayloft and watering trough, not far from the ruins of the old Forum where market-bound cattle were pastured. Gussie approached an austere medieval church dominated by a square bell tower. A priest sat on a three-legged stool before the portico; which was gated with iron bars. Gussie handed him a few coins.

The priest opened the middle gate with a sly smile. "Watch yourselves, Signori—not many visitors today—he may be getting hungry."

We passed into a deep portico that was paved in stones the color of aged salami. As I waited for my eyes to adjust to the shadowed interior, I asked, "Who's getting hungry?"

My question sounded hollow in the eerie quiet. The lowing of the cattle and the whistles of the drovers on the square had faded. The portico had a dank chill about it, like a rocky overhang rarely touched by sunlight.

Gussie touched my shoulder and jerked his chin toward a low plinth that held an odd sculpture. It was a worn and weathered face of a man chiseled onto a large stone disk. A tangled mane of hair and beard surrounded a countenance frozen at the beginning of a scream. The eyes, widened by fright or astonishment, sported hollowed-out pupils that I could have poked a finger through. The mouth was another dark hole, just the width of a man's palm.

"*La Bocca della Verita*—the Mouth of Truth," Gussie said. "If you tell a lie while your hand is in his mouth, he'll bite it off."

"What a preposterous notion!"

"Is it? Suspicious wives have been bringing their husbands here for hundreds of years." He nodded to the gaping mouth. "Will you humor me?"

"Gussie, you amaze me. I thought you considered yourself the levelheaded one."

He gave a broad-shouldered shrug and again gestured toward the black slit.

More tentatively than I liked to admit, I flattened my hand and inched it over the polished stone until the unyielding lips enveloped my wrist. My fingers disappeared into a cool void, and I shivered, suddenly gripped by irrational doubt and dread.

"Do you love Liya, forever and always?" Gussie's solemn baritone bounced off the walls and ceiling.

My fingers tingled as if I gripped a handful of Alpine snow: forever was a long time. I squeezed my eyelids shut and pictured Liya's exotic beauty, her graceful demeanor, her lively intelligence leavened by tenderness and love. I steeled myself against the judgment of La Bocca. But I knew the truth; I should be able to speak fearlessly.

"Yes," I proclaimed, "no matter what hurdles we may face, a future without Liya would be unlivable." Warmth flooded back into my hand, and no sharp teeth pierced my skin. I jerked away from the stone disk, feeling like an ancient gladiator who had survived the Coliseum.

Gussie shook his head as though despite himself, but he threw his arm around my shoulder and agreed to speak no more against my love. It was as much as I could hope for. My brother-in-law and I left the strange church in an uneasy truce.

❧

The Vatican Hill was the traditional site of the Holy See, but by the sixteenth century, a nearby swamp had given it a reputation for malaria during the warm months. The air of the taller Quirinal Hill in central Rome was deemed more salubrious, and a splendid palace was built there as the pope's summer residence.

Given that its spacious corridors and gilded apartments contrasted so favorably with the dark labyrinth of the Vatican, it took little time for the papal court to take up permanent residence. Cardinal Fabiani conducted me there on a chilly afternoon in early February.

My guide traversed the Quirinal Palace as if it were his personal preserve. In the grand reception hall, a mass of prelates and courtiers had gathered to wait for news of the pope's condition. The mirrored walls amplified their number from hundreds to thousands. To a man, they all suspended their conversations and bowed to Fabiani as we passed. Scanning their faces, I saw craft and guile peeking through masks of respect and concern. Were they calculating how rapidly Fabiani would fall from power once his patron had succumbed to his physical ailments?

At the far end of the hall, a canopied throne exuded a lonely air of disuse. Fabiani paused. "Our pontiff started his reign right here, Tito. On a tide of goodwill. He was expected to govern with caution and good sense, and to restore the pomp and magnificence of the court that his austere Dominican predecessor had all but abolished."

"Did he?" I asked. "Before he became ill?"

"Very much so. Pope Clement's taste has always been of the highest order. He hired the most talented craftsmen to effect repairs both here and at the Vatican. But he didn't stop at artistic beauty. His personal library is one of the finest in Europe—he donated many volumes to the papal library and encouraged the study of literature in the academies and universities."

"Did he also receive top marks for governing?"

Fabiani seemed to squirm beneath his scarlet cassock. "He instituted some very good works."

"Like the Ancona project?"

"That, and others. He widened the Corso and commissioned the construction of the Trevi Fountain that is sure to become one of our city's noted ornaments. He also showed remarkable proficiency at stamping out banditry in the wilder areas of the realm."

Summoning an innocent smile to my mouth and eyes, I asked a question whose answer was known to all of Italy. "Wasn't there some difficulty with the Spanish, though?"

"Pope Clement weathered that little contretemps."

"By making one of the young Spanish princes a cardinal at age seven?" I continued, watching Fabiani's pointed nose sniff the air as if we stood over the royal sewer. "I wonder if his mama will allow the little cardinal to leave his nursery and attend the conclave?"

Fabiani fingered the cross on his chest. His deep-set eyes were not amused. "I thought you came with me to honor His Holiness in song."

I inclined my head. "Your servant, Eminence."

Fabiani escorted me around the back of the throne and down a short hallway. We stopped at a door flanked by Swiss Guards bearing crossed halberds tipped with steel spikes. At a sign from Fabiani, the soldiers rapped their halberds on the floor in perfect unison, then stepped aside with a double-quick march.

A major-domo wearing a white ruff and red uniform conducted us to the bed chamber, announced our names, and immediately withdrew. It was clearly the nuns who ruled here, and by my guess, there wasn't one a year under seventy. Their severe gray habits provided a stark contrast to the magnificence of the surroundings. Precious materials, the heritage of centuries of pious tithes and devotions, shone from every surface and corner. The bed hangings were spun of gold and silver threads. Golden caskets and book covers blinked with a rainbow of rubies, sapphires, and emeralds. Huge, age-darkened paintings of the Crucifixion and the Ascension were framed in gilt inlaid with jet and ivory. But all this I noticed from the corner of my eye. My chief concern was the old man half hidden behind the partially drawn bed curtains.

As Fabiani spoke with a trio of nuns clustered around the brightly burning fireplace, I approached the leader of all Christendom. Pope Clement was clearly on his deathbed. His face was haggard, and his mouth pulled to one side. The sharp bones of his aristocratic nose threatened to break through brittle, translucent skin. With each gurgling breath, his coverlet rose and fell even more shallowly than Benito's. His eyes were closed.

"Not long now," whispered the oldest nun, who had come up behind me with so noiseless a tread that the hem of her habit seemed to hover above the thick rug. She gave me a small push, and I realized that I'd been hanging back, repulsed by the smell of sickness that flowery unguents and incense could not overcome.

"You must sing right over him—right in his ear. We're not sure how much he can hear," she explained. Still I hesitated. "Don't be afraid." She nudged the small of my back. "His Holiness has one foot in heaven. Even now, Our Lord may be tugging on his hand."

I sank to my knees on the prayer stool provided for visitors and did as she commanded. In the clearest tone I could produce, I sang a Monteverdi Adoremus. Fabiani and the other sisters crowded at the foot of the bed. He sighed and whispered, "I told you, the voice of an angel."

They nodded. One of the nuns had tears streaming down her cheeks.

The oldest nun stayed beside me. She took one of Pope Clement's mottled hands in hers, pressing it between her palms as if she could rouse him with her warmth. I willed him to rouse, as well. It was torture hovering right over the man and not being able to uncover the information I needed. Was Pope Clement the brown-eyed model for the lover's eye in the marchesa's ring? The answer lay beneath his shaggy white brows, behind his tissue-thin lids.

As I followed the Adoremus with a Gloria Patri, I became convinced that the man before me was highly unlikely ever to open those lids again. I was already wondering how many people I could quiz about the color of Pope Clement's eyes without provoking suspicion when the door of the bed chamber opened. A maid entered, wheeling a cart packed with steaming pitchers and fluffy towels.

I prolonged one last sweet cadenza. My serenade must soon give way to the papal bath.

The cart clattered over the terrazzo flooring, then quieted as the maid pressed the handles to raise the front wheels onto the carpet.

"*Dio mio*," she cried with a yelp. A metal pitcher clanged and bounced, splashing hot water in a crystal arc.

The nun beside me pivoted and raised her skirts to skitter across the room. The group at the foot of the bed turned to assess the damage.

Fortune would never hand me a better opportunity. Using my thumb in the maneuver I'd seen the doctor perform on Benito, I flicked Pope Clement's eyelids back.

Blue. His eyes swam in a miniature lake of milky rheum, but they were blue. Most definitely blue.

I straightened quickly, hiding a triumphant grin. This was Cardinal Fabiani's secret: the Villa Fabiani was built on sand.

Chapter 22

Once back in the carriage with the team of glossy Arabians clip-clopping down the Quirinal Hill, I sought to introduce the subject of fathers.

"How much longer, do you think?" I began.

Cardinal Fabiani pursed his lips, then shrugged. "Who can say? He's entirely in God's hands, and we can only wait."

"It must be very trying—losing someone who has been a great influence in your life." I maintained a careful, but sympathetic tone. "Especially a father."

"You would know." The cardinal raised an eyebrow. "Your father met a particularly violent end. Just about the time your younger sister disappeared in rather mysterious circumstances, wasn't it?"

"Now where did you hear about that?"

"The retinue of the Papal Nuncio in Venice includes several men whose job consists solely of collecting useful information. I like to know as much about the people who live in my house as possible. Can you blame me?"

"I suppose not." I shrank inside my cloak and turned up the collar. I doubted that the papal spies had more than scratched the surface of my life, but I didn't intend to discuss even a jot of my painful personal history with the cardinal. I turned the conversation back to Pope Clement. "At least it appears that the pope will sink into his last sleep without undue pain."

Fabiani nodded. "It will be a blessing. My father of record, the Marchese Fabiani, was not so fortunate. He was thrown from a horse and lay in the woods in pain for many hours before succumbing."

"I'm sorry to hear it, Your Eminence. When did this tragic event occur?"

"It must be over ten years now…shortly before I moved to Rome."

"With the marchesa?"

He smiled thinly. "Some would have had my mother shut herself away in perpetual mourning, but Olimpia Fabiani wasn't made for disappearing quietly into widow's weeds. I wish you could have known her in her prime, Tito. This terrible rotting of the brain…"

He pressed himself stiffly upright against the leather cushion, eyes on the changing street scene. His tone was distant. "I look at her and see the familiar face, but in her gaze, the woman whose unwavering hand guided me for so many years is simply not there. Mama used to have such courage, such ambition. When we made the move to Rome, Pope Clement had just risen to the throne. She didn't waste a moment setting herself up as a fashionable hostess, meeting the right people, reestablishing relations with the pope. Before I knew it, she had burrowed a path into his inner circle for both of us. Mama is responsible for everything I have today, but because of her despicable condition, she's barely aware of—"

Fabiani quieted abruptly. He stuck his head out the window and called up to the driver, "Stop here."

My attention had been consumed by the cardinal's expression, as unguarded in its emotion as I'd ever seen, so it took me a moment to get my bearings. I was facing the front of the carriage. Looking back, I saw that we had just come through the Porta Settimiana on the way back to the villa. Old Benelli's hut stood on our right. A plain, black carriage waited at its door.

The grooms had jumped down as soon as we rolled to a stop. They bent to unfold the steps, but Fabiani instead ordered them to inquire whose carriage we were looking at.

I strained my ears as the senior groom conferred with the other driver but heard nothing until the man returned to say, "Your Eminence, it is the carriage of Magistrate Sertori."

I felt the hackles rise on the back of my neck. Fabiani appeared no less affected. His eyebrows registered surprise, then shock.

Before the cardinal recovered sufficiently to speak, Sertori himself ducked through the doorway of the mean hut. He took one look at Fabiani's startled face framed by the carriage window and bowed his solid, phlegmatic frame. The curtains of iron gray hair fell forward to cover his face, but I would have wagered my remaining gold pieces that he was smirking.

For half a moment, I thought the cardinal meant to call the magistrate over. Instead he commanded the driver to move on. We jolted up the Via della Lungara in silence. My thoughts tumbled furiously. The cardinal was clenching his jaw like a man with a bad toothache.

Once we'd turned down the lane to the villa, Fabiani said, "Someone has been talking out of turn, Tito."

"Not me, Your Eminence," I replied quickly.

"Of course not." He eyed me with a thoughtful gleam. "Calling Benelli to Sertori's attention would hardly be to your advantage."

"What should we do?" My tongue was so dry, I could barely form the words. I could almost feel the bite of the constables' irons on my wrists.

As the carriage halted at the villa's portico, he replied, "You should do nothing. I'll take care of this."

"But—"

He lifted three fingers, but not in blessing. It was a warning gesture.

"Anything you might do would only make things more difficult, Tito. I can squash Sertori like a maggot at any time I choose. Trust me, my friend."

At that moment, I was hard pressed to think of anyone I trusted less.

⌒〜〜〜◡

"You shouldn't have come. Sertori's constables could pick you up on the street—he could have you beaten until you tell everything you know about Gemma's death." Liya was still shaking over my latest news. She slid her arms under my cloak and hugged me close. My mouth sought hers. The rats making their midnight forage in the passage behind Maddelena's cookshop were treated to the sight of a long, ardent kiss.

"Perhaps that wouldn't be a bad idea." I had disengaged my lips, but kept my hold on her slender waist.

"What?"

"Telling Sertori what I know, I mean—about the night Rossobelli called me to the pavilion to move Gemma's body."

"How would that help?"

"Sertori has found Benelli. He must know that I was the one who summoned the old man and his boat. I could explain that both Rossobelli and Cardinal Fabiani had reasons to kill Gemma, where I barely knew the girl."

She shook her head. "Tito, you're exhausted from serenading that infernal cardinal and sick with worry over Alessandro and Benito. You're not thinking straight."

I was exhausted, but from pondering possibilities, not singing. Rossobelli was never far from my thoughts, but since I'd lifted the pope's eyelids, the knowledge that Cardinal Fabiani was not the man Rome believed him to be towered above all. Fabiani's position rested squarely on the widely held belief that he was Pope Clement's bastard son. Instead, he'd been fathered by the unknown man under the marchesa's ring. Perhaps I'd got it wrong in springing to the conclusion that Gemma died because of what she'd witnessed at the Palazzo Pompetti. Perhaps Gemma had teased the secret of Fabiani's true parentage out of the marchesa's ramblings. What would he have done if she had confronted him, demanding money perhaps? Would the proud cardinal have allowed a serving maid to possess his secret?

I babbled as much to Liya.

She stroked my cheeks. "But Tito, you said his hands weren't scratched. Of the two men you found in the pavilion with poor Gemma, Rossobelli was the one who had claw marks."

"It doesn't signify. Rossobelli could have hurt himself when he fell in the tunnel, and the cardinal must have scores of gloves. I've watched him. Besides his cold weather gloves, he wears a fresh pair of white ones to celebrate every Mass."

She shook her head adamantly. "You mustn't even think of going to Sertori. These petty officials like quick arrests and quicker hangings. Sertori would probably have a secret laugh, taking a member of the Cardinal Padrone's household into custody, but he knows better than to spar with the cardinal himself. Besides, the body is safely on the bottom of the river, and Gemma's spirit has returned to the Great Mother. All these troubles will sort themselves out, you'll see. We'll soon be safe and happy, every one of us. Alessandro, too."

"Liya…" I breathed the scent of her hair, felt the warmth of her body against mine. "How can you possibly believe that?"

"I've seen it."

"In your pot of glowing coals?" I was too tired to muzzle my skepticism.

She wriggled free. A sudden chill came between us.

"Oh, Liya. I didn't come to argue about your convictions or who killed Gemma or what I should do about it or…anything." I cupped her chin in my hand, meeting her irritated gaze with the eyes of longing. "Please, let's just go upstairs."

Her face softened in the moonlight. She leaned close, to kiss me, I hoped, but a scraping sound followed by a soft thump stopped her.

"A cat, after the rats," she whispered. "Let's go inside."

Biting her lip, Liya pulled me through the door and up the stairs to her attic. Little Tito was fast asleep on his cot. She brushed the tumbled curls from his forehead, tucked his favorite rag animal in his arms, and wrapped the covers tight around him. I held the door as she carried the boy to Maddelena's room.

I stood very still, watching Liya's straight back move down the stairs. I hadn't stirred when she returned, sleeves rolled back from bare forearms, white apron covering the front of her blue gown, delicately molded scallops of pink flesh rising from the bodice. This was the moment I'd anticipated for so long. Unfortunately, the memory of little Tito's father came crashing in.

Luca Cavalieri had been a charming, handsome, abundantly virile man. No matter how Liya disparaged him now, I knew that he had once fascinated her. Of course, I had not lacked for amorous adventures. As many of my fellow castrati were well aware, a certain type of woman was drawn by our celebrity and passionate stage performances. I had learned to please these moths to the flame, but the spark of lust they engendered was nothing compared to the burning desire that flooded my loins whenever I embraced Liya. Still, after Luca, could the love of a eunuch possibly be enough for her?

Liya met me with a smile, the flat planes of her cheeks plumped with delight. She took my hand and we entered her room. While I stood nearly paralyzed with doubt, Liya latched the door and moved to a bureau in a shadowy nook. I heard the clink of glass on glass, then a drawer sliding open and shut. She returned bearing two goblets.

Almost in a daze, I sat on the shabby sofa and accepted a glass. "I know what this is." I swirled the golden liquid. "Liquore Strega—the same that Prince Pompetti served."

"Not exactly the same. I'm adding a special ingredient." She placed her clenched fist over my goblet and released a stream of tiny crystals that dissolved on the yellow surface.

"None for you?" I asked, as she wiped her palm on her apron.

She shook her head. "It wouldn't have any effect on me."

"What is it?" I took an experimental sip.

"Don't worry about what it is. Just enjoy. You may find it…energizing."

I rolled the liqueur over my tongue. Competing flavors melted into one warm, sweet swallow.

"Is this more of your magic?" I found myself relaxing back against the cushions.

"Not magic. It's the dried juice of a plant, actually a common plant that can be found in most any hedgerow. It's there for anyone to use, but of course, you must know what you're looking for and how to extract its essence."

"You learned many things in Monteborgo."

She nodded. "One of the elders was an expert herbalist. She taught me what leaves and roots to gather to make everything from fragrant hair wash to medicinal brews."

I stroked the loose curls that fell from a center part to cover Liya's shoulders. "Is that why your hair always smells so lovely?"

She nodded, moving closer. "Black malva to make it shine. Bergamot and lavender for the scent."

As she twisted and curved her back against me, I buried my nose in her raven locks and asked, "Is there no magic, then? Only knowledge that has been forgotten except by a very few?"

She remained silent a moment. We sipped at our glasses until she finally replied, "True magic is rare, but it exists. That's why I'm here…Have you never wondered why I came to Rome? Doesn't it seem like a miraculous coincidence that we met in a city where we have no family or other ties?"

The thought had occurred to me. I just hadn't had the leisure to contemplate it. "Go on," I replied.

"When I traveled to Venice several years ago and found you gone, I took it as a sign that we were not meant to be together. I returned to Monteborgo and tried to forget all about you. But I couldn't. No matter how busy I kept, you were always there. In my waking thoughts and even in my dreams. I decided I must find you, but I didn't know how to go about it. I needed advice. So at the Festa Dell'Ombra, when the veil between the living and the spirit world grows thin, I climbed to a sacred chestnut grove farther up the mountains. There a priestess of Diana lives in solitude and serves as an oracle of the goddess."

"She told you to come to Rome?"

"It's hardly that simple. The ritual of petition is long and arduous, but finally, the priestess agreed to guide my steps."

Liya snuggled against my chest, tilted her head, and whispered her words directly into my ear. "She told me that my future happiness depended on meeting my true love in Rome when the next Holy Strega would seek to turn the new religion inside out. I had no idea what that meant, but now I begin to see."

"Cardinal Di Noce."

She nodded.

"Is that all your sibyl told you?"

"She encouraged me to leave for Rome immediately, but to be patient, as the coming events were of great pith and significance. They would play themselves out according to their own fashion, she said, and were difficult to foresee with respect to time. I followed her advice and have been waiting over a year."

"Did she mention me by name?"

"No."

"What if I'm not the true love she predicted?" I asked the question with a chuckle. Nevertheless, I held my breath in anticipation of her answer.

"Don't tease, Tito. It's always been you—even back in Venice. I was just in too much turmoil to see it."

I kissed her shoulder, then thought of all the wickedness an unescorted woman with a child would find along the road: greedy officials, churlish innkeepers, bands of robbers, and worse. City life would hardly be easier. "How have you managed alone all this time?"

"I'm not alone. Maddelena is from Monteborgo. Her aunt and uncle who still live there accompanied me to Rome and helped me with Tito. Maddelena was glad to give us shelter. But even without them, I would have been all right. Followers of the Old Religion never turn our backs on a fellow devotee, either friend or stranger."

"How do you find each other?"

"We have ways."

"Like the cimaruta?"

"That's one way. There are also certain signs on gates and buildings."

I remembered the crude drawing by Maddelena's door and the figure on Pompetti's gate. With my head lolling on the cushions, I asked, "Would frogs have anything to do with that?" My voice sounded odd, booming and fragile at the same time.

Chuckling, Liya took my empty glass and set it aside. Her face seemed to glow with a radiant light. "How do you feel?" she asked.

I stretched my arms high, surprised at how light yet powerful they felt. I closed my eyes and tried to remember what had happened earlier that day, but the Quirinal Palace and old Benelli's hut seemed as distant and unimportant as a Chinaman tending his field on the other side of the world.

Liya was all that filled my consciousness: the smooth flesh of her shoulders, the curve of her hips, her tiny ankles. Her mouth closed on mine, and a moment later, I was untying her apron and pulling at the laces of her bodice. A musky scent filled my nose. Her soft breasts seemed to spill into my hands. She stopped me then, but only long enough to blow out the candle and pull me toward the bed.

Whether it was the mysterious herb or the magic of two bodies that sought to become one, my love flowed sure and strong. Liya's ardor matched my own, and we surrendered to forces that had been building since we'd met in Venice so long ago.

༄

Hours later, I awoke to a rhythmic shudder that seemed to emanate from the surrounding walls. For the duration of one lurching heartbeat, I forgot where I was. A warm, soft weight lay across my chest, and something was tickling my nose. I inhaled cautiously—bergamot and lavender—and smiled as the memories came flooding back.

Moving gingerly, I eased Liya off my chest and looked up at the window. The barest trace of dawn shone there. The pulsing shudder continued.

"What is it, Tito?" Liya shook her hair back and propped herself up on one elbow.

"I don't know. Listen."

Very near, a series of mournful bongs sounded in *basso profundo*.

"That's the bell from the church on the square," Liya said.

It was answered by a peal of higher pitch.

She drew her knees up under the cover. "That's Santa Cecilia down by the river."

The bells continued to peal, joined by others near and far. It seemed that every minute a hundred more entered the clanging, jangling fray. The din flew through the air above the city, coursed through stone and timber, and shook the very bowels of the earth. I had never heard anything like it.

"Every bell in Rome must be tolling," I said wonderingly.

Liya nodded, then winced as the looking glass above her dressing table trembled and fell with a tinkling crash. Pressing closer, she enfolded me in a ferocious embrace. We clung together, rocking softly back and forth. We both understood. The monstrous clanging was a wordless message, more profound than words could ever be.

Pope Clement was dead.

Part Four

*"Seek thee out some other chase, for I myself
must hunt this deer to death."*

—William Shakespeare

Chapter 23

"Zio Antonio is here. His coach arrived just before dawn." Abate Lenci gave me a sidelong glance as he plucked a dead leaf from a vine in the walled garden of the Palazzo Venezia. We were quite alone; a gardener raking the gravel path had shuffled off at our approach.

"Your uncle traveled at night? Over those mountain roads?"

Lenci raised his boyish face to the tenuous warmth of the midday sun. "He left Venice the instant the news of the pope's death reached San Marco's—in a coach and six that changed horses at short intervals, decked out with extra lamps so the darkness couldn't stop its progress."

I shouldn't have been surprised. Mourners had been pouring into Rome for several days. The natives spent half their time hawking food and souvenirs and the other half cursing the clogged streets. Senator Antonio Montorio had more reason than most to make the journey. Tradition set the opening of the conclave for nine days after a pope's death; six days remained. During that time, the senator would be up to his neck in negotiation with Fabiani and the other cardinals, who would soon be under lock and key in the Vatican.

"I suppose the senator wants to talk to me," I said over the lump in my throat, "since he sent a carriage to fetch me."

"Oh yes. He was quite distressed when Zio Stefano told him you'd been avoiding us."

"What? But I haven't...it's so hard to get away...Fabiani summons me on a whim." I paused, realizing that my voice was rising to a screech. I continued in a more dignified tone, "I've been ill, as well."

"Yes, unfortunate for you." He plucked another withered leaf and crumpled it in his fist. "I hope that Magistrate Sertori hasn't been leaning on you too hard, given your weakened state." He regarded me with eyes that could have been twin spheres of blue ice.

"Lenci, I—"

He grabbed the front of my coat, pulling me off my feet. As I stumbled, he shook me, growling. "You knew. That day on your balcony, before we were interrupted, you were going to tell me that Gemma was dead. Then you thought better of it." I gripped his wrists. His face was inches from mine. "Didn't I deserve to know—the one who loved her above all others?"

I broke his hold. He shoved me hard, his palms flat to my chest. I scrambled for balance, but ended up splayed like a starfish on the gravel path. Wincing, I blinked up at the young man with his arms stiff at his sides. His breath was coming in short gasps. So was mine.

"You have a right to be angry, but will you just listen a moment?" I bent my knees and pushed up on one elbow, tensing in expectation of another outburst. "Please?"

Grimly, he extended a hand. I took it, and he pulled me up.

"My hat," I said, pointing to my tricorne, which now crowned a bare rose bush.

Lenci jerked the hat off the thorns and squashed it into my chest. "Enough stalling. Tell me what you know."

I would rather have kept my own counsel, but it wouldn't do to have Lenci feeling that I'd betrayed him. I didn't need to create an enemy. I had enough of those already. I said, "I don't know how you found out, but yes, Gemma is dead. Rossobelli found her in the little pavilion by the cardinal's garden wall."

The color drained from his cheeks. "How?" he asked gruffly.

"She was strangled with one of the marchesa's scarves."

He inhaled sharply. "The old lady killed her?"

I shook my head. "Someone else used Marchesa Fabiani's scarf as a weapon of convenience."

"Who?"

"That's what I've been trying to discover. But tell me, how did you learn that Gemma was dead?"

"Magistrate Sertori received a note advising him to question a woodsman about Gemma's disappearance, an old retainer of the cardinal who lives on the river."

I twisted my hat brim. "Atto Benelli."

"Yes, Sertori questioned him a few days ago. Benelli kept mum at first, pretending that he was hard of hearing. But Sertori is relentless. He badgered the old man until he finally admitted that he helped a tall, beardless man from the villa dispose of a mysterious bundle in the Tiber." Lenci gulped, wiping sudden tears from his eyes. "A bundle that could only have been my Gemma."

"You've been talking with Sertori, then."

The abate nodded in a quick jerk. "Absolutely. He's the only one trying to get to the bottom of this horrible business. Yesterday, he took Benelli out on a boat to show him where you two dumped Gemma. He intends to drag the river."

Lenci finished with such a dreadful look that I took a step back. I put my hand to the dagger in my waistcoat pocket. I could overlook one grief-stricken outburst, but if the abate attacked me again, he'd be facing a blade. "I didn't hurt Gemma," I said, regarding Lenci with a steadfast gaze.

He nodded stiffly. "If I thought you had, you'd be at the bottom of the Tiber with her."

"And Fabiani coerced me into helping with her shameful burial."

"How? A pistol to your head…or did he threaten to have Rossobelli crush you to death with fawning and flattery?"

"You forget. My brother is being held hostage to the outcome of an election that Cardinal Fabiani will control."

"I could hardly forget—my ears are stuffed with the conclave every minute of the day. Is that why Gemma was killed? Because she allowed Fabiani to draw her into his schemes? Could it have been one of Pompetti's bravos?"

"I don't believe so. Despite knowing that Gemma was spying at Fabiani's behest, Lady Mary had taken a liking to her. She saw promise in the girl and wanted to further her education. She was tutoring her in…ahm…historical matters and such." I gulped at that innocuous version of events, but it would be folly to reveal every card in my hand.

"So what do you believe?"

I looked around. The garden paths were deserted, and the bare bushes provided no cover for spies. Still, the back of my neck crawled as if we were being observed. The windows of the hulking palace were shut tight against the February chill. No human figures were evident, but that didn't mean there weren't eyes peering through a slit in the drapery. I turned down a path that directed us away from the building, then told Lenci about the theft of my letters and my conviction that Gemma's murderer was someone from the Villa Fabiani.

Lenci's brain worked quickly. "That someone wants Sertori to think you killed Gemma."

I nodded gravely. "It would be most instructive to know who sent the note pointing him toward old Benelli."

"I saw it. It was signed 'a concerned citizen.'"

"The paper, the writing itself—do you recall anything about those?"

The gravel crunched beneath our feet. Lenci appeared deep in thought, with chin lowered and hands clasped behind his back. The gears of my own brain were grinding as well. Who had sent that damned note? Fabiani? Rossobelli? The men who attacked Benito? Or some faceless villain that I'd not even considered?

"Well," Lenci finally responded, "the paper didn't carry a letterhead, if that's what you mean."

"Just describe it as best you can."

"It was common notepaper. The words were written in a running hand, no blotches."

"Composed by a person of higher learning?"

"Santa Maria, the questions you ask—I don't know." He rubbed his forehead. "The language wasn't particularly fancy. Actually, it reminded me of those letters written by clerks who set up at markets to read or write for folks who've had no schooling."

As I bit my lip in thought, a footman trotted up to summon us inside. I steeled myself. It was time to face the man who had set me on this fatal path to Rome.

Once through the door, Lenci headed for the main staircase that rose to bifurcate like a T. A delegation headed by a dark man of military bearing descended toward us. The wide skirt of his coat and the crimson sash that girdled his chest told me he was Spanish. Several other soldiers were sprinkled among the cardinals and bishops who made up the bulk of his retinue. They all appeared slyly gratified, like the cat who has wangled an extra saucer of cream from a stingy master.

Lenci turned right at the top of the stairs, but the footman stopped him. "*Scusi*, Signori. You are wanted in Cardinal Montorio's suite."

Leaning close, Lenci covered his mouth and whispered, "Zio Antonio had planned to dazzle you by holding court in the main salon. I wonder what happened?" We mounted the opposite staircase and started down the long corridor to the family wing.

We heard the uproar before we had gone twenty paces. "No, no. Put that down this minute. You vandals—stop—" An agonized wail followed.

"That's Zio Stefano." Lenci broke into a run. I was right on his heels.

At the doorway, we plowed into a footman packing a glass case that hit the floor with a shattering crash. Its contents, a preserved species of fox, broke into several pieces. I kicked the head from under my feet, and it went bouncing along the corridor like a *bocce* ball.

The man ran for a broom; we entered the suite and pressed ourselves against a folding screen painted with Venetian landmarks. Servants were streaming through the open door of Stefano Montorio's workroom, carrying a variety of brass instruments,

250 Beverle Graves Myers

sealed cases, bellows, and oddly shaped glass vessels. The cardinal himself, stumbling on the hem of his scarlet cassock, ran back and forth, emitting squeaks of despair and filling his arms with the treasures that still remained. With expressionless faces, the footmen pried them from his grasp and continued the despoliation of his workroom.

When the apparatus that had shown me the louse was borne away, the cardinal threw himself on a gilded stool with a pitiful moan. He hugged his belly and rocked from one rounded hip to the other. "Antonio, for pity's sake. Leave me my microscope." His fleshy jowls ran with combined tears and sweat. "Just the one instrument, I beg you. Where is the harm?"

Antonio Montorio had been gazing silently out the window. He turned and strode over to his brother. The senator's face was more lined than I remembered, but he was as elegantly attired as before. His traveling clothes had been replaced with a suit of bottle green silk over a flowered waistcoat worked in gold thread. His lace was exquisite.

I realized that I had never seen the two brothers together. Though their features were similar, the contrast was striking. Where the senator displayed an implacable bearing, with flashing eyes and a hard mouth, the cardinal was a blubbering lump of craven flesh who couldn't raise the resources to save his own possessions. I'd been a fool to think that he might have been able to arrange Alessandro's escape.

The senator addressed his brother with the verve of a dramatic orator. "I now see that I should have come to Rome much sooner. People have been talking. There are rumors of impious activities at the Palazzo Venezia—experiments in natural philosophy that dishonor God's work."

The cardinal straightened. "There is nothing impious in studying the laws of the knowable universe."

"Theologians teach otherwise," his brother shot back.

"The church fathers cling to hopelessly outdated theories. When they preach that demons of the air create thunder and lightning, they ignore the evidence of electrical sparks jumping from cloud to cloud. When they speak of miracles effecting—"

"All that isn't worth a soldo." The senator was adamant. "I'm bleeding our family coffers dry to see you elected head of the Church, not president of some chin-wagging scientific society." He stabbed his finger through the air. "You know as well as I do, Venice is on her last legs. Trade has nearly perished for lack of custom, and our neighbors are peddling their treasures from palaces that are crumbling at the foundation. The majority of common citizens exist only by grace of the public dole. A Venetian papacy could turn all that around, send wealth flowing back to our city." He spread his arms wide. "Now, who do you suppose would be first in line to receive that silver and gold?"

The cardinal maintained a sullen silence.

The senator swiveled his head toward Abate Lenci. "Tell me who."

"The house of Montorio, Zio."

"Exactly." The senator turned back to his brother. "And you would risk this so you can muddle about with your toys? It's outright rebellion against your family and your government. I won't allow it. In fact, I absolutely forbid you to read, discuss, or perform any more natural philosophy under this roof."

"You're taking the journals, too? What about my notes?" The cardinal half rose from his seat, stretching a hand toward a footman with a bundle of stained, tattered notebooks under each arm. "Please Antonio, those are written in my own hand, with great labor."

In reply, the senator grabbed one of the books, crossed the room, and threw it in the fire. The thin papers caught flame and curled into ash almost immediately.

Cardinal Montorio sank down and pressed his hands to his mouth. His eyes had widened to tea saucers. A whispery whine escaped his lattice of fingers: "I could be more careful—set up a workroom outside of the palazzo, in a warehouse somewhere— do my experimentations in absolute secrecy."

His brother braced his hands on the firemantel and stared down at the creeping ashes. He shook his head. "Your experimentations are over, Stefano."

"But Antonio—I deserve a tiny place of my own—I do—and no one would be the wiser."

The senator moved to tower over the cardinal. "You are spouting nonsense and you know it. Secrecy doesn't exist in Rome."

I had to raise my eyebrows at that and saw Lenci do the same.

Cardinal Montorio dropped his hands, gripped the edges of his stool, and raised his chin. His eyes narrowed to slits. "You'll be sorry, brother." His voice was husky with rage. "You may have won today, but there are other battles to come."

Senator Montorio snorted. He consulted a watch on a short, heavy chain and seemed to notice me for the first time. Waving a hand, he moved toward the corridor. "Come with me, Tito. I'll take your report elsewhere."

I drew a deep breath and started after him. Lenci followed, but halted when Senator Montorio commanded, "See that your uncle pulls himself together. I'll need him later—in good form and wearing a fresh cassock."

The senator ushered me to a study a few yards away. The room contained a large globe in a bronze stand, a square table, and several comfortable chairs. The senator didn't sit, so neither did I. He paused and traced his finger over the globe's brown continents and blue seas. Was he following one of his company's spice routes? Or contemplating how many of the world's Catholics would come under Stefano's domain if he managed to get the reluctant cardinal elected?

After a long moment, the senator raised his gaze to glower at me. His fingers dove into his embroidered waistcoat and produced a small object which he displayed at arm's length. "Do you see what this is?"

I stepped closer. He held a steel key with a heavy shank and simple looped head. "It seems to be a key, Excellency."

"Not just any key—it opens the lock of your brother's cell. What information do you have to trade for it?"

I sighed. "I have information, but I'm afraid you won't find it pleasing."

"Proceed."

"I've observed Cardinal Fabiani closely, hovering near as he talked with influential guests and sifting every scrap of conversation or unguarded musing for—"

"Yes, yes. I know how you gain your information. What have you found out?"

I attempted to keep my voice steady, but a note of wild desperation crept into my answer. "I'm sorry, but…Cardinal Fabiani intends to throw his votes to Di Noce. I find it highly unlikely that he will change his mind in the next few days."

Montorio studied me, calmly nodding. "That tallies with what others have reported. For some reason, our old friend Lorenzo Fabiani doesn't trust us to keep our bargain."

"At least your spies agree," I said, wondering if I had unknowingly stumbled over any of them and if they had managed to penetrate Pompetti's Academy of Italia.

Continuing to nod absently, the senator turned his attention back to the globe. He gave it a spin and let it whirl beneath his brushing forefinger. His thumb and other fingers enclosed the key to Alessandro's cell in a tight grasp.

I searched the senator's downcast profile. What else could the man want from me? I'd done as he commanded, and every cardinal that was able to make the journey to Rome would soon go into conclave. Yet I sensed that Antonio Montorio wasn't finished with me.

I decided to test that notion. "When will Alessandro be released?" I asked.

He looked up with a sardonic smile. "When Stefano Montorio sits on St. Peter's throne."

I felt as if a mule had just kicked me in the stomach. "What do you mean? I've fulfilled my part of this forced bargain. It's not my fault that Fabiani has decided to back Di Noce. Just having that information should be of value to you."

"We're striking a new bargain." He sent me an exaggerated wink and pocketed the key. "Your brother's cell will open only when my brother gains the papacy. If the Sacred College elects anyone else, Alessandro's case will go to trial. I don't need to remind you of the penalty meted out to salt smugglers."

I looked away, barely able to keep myself from flying at his throat. "That's ridiculous. You expect a musician to bend a cardinal to his will?"

"You have Fabiani's ear. He squires you around the city. You are admitted to his bed chamber at all hours. You share his intimate moments."

I gazed back at him in furious amazement. "If you're suggesting what I think you are, your informants have made a big mistake about Lorenzo Fabiani. And about me."

"I'm not suggesting that you are Fabiani's bedmate, merely that you have more access to him than anyone else in my pay. As you said yourself, there is little time left. The battle is nearing its climax, and I must use every weapon at my disposal."

I remembered the Spaniards I'd seen on the stairs. "Surely I'm a dull blade compared to the others in your arsenal."

"Your brother's peril will serve as a whetstone. With the proper motivation, you may yet find a way…" He shrugged. "And if you don't, Alessandro will die as a martyr to the cause of rebuilding the Republic of Venice."

My jaw clenched. My arms began to tremble. My bowels had turned to water, and I fleetingly wondered if I would lose control of them entirely. "This is unjust." My words came out in a hoarse growl.

Montorio's features arranged themselves into a mask of hypocritical concern. His voice was as sweet and smooth as honey. "My poor Tito. Surely you, of all men, have learned that we cannot expect justice until our souls reach Paradise."

Chapter 24

I charged out of the Palazzo Venezia like a madman, legs pumping and heart pounding. Once I'd left the protection of the compound, a number of street processions slowed me to a more dignified pace. As part of the nine days' mourning for Pope Clement, priests were conducting bands of pilgrims robed as *penitenti* from church to church.

I fell in behind one such band that was waving the banners of Liguria and singing hymns with a painful want of harmony. We had progressed only a few blocks when we halted at a cross street. Edging forward impatiently, I saw the leader arguing with a priest at the head of a Piedmontese procession that bore an effigy of Pope Clement wreathed in flowers and streaming with tinsel and ribbon. Muttered oaths rippled through the crowd. Black-robed pilgrims pressed forward from both sides.

The man next to me said to no one in particular, "By the blood of San Giorgio, we can't let a gang from the Piedmont back us down." His fellows nodded vehemently.

Recognizing the overture to a brawl, I darted back the way we'd come, only to find the next through street blocked by a delegation of Austrian cardinals. As if their endless cortege of carriages and brightly uniformed cavalrymen did not provide sufficient display for us peasants of the pavement, a mounted official with a money sack girt across his chest flung a handful of *quattrini* every few paces. I pressed myself into a doorway as a multitude of hands grabbed for the coins. In that moment of forced inactivity, I realized that I didn't even know where I was rushing to. Antonio Montorio's threat had riled my blood and spurred me to flight, but pounding my heels wouldn't help Alessandro. I must keep my head.

There was a small café across the side street. Slipping through the fringe of the crowd, I went inside, ordered chocolate, and attempted to shut out the hubbub.

The senator had complicated my situation considerably. Several days ago, after Liya and I had wakened to the clamor of the bells, I had hurried back to the Villa Fabiani to search for the portrait of the marchesa's brown-eyed lover. Seeing Magistrate Sertori coming out of old Benelli's hut had shaken me deeply; even without Lenci's information, I knew that the magistrate must suspect me. The painting inscribed with Fabiani's true genealogy could deflect that suspicion from me to Cardinal Fabiani. But first I had to find it.

The news of the pope's death had turned the villa's routine topsy-turvy. No one missed me at Mass because there was none. Cardinal Fabiani had sped to the Quirinal the minute the tolling penetrated the villa's walls. Rossobelli must have gone with him. Clerks with bulging portfolios trotted through the corridors and in and out of the cardinal's study, but the self-effacing secretary was not among them. The old marchesa was the only inhabitant of the villa who sought my company. Unfortunately, her mind had retreated to her childhood and all she could talk about were her playmates and her pets and her dolls.

The villa's confusion, combined with Benito's unfortunate absence, gave me an excuse to visit the kitchens in search of a meal. Signor Tucci had suggested the larder as one of the marchesa's favorite hiding places, but when I entered the low-ceiled warren of rooms where the villa's meals were prepared, I saw the futility of a daytime search.

In three separate kitchens, great fires blazed to bake the day's bread or roast the day's meat. A bit of ferreting around told me each of these areas stored supplies in its own larder. The head cook gave me leave to take a freshly baked leek and mushroom tart from one. I lingered in the fragrant storeroom as long as I dared, lifting bin lids and snaking my arm into onion and potato baskets, but the frequent appearance of maids and kitchen boys made a thorough search impossible.

The café waiter plunked a heavy china mug and plate of rolls onto my table. Startled back to the present, I glanced out the window. The Piedmontese pilgrims seemed to be winning the day. Using their outsized bust of Pope Clement as a shield, they pressed the Ligurians back in an untidy rout. I took a sip of chocolate. It was perfect: thick, bittersweet, and almost hot enough to burn the back of my throat but not quite. I drifted deep into thought.

I had planned to search the kitchens during the deserted night hours, but my efforts were hampered by a series of summons from Cardinal Fabiani. A host of details claimed his every waking minute. He was supervising the construction of Clement's magnificent catafalque, organizing the funeral procession, and deciding how the cardinals would be bedded and fed during their sacred retreat. All this as he was besieged by people seeking favors while he was still in a position to grant them.

The strain told—on both of us. Each night, the bell above my bed jangled as I awaited the hour when I thought the kitchen staff must place the last clean dish in the cupboard, cover the fires, and go off duty. Plodding down the corridor as if my ankles were shackled by a ball and chain, I found the cardinal squirming on his huge bed, scowling from headache and unable to toss off the cares of the day. The first night had required two hours of singing to soothe him to sleep. Last night, closer to three. My frustratingly brief forays to the night kitchens had left me empty-handed.

Now that Antonio Montorio had delivered his brutal ultimatum, I saw that I must redouble my efforts. My search for the painting had started as a way to save myself from arrest, but with a bit of daring, it could turn out to be the miracle that would save Alessandro from the gallows. I pushed my empty cup away and raised my face to the ceiling of the noisy café. From somewhere in God's heaven, I imagined Mama smiling down on me.

༺══༻

Gussie was expecting me to call, and I sorely needed his frank observations. But Benito needed me more. Despite all the gold I'd deposited with Father Giancarlo, I was worried about my manservant's care. The congestion in the streets had invariably led to many accidents, and the victims had stretched the hospital's capacity to the limit. Yesterday, the beds on the men's ward had been squeezed so close that the nuns were forced to turn sideways to move down the aisles. Sister Regina had appeared harried and harassed and barely raised her hand in greeting before being called away.

Today, I found yet more beds spilling into the corridor. Within the crowded ward, my manservant was restless and feverish, as mute as ever. I wrinkled my nose at the smell of human waste hovering around him. Where was Sister Regina? I saw no nuns tending the patients, though many of the poor unfortunates moaned or called out as I passed.

I went out to the corridor. "What's going on?" I asked a fellow in an invalid chair with a bandaged foot propped up on a thick pillow.

He nodded his chin southward. "My fool pack horse stepped on it."

"I mean, where are the nuns?"

"Oh. They're upstairs. Dropped everything when they heard Cardinal Di Noce was in the building. You know, the one they say will be our next pope?" He compressed his lips. "I just hope they don't forget my dinner—it's over an hour late. I don't suppose you…" I was already heading toward the stairs.

In the corridor above, Cardinal Di Noce was just coming out of the children's ward, flanked by two priests who were shielding him from a mob of women. There were women in silk gowns with cameo-chiseled features; crudely rouged women in bodices of tattered satin; pious matrons wrapped in black shawls; and women barely out of girlhood with long plaits hanging to their waists. They were all striving to gain the attention of the cardinal, who looked so fatigued that he could barely take a step.

Sister Regina appeared at my elbow, a little out of breath. As far I was concerned, the desperate women might as well have been a cloud of gnats. It was Benito that mattered. I grasped the nun's shoulders. If she had been a man I would have shaken her. "What are you doing up here? Why have you left Benito in such a state?"

The young nun barely registered a grimace at my brusque behavior. "I was needed. Whenever Cardinal Di Noce comes, it's always the same. Wonderful, but difficult."

I shook my head, puzzled.

"His Eminence has been gifted with the healing touch of Our Lord. He tours the ward placing his hand on first one child and then another. He can ease pain and strengthen breath and bring roses back to pale cheeks."

I understood then. The women clamoring after Di Noce were mothers. Dozens of mothers from every social class, all sharing a single plea: Help my child!

Releasing my grip, I asked, "He doesn't go to all the children?"

"Even such a holy man as Cardinal Di Noce has limits." She nodded gravely. "Somehow he senses which ones will respond. I've seen him try with others until sweat pours from his head and he is near collapse, but…nothing."

Di Noce appeared near collapse now. As Father Giancarlo and several nuns herded the mothers back into the ward, the pale cardinal leaned on the nearest priest. They moved slowly, as if mud sucked at their feet.

I stepped aside to let them pass. I did not intend to speak, but Di Noce paused. His sagging face revived as he noticed me standing with Sister Regina.

"Ah, Tito," he murmured. "Sister tells me that we have you to thank for the new blankets and fresh dressings. You are a selfless man indeed—to think of the children when your own position is fraught with so many demands."

I raised my eyebrows. That was one way of putting it.

"You must feel the distress of the little ones as keenly as I do," he continued.

"I am fond of children, Your Eminence, but don't give me too much credit. If someone I know wasn't a patient here, I probably wouldn't have thought of making donations."

Di Noce gazed at me intently. He wore his humble black cassock, but I couldn't forget his appearance in the fire-kissed robes of the priest of Lupercus. What a strange confluence of events! The entire hospital acknowledged this astonishing man as a sacred hero, as close to sainthood as he was to St. Peter's throne. I was the only one in attendance who knew him for the pagan he was. I bowed stiffly, expecting Di Noce's party to continue down the corridor, but the cardinal stepped away from his companions.

"It is not just someone you know, but someone very dear to you who has been hurt." Though he stopped inches from me, Di Noce's voice was distant and he focused his gaze over my left shoulder. He was still pale, but a peculiar radiance had taken possession of his features.

"That's right," I answered, unable to look away from his shining countenance. My scalp prickled in sudden anticipation. The rustle of Sister Regina's habit told me she was attending closely.

Di Noce placed the tips of his stubby fingers on my chest and closed his eyes. His whisper was a warm breath passing over my face. "Yes, Benito's spirit hovers near. He has been with you every minute since the cart struck his head."

"With me? I don't understand."

"What is not to understand? His body rests while his spirit guides and protects you."

"He's here now?"

Di Noce nodded emphatically, eyes still closed. "He is here, though he will soon be ready to return to his earthly vessel."

Sister Regina inhaled sharply and made the sign of the cross over her apron.

"Then for heaven's sake, ask him who ran him down."

Di Noce cocked his head like a dog who hears a whistle in the distance. Then he whispered, "The name alone is of no use."

"Let me be the judge of that."

Silence.

I batted the cardinal's fingertips away. "You don't know. This is a sham—total foolishness."

His eyes flew open and his face went slack. Once again, Cardinal Di Noce looked like nothing more than a kind, but very tired, man of middle years. Shooting annoyed glances at me, the priests stepped to his side and encircled him in supporting arms.

Before they led him away, Di Noce smiled and said, "Go to Benito, my son. Then talk to me of foolishness."

Simmering with anger, I followed Sister Regina downstairs. The nun immediately clucked her tongue at the filth in Benito's bed and sent me off so she could make him clean.

I spent a quarter hour wandering the hospital corridors and a similar measure of time trying to distract myself with a discarded news-sheet from several days earlier. When I returned, Sister Regina met me with an encouraging smile. "He does seem a bit better," she said.

I pressed my palm to Benito's forehead. His skin was cool and dry. No fever. Behind closed lids, his eyes seemed to roll and twitch. I couldn't explain what I was seeing, but somehow, Benito just seemed to be more *there*. Suddenly, he gave a jerk and a whimper.

"Sister?" I called. "Is he all right?"

She heaved her basket of dirty linen onto one hip and placed her fingers on his wrist. Nodding judiciously, she said, "Benito seems to be coming awake." She admonished me with a glance. "As usual, Cardinal Di Noce knew what he was talking about."

I ignored her look. "Should we get the doctor?" I asked.

"No need. This is a good sign. Besides, all the doctors are in the operating suite." As she slipped through the screens, she added, "Just don't expect too much. After such a serious bump on the head, returning to normal takes time."

Benito whimpered again and fluttered his eyelids. A shudder ran over his small frame.

I sank down on the edge of the bed. Bending at the waist, I pressed my chest and cheek to his. The fragrance of Sister Regina's soap filled my nostrils. If she were stillthere, she would have chided me, but I couldn't help myself. I squeezed Benito tightly and begged him to speak.

The little manservant's chest heaved in a ragged breath. A rattle came from his throat. I turned my head to put my ear to his mouth.

The name sounded softly, brokenly, repeated several times: "Guido."

I straightened. Sighing, I tucked an errant strand of hair back under his bandage. Di Noce might possess mystifying abilities, but his claim that Benito's spirit had been following me around like a transient guardian angel struck me as ridiculous. True or not, it meant little for the future. It was clear where my manservant's heart lay.

⚭

Outside the hospital, thick clouds obscured the late afternoon sun, and a gusty wind sent scraps of straw and paper dancing along the pavement. The scent of rain permeated the air. Despite the looming storm, many people remained out of doors.

A footman approached as I descended the front stairs of the Consolazione. His rust red livery and gray cloak both bore an unusual coat of arms: a pair of frogs, canted, on a shield topped by a spiked crown.

"Signor Amato?" he asked with a brief but respectful bow.

"Yes."

He handed me a note sealed with a scarlet blob of wax. "Prince Pompetti sends his compliments."

I waited until the man was well away before breaking the seal. The thin paper rattled in the breeze as I unfolded it. The message was short and to the point: *Don't forget. I'll be watching you.*

Laughing without mirth, I held the note aloft and let a gust of wind sweep it away. If he wanted to take me on, Prince Pompetti would have to stand in line, right behind Magistrate Sertori and Antonio Montorio.

Chapter 25

I slouched into my room at the villa a half hour later. The lamps were lit, and a freshly ironed shirt and my best brocade jacket lay across the bed. Sounds of rummaging came from the dressing room. Guido.

"What are you looking for in there?" I called wearily, craning my neck around the doorway.

"Oh, Signore, there you are!" Guido slammed one side of the wardrobe shut. His eyes bulged in surprise. "I was searching for a fresh neckcloth. All the ones in the bureau drawer are stained."

"Just make do. This evening, I don't have to be perfectly turned out. It's only a small gathering, and I'm sure they'll be more interested in discussing politics than attending to my music."

"But, Signore, I can't send you down looking tatty and shopworn. There are those who say I'll never make a valet, but I mean to prove them wrong."

Despite all the worries crowding my mind, I raised a chuckle. "So I'm to be your *chef-d'oeuvre?*"

Guido cocked his head suspiciously. "My what?"

"Your masterpiece."

A smile cracked his heavy face. "That's right, Signore."

"Do what you must, then."

I left Guido to his labors, shed my day garments, and poured warm water into a china washbasin, all the while plotting my next move. Cardinal Fabiani would be leaving the villa after the reception. I didn't know his destination, but it couldn't be the opera. As a demonstration of Rome's grief, the theaters had been shut down and would remain so until after the pope's funeral. All that mattered was that the cardinal would be supping elsewhere. After the household staff had been fed, the villa's kitchens would close down for an early night.

I washed and toweled dry, recalling all the places I had searched for the marchesa's portrait and considering the possible hiding places that remained. The list of the latter grew longer and longer. Beneath the towel, my shoulders tensed and my stomach fluttered like it used to before my student performances.

"Here, Signore." Guido took my towel and floated a shirt past my ears.

I stretched my arms through the sleeves, then sought to calm myself by giving him some good news. "Have you seen Benito lately?" I asked. "He's doing much better today. He asked for you."

Guido's fingers trembled as he tied the snow-white neckcloth he had unearthed from the wardrobe. "Really? I haven't been able to get away for several days. With all the visitors, Rossobelli has put the whole staff on double-duty." Guido gave the lace a final tweak and stepped back to gauge the effect. His eyes sought mine as he went on haltingly, "I had almost…given up hope…Benito actually said my name?"

"Yes. Nothing else, though. Sister Regina says we must be patient. He will take a long time to mend."

Guido nodded slowly, face pink and blotchy with emotion. He seemed too overcome to question me further. He must be as enamored as Benito, I thought, struggling to feel magnanimous. After all my manservant had been through, I would hate to see Benito's heart broken.

"Come," I said. "Complete your *masterpiece* so I can get to the music room and look over my scores."

In silence, Guido worked pomade into my hair and brushed it flat. After positioning my wig just so, he reached for the bellows and a box of powder. The open box slipped from his grasp and fell to the floor.

"*Santo cazzo!*" he exclaimed, glaring at the trail of powder. He quickly stepped toward the door and modulated his tone. "A hundred pardons, Signore. I'll go for a dust pan."

"No, Guido." I motioned him back. "I'd rather you left it for now. You can clean up later."

For someone who professed to take his valeting so seriously, Guido finished me off in haste. It was of little import; my plans for the night would soon dismantle his work. After a quick check in the mirror, I dismissed the footman to his other duties and went downstairs to fulfill mine.

⁓

Prince Pompetti was as good as his word. In the music room, after the guests had been seated and wine and biscuits had been dispensed, he clapped his eyes on me and followed my every trill and gesture with unwavering gravity. Lady Mary whispered in his ear, tapped his arm with her closed fan, and at least once, I saw the tip of her satin slipper inch over to kick his ankle. All to naught. His gaze never left my face.

Even the harpsichordist noticed the intense scrutiny. When he handed me my second aria, he whispered, "You've made quite an impression on Pompetti. Looks like he either wants to hire you away from the cardinal or have you flogged for some indiscretion. You haven't been making love to his blond Inglesa, have you?"

I took the score with a withering stare and went on with my serenade. As I had thought, most of the guests were drawn from Rome's aristocratic clans: the Colonna, Orsini, Savelli, and twenty-some others who had been struggling for dominance throughout the centuries. I wondered how many of them also belonged to the Academy of Italia and whether Fabiani knew about the organization that was backing a secret pagan for the pope's throne.

The cardinal himself was all smiles, moving gracefully from group to group, generous in calling for more refreshment. Several times, Rossobelli appeared at the doorway, provoking short silences and uneasy glances from Fabiani. But when the abate gave a subtle shake of his head, the cardinal turned back to his mingling with renewed cheer.

At the conclusion of the reception, I bowed to tepid applause and retired to my room. I anticipated an anxious vigil of several hours, but I did have a few things to attend to. First, I returned my peruke of powdered curls to its stand. After toweling the pomade from my own hair, I gathered the strands into a black ribbon at the nape of my neck. Then I exchanged my formal clothing for a traveling suit of dark blue broadcloth. A flint, my stiletto, and several other useful items found their places in my pockets. I kicked my white stockings and heeled court shoes onto the pile of dirty clothes that lay where I'd left them earlier. Thick socks and dark boots were what I needed. Tonight, I would become a creature of the shadows.

Once I was attired to my satisfaction, my pent-up energy sought release in pacing. On one of the numerous circuits of my bed chamber, I stumbled on the powder box that Guido had dropped. The aspiring valet must have fallen into Rossobelli's clutches and not been allowed to return and tidy up.

I headed for the dressing room. Somewhere I'd seen a whisk broom and dust pan—there, on a shelf above my stacked trunks. I returned to the bed chamber and knelt on the royal-blue carpet. The powder looked just like a spill of flour on the dark surface. Rubbing a pinch of the white substance between my fingers, I realized that I had never wondered where this product I used so frequently actually came from. Perhaps hair powder was nothing more than flour, milled very fine, then mixed with scent and a whitening agent. An errant memory flitted through my mind. Someone else had mentioned something about flour recently— flour spilled all over a floor. I had stored that bit of information at the back of my mind, hoping it would be of value one day.

I shifted my weight to a more comfortable position and cast my mind back to several conversations with Rossobelli. Yes! The broom and pan fell from my hands. I remembered who had spilled flour—and where.

I sprang up to rush to the kitchens but stopped myself at the door. Pressing my forehead and splayed palms against the cool wood, I willed myself to take a few deep breaths. It was not yet time.

∽∽∞

At half past ten, I was hovering in a back corridor on the first floor of the villa. The light was dim, barely illuminating the landing where the kitchen stairs turned a corner. I strained my ears and listened for any signs of activity. All was quiet.

Treading lightly, I scurried down to the landing and, after a pause, to the kitchen level. A wide, red-tiled corridor stretched before me. The servants' dining hall lay on the left. Its entrance was dark. The cook's parlor was on the right, almost to the archway that led into the first kitchen. The parlor doorway cast a thin wedge of light across the tiles.

Hugging the wall, I drew equal to the door, which was open only a few inches. I heard the cook's curt alto melding with another, softer voice. Someone counted in an undertone and made an exclamation of disgust, then the alto cackled and said, "I told you. I took that last trick, so I win."

"So you did, but I'll have my revenge. Deal another hand." Now I recognized the soft voice. The cook and the housekeeper were playing two-hand Tarocchino.

I held my breath, waiting for the unmistakable sound of the shuffle. The cook's gaze would be trained on the cards riffling through her fingers, and the housekeeper's too, making sure her friend kept all the cards on the table. There!

I sprinted for the kitchen on tiptoe and recited a silent prayer of thanks when no cries erupted from the cook's parlor. Most of the vast, low-ceiled kitchen lay in shadow. Beneath an overhanging mantel, the main fireplace was a seething bank of orange pierced with pinpoints of yellow flame and ringed by a moat of gray ashes. Huge copper pans and basins that hung from ceiling hooks reflected the mellow glow. I started when a movement to one side of the fire caught the corner of my eye.

It was one of the kitchen boys, turning over on his pallet, kicking a blanket away. His regular breathing told me he slept like a typical twelve-year-old who had carried fuel and hefted pots all day. A brass band couldn't have awakened him.

From my earlier searches, I knew where the baking supplies were kept. My target was the capacious flour barrel that supplied the raw material for the villa's bread and pastries. When I had questioned Rossobelli about how he found the marchesa on the night of Gemma's murder, the abate said that he had chanced to notice her shawl caught in the larder door and discovered the poor lady in a mess of spilled flour. I only wished that I had remembered the detail of the flour before now.

The larder door wasn't locked, but the dim light from the banked fire didn't penetrate its planks. A handy shelf outside the door supplied a lamp. I considered it a sign of good fortune when I managed to light it on the first try. I set my little flame on a marble slab among some cold tarts and tilted the flour barrel's lid. Using the wooden scoop chained to the rim, I dug down into the cool, soft billows.

Nothing.

I'd have to go deeper, of course. Flour was scooped out many times a day. If the marchesa had buried her treasure near the top, it would have been found already. I noticed several plump sacks piled nearby. The barrel was probably replenished whenever the level sank low enough to accommodate a full sack, thus ensuring that the flour near the bottom had been undisturbed for a long time.

I threw off my coat and pushed up my sleeves and soon discovered that flour is worse than sand for staying where you want it to. Stretching over the rim, barely keeping my nose out of the smooth drifts, I tunneled my fingers along the inside of the oaken staves. Sometimes having a eunuch's long limbs is an advantage. I found what I sought at about the level of my knees: something flat and solid that had no business in a barrel of flour.

A wooden rectangle anchored the stretched canvas. There was no exterior frame. The painting itself was small: about the width of my arm from wrist to elbow and a bit less in height. I tapped it on the side of the barrel to release the clinging flour and cleaned it further with the cuff of my sleeve.

You could call the thing a portrait, I suppose, but its subject was a horse. A magnificent bay stallion with a pulled mane and bobbed tail. The man who clutched the reins seemed to have found his way onto the canvas only to form a pleasing composition.

Holding the painting as close to the lamp as I dared, I examined the man more closely. He was tall, broad-shouldered, and attired as a groom. Dark brown locks escaped his brimmed cap. Just as in the lover's eye hidden in the marchesa's ring, his eyes and prominent brows were also brown. Beneath a pointed nose, his wide mouth appeared about to break into a smile. If I covered the top half of his face with my forefinger, I was staring at Cardinal Fabiani's nose and mouth.

I turned the canvas over and studied the back side. Here the marchesa had noted names and dates so that she would never forget the love of her life. The groom's name was Desio Caporale, but his son, Lorenzo, carried the name of Fabiani. Beneath the genealogy, the marchesa had signed her full name with many loops and flourishes. She had added a date, June 21 of last year.

Another line of writing was squeezed in above the junction of the canvas and the stretcher board. I tilted the painting in the feeble light. This writing was in a different hand than the marchesa's. I squinted and the disconnected block letters suddenly became readable: *On this day, I witnessth—Gemma Farussi.*

I exhaled deeply. This was it. Proof that went far beyond a senile woman's ramblings. Lorenzo Fabiani was the son of a common groom and Gemma Farussi knew it. A word in the right quarter, backed up by the evidence in my hands, and the cardinal would be the laughingstock of Rome. Rude jokes would spring up immediately; dirty songs about him and his mother would circulate round the taverns; journalists would pen bravura essays on the pernicious lies of the Cardinal Padrone; the Fabiani carriage wouldn't be able to navigate the streets without being pelted by rotten fruit. Like a dish of *gelato* left in the summer sun, the proud cardinal's power would melt away to nothing.

I had known Gemma for a short two days before she was killed. Like Gussie at his sketching, I had formed only a bare impression of her character. Her strength and ambition stood out in bold relief, but it was my conversations with Abate Lenci and Lady Mary that added hues and shadings. The maid had been desperately in love with Lenci and determined to wed him. Lacking rank, she needed a great sum of money to tempt him to turn his back on his uncles—much more money than could be gained by serving as Fabiani's eyes and ears in the Pompetti camp.

I had no doubt that Gemma had turned to extortion to raise her dowry. But threatening Lorenzo Fabiani had proved to be a very bad idea.

Clutching the painting, I imagined the cardinal weighing his prospects. The amount of money that would seem like a fortune to Gemma would barely leave a dent in his purse, but allowing an ambitious, determined young woman to walk away with his secret carried a dangerous risk that would follow him forever. What had the cardinal called Gemma: a person of no significance in society or government? I sighed as I stared at the untutored letters of her signature. Cardinal Fabiani had strangled Gemma with no more compunction than swatting a mosquito.

Now what? I intended to use the painting as leverage to induce Cardinal Fabiani to transfer his support from Di Noce to Stefano Montorio, but if I weren't careful, I could end up as dead as Gemma. One thing was certain, it would be folly to confront him with the evidence in hand. I needed to find my own place of concealment, but where? I spent several minutes in furious concentration. My room? The garden pavilion? One of the passages behind the tapestries?

"Idiot!" I gave myself a sharp knock on the forehead. The marchesa had handed me the best hiding place of all. The flour barrel had sheltered the painting for several weeks, at least. Who knows how many times Gemma and the old lady played their desperate game of hide and seek with the painting? But Gemma was gone, and the marchesa's memory no longer extended beyond her childhood. I was the only one who knew.

I must hurry. Digging like a dog burying a bone, I returned the painting to its floury cache. The dusting of white I'd created on the red floor tiles and marble shelves also had to be dealt with. I didn't dare leave any trace of unwarranted interest in the villa's flour stock. By the time I'd cleaned every surface and stowed my rag and broom, it must have been almost midnight.

The cook's parlor door was shut and the servant's staircase deserted. I took those stairs two at a time, intending to wait up for the cardinal and confront him as soon as he came in. When I reached the second floor, I stepped into blackness. The small lamps that usually illuminated the night hallways had been extinguished.

Pausing to let my eyes adjust, I palmed the hilt of my dagger. A stealthy click met my ears. I could just make out a dark figure letting himself out of my room. It wasn't Guido. The footman was much stockier and had no reason to skulk in the shadows.

The figure scuttled away toward the cardinal's suite. I could have stayed where I was, but I was sick to death of secrets. I wanted to know who had been in my room. I launched myself down the hall. The collision with the dark figure sent us both staggering. After wrestling the slight man to the carpet, I found myself astraddle a squirming, whimpering bundle of bones.

"Shut up!" With my left hand, I pinned his jaw askance. With my right, I positioned the blade of my dagger behind his ear. "Who are you and what do you want?"

"Tito! It's me—Rossobelli." The abate made a pitiful squeak. "Thank the good Lord, I've found you in time."

Chapter 26

"You must flee! Now!" Rossobelli whispered frantically as I pushed him into my room and shut the door. "Take what money you'll need to get out of Rome and go. Just go, for God's sake."

I lit a candle and located a decanter of brandy. The abate needed a glass badly. He was trembling, near hysteria.

"Here, calm yourself." I handed him a glass. "Take your—"

"You don't understand," he cried, knocking my hand away, splashing brandy onto my waistcoat. "Sertori is at the front entrance. He's brought constables, Tito. He means to arrest you for Gemma's murder."

I let the brandy soak into my waistcoat unchecked. "He found the body?"

"They brought her up just before the light failed, and he had a warrant drawn up this evening."

"Has Cardinal Fabiani returned?"

"No. He's meeting with the Montorios tonight."

"At the Palazzo Venezia?"

The abate gave a quick nod. "Yes. But…Tito…I don't think you can count on him for help. If it comes down to a choice of giving up you or the marchesa…"

Or himself, I thought, as I swiveled my head at the sound of distant commotion.

Rossobelli stepped to the door and opened it a fraction. "They're inside the villa. I told Guido to make them wait outside, but the constables must have pushed through." He spied my cloak thrown over a chair, grabbed it, and shoved it into my hands. "Come. His Eminence's suite is empty. I'll send you out his private entrance. Do you remember the way through the aqueduct passage?"

I nodded, suppressing a shiver. How could I ever forget?

Darting glances over my shoulder, I followed the abate down the corridor and into the cardinal's bed chamber. With a grunt, he shifted the priedieu with the flickering candles that were kept continuously lit. As he illuminated a lantern from one of their flames, a question rose to my lips.

"Why are you doing this?"

"Doing what?" he asked with a gulp.

"Helping me escape Sertori. I always thought that you considered me more enemy than friend."

Rossobelli clenched his jaw. Fine beads of sweat had formed on his sharp, red cheekbones. He had the look of a man who might be sick at any moment. He handed me the lantern and unhinged the bookcase that concealed the stairway.

"Just go," he said.

"Not until you have told me why."

"Ancona," he answered in a faraway tone, "my boyhood home. The prettiest town on the Adriatic seacoast. My father should be supervising a harbor full of ships, and Ancona's people should be well-fed and comfortable."

"You're warning me away because of the Ancona project?"

"No." He hung his head. "It's because of Ancona that Magistrate Sertori is here. I suggested that he question old Benelli about dumping Gemma's body."

"I see. You're the one who sent the anonymous note."

He writhed miserably. "It was wrong, I admit it. It's just that His Eminence is so taken with you. Before you came to the villa, I felt sure that Di Noce would carry the day and shepherd the Ancona project to conclusion—Prince Pompetti and His Eminence seemed in such perfect sympathy. But then, with a Montorio supporter practically living in the cardinal's pocket…"

"It's the music I make that he admires, not my clumsy attempts at politicking."

"Perhaps, but I was determined to make the most of every opportunity that might benefit Ancona."

"Including my arrest for a murder I didn't commit?"

"It must have been the Devil himself who tempted me. I was weak…and too quick to sin. Can't you see that I'm trying to make reparation?" He opened the bookcase a little wider. "Please, Tito, get out of Rome before Sertori finds you. Once you cross the boundary of the Papal States, you'll be safe. Otherwise…I won't be able to live with myself."

I entered the dark passage, lantern in hand, but paused on the top step. "Did the Devil also give you the idea of sending some ruffians to run Benito down? Was that your first attempt to get me out of the villa?"

Rossobelli's jaw dropped. He appeared horrified. "No, nothing of the sort. Benito met with a tragic accident…did he not?"

"There was a witness who saw the cart run him down deliberately, and you seemed most interested in his condition."

"I was, but only because I felt sorry for the little man. I would never—" Drawing a quick breath, the abate looked over his shoulder. "They're in the corridor. Run, Tito. Godspeed."

The bookcase clicked shut.

I am as fond of my skin as the next man. I cannot claim that I gave no thought to hurrying straight to the kitchens, digging the painting out of the flour, and presenting it to Sertori with my theory about why Fabiani strangled Gemma. But I couldn't desert Alessandro in that cowardly fashion. If our places were reversed, I knew that he would move heaven and earth to save me. Besides, I tended to agree with Liya that Sertori would prefer the quick arrest of a powerless singer to a pitched battle with a prince of the Church.

The aqueduct at the bottom of the stairs was just as narrow, still, and damp as I remembered, but I scuttled through the first section clinging to one firm goal: find Fabiani. At the stone steps that led up to the pavilion, I paused and gathered my cloak tight. It wasn't the chill, but the act of passing over the very route that Rossobelli and I had traversed with Gemma's lifeless body. I pushed forward. The tunnel seemed to stretch for miles. Finally, a draft of fresh air touched my cheeks. Mindful of the bats I had encountered before, I covered the remaining yards to the mouth of the aqueduct in a stumbling crouch.

A rumble of thunder greeted my clumsy exit. Lightning flashed above the hills to the east, its jagged silver threads providing a glimpse of angry clouds swirling against the dark sky. At least the rain had held off. With the help of my lantern, I located the twisting path through the bushes whose tops were whipping to and fro in the wind. Pulling the hood of my cloak well forward, I began the long walk to the Palazzo Venezia.

It was late, I wasn't expected, and my muddy boots and stained waistcoat failed to impress. I had to produce my card and shuffle my feet in the drafty entryway while a footman sailed off with my bit of pasteboard on a silver salver. He soon returned in a dignified version of a trot.

"This way, Signor Amato."

I followed him with my heart in my throat and was announced at the door of the study where Senator Montorio had delivered his ultimatum. I found both Montorio brothers and Cardinal Fabiani seated before a dwindling fire with all indications of having a companionable chat. A tray of fruit and cheese had been set out, along with a decanter of amber liqueur. The globe of the world had been removed to one corner, and the wide writing table was piled with papers.

Antonio Montorio greeted me with a smile. He stepped forward and, for one dizzying moment, I thought he meant to embrace me. "Ah, the wind has blown our nightingale to us," he said. "This is a surprise, Tito, but a welcome one. Cardinal Fabiani has been singing your praises."

Stefano Montorio did not rise. His armchair was slightly removed from the group, and he stared into the fire with shoulders slumped and chin resting heavily on one hand. I knew that pose. I used it whenever I had to play the role of a general whose army had just been decimated.

Across from him, Cardinal Fabiani sat ramrod straight, eyes brilliant and pointed nose twitching in outright curiosity.

The senator continued in an ebullient vein. "The weather is fierce tonight. You must be chilled. Won't you join us in a glass?"

I almost refused, wary of disordering my senses with drink when I had not dined or supped. But I needed a restorative; the fine French Cognac proved to be the very thing. The warmth that spread over my chest emboldened me to ask to speak to Cardinal Fabiani alone.

"Lorenzo?" Senator Montorio questioned his guest with a raised eyebrow.

Cardinal Fabiani nodded. After the senator had roused his brother with a tap on his shoulder, the two Venetians left the room.

"Come near the fire, Tito." Fabiani sat forward and bumped his chair so close that the tips of his satin slippers were nearly in the ashes.

I followed suit.

"Just a precaution," he elaborated. "Even Montorio's practiced spies cannot stand in a flame without getting burned. Now, what do you want?"

"Magistrate Sertori came to the villa with a warrant for my arrest."

He grimaced, casting an eye toward my muddy boots. "It appears that you put the old aqueduct to good use."

I saw no point in reciting the facts of my flight from the villa. Time was of the essence. "Desio Caporale," I said flatly.

"Who?" he inquired smoothly, politician to the hilt.

"Desio Caporale, groom on the Fabiani estate in Tuscany. You know—your father?"

The cardinal opened his mouth, then shut it and pressed himself back into the chair. "Tito, Mama doesn't know what she is saying anymore. Her mind is completely addled. Whatever she told you, you can't believe—"

"She didn't tell me anything," I put in. "And I know that she didn't kill Gemma."

Fabiani's face was covered by a sheen of sweat that glowed in the firelight. "You had better tell me what is on your mind, Tito, and be quick about it."

I let him stew a moment, then commenced. "There exists a certain painting of a bay stallion held by the groom, Desio Caporale. When her mind was clearer, your mother recorded your birth history on the back of the canvas. It was witnessed by her maid Gemma. But then, I'm not telling you anything you don't know."

The cardinal would neither admit nor deny. He regarded me with his lips pressed in a tight line.

"Gemma had ambitions far beyond her station. You paid her to be your spy in the Pompetti household, but she wanted more. In her time with the marchesa, she had managed to discover that Pope Clement was not your father, and she knew where the proof could be found. Gemma asked you for money." My throat faltered. It was getting very hot.

Fabiani wiped his brow with a snow-white handkerchief. He sighed. "Is that what you want? Money?"

"I don't need money. What I need is my brother out of prison, safe and sound. That will only happen when Stefano Montorio is elected to the papacy. I will trade you the painting of Desio Caporale for your unqualified support of the Venetian cause."

Fabiani made a weary gesture. "As you see, Senator Montorio is quite pleased with my promises."

"But you have made the same promises to Prince Pompetti," I replied in a bitter tone.

Fabiani rose and poured Cognac into his heavy-bottomed goblet. He raised the decanter in question, but I shook my head. He returned to lean over the back of his chair with glass in hand.

"That's the way the game is played, Tito. Once we go into conclave, there will be many rounds of balloting, with cardinals switching loyalties right and left. I won't know who I'll deliver my votes for until the last minute."

"I need your solemn word that you will support Stefano Montorio."

He stared at me with something close to admiration. "You're as determined as that sly vixen Gemma."

"So you admit that she tried to extort money from you?"

He nodded. "I met Gemma in the garden pavilion to hear her report on Prince Pompetti's ridiculous revels. Aurelio was once my best friend in Rome, but since that misdirected Englishwoman put him under her spell, his harmless fascination with his ancestors has turned into something that could lead to a great deal of trouble." He glanced down, swirling the Cognac in his glass. "I was digesting Gemma's latest information when the maid started making demands. She was so sure of herself, so resolute. You would have thought that she was a queen and I her servant."

"Of course you couldn't allow that. Did you use the scarf to throw blame on your mother? Or was it just the nearest thing to hand?"

The goblet slipped from his grasp and bounced to the hearth with an explosive crash. We watched in horror as a tongue of fire shot from the smoldering logs to the Cognac. Jerking his scarlet robes around his knees, the cardinal jumped aside. I stomped on the blue flames until my boots had driven them down. By common consent, Cardinal Fabiani and I backed away from the fire until we had reached the globe in the corner.

"I didn't kill Gemma," he said in a fierce whisper. "It was Mama. You know that."

"I know nothing of the sort. I've spent many hours with the marchesa. I don't believe she possesses the strength to strangle Gemma, even in anger. It was you. You are ashamed of your real father and terrified that all Rome would know of your deception."

"Ashamed? Ah, Tito, you are very much mistaken."

"Am I?"

He narrowed his eyes and leaned over the globe. "Do you really have time for this? Shouldn't you be taking a fast coach out of Rome?"

"The painting is safely hidden for now, but if I leave the city tonight, it will eventually be found by…" I shrugged. "Who knows?"

He spun the globe in thought for a moment, then spoke softly. "I could hardly be ashamed of Desio. He first set me on a horse when I was four years old. Over the years, he introduced me to every stream and badger hole on the estate. Those rides with him represent the happiest memories of my life."

"Did you know that he was your father?"

"Not then. Like everyone else, I believed my father to be the Marchese Fabiani, a mean-tempered bully who'd as soon cuff me as look at me. I didn't know the truth until after…"

"After what?"

He stopped the spin of the globe with a smack from his palm. "The history of my family isn't pretty, Tito. Our lands are too low for grapes or timber, the soil too poor to support a rice crop. Over the years, we survived by currying favor at the Medici court. My mother wielded her influence in the bed chamber, and her husband was a favorite drinking companion of Grand Prince Ferdinando. I was left behind on the estate. As a small child I would be in the way, and as I grew, I could only make my mother appear older than she wished. I didn't mind. I grew to manhood with Desio as my mentor and friend. If only those golden days could have lasted," he reflected with a yearning smile that changed the whole nature of his face.

"What happened?"

The cardinal's smile disappeared. "Ferdinando liked his women highborn and lewd. He dallied with my mother for a time, and when he got bored, the Marchese Fabiani found him an accommodating noblewoman from your country. Unfortunately, this Venetian presented the grand prince with the French disease, and the Marchese Fabiani was never forgiven. My mother and her husband were banished to the country, where he sank into indolence and drink. When my mother wasn't consoling herself with Desio, she nearly fretted herself to death about my future. Lacking prospects to link me to a wealthier family by marriage, Mama finally sold off the last of our decent land to buy a small bishopric for me."

"In Rome?"

"No, Milan. It was quite nice. They have a wonderful opera there, and I would have been happy to stay forever. But it wasn't good enough for Mama. She was determined that I rise to the top. She saw our chance when it appeared that another of her old lovers would be elevated to the papacy."

"Pope Clement," I observed.

He nodded. "He was Archbishop Lorenzo Corsini when Mama first knew him. I think she always had a feeling that he would go far—much farther than her husband. That's why she insisted that my name also be Lorenzo."

"And when Corsini became pope?"

"Mama was intent on coming to Rome, but not with an overfed, slovenly embarrassment of a husband. She went to her faithful Desio with a request. Being the kindest of men, he refused many times. But when Mama wants something…" He shook his head, shrugging. "She finally wore him down. One day he accompanied her husband on a ride—the Marchese Fabiani never came back—I don't know exactly what Desio did and don't want to."

"Perhaps it was simply an accident."

"No. Desio was eaten up with guilt and grief." The cardinal took a deep breath. "He hanged himself from a rafter in the stables a month later. I was desolated when I heard."

"Yet you left Milan and came to Rome to secure your fortune."

"I took no satisfaction in the way things turned out."

"You could have refused."

"Refuse Mama? You can't imagine how she was—it would have been easier to stem a flood tide. And then, it may sound strange, but I couldn't stand the thought that my true father, my beloved Desio, had sacrificed himself for nothing. I fell in line with Mama's plan, but everything I've done since has been dedicated to Desio's memory."

"Eminence…" I shuffled uneasily. "Your mother would make Lucrezia Borgia blush."

He widened his eyes. "Do you see why I have no problem believing that Mama strangled Gemma? I left the maid in the pavilion while I went to get her purse of money. The sum she asked for showed a shocking lack of imagination. It would have been worth ten times that amount to send her packing. When I returned, Gemma had been strangled with Mama's scarf and Rossobelli stood over her, about to lose his head and wake the villa."

I thought for a moment. I still wasn't sure that he hadn't killed Gemma, but Fabiani's tale had led me to see him in a new light. In some ways, the seemingly all-powerful cardinal was trapped as surely as I was. "What do we do now?" I asked.

"Do?"

"We've come to something of an impasse. The painting of Desio Caporale is not on my person, and circumstances make it too dangerous for me to retrieve it. I can only hope you will believe me when I tell you where it can be found."

"And when it comes to getting Cardinal Montorio elected, I can only give you my word that I will deliver my votes for Venice." He sent me a sweet smile. "It looks like we'll have to trust each other."

Chapter 27

The rain had come, showers of it, driven slantwise by the tireless north wind. I was trying to reach Liya's to pass the rest of the night, but Gussie's rooms were closer. When I staggered up to his lodging house, I was so cold, wet, and weary I could barely take another step.

I hardly wanted to call attention to myself by waking Gussie's landlady, so I searched the slick flagstones for some small pebbles to throw on his windowpanes. My stratagem worked, and Gussie soon came down to unlatch the door.

"By Jove, Tito, where have you been? I thought I'd see you yesterday or the day before. And what a state you've got yourself into. Your cloak is sodden clear through."

I let Gussie bundle me upstairs and fuss over me like a mother cat with a wayward kitten. I fended off his questions until I was warm and dry in a dressing gown that was several inches wider than I was. Then I inquired about food.

"I've only this bread. If I'd known you were going to show up…" He handed me the end of a day-old loaf.

I stuffed a hunk in my mouth without ceremony and looked around the room as I chewed. On his desk, Gussie had several candles burning over a half-finished letter. Dirty clothing, sketches, and used crockery were spread throughout the shadows.

I pointed toward the desk. "Are you writing Annetta?" I mumbled between chunks of bread.

He nodded, not looking at me.

"Any news from home?"

"You would know if you had called for me as you promised." Now that he thought I was safe, Gussie had turned sulky.

"You have my heartfelt apology. If I could have spared a moment, I would have been here."

"You don't fool me. If you had only a moment, it would belong to a certain Jewess." Gussie smiled ruefully, but at least he smiled. He threw himself into the chair behind the desk. "I had my last letter from Annetta several days ago, but it was old news. All the pilgrims on the roads between here and Venice must have slowed the post. She wrote that Alessandro was well—still keeping mum about the Turkish business."

I nodded, swallowing the last of the bread.

"I've been waiting to send an answer until I could learn what is going on with you. What shall I tell her?" Gussie dipped his quill in the inkwell and let it hover above the paper. "Did you manage to discover the color of Pope Clement's eyes before he died?"

I clapped my hands to my cheeks. Fabiani had taken me to the Quirinal only four days ago, but it seemed like a lifetime had passed. Sliding my fingers down to my chin, I said, "I haven't seen you since then?"

He shook his head.

"What have you been doing?" I asked.

"Going about the city, doing a watercolor whenever I spot something interesting." He gestured toward sketches that covered the chest and sat on the windowsill. "More importantly, what have you been doing?"

I sighed. "I doubt that your ink will hold out."

He raised an eyebrow and dipped his quill again. "Let's see, shall we?"

I began with my adventure in the pope's bed chamber, which Gussie dutifully transcribed for Annetta. When I reached the part about Magistrate Sertori questioning Benelli, Gussie put his quill down. And when I told him that Antonio Montorio thought Alessandro would make an inspiring martyr, my brother-in-law sprang from his chair.

"Damn that devil. We can't let this go on. I'll get back to Venice. I'll demand to see the doge…I'll speak to the British Envoy…" Gussie dropped to his knees, retrieved his case from under the bed, and transferred it to the top.

"No, I'm the one who'll be going, Gussie." I grabbed his shoulders and spun him round to face me. "Listen."

By the time I finished explaining the latest developments, Gussie had steadied himself. "We must leave at dawn," he said, as he began to pack slowly and deliberately.

I stayed his hands. "I can't let you come with me. If I am caught, they'll arrest you, too—for aiding a fugitive. You must follow at a safe distance. And not alone, I hope."

His worried blue eyes opened a little wider. "You want me to bring Liya and her son."

"Will you do that for me? And make arrangements for Benito? If I know that he is safe and you three are on the road behind me, it will give me the strength to face whatever I must."

He peered at me for a long moment. "Of course," he answered staunchly. "But…" A doubting tone crept into his voice. "…what if Liya won't come with me?"

"She will."

Gussie's expression remained dubious.

"On my way out of the city, I'll stop by the cookshop and tell her what is going on. I couldn't bear to set off without seeing her again, anyway."

"No." Gussie chewed at a knuckle. "We want you on the streets as little as possible. At first light, I'll go get Liya and bring her here. We'll perfect our plans together."

I would have sworn that sleep was impossible. I intended merely to close my eyes and give some thought to the uncertain journey ahead, but the moment Gussie covered me with a blanket, I was dead to the world. I awoke to find my brother-in-law gone and his room barely visible in the fuzzy, gray light.

I swung my feet to the floor. Gussie had brushed the mud from my boots and hung my breeches and jacket before the smoldering stove. They were still slightly damp, but they would serve. I lit a candle and dressed quickly, picturing Liya's look of surprise when Gussie appeared at the cookshop.

The minutes passed. My stomach rumbled. I rummaged among shelves and cabinets and found a forgotten, withered apple. It tasted as good as Eve's must have. What time was it? I consulted my watch, only to find that I had neglected to wind it. I threw the window drape back, scattering some of Gussie's sketches. A light mist had taken the place of the rain. The windows across the way were still dark and the street was quiet. It must be very early.

As I retrieved the watercolors from the floor, I saw that Gussie had been sketching all over the city. In turn, I admired a saucy angel that graced the Ponte Sant'Angelo, a tidy courtyard with a clipped box hedge, a swarthy woman plaiting garlic bulbs into a wreath, and some porters with bulging muscles rolling casks down a ramp and heaving them onto a cart.

I started to lay the papers aside, but something prodded me to take a closer look at the last sketch.

I pressed my shoulder into the corner of the window to make the most of the weak light. The sketch clearly showed men loading olive oil casks. Gussie had taken care with the image on the sign over the loading ramp: an olive branch heavy with fat golden olives. But that wasn't what sent my heart racing. Gussie's practiced brush had also sketched the cart's driver with precision, right down to his floppy blue cap, studded gloves, and turned-up jaw. Blood pounded in my ears. This was the cart and driver that the beggar had described—the cart that had crushed Benito like he was no more than a gutter rat.

As was his habit, Gussie had noted the sketch's date and location in the upper left-hand corner. In a lather of rage, with no thought in my mind but revenge, I ripped the sketch in half, shot out of Gussie's lodgings, and launched myself into the fog.

༺∞༻

Via Verdi near the Porto Ripetta. I didn't know the street, but the port that supplied Rome with goods from the countryside should be easy to find. It lay north; all I had to do was cross the

Tiber and keep the river on my left shoulder. In my haste, I had neglected to don cloak or hat, so I slunk through the mist with my hair clumping about my cheeks and my chin on my chest. I threw in a subtle stagger now and then. If any constables noticed me, I wanted them to see a man heading home after a night's debauch, not a castrato singer avoiding the law.

By the time I reached the Ripetta, a pale sun was thinning the mist and the day's business had begun. A flock of boats with high curved prows and single masts bobbed at the quay, almost like a little Venice. Porters were unloading casks and crates from wheeled vehicles and transferring them to the jetty to be loaded onto boats. I stopped several draymen before I was directed to the Via Verdi.

I recognized the warehouse immediately. It seemed to be the only oil business among establishments that dealt in corn and wheat. Its stone façade was cracked and discolored, and though the rest of the street was coming to life, its ramp was not in use.

Approaching cautiously, I ducked under a slanting portico littered with broken casks and other debris. A street door fashioned of heavy planks was wide enough to admit an average-sized cart. The door sagged on its hinges. I pushed it open a few inches, stopping when it creaked like a dungeon gate.

I glimpsed a vast interior stacked with oil casks, then stepped back. I didn't know what to do. The walk through the mist had cooled my white-hot anger to a temperature that allowed reflection. I could barely contemplate leaving Rome while Benito's attackers went on as if the evil deed had never occurred. But I obviously couldn't alert the authorities. Had I thought I was going to leap on the man with the blue cap and pummel him to a pulp? Alessandro could have carried that off, but not I. Heaving a sigh, I realized it had been a mistake to come to the warehouse at all.

I turned to go, but I was too late. The man in the blue cap blocked my path, his dark eyes narrowed and his lantern jaw pushed forward in a scowl. His sinewy hands gripped a stout leather bludgeon. I knew him only from the beggar's description and Gussie's sketch, but he knew me by sight. He pronounced my name in a raspy growl.

A wave of panic rose in my chest. I feinted to my left, and then sprang to my right, hoping to throw him off balance, but his big body moved with the grace of a dancer. The blow struck my forehead and sent me staggering back. A rainbow flash rent the air, then darkness.

⁂

A splash of cold water startled me to consciousness. Lying on my side, atop some lumpy sacks smelling of garlic, I coughed and spat only to have another bucketful flung in my face.

I was in a small storeroom. Blue Cap squatted beside me. He poked my chest with his bludgeon, and I realized that my wrists were tied behind my back. "He's awake," he called to someone moving around behind me. "We don't need no more water."

I endeavored to move my feet and found those restrained as well. A wave of dizziness engulfed me as the white stockings and buckled shoes of the water flinger came into view. I raised my gaze to his face. Hope exploded in one delirious heartbeat, then the truth struck me with the force of Blue Cap's club.

"Guido," I whispered.

The footman looked down on me with a nasty smile. "Not very clever of you to show up here. If I were you, I'd be putting as much distance between myself and Magistrate Sertori as possible. What are you doing at my uncle's place, anyway? Did Benito revive enough to tell you that I took your letters?"

"No." I thought quickly. "Benito is a little better, but the doctor says he will never be able to remember what happened."

"Then what brought you here?" Guido asked.

I glanced at Blue Cap. More lies designed to protect the people I loved sprang to my lips. "People in the street where Benito was struck described the cart and driver. I've been on the watch ever since. I spotted a likely cart one day and followed it here, but there were a lot of porters milling around. I returned to have it out with the driver in private."

Guido squatted and nudged Blue Cap aside. The footman produced a dagger and caught the tip in the notch of my jaw. "Now, why don't I believe that?"

Barely moving my mouth, I answered, "I'm telling you how I found this place. I can't help it if you don't believe me. Why did you want my letters, anyway?"

"You know that as well as I do."

He was right. Guido had played his valet role as skillfully as the most seasoned actor, but now that he had dropped the respectful servant's persona, he looked every inch a killer.

"You were trying to find out what I knew about Gemma's murder."

"Of course. Once Gemma was found with the marchesa's scarf around her neck, I thought the old bat would finally be packed off to the madhouse where she belongs…but the cardinal surprised me. He decided to keep things quiet and involve you. I had to know what was going on."

"At Benito's expense," I replied grimly.

Guido released the dagger and sank back on one knee. He lowered his eyes. "I didn't want things to end up that way."

I thought I saw real regret in his face, but it passed with a flicker.

"Why did you kill Gemma?" I asked boldly. "Surely it was not just to get rid of a troublesome old lady."

"You really don't know?"

I shook my head.

Guido snorted. "You're all the same. We servants live right under your noses, but we might as well be invisible unless we're shoving food at you or wiping your precious asses."

"You're lumping me in with aristocrats like Cardinal Fabiani and Prince Pompetti?" Even in my dire situation, Guido's point of view amazed me.

"You wear silk coats, don't you? And full dress wigs made of real hair? And you have a trunkful of snuffboxes and silver buckles and other such gewgaws." He and Blue Cap shared a nod, setting anyone above their station squarely in the enemy camp.

Another truth burrowed its way through the pounding in my head. Despite my bonds, I managed to raise up on one elbow. "You're a thief! Some of my things have gone missing. The marchesa's, too. Is that why you killed Gemma—because she found you out?"

Guido laughed outright at that. "Gemma was partners with us. She took things the old lady wouldn't miss. And stood guard when need be."

I nodded. Everything was becoming clear. "Because of the marchesa's wandering, Gemma could find an excuse to be idling almost anywhere…by a tapestry that leads to a concealed staircase, in the pavilion that has a secret entrance to the old aqueduct…" I remembered the carefully clipped path from the aqueduct to the river. "It's all so very convenient. You pack your booty through the tunnel and a boat picks it up. Under cover of night, of course. Where do you store it until it can be sold, I wonder."

Guido's quick glance toward the casks stacked along the back wall of the storeroom wasn't lost on me.

Blue Cap drew his truncheon arm back. "Here, this capon knows too much."

I tensed in expectation of a blow, but Guido jerked his confederate's arm down. "It doesn't matter how much he knows." The footman gazed at me, a smile playing around his brutish mouth. With a sinking heart, I realized that he was going to recount the murder scene—and that I wouldn't live to tell another soul.

"Old Red Chaps had me on duty at the front entrance that night, but as no one was about, I decided to do a little scouting for a pretty trinket or two. Those hidden passages make it easy. All the servants know about them. How else would they keep 'em clean? But the passages are off limits for anything else, and no one breaks that rule for fear of being let go."

"Except you and Gemma."

He shrugged. "A fellow like me takes risks when he has to. Gemma had her own fish to fry. Anyway, when I saw the cardinal duck into the tunnel, I wondered what was up. I followed him. Gemma was waiting in the little garden house. I cracked the door open and listened from the other side. They were walking around—talking low—made it hard to hear every word. But I got the most important bit—Gemma wanted a hundred gold sequins to keep quiet about something she knew, and Fabiani was going to give them to her.

"Well, I could hardly let that go by, could I?" Guido stood and began pacing, warming to his sense of injustice. "I had cut her in on my deal. The gardener didn't trust her, but I said we needed her. I told him, 'Either she's partners with us or I go.' You see? I did right by her in the thieving business—so half those sequins were mine by right. I waited 'til the cardinal left, then came out and told her how it was going to be."

I squirmed upright so I could watch Guido's face. "She wouldn't share."

"It was pathetic." His lip curled in a sneer. "She refused me because she was saving up for a dowry. Gemma thought that she could buy a marriage proposal from that custard-faced abate of hers. As if a Montorio would ever wed a serving maid."

"There must have been more, though," I said, observing the deep-seated anger that had bunched Guido's shoulders and balled his hands into fists. "You weren't thinking very clearly—leaving a dead body at the entrance to the tunnel where your gang shifted your goods was the work of a dolt."

The footman stooped and stuck his face close to mine. Blue Cap was right behind him. "The little whore called me a finocchio."

I raised a questioning eyebrow.

Guido shook his head vigorously. "Benito is a finocchio. I'm as much a man as they come. I just like fucking the finocchio."

Before I could contemplate the distinction, Guido gave Blue Cap a nod, and my world went dark once again.

Chapter 28

Wheels clattered. A fishy smell filled the air. Boatmen cried their distinctive calls. Had I somehow got to Venice? With a pounding ache in my head that felt like it had swelled to twice its normal size?

I opened my eyes and squirmed tentatively. The light was faint, filtering through seams between boards that encased me in a tight, uncomfortable ball. Despite the chill, I broke into a torrent of sweat. Guido and Blue Cap must have stuffed me in a crate and hauled me to the Ripetta. I nearly vomited when I realized how simple it would be to dump this crate from a boat once it was out on open water.

My hands and feet were still bound, and a gag that tasted of rancid oil covered my mouth. I made short work of that by scraping my jaw against the rough boards until the fabric loosened and I could wriggle it down my neck. With frantic energy, I went to work on my bonds. My captors must have tightened them as I lay helpless. I couldn't do more than hunch my shoulders or draw my legs back a few inches. This I did, using my boot heels to drum a tattoo on the boards. I yelled at the same time, but my feeble efforts produced no effect.

I quieted when I heard the sound of several voices above my crate. Guido's I recognized at once. The footman assured someone that "all would soon be taken care of," and my prison was lifted aloft, rocked along for thirty paces or so, and deposited on a hard surface.

The voices of Guido and the others drifted away. Against the background clamor of the busy port, I heard water lapping against stone, very near, then the sound of rigging lines slapping wooden masts. My crate was on the jetty, ready for loading. If I couldn't summon help within the next few minutes, I was a dead man.

Poor Gemma had been no match for Guido, but I wasn't about to let a greedy street tough do away with me. I craned my neck to find the widest crack between the boards. Behind my left shoulder, a knothole admitted a circle of light the size of my pocket watch. By painful degrees, I twisted around until my mouth could reach that hole.

I shouted and screamed for all I was worth. My lung power was prodigious, but I might as well have been crying to the deaf. I was competing with haulers, porters, boatmen, and harbor agents—all raising their voices on urgent matters, all striving to be heard against the chaos of rattling drays, stamping horses, and casks rumbling over paving stones.

Tears of frustration wet my cheeks. I couldn't end like this. Not when I'd just found Liya again, with so much to look forward to and so many triumphs before me. I beat my head on the boards, oblivious to the piercing pain. I had to sing again, to fill the opera house with my voice.

I inhaled sharply. Of course! There was one sound I could make that might cut through the din. If one note had the capacity to inspire rapture in an audience intent on dining, gossiping, and romancing, surely it could catch the attention of those who would never expect to hear such a sound emanating from a crate on the jetty.

The maestros called it a *messa di voce*. I had never performed that vocal marvel from such a cramped position, but I had to try. Pushing my knees against the opposite end of the crate to make as much room for my ribcage as possible, I took a deep breath.

I covered the hole with my mouth and sounded a soft, clear tone. Slowly, with exquisite control, I swelled that note louder and louder until it throbbed with the majesty and power of an organ pipe vibrating in a vast cathedral. Many a lady in a sixth-tier box had been driven to a swooning frenzy by my messa. With the accuracy of a marksman, I projected this one straight toward the sounds of the thickest activity. Surely someone on the Ripetta would hear and come to investigate.

I sustained the height of my crescendo until black spots danced before my eyes and I slumped down, lungs utterly spent. For a moment, I thought I had failed. Then, as welcome as Saint Gabriel's trumpet, a very British voice called my name.

"Gussie," I shouted through the hole. "Over here."

The crate shook. My brother-in-law continued to call my name, along with another voice that made no sense. The sounds of a fight erupted: fists pounding flesh, Guido snarling oaths, a woman screaming, yelps of pain and anger. Through it all, I could only kick at the boards and pray in helpless, barely coherent anguish.

Suddenly, the lid of my crate was ripped away. Blinking in the bright sunshine, I was overjoyed to see Gussie and Liya reaching in to pull me to freedom. I added my clumsy efforts to theirs and was soon rising to my feet.

I emerged from the crate to face an audience, a crowd of onlookers packing the Ripetta. When they saw that I was unharmed, spontaneous cheering and clapping broke out, then several cries of "bravo." A grin split my face—never had applause sounded so sweet to my ears.

Gussie sprang to my back to work at my bonds, and Liya threw her arms around me and buried her face in my chest. In the excitement, I had barely noticed my third rescuer, a man whose bearded face was hidden by a handkerchief stanching a wound over his cheekbone. Who was this?

He lowered the bloody cloth.

"Alessandro!" I gasped. "How in Hades did you get here?"

⟡

Magistrate Sertori had not been far behind my rescuers. As I later learned, he had set his most intelligent constable on my trail the moment he heard about my part in Gemma's watery burial. I had been watched as I kissed Liya in the alley behind the cookshop, as I mixed with the pilgrims in the street, and as I hovered at Benito's bedside. Only the fact that I'd been too busy to visit Gussie's lodging had kept Sertori from discovering that my brother-in-law was in Rome.

When the retrieval of Gemma's body set my arrest in motion, Sertori was furious that I couldn't be found at the villa. I can imagine how he must have raged and fumed, but all he could do was put a guard on the place he most expected me to turn up: Liya's cookshop.

The dawn appearance of an English stranger who swept Liya away in great excitement signaled his men to summon their master and give chase. They hung back as Gussie and Liya hurried to his lodging and entered the building. When Sertori arrived, he and his band of sbirri waited in anticipation of an easy arrest. They were puzzled to see Gussie and Liya leave and proceed toward the Ripetta, not with me, but with yet another tall stranger.

The magistrate created quite a stir when he waded into the appreciative crowd on the jetty. Recognizing a person of authority, Alessandro pointed out Guido and Blue Cap, who were being restrained by some boatmen. While my brother accused them of kidnapping me and attempting to murder Benito, they yelled stout denials and identified me as "the vicious capon who had killed poor Gemma Farussi." Liya took great exception to this and pulled at Sertori's sleeve to induce him to listen to her. Magistrate Sertori had no interest in conducting an open-air interrogation. Brandishing his walking stick, he barked orders for the lot of us to be taken into custody.

Thus it was that we were carted to the building that housed the magistrate's court and lock-up. The constables sat us down on hard wooden benches lining a gloomy hallway and took up positions at each end of the corridor. Liya, Gussie, Alessandro, and I faced Guido and Blue Cap as Sertori paced the floor between us. He fingered his lower lip as he regarded us from between lank curtains of hair. Like a cat with some captive mice, he was keeping us in suspense. I had the feeling he enjoyed every minute.

When Sertori paused to take a folded missive from one of the constables, I took the opportunity to question Alessandro in whispers.

"When did you arrive?"

"Just this morning. I came straight to Gussie's address." He stroked his beard, answering from behind his hand. "I couldn't think where Gussie would have gone so early, but he and your lady soon showed up and let me know what was going on. It gave them quite a jolt to find you'd disappeared."

"How did you find me?"

"The torn watercolor that you left on the floor. We started at the oil warehouse and were told the cart had just left. We fanned out looking for it and its driver."

I nodded with a great exhalation of breath. At least my anger had served one good purpose. If I hadn't ripped up Gussie's sketch, they would never have found me in time.

I leaned close, my chin nearly resting on my brother's shoulder. "But how did you get out of prison? You must tell me."

Alessandro kept his gaze trained on Sertori, who was having an increasingly agitated conversation with his officer. "Later, little brother. Right now, we need to finish rescuing you."

Sertori sent the constable away with a stern shake of his head, then came to stand before me. "Tito Amato, we know you murdered Gemma Farussi. Did your confederates assist you or were they merely conspiring to help you escape?"

His penetrating gaze slid down the bench. Liya gave a startled gasp and sent me a wide-eyed look. Gussie set his chin defiantly.

"I didn't kill Gemma," I said. "The man who strangled the life out of her is sitting right behind you."

I listed to one side and flung my words at the footman. "Guido killed her and was about to get rid of me, as well."

"He's lying!" The footman erupted in fury. "We had him all trussed up for you, Magistrate. You know me, I let you in the door at the villa last night. I saw Tito on the Ripetta this morning. You can thank me and my cousin for blocking his escape."

"And the crate?" Alessandro sneered. "I suppose you stuffed Tito in there to—" My brother broke off as a regal figure appeared at the end of the corridor.

"I believe I can be of some help in this interrogation, Magistrate." Cardinal Fabiani approached with the air of an avenging angel clad in scarlet and lace. His voice was dangerously smooth. "Surely your man must have misunderstood when he said you wished me to wait outside in my carriage."

Sertori drew himself up in a defiant column. "Your Eminence must have many spiritual duties to attend to. There's no need for you to waste your time here. Leave this to me—it is a matter of law, after all."

Fabiani floated to a halt an arm's length from Sertori. "Do you forget, Magistrate? I'm the Cardinal Padrone. Until a new pope is elected, I am the law."

Sertori ground his jaw back and forth. The power of the constabulary and the power of the Church faced each other in an unequal duel. Very slowly, never breaking the magistrate's gaze, Cardinal Fabiani extended his hand. Even in the dim corridor, his ring of office seemed to concentrate all the available light. It twinkled on his forefinger like a miniature star.

Sertori was beaten. In the seconds it took for him to bow and kiss Fabiani's ring, the man changed from a rod of granite to a piece of half-boiled spaghetti.

"Now, Tito," Fabiani said after Sertori had released his hand, "explain yourself. How did you manage to get boxed up on the Ripetta?"

I told my story, beginning with Gussie's watercolor sketch of the cart that had ambushed Benito. I admit to being intentionally vague about how Gemma expected to obtain the money that Guido claimed as his right, but it wasn't my evasion that drew yells of protest from the footman. Guido strongly denied he had ever stolen anything from the villa.

"Prove it," he demanded, jumping up from the bench, only to be shoved back down by a constable.

I remembered the footman's guilty glance when I had inquired where his gang stashed their ill-gotten baubles. "Eminence, send someone to check the casks in the little storeroom at the warehouse. They should fetch us the ones that clank when they're shaken."

Within an hour, the casks had been broken open to reveal a treasure trove of rings, bracelets, watches, gold tableware, small carvings made of ivory or precious stone, silk garments, even several unmated dueling pistols. Some the cardinal was able to identify; he sent for his housekeeper to look through the rest. Once the proof of their thievery lay before us, Guido and his cousin shut their mouths as tight as clams. They were jailed in Magistrate Sertori's lock-up to await further questioning.

There still remained the matter of my role in disposing of Gemma's corpse. Magistrate Sertori could have chosen to have me locked up as well, but he wisely decided not to press the issue. I foresaw a time when the statutes of a state might overrule the Church, but that time was not now, and I fancied that neither I nor Magistrate Sertori would live to see it.

The sun rode high in the sky when we left the magistrate's court. While my loved ones clustered around me, cheerfully arguing over the quickest route back to Venice, Cardinal Fabiani laid a light hand on my shoulder. "Tito, I hold you under no obligation, but I wonder if you would consider a request."

"What is that, Your Eminence?"

"No other singer's songs have eased my wakeful nights as completely as yours. Is there any chance that you would stay on in Rome? Make no mistake, you would be well paid for your serenades."

His request required little thought. I shook my head firmly. The cardinal's nightingale had burst through the bars of his cage, never to return.

⚬⟁⟆⚬

My bride wore a green satin gown of her own design. In the mellow summer twilight, in a garden of flowers and pomegranate trees, Liya and I pressed forearms together and a wise woman bound them with a silver cord. Thus we were "twined as the vine as long as love shall last." What matter if the Christian world that surrounded us would never acknowledge our marriage? Liya and I had found true happiness that could not be extinguished by doctrine or convention.

I admit to first petitioning the new pope for dispensation to marry in the traditional manner—lifelong ways of thinking die hard. I was summarily refused, and not really surprised. Though Pope Benedict was an amiable man and a tolerant pope, he was known for his bookish theology and had no love for opera or eunuchs. My petition might have stood a better chance with either Montorio or Di Noce, but the man who took the name of Benedict the Fourteenth was neither of these.

The Sacred College had gone into conclave with fifty-four cardinals split into several parties. I had released Fabiani from his promise, but for reasons of his own, he remained in support of Cardinal Montorio. The opposing Di Noce contingent was strong enough to force weeks of tedious debate and corridor intrigue. As spring turned into one of the hottest summers Rome had ever seen, a completed election seemed no nearer than it had in February.

The cardinals, many among them elderly and stricken with gout, suffered in the oppressive heat. Fever-filled air crept up the slopes of the Vatican and entered the palace, sending cardinal after cardinal to their sick beds. Cardinal Di Noce distinguished himself by ministering to their needs as diligently as any nursing sister—until the malarial fever extinguished his genial spirit forever.

With the saintly Di Noce out of the running and the Roman cabal in disarray, Fabiani should have attained an easy victory.

It was Stefano Montorio who orchestrated his own defeat. He took his revenge on his brother Antonio by giving the speech of his life—in support of Prospero Lambertini, a pious nonentity who had never been considered papal material. Zio Stefano had judged his moment well. The cardinals were eager to divine the Will of God and go home. In the next round of voting, Lambertini easily carried the necessary two-thirds majority.

As for my brother, he had been hiding a secret. Yusuf Ali Muhammad was Alessandro's business partner in Constantinople, a highborn merchant with ties to the Ottoman court. He was a man of sixty who embodied the wisdom of thought and purity of philosophy that our father had never aspired to. This worthy Turk had taken Alessandro under his wing and tutored him in the essence of Islam along with good, hard business principles. Yusuf Ali also had a perfect beauty of a daughter named Zuhal. Alessandro had changed his religion and married her two years ago.

On receipt of Alessandro's letter, Yusuf Ali had raced to Venice. Packing letters and promises from the Grand Turk himself, he arranged a meeting with the doge and several influential senators who were not in thrall to the Montorios. A generous inducement of cash, along with a favorable contract for the purchase of Venetian salt, secured Alessandro's release and complete vindication. To my brother's mixed relief and disgust, the doge sent one of his most courteous noblemen to unlock the door of Alessandro's cell and fill the noxious prison air with cloying regrets and apologies.

The release had taken place right before Antonio Montorio set out on his swift journey to Rome. When the senator had waved his key in my face, he was merely playing the odds. He knew that Alessandro could show up in Rome any day, but was hoping I would snare Cardinal Fabiani for Venice before I learned that my brother was at liberty to go where he pleased.

I was in Alessandro's debt for much more than helping Gussie break open the crate and expose Guido as a thief and a murderer. My brother had done me a tremendous favor by embracing Turkish ways and customs. Annetta was so aghast at those developments that she barely blinked an eyelid at my unconventional marriage to an apostate Jewess.

"There's just one thing," Liya said, as Gussie and Alessandro lit torches around the perimeter of the fragrant garden.

"What is that, my love?" I raised her hand and bestowed a kiss on her delicate fingers.

"Not everyone we love is here to share in our wedding feast."

I tore my satisfied gaze away from my bride. Little Tito was tumbling on the soft grass with my niece and nephew. An obviously pregnant Annetta was in earnest conversation with Maddelena and the wise woman who had performed our hand-fasting. And Benito was hobbling around on a cane supervising supper preparations.

"I know. Pincas and the rest of your family are missing."

She nodded wistfully. "At least I'll be living back in Venice. I don't think they'll be able to ignore me forever. Mama maybe, but not Papa." She squeezed my hand. "But there is someone else."

"Who?"

"Your other sister—Grisella. Don't you ever wonder what has become of her? She must be over twenty, quite old enough to have a husband and family of her own. Now that Alessandro has so many contacts in Constantinople, I think you two should track her down."

I raised a bemused eyebrow. Another adventure, for another time.

Author's Note

Readers of the first two Baroque Mysteries will notice that *Cruel Music* takes more liberties with recorded history than Tito's previous adventures. Clement XII was indeed Lorenzo Corsini of Florence, a blind, chronically ill pope who sat on St. Peter's throne from July 12, 1730, to February 6, 1740. And his successor was Prospero Lambertini, a bookish cardinal who was amazed to be elected. However, Cardinal Fabiani, his scheming mother, and the political tangle that Tito faced are pure fiction.

The notion of a pagan infiltrating the ranks of the Catholic Church is not as strange as it might appear on first glance. There are many indications that the Old Religion survived in Italy into the eighteenth century and beyond. Those interested may consult *The Rebirth of Witchcraft* by Doreen Valiente (1989); *Aradia, The Gospel of the Witches* by Charles Godfrey Leland (1899); and *Etruscan Roman Remains in Popular Tradition*, also by Leland (1892). One inspiration for Prince Pompetti's Academy of Italia was the Academy of Rome, an earlier confraternity that espoused a return to the ideals of the pagan world and earned its followers a nasty reprisal from the Church.

Tito's enforced stint as a baroque music therapist also has its roots in historical fact. Farinelli, the most acclaimed castrato of the eighteenth century, gave up his stage career to serenade King Philip V of Spain. The king often suffered from bouts of depression and madness that prevented him from leaving his bed chamber. His queen, Elizabeth Farnese, employed Farinelli to soothe her husband with song. Thanks to the singer's nightly visits, King Philip recovered his taste for life and was able to reign more or less appropriately until his death in 1746.

A few other matters that may be of interest: Pope Clement's port project was completed, and Ancona remains a busy seaport today. Liquore Strega is still produced in Benevento and is known as one of Italy's most distinctive liqueurs. It can be found in well-stocked stores in the United States. It was not until 1870, during the foundation of the modern Italian state, that the temporal dominion of the pope was restricted to the Vatican. The Quirinal Palace eventually became the residence of Italy's president.

I wish to express my gratitude to everyone who provided assistance in bringing this novel to completion, particularly my family, the late Father Lee Trimbur, the staff at the Louisville Free Public Library, the staff at the University of Louisville Ekstrom Library, Kit Ehrman, Joanne Dobson, and my editor at Poisoned Pen Press, Barbara Peters. Thanks also to Jeanne M. Jacobson for calling my attention to the Benjamin Britten quote that lends this novel its title.

Special words regarding the late Dan Hooker are in order. Dan was a creative, caring, eminently dependable agent who gave me consistently good advice. He will be sorely missed.

To receive a free catalog of Poisoned Pen Press titles, please contact us in one of the following ways:

Phone: 1-800-421-3976
Facsimile: 1-480-949-1707
Email: info@poisonedpenpress.com
Website: www.poisonedpenpress.com

Poisoned Pen Press
6962 E. First Ave. Ste. 103
Scottsdale, AZ 85251

09 06